CANADA, QUEBEC, AND THE
USES OF NATIONALISM

Canada, Quebec, and the Uses of Nationalism

Second Edition

Ramsay Cook

M&S

Canadian Cataloguing in Publication Data

Cook, Ramsay, 1931-
Canada, Quebec, and the uses of nationalism

2nd ed. rev. & updated.
Includes bibliographical references and index.
ISBN 0-7710-2254-9

1. Nationalism – Canada.   2. Nationalism – Quebec (Province).
3. Canada – Politics and government.   4. Quebec (Province) – Politics and government.   I. Title.

FC97.C66 1995   320.971   C95-930234-4
F1034.2.C66 1995

Typesetting M&S, Toronto
Printed and bound in Canada

McClelland & Stewart Inc.
The Canadian Publishers
481 University Avenue
Toronto, Ontario
M5G 2E9

1 2 3   99 98 97 96 95

Contents

Acknowledgements

The essays in this book have been published, often in different form, or delivered as lectures. I would like to thank the following publications for providing me with an opportunity to present my views and for allowing me to use this material again: Yale University Press, the Robarts Centre for Canadian Studies, *The British Journal of Canadian Studies*, Oxford University Press, Viking, *Saturday Night*, the Centre for Constitutional Studies, University of Alberta, University of Ottawa Press, the Japanese Association for Canadian Studies, New York University Press, *Canadian Literature*, University of Toronto Press, Swedish-Canadian Academic Foundation, *The Journal of Canadian Studies*, *Cité libre*, the *Canadian Literary Review*.

The index is the careful, much-appreciated work of Molly Ungar.

The first edition of *Canada, Quebec, and the Uses of Nationalism* has recently been published in Japanese by Sankosha. It received the Prime Minister of Canada's publishing award for translation, presented annually by the Canadian Embassy in Tokyo. I owe a deep debt of gratitude to my translators and good friends, Professor Takashi Konami and Ms. Norie Yazu Kagegawa, both accomplished students of Canada. Their excellent translation of my work is only one of many examples of Japanese interest in Canadian cultural and intellectual life and of the willingness of my Japanese friends to welcome a wandering Canadian into their midst.

For Carl Goldenberg

ONE

Who Belongs Where?

"God put the English in England, the French in France, and the Germans in Germany. I figure he put us in the Queen Charlotte Islands because that is where we belong."
Fred Russ, Haida elder, Skidegate

"I suppose that a Canadian is someone who has a logical reason to think he is one."
Mavis Gallant, *Home Truths*

EVERYONE BELONGS SOMEWHERE. Yet much of the conflict in the history, and the pre-history, of mankind has been about who belongs where. [1] Some peoples are entirely satisfied with their place on the earth. Others are utterly discontented. That makes population movement both certain and a source of conflict; the movement of people can be peaceful – emigration – or it can follow military conquest. While possession may be nine-tenths of the law, in the modern world it usually requires ideological justification. That is the function of nationalism, a doctrine asserting that humanity is naturally divided into groups with common characteristics and that by virtue of those collective traits they have a right to exercise control – sovereignty – over the particular place. [2] If they occupy that place their national aspirations are satisfied; if some other group controls it their nationalism is frustrated. The history of the Jews, especially of Zionism, provides the archetypal case. [3]

In the early nineteenth century many exponents of nationalism claimed that God had arranged peoples by national groupings and assigned them their places of belonging – though even a casual glance revealed that God favoured the largest armies. Later, as secular social science replaced religion as the accepted explanation of human affairs,[4] God gave way to such mundane matters as language, culture, and historical experience as the justification of nations – though the social sciences, like God, still favoured the powerful. The reason was simple: since there was no court to enforce either divine or natural right, the essential basis for a nation's claim to belong in a particular place rested on power and possession. Nationalism, then, is a doctrine that provides emotional and intellectual justification for a people's power over the place they claim is theirs. Or it is the justification for a people's desire to take control of a place occupied by someone else. The strength of nationalism is a measure of the extent to which a people feels that its claim to its place is secure or threatened. When nationalists say that their culture or identity is threatened, that their nation's survival is at stake, what they mean is that they fear they are losing control over the place where they claim to belong. Control can be cultural, political, or economic, or perhaps all three.

The trouble with the nationalist view of the world as a place where each "nation" has its place is obvious. Neither God nor social science succeeded in assigning any one cultural group to the exclusive occupancy of a defined territory. For many reasons, movements of people, money, ideas, and even armies have ensured that most nations are composed of a variety of cultures. (If every linguistic group became a nation, there would be approximately 8,000 nations; in fact, there are only some 200 nation-states.)[5] But that very movement of people, money, ideas, and armies raises the fundamental nationalist questions: who belongs where, and what belongs to whom? Though posed in less direct terms, these have been central questions in Canadian history. Who were the "first Canadians"? Do Aboriginal peoples remain permanently dispossessed or are "historic claims" valid forever? Do French Canadians have rights equal to those of English Canadians? Does Quebec have the right to self-determination? What kind of immigrants should be allowed into Canada? And, once admitted, do they have collective rights like French and English Canadians, or must they assimilate? Will ideas and capital from the United States destroy the Canadian identity?

The essays in this book examine some of the ways these questions have been answered. They are studies of nationalism and its uses in Canada, especially in recent decades.

Since the middle of the 1960s one of the principal themes of public debate in Canada has been nationalism – Quebec, Canadian, cultural, economic, and political. In this, Canada was far from unique, for many parts of the world, including some quite unexpected ones, witnessed a rebirth of ethnic identity and a reinvigoration of nationalist aspirations. Some African Americans, dissatisfied with the rate and results of integration in the United States, began to advocate a nationalism that at least implied political separateness. Great Britain and France, seemingly the most stable and indivisible of nations, both experienced the growth of nationalist groups – Welsh, Scottish, Breton, and Occitanian – demanding various forms of recognition. And what was true of long-established European nations was even more the case in those parts of the world where the post-war process of decolonization continued to work itself out. Even the decolonized were not immune – Biafrans tried to get out of Nigeria; Pakistan split in two; Punjabis called for the creation of Kalistan; federations in the West Indies and Central Africa disintegrated. Though the languages in which these demands were expressed were often foreign, the meaning was familiar enough to Canadians: Canadian nationalists demanded increased economic and cultural independence from the United States; Quebec nationalists advocated political sovereignty; and virtually every provincial premier learned that the language of regional identities was an excellent weapon in the battle for a larger share of the Canadian pie.

These nationalist movements, in Canada and abroad, shared a number of common characteristics, though local circumstances were always important. One was a sense, real or imagined, of deprivation – the denial of a fair share of political and economic power. Evidence of that deprived condition was often either the complete absence or at least the under-representation of the group in the political or economic structure of the nation. That condition, in turn, was symbolized by the exclusion or subordination of the language of the minority from the higher levels of government and business. Thus, socio-economic and cultural grievances converged in a set of demands that, if they sometimes stopped short of advocating complete independence, always moved several degrees in that direction. If Scottish nationalists contented themselves with demands for limited home rule and moderate Sikhs were prepared to accept a special status for Punjab in the Indian federation, other nationalists, Basques, Catalans, and Palestinians, insisted that only full statehood could protect their place of belonging and ensure that they would have a fair, meaningful share in the political and economic life of their society.

Another characteristic shared by these new nationalist movements was the prominence of intellectuals in them. This, of course, is a category of men and women that is not easily defined. It includes those who live for and those who live by ideas, those who generate ideas, and those who apply them – artists and lawyers, philosophers and journalists, poets and computer programmers, humanists and technocrats. What united these seemingly distinct groups, at least in opposition, was the importance of creators of culture and manipulators of technology to the state and politics in modern industrial society. The new "état-providence" (a much more revealing term than "welfare state") provided an enormous range of new possibilities for those who lived for and by ideas. But those opportunities were severely limited if the new state's operational language did not coincide with the language of the intellectuals. If the dominant or working language was English, French Canadians felt excluded or at least disadvantaged. Where the intellectuals were marginalized because of their language, they sought to mobilize other groups in their society behind demands for the recognition of collective ethnic rights. One option was the promotion of bilingualism. Another was the establishment of a separate "état-providence" where state and language would coincide. In that state, groups previously deprived of power would take control. And in that state the "intellectuals," especially those with applicable skills – economists, teachers, specialists in administration – would assume leading roles. When French was established as the official language of the state both teachers and agronomists who worked in French would win higher status. When Canadian literature received recognition, not merely as literature but as a source of "national identity," then Canadian writers (and filmmakers, historians, and painters) could claim special recognition. A government with a cultural policy might even pay them to visit some of the most exotic watering places in the world in the promotion of "Canadian studies." In this, it should be added, Canadian intellectuals – French teachers and English-Canadian poets – were merely adopting a strategy long exploited by Canadian businessmen: tariffs and subsidies for businessmen were justified because national survival depended on a national economy.

Nationalism, then, is about ethnic survival and growth. It is also about self-interest and power. But nationalism is more than the ideology that different groups summon up as a weapon in the struggle for status and power. It is also an ideology that plays an important part in the clash of values and the struggle for power *within national communities.* "The movements are ostensibly directed against the foreigner, the outsider," Elie Kedourie has written, "but they are also a manifestation of a species of civil strife between the generations; nationalist movements are children's crusades. . . ."[6] For the rising generation, impatient to assume the leadership of society, nationalism takes the form of a claim that the older generation has failed to defend adequately the national identity and interest. Consequently, nationalist struggles are not only about home rule but also, perhaps even primarily, about who should rule at home. Young Quebecers in the 1960s condemned their elders as "federalists" or even *"fédérastes,"* a word that was made to mean *vendu* or traitor. Its English-Canadian equivalent was "continentalist."

Within these general, almost abstract, terms the great debate about the national question in Canada can be examined. Our nationalist history reveals a drama that is central to the Canadian experience. Here, in a country that is geographically huge and demographically small, some quite fundamental issues are being played out. At centre stage in Canada's history has always been the question of how, or indeed whether, peoples of different cultures can live together successfully: Canada is the product of that population movement – people in search of gold, land, freedom, or adventure – that has almost everywhere brought different cultures together. When different peoples meet they must find ways of answering the question: who belongs here and what belongs to whom? There are many ways of answering the question: conquest, domination, and assimilation of the weak by the strong are perhaps the most common. But there is also the possibility of sharing, co-existence, and even co-operation. The history of Canada provides illustrations of all of these possibilities, as the essays in this book are designed, implicitly or explicitly, to show.

In the beginning was what was once known as "the Discovery of America" but which is now often, and more accurately, known as *The Invasion of America* or *The Conquest of America.*[7] The meeting of the European and the Amerindian, in its various phases, involved both conquest and sharing, domination, co-operation, and assimilation. In the end it came very close to genocide and annihilation. It is a prime example of the expansion of one society, European, at "the cost of another's destruction," the Amerindian.[8] Here is a major feature of the Canadian past that historians have begun to re-examine from the perspective of invaders rather than discoverers. This is where my book begins.

Once the French and the English had dispossessed the indigenous peoples of North America they turned to warring with each other over who should be dominant. Conquest, this time of the French by the English, again marked a beginning in Canadian history. But the consequences of this second conquest differed markedly from the first. The British were dominant, but for geopolitical, demographic, and perhaps even humanitarian reasons, they lacked the will and the power to assimilate the *canadien*. Gradually, co-existence and even co-operation became the almost inevitable outcome of a situation in which the conquered refused to assimilate voluntarily and the conqueror was unable to force the process. By the mid-nineteenth century British North America was a colony where two cultures existed in uneasy equilibrium. But the basis of a co-operative relationship was laid, and its first achievement was the federal union of 1867 in which cultural duality received constitutional recognition.

This second coming together of different cultures – this time both European – became the central theme of Canadian history. Over more than two centuries the minority culture developed a defence system of institutions and attitudes to protect it against the threat of assimilation and to prevent domination. Co-existence became inevitable; co-operation became possible only if English Canadians relinquished the role of conqueror and accepted that of partner. The attitude that French Canadians, especially the political and religious elite, developed over this period was nationalism. But it was a nationalism that emphasized cultural survival and rarely, after the failure of the 1837 Rebellion, aspired to political nationhood. In the period after the Second World War, however, fundamental social and economic changes produced a new intellectual class determined to modernize Quebec society and to re-invent its nationalism. In pursuit of these goals the new intellectual class conducted a war on two fronts: against the "foreigners" in Ottawa bent on undermining Quebec's autonomy and against those who held power in Quebec who had failed to prepare Quebecers for the modern world. This is the tale so well told in Gratien Gélinas's play *Yesterday the Children Were Dancing*. This double offensive has entered our history as the Quiet Revolution and is the subject of the second group of essays in this book.

The issue of nationalism among English-speaking Canadians has always been a different one. For English Canadians the problem of maintaining a distinctive identity has not been one of fending off the threat of assimilation by a conqueror but rather of differentiating itself from nations with which it shares many cultural characteristics, most obviously language. During the first fifty years after Confederation, English-Canadian nationalists insisted that our British heritage made Canada distinct from the revolutionary United States. The next generation described that attitude as "colonial," arguing that Canada was not British but rather North American. By the 1970s, being North American seemed increasingly difficult to distinguish from being part of the United States. And so a new cultural and to some extent economic nationalism was born. For the most part it was articulated by producers of ideas and culture – writers, painters, professors, and publishers – who, in a manner similar to their counterparts in Quebec, demanded that steps be taken to protect and develop the Canadian identity and, not incidentally, their market.

In English Canada this renewed quest for a distinctive identity was more complicated than the parallel demand in Quebec. It was complicated not only by those regional loyalties that have always been strong in Canada, but also by the heterogeneous ethnic make-up of English-speaking Canada. Those who spoke about an English-Canadian "nation" assumed a homogeneity that simply did not exist. The movement of people from Europe to British North America had not stopped with the French and English. Canada's continuing manpower requirements ensured that Irish, German, Ukrainian, Italian, and other groups would join the almost uninterrupted flow of British and United States immigrants into the country. To these Europeans was added a trickle of people from China, Japan, India, the West Indies, and Africa. Once again, different cultures came together, not by conquest this time but certainly not in a relationship of equality. All of the old questions were once again raised, summarized in such catch phrases as "melting pot" and "mosaic." In the years before 1945 the tendency was strongly toward assimilation, though the process was never complete. Since the 1960s the official rhetoric has emphasized multiculturalism, though it, too, has meant less than meets the ear. The non-French, non-British population, then, occupies a special, if vaguely defined, place They are neither marginalized, like the Native people, nor "founding people," like the French and English. Consequently, the idea of a national identity based on a single culture, as in Quebec, was unrealistic in English-speaking Canada. In fact, several ethnic groups, or at least their leaders, argued that cultural pluralism should not only be preserved but even promoted in the same fashion as French and English.

And there were further complications. While English-Canadian nationalists, preoccupied with the growing United States influence on Canada, called for measures to strengthen the central government, Quebec nationalists demanded a reduction of power at the centre, especially in matters touching culture. Moreover, nationalist economic policies – the National Energy Program and the Foreign Investment Review Agency, for example – struck provincial governments in the West and the Atlantic region as reflecting the interests of central Canadians rather than of all Canadians. Ironically, then, the new nationalism of the 1970s was accompanied by an intensification of cultural pluralism and of regional economic and, sometimes, cultural dissatisfaction.

From the perspective of the late 1980s there seemed something rather artificial about the nationalist sound and fury of the previous decades. In both French- and English-speaking Canada nationalism was suddenly becalmed. In 1980 the people of Quebec by a modest majority – a tiny majority if only the Francophone votes are considered – rejected their nationalist government's plans to begin negotiations leading to sovereignty. In the next five years the idea that had dominated Quebec public life for over twenty years slipped from sight, buried hastily by many of the very people who celebrated its birth. The mourners were distinguished but few. Whatever the future of the Parti Québécois, it had lost its determination to make even limited independence its principal goal.

Similar poorly attended obsequies were held in English-speaking Canada. In 1984 a moderately nationalist government, which had implemented some limited measures designed to modify the glaring imbalances in foreign investment in Canada, to strengthen central supervision of the national economy, and to promote Canadian cultural development, was soundly defeated in a federal election. The Liberal government was replaced by a Conservative administration committed to dismantling or reducing the impact of virtually all of these policies. Those most directly hurt protested mildly while most of the country yawned. Prime Minister Brian Mulroney even broached a subject that historically was the red flag to the Canadian nationalist: free trade with the United States. And in this he had the support of the report of a royal commission whose chairman was once thought of as an economic nationalist. Virtually every provincial government, Ontario excepted, agreed that the time had come for a final dismantling of the central structure of the post-Confederation National Policy.

But the nationalism of the previous decades was more than smoke and mirrors. While its decline in Quebec and in the rest of Canada was partly due to exhaustion and boredom, it was also a victim of its own successes. In Quebec, in particular, the social transformation that had aroused nationalist fervour had run its course. The Quiet Revolution largely succeeded in its main objective: the modernization of Quebec's public institutions. Many of the individuals who formulated the new values and goals of Quebec society succeeded with their revolution: in politics, the arts, education, the bureaucracy, and even the economy. French had become the dominant language in virtually every aspect of Quebec life and French-speaking Quebecers were no longer largely confined to the lower ranks of the province's economy.[9] Temporarily at least, nationalism as a tool for social promotion could be abandoned.

In the rest of Canada the results of the great national debate were more mixed, perhaps because the debate had never been resolved and because of the divisions in English-Canadian society. Nevertheless, there were successes. Canadian culture has won more recognition and support and its presence in public places – bookstores, art galleries, newsstands, universities, and perhaps even movie theatres – is more obvious. Petro-Canada signs multiply and even Arctic sovereignty may be more secure. And those who cried wolf – professors, novelists, publishers, journalists, and the occasional businessman, especially in the oil industry – have also reaped modest rewards. But the changes were incremental, not revolutionary, not even in the moderate Quebec fashion.

Yet nationalists, in Canada as elsewhere, have always promised something more than mere piecemeal changes; they have promised to "create a new man and society through the revival of old identities."[10] But that apocalyptic promise has never been fulfilled – not in nineteenth-century Europe, not in the twentieth-century Third World. The cases of Quebec and of Canada suggest that in developed countries, at least, nationalism may serve as a defensive doctrine, one that may help to promote certain specific changes. But it is not a doctrine that can mobilize and unite a population in favour of extensive political, economic, or social change. Nationalism is often expressed in the evangelistic rhetoric of a secular religion, offering redemption and salvation to sinners. But like other missionary religions, nationalism has never solved the problem of the backslider, how to keep the flock true to the faith. This world's temptations or necessities are too demanding, the promise of a "new man" and a "new society" too ethereal.

Canadians, English- and French-speaking, in the last analysis are sceptical about the promise of nationalism. They are not, as nationalists sometimes claim, somehow spiritually crippled or "colonially minded." They are either innately aware or, more likely, have learned from experience that the outcome of nationalist policies are rarely the ones predicted. Too often the claims advanced on behalf of the nation in practice benefit only a part of that nation. In responding to Alexander Solzhenitsyn's claim that only a revival of nationalism could save Russia from the evils of the Soviet system, Andrei Sakharov, a fellow dissenter, replied that "It may be said that Solzhenitsyn's nationalism is not aggressive, but mild and defensive in character, only aiming to save and revive one of the most long suffering of nations. History shows, however, that 'ideologists' are always milder than the practical politicians who follow in their footsteps."[11] Solzhenitsyn has now returned to his motherland, a country abundantly fulfilling Sakharov's prophecy.

POSTSCRIPT 1995:
A SAD THING HAPPENED ON THE WAY TO MEECH LAKE

Dormant or drowsy nationalism is easily awakened and aroused. That, at least, would seem the most obvious conclusion to draw from the most striking events of the nine years that have passed since *Canada, Quebec, and the Uses of Nationalism* was first published. In Europe, especially eastern Europe where Communism and the Soviet Empire claimed to have replaced the bourgeois ethnic national with a "new Soviet Man," nationalism is once again a central issue in international politics and in intellectual discourse. As the Soviet Union collapsed into a series of jealous national states, some of those nations – Georgia, for example – were torn apart by ethnic conflict. In Czechoslovakia the inspiration of the "Velvet Revolution" proved insufficient to prevent a "velvet separation" into two national states. And then came Yugoslavia: first the secession of Slovenia, then Croatia, followed by Bosnia, bringing with it the savagery of civil war and "ethnic cleansing." The essential danger of the "ethnic revival" is brilliantly captured in Zlatko Dizdarevic's *Sarajevo: A War Journal*, a book that may one day rank with George Orwell's *Homage to Catalonia* as the truthful witness to a critical period in modern history. Reflecting on the meaning of the old Lion Cemetery in Sarajevo, he writes: "Here are hundreds and hundreds of people who probably never knew each other, but who belonged to the great family of regular people who looked to the future and weren't crazed by their genes, or by the phony myths about the past; people who weren't trapped inside a tight flock where survival can only be collective and ruled by the authority of a leader and the blood oath."[12] The civil war in Bosnia continues, sometimes raging, sometimes sputtering (while the Great Powers that control the United Nations – and Canada – stutter and temporize); its only certain outcome is death, mutilation, dislocation, and the intensification of ethnic hatreds. The new world order teeters on the edge of what U.S. Senator Daniel Moynihan, following John Milton, calls "pandaemonium."

Nor has Canada been insulated from the divisive forces of revived ethnonationalism, indicating that the "pernicious and perhaps unrealistic principle termed 'self-determination of nations' is far from spent as a significant force."[13] In the years between 1987 and 1992 drowsy nationalisms were reawakened in both Quebec and among many Canadians in the rest of the country. It was aroused by Prime Minister Brian Mulroney's ill-advised decision in 1987 to reopen the constitutional question in an effort to satisfy the Quebec government's insistence that the 1982 constitution was unacceptable to the legislature of that province. The result was the Meech Lake Accord with its ambiguous recognition of Quebec as a "distinct society." That Accord ended in discord in the spring of 1990, when Elijah Harper refused the unanimous consent necessary before the Manitoba legislature could consider the agreement. The acrimonious debate leading up to this dramatic denouement stimulated the revival of nationalist forces, notably the Parti Québécois, in Quebec and provoked a form of nationalist emotion – anti-French nationalist emotion – in parts of English-speaking Canada. It was not the failure of Meech Lake that produced this revival and reaction, it was Meech Lake itself. Reopening the constitutional issue allowed Jacques Parizeau to pull his party together to a degree that had not been possible since the defeat of the 1980 referendum. That was demonstrated in the gains the Parti Québécois made in the 1989 provincial election, while Meech was still alive. That set the stage for the slim victory Parizeau and the PQ managed in the Quebec provincial election on September 12, 1994. Meech also gave Preston Manning's developing Reform Party a boost and, of course, transformed Lucien Bouchard, a moderately capable Conservative cabinet minister (his strength in the party deriving from his close friendship with the Prime Minister), into the leader of the Bloc Québécois. The total cost of Brian Mulroney's attempt to appease his nationalist allies in Quebec can still not be fully calculated, for that must await the outcome of the next Quebec referendum promised for 1995 by Premier Jacques Parizeau and, more ambiguously, by the federal leader of Her Majesty's Loyal Opposition, Lucien Bouchard.[14]

The eight new essays I have added to this collection, replacing four that I have dropped, develop some of the themes introduced in the earlier edition: the clash of values that marked early European contact with the Native people of Canada, the evolution of nationalism in Quebec, the constitutional debate. One essay explains the "fatal flaw" of the Meech Lake Accord and two others set out my views on the way to make Canada, in Daniel Moynihan's phrase, "safe for and from ethnicity."[15] My argument is simple enough: though it is the nature of federalism that there will be regular disputes over jurisdiction, those pragmatic questions can only be satisfactorily tackled once the essential issue of principle is confronted: ethnic nation or civic nation?

That this is the essential issue has once again been made plain by two recent political debates-cum-slinging matches. The first was the parliamentary debate initiated by the Reform Party in April, 1994, on the subject of the Official Languages Act. Implicit in the Reform Party's attempt to modify that legislation was the view that language is territorial, a collective right imposed by majorities on minorities. For the Liberal architects of the policy, language is a human, not a territorial right, guaranteed to minorities and majorities. For reasons of either confusion or opportunism the Bloc, which should logically have joined Reform, chose to defend those French-speaking minorities outside Quebec, once pronounced "dead ducks" by René Lévesque.[16]

The same conflicting assumptions underlie the simmering debate over the "right of self-determination" – that of Quebec itself and of the Native peoples within Quebec. In asserting Quebec's right to secede from the federation with its provincial borders intact, the PQ and the Bloc – and the provincial Liberals, for that matter – affirm an ethnic right of self-determination for Francophones but deny it, on the territorial principle of majority rule, to Native people. Not surprisingly, Native people in Quebec and elsewhere have reacted by insisting that they, too, have that quintessential European right to ethnic self-determination in majoritarian terms. Ethnic nationalism confronts ethnic nationalism, Canadian-style. The historian Tony Judt has recently remarked pessimistically that, if federal Canada, "one of the world's most fortunate places," cannot contain these forces, then "the prospect for non-territorial, state-sharing, overlapping cultural nationalisms of a liberal (or any other) kind is slim indeed."[17]

Here, then, is the challenge to Canadian federalism in the 1990s: "la nation-génie" or "la nation-contrat." That challenge may exceed our talents and imagination. But if it is to be met, at least two essential principles will have to be accepted – and applied. The first, expressed long ago by Lord Acton, has been forcefully reiterated recently by the cultural critic Tzvetan Todorov in *Nous et les Autres*. He writes: "Any identification of the State with one particular cultural group clearly signifies the oppression of other groups ('minorities')."[18] The second, integrally related, principle is most convincingly stated in Alain Finkielkraut's defence of the values of the enlightenment against Herderian romanticism. In *La Défaite de la Pensée*, he writes that "The whole spirit of the Modern Age . . . is very receptive to the presence of national or religious minorities, provided that they are composed, on the model of the nation, of free and equal individuals. This requirement involves treating as illegal all and any practices – even those which reach far back into history – which flout basic personal rights."[19]

Adherence to those principles might just see us through the challenges to Canadian federalism in the 1990s, and perhaps even prepare us for the multicultural global challenges of the twenty-first century. If not, we might want to observe a piece of advice that, according to E.J. Hobsbawm, an Italian peasant woman once gave to her son: "Scappa, che arriva la patria" ("Run away, the fatherland is coming").[20]

TWO

The White Man Cometh

I

A NORTH AMERICAN revolution began with the arrival of the first European fishermen, explorers, and traders in the late fifteenth century. An expanding Europe opened a new frontier on which two distinct societies and cultures made their first contact. Over the next four centuries the European intruder gradually engulfed the indigenous Amerindian. While it was not obvious at the beginning, the long-term advantages in the clash between these two "integral cultures"[1] lay with the Europeans: a growing economy, an increasingly complex technology, an expanding population, and a centralized political system supported by military power. Though the Amerindians "were not at all behind us in natural brightness of mind and pertinence," as Montaigne remarked, the Old World sold the New "our opinions and our arts very dear."[2]

Montaigne's comment places the emphasis in the right place. To understand fully the social and economic processes on the new frontier, it must be clearly seen that the newcomers were more than just fishermen, explorers, and traders: they were agents of Europe. The process, whose beginning their arrival announced, was the Europeanization of North America. That did not mean simply the creation of replicas of Europe – though names like New France, New England, and Nova Scotia are more than just suggestive. But the North American environment inevitably induced substantial modifications.[3] North America was Europeanized in the sense that, in the conflict on the new frontier, it was European "opinions and arts" that became dominant and Amerindian "opinions and arts" that became marginal. "In the beginning," John Locke maintained, "all the world was America."[4] By the end of the nineteenth century, most of North America was Europe.

The idea of the "frontier" as an interpretive device originated with Frederick Jackson Turner; he viewed it as a process of Americanizing the European settler, a process that "takes him from the railroad car and puts him in the birch bark canoe." Others, like Harold Innis, the fur-trade historian, viewed the process from an opposing perspective: Europe reached out to draw North America into its orbit.[5] But the distinction was perhaps not so radical. Innis certainly recognized that, to a degree, European survival in North America depended on "borrowing cultural traits" from the Amerindian: indeed, he argued that the beaver, the birch, and the Indian laid the foundations of Canada.[6] And Turner was certainly aware that whatever the frontier did to the European, the outreach of the European also had its impact on the frontier, specifically on Native Americans. In fact, two years prior to his most famous pronouncement, he published a little monograph entitled *The Character and Influence of the Indian Trade in Wisconsin*. In that study, whose conclusions were quietly re-echoed in the essay on the frontier,[7] Turner set out the broad outlines of the impact of European trading systems on Native American societies. His conclusions were similar to those reached by Innis forty years later, and have a strikingly modern ring:

> Upon the savage it [the trading post] has worked a transformation. It found him without iron, hunting merely for food and raiment. It put into his hands iron and guns, and made him a hunter for furs with which to purchase the goods of civilization. Thus it tended to perpetuate the hunter stage; but it must also be noted that for a time it seemed likely to develop a class of merchants who should act as intermediaries solely. . . . The trading post left the unarmed tribes at the mercy of those that had bought firearms, and thus caused a relocation of the Indian tribes and an urgent demand for the trader by remote and unvisited Indians. It made the Indian dependent upon the white man's supplies. . . . Instead of elevating him the trade exploited him. . . . By inter-marriage with French traders the purity of the stock was destroyed and a mixed race produced. The trader broke down the old Totemic divisions, and appointed chiefs regardless of Indian social organization, to foster his trade. . . . The sale of their lands, made less valuable by the extinction of game, gave them a new medium of exchange, at the same time that, under the rivalry of trade, the sale of whiskey increased.[8]

Both Turner and Innis recognized that the frontier was the scene of a clash between a "relatively complex civilization and a much more simple civilization,"[9] between the agents of Europe and the inhabitants of North America.

II

Innis's contrast between two "civilizations," though at different stages of development, was much nearer to the truth than Turner's conflict between "savagery and civilization."[10] Indeed, it is all too easy from the twentieth-century perspective to exaggerate the disparity between pre-industrial Europe and pre-Columbian North America. Once the differences in environment have been taken into account, as Nancy Lurie has argued, "there was actually little in the European bag of tricks which the Indians could not syncretize with their own experience . . . despite guns and large ships the Europeans could not wrest a living from a terrain which, by Indian standards, supported an exceptionally large population."[11] Recognition of that fact helps to explain the relative ease and self-confidence that characterized the Amerindian reception of the first Europeans. For the most part, the Native inhabitants welcomed their unexpected visitors, offered hospitality, showed a willingness to trade, and provided advice on everything from food and transport to the healing arts. At first the Europeans acted more like tourists and peddlers than like prospective permanent residents. They were impressed with what they saw in this (to them) new world. "Throughout the eastern woodlands," Carl Sauer concluded in his survey of the earliest contacts, "the observers were impressed by the numbers, size, and good order of the settlements and by the appearance and civility of the people. The Indians were not seen as untutored savages, but as people living in a society of appreciated values."[12]

Yet on closer examination even those earliest contacts bore the seeds of future developments. Jacques Cartier's first meeting with the Native people who lived around what he christened the Baie des Chaleurs was typical, and its symbolism unmistakable. On July 6, 1534, just after mass, Cartier and his crew, travelling by long boat, were surprised by two fleets of Indian canoes whose occupants signalled their desire to trade. The Europeans, substantially outnumbered, were uneasy, and rather than trade they chose to frighten off their pursuers by loud gunfire. But the Amerindians were undaunted and returned the following day, apparently determined to exchange goods. This time a meeting took place, which Cartier recorded in a well-known passage:

> The savages showed a marvellously great pleasure in possessing and obtaining these iron wares and other commodities, dancing

and going through many ceremonies, and throwing salt water over their heads with their hands. They bartered all that they had to such an extent that all went back naked without anything on them; and they made signs to us that they would return on the morrow with more furs.

The inhabitants of this region had obviously met Europeans before. That they wanted to trade was one sign; that they left their women behind was another. Equally interesting was their almost insatiable desire for goods from Europe. Then there was the European sizing up his new acquaintances; there was obviously profitable trade to be had here. But there was still more. "I am more and more of the opinion," Cartier wrote, "that these people would be easy to convert to our holy faith."

With visions of commerce and Christianity in his head, Cartier on July 24, 1534, erected at the mouth of Gaspé harbour a thirty-foot cross emblazoned with the fleur-de-lys. An engraving in gothic print read, "VIVE LE ROY DE FRANCE." Here was a new turn of events, and one the Indian leader, Donnacona, did not expect. He protested vigorously, but to no avail. Under the duress of what amounted to abduction, he apparently accepted Cartier's claim that "the cross had been set up to serve as a land mark and guide post on coming into the harbour." But this, surely, was no ordinary traffic-control device. Rather, it was a claim to French possessory rights, directed not so much against the Native Americans, whose rights seem not to have been consulted, but against other European powers engaged in establishing overseas empires. Cartier's first meeting with the Native people of North America, his assessment of their trading and religious potential, and his cavalier assumption that he had the right to erect a traffic sign typify a whole series of similar events that took place along the Atlantic coast of North America.[13]

The European newcomers had little idea that they had made contact with peoples who had been developing over many centuries as hunting, gathering, fishing, and agricultural societies.[14] Pre-contact Huronia represented one type of society. It existed on the produce of its natural surroundings: the soil for corn, squash, and beans, "the three sisters"; the lakes for fish; and the animals of the woods and forests for clothing. These were the people of the "Long House." Rivers and streams provided natural roads for their birch-bark canoes. Their travels rarely carried them far.[15] The life of the

Plains people was different to the extent that their environment required other responses. The buffalo was basic to their domestic economy, providing food and shelter. The bow and arrow and spear were their weapons. When they moved, distances were short, for the carrying had to be done by women and dogs.[16] On the west coast a distinctive culture based on salmon-fishing, the collection of shellfish, and the trapping of land and sea animals thrived. Woodworking was highly developed, producing large houses in permanent coastal villages. These peoples' canoes were dugout cedars, suitable for heavy water, their fishing gear highly sophisticated, their sculpture and painting second to none in North America.[17]

In pre-Columbian North America the rhythm of life coincided with the cycle of the seasons. The Amerindian's cosmology provided an understanding of the world as he knew it.[18] Ceremonies like the Huron Ononharoia, the Mandan O-Kee-Pa, the Kwakiutl potlach, or the Ojibwa Midewiwin formed part of a rich religious and social life. Pre-contact society included some 200 separate cultures with perhaps as great a variety of languages. Those cultures were not static, but rather growing and changing. But that growth and change had taken place in virtual isolation from the European world.[19] The cultural and biological consequences of that separate existence only became evident after the Europeans arrived, bringing new animals and plants, new technologies, new diseases, new religious beliefs, and new views of social and economic organizations.[20]

III

The expansion of Europe into North America was, in part, the extension of the developing commercial system of early modern capitalism. That economic system, as it spread throughout the new continent, drew North America and its original inhabitants into the European mould. Settlement sometimes accompanied, sometimes followed, commercial contact. Christian missions were the third, sometimes uneasy, partnership in the Europeanizing project. Nascent capitalist economic structures brought market economics with profit-oriented trading practices and concepts of private property ownership that were, in most respects, alien to Amerindian customs. The rules of capitalist society, especially those relating to property relations, were contained in complex legal systems that had no real counterparts in North America.[21]

The Amerindians' initial contact with European economic organization came through the fur trade. At least in its early phases, that relationship proved satisfactory, even beneficial, to the Native Americans. But it also demonstrated the obvious importance of controlling some of the terms of the trade. As the fur trade was succeeded by agricultural settlement and industry, the Amerindian was gradually pressed to the margins of North American society. His way of life was an obstacle to agricultural production organized through private land ownership. His technology and skills, so important in the fur trade, were no longer in demand in the more diversified society. He rarely fitted into the new capitalist economy, even at the lowest level. In North America the proletariat also came from Europe.[22]

In the New England colonies, New France, and the vast territories of the Hudson's Bay Company, the fur trade provided the framework for a mutually profitable partnership.[23] Indeed, in the early stages the Native American had the upper hand because he had so much that the European needed if the trade was to be profitable.[24] Native technology, geographical knowledge, and country foods made penetration of the continent possible.[25] And most important, it was the harvest of furs that financed the founding of European empires in the New World.

The French were quick to recognize the superiority of Indian means of transportation. In 1602, facing the treacherous Lachine Rapids, Champlain wrote:

> The water here is so swift that it could not be more so . . . so that it is impossible to imagine one's being able to go by boats through these falls. But anyone desiring to pass them should provide himself with the canoe of the savages, which a man can easily carry. For to make a portage by boat could not be done in sufficiently brief time to enable one to return to France if he desired to winter there. . . . But in the canoe the savages can go without restraint, and quickly, everywhere, in the small as well as the large rivers. So that by using canoes as the savages do, it would be possible to see all there is, good and bad, in a year or two.[26]

Champlain was too optimistic about the time needed to tour the country, and he still had to learn that in winter another Indian invention would be necessary for the traveller: the snowshoe. Travelling in the interior, by canoe or snowshoe, meant travelling light. For heavy, complicated, and perishable food the Indians substituted *sagamité*: ground corn to which other ingredients could be added if available. At first the French palate revolted against this, especially when, as Father Sagard noted, it was eaten from the same bowls the Indians used when they "found themselves under the necessity of making water" in the midst of a canoe journey.[27] But *sagamité* quickly became recognized as indispensable for those who wanted to make the long journey into the Huron country. And when corn was not readily available, the Plains Indians provided another readily transportable food: pemmican. It was pemmican that got the Connecticut trader Peter Pond to Lake Athabaska before any other trader in 1777-78,[28] and it was soon a staple of the trade. With canoes and snowshoes, ground corn and pemmican, and, above all, with the aid of Indian guides, the European traders and explorers – the French on the St. Lawrence, the British on Hudson Bay, and then the Americans from St. Louis – were able to tap the rich fur resources of the interior of the continent. The fur trade, which magnetically drew the Europeans toward the unexplored interior, was of critical importance in the history of Amerindian-European contact.

In examining the fur trade and the Amerindian place in it, three initial points need to be emphasized. The first is that trade itself, and some of its consequences, preceded the coming of the European. While the pre-contact trading network of the Hurons, for example, has sometimes been exaggerated in size and importance,[29] there is no question that the trade and the rules of trade between Hurons and their neighbours, especially the Algonkians, had a lengthy history. From that long experience, the Hurons gained the knowledge that helped them in their later trading relations with the French. "The introduction of European goods," Bruce Trigger, a leading student of the Hurons, notes, "did not alter the pattern of Huron development so much as it intensified it."[30] In the southern part of the continent another member of the Iroquois linguistic group, the Cherokees, readily developed the techniques and rules of a trading people.[31] Similar pre-contact trading patterns existed in the Plains areas, where the Mandans, for example, played a leading role as middlemen.[32] In 1738, La Vérendrye observed the Mandans at first hand and was impressed with their business acumen. The Mandans, he recorded, "are sharp traders and clean the Assiniboine out of everything they have in the way of guns, powder, balls, knives, axes and awls."[33]

The role of middleman was well understood by many Indian groups, who jealously guarded that position once the European trade began. Donnacona's reluctance to provide Cartier with information about routes inland in 1535 may have stemmed from his desire to preserve the economic and political advantages his position as go-between gave him.[34] In the Hudson's Bay trading orbit, Assiniboine and Cree middlemen established their dominance in the trade at York Factory. That gave them the power to demand the best terms from the Blackfoot and Gros Ventres, on the one hand, and the French or British on the other.[35] A similar pattern was repeated on the Pacific coast, where Kwakiutl traders outbid the Hudson's Bay Company and sold to U.S. coastal ships, while Tsimshian and Tlingit chiefs monopolized trade on the Skeena and Stikine rivers.[36]

Although the fur trade unquestionably contributed to intertribal conflict and bloodshed, those conflicts were not initiated by the trade. The serpent, as John Ewers and others have shown, was already in the American Eden. Champlain discovered on his arrival in America at the beginning of the seventeenth century that Hurons and Algonkians were at war with the Mohawks and were anxious to engage the French on their side in the struggle.[37] Pre-contact Plains Indians fought over hunting grounds, women, and for revenge and prestige.[38] Indeed, one of the trader's main tasks was to attempt to pacify ancient tribal enmities, for in North America, as elsewhere, trade flourished best in conditions of peace and stability. The European peacemakers were not always successful, nor, indeed, were they always peacemakers. They were certainly not above exploiting intertribal rivalries for their own benefit. But war was not a preferred policy, for peace meant better profits.[39]

A second general, if somewhat obvious, point should be mentioned. In the fur trade, as in other aspects of contact, inland tribes were able to preserve their cultural integrity and bargaining power over a longer period than those tribes that came into earliest and most direct contact with the Europeans. The coastal tribes were the first to face the pressures of settlement, disease, and warfare.[40] While, in an unusual case like that of the Micmacs of Acadia, Indians were able to establish "a symbiotic relationship of mutual tolerance and support" with the French, the more common fate of the coastal Algonkians was defeat and subjugation. From the very outset of contact, the trade brought dramatic changes to the life cycle of the coastal tribes. The demands of the trade disrupted the usual winter movements of the Micmacs toward the coast. This meant that they gave up a traditional food source and became dependent on Europeans for subsistence.[41] What saved the Micmacs in Acadia was the confinement of the settlers to the coast, which left the Native peoples their interior hunting grounds while "neither group coveted the other's territory."[42] Most other areas on the coast had the opposite experience: white settlers did covet Indian lands. Moreover, the coastal Algonkians sometimes became pawns in a power game between the Europeans and the interior tribes, notably the Iroquois, who used them both as protective buffers and as conduits for trade with the Europeans.[43] The social revolution that followed this first phase of contact was rapid, much more so than in the interior.[44] For nearly two centuries, the distant tribes benefited from continued isolation – an isolation the fur traders encouraged in the realization that large-scale settlement would destroy their livelihood.[45]

A final general point is that, within the fur-trading system, the role of the Native people was certainly not a passive one. Cartier's initial experience was a common one: the Amerindians wanted to trade. They wanted to obtain European goods that were useful to them, and they early demonstrated a penchant for what might be called luxuries or novelties. That the Native Americans understood the benefits of competition was apparent from the outset. In 1611 Champlain wrote that the Montagnais "wanted to wait until several ships had arrived in order to get our wares more cheaply. Thus those people are mistaken who think that by coming first they can do better business; for these Indians are now too sharp."[46] Nor had the importance of profit escaped them; guns obtained at York Factory in the late eighteenth century for twelve beaver by the Crees were later sold to the Blackfoot at a 200 per cent markup. As long as fur-bearing animals remained plentiful, the fur trade provided a mutually profitable framework for Amerindian-European relations. The Indians, Arthur J. Ray has made clear, "were sophisticated traders, who had their own clearly defined set of objectives . . . they were astute consumers and not people who were easily hoodwinked."[47]

Many of the complexities of the fur trade can be illustrated by looking at the French-Huron experience. From the outset the part played by the Hurons in that relationship was that of a partner; it was, as W.J. Eccles notes, "a commercial alliance."[48] Since the

Hurons had already, in pre-contact times, developed a significant trading network based on their large agricultural output, the French found it necessary to adapt themselves to Huron trading practices. That meant at least a partial conformity to the Huron idea that trade had to satisfy more than mere economic motives. It was part of the politics of prestige.[49] Champlain quickly recognized that a successful trading relationship would have to include gift giving, treaties of friendship, exchange of European and Huron representatives, and perhaps even intermarriage. Father Sagard, for example, recorded his embarrassment at the repeated suggestion that he take a Huron wife "or at least . . . make a family alliance."[50] While Huron youths went off to Quebec to be educated and Christianized, the *coureurs de bois* took up residence with the Hurons at least partly as tokens of French trust. As the missionaries soon discovered, however, the *coureurs de bois* frequently adopted Indian customs and were thus poor examples of what civilization was supposed to offer.[51] Consequently they were replaced by *donnés*, laymen employed and controlled by the Jesuit missionaries. The Huron acceptance of the Jesuit presence was only a matter of convenience, not a demonstration of a willingness to convert. They wanted the benefits of the trade, especially European goods, which they believed could be readily integrated into their way of life. If, as Champlain and his successors insisted, acceptance of the missionaries was the price to be paid for the trading partnership, then they tolerated Brébeuf and his brethren. But only just.[52]

Yet even in the case of the relatively powerful and economically sophisticated Hurons, the fur trade had its disadvantages. It led to a gradually growing dependence on the French. The Iroquois threat increased that dependence. As Conrad Heidenreich and others have pointed out, the most important change was that, prior to contact, the Huron trading system was based on commodities they themselves produced; after contact it relied increasingly on furs and European goods.[53] It is true that Huron dependence never became as total and debilitating as that, for example, of the Montagnais, and at least until the 1630s trade seemed to bolster rather than undermine the Huron culture.[54] But by the late 1630s, the complicated relationship with the French that focused on the fur trade led to the destruction of Huronia and the assimilation of most of the survivors into the Iroquois Confederacy. In simple terms, the Hurons believed that the preservation of the French trading alliance depended on the missionary presence in Huronia. While the trade might not have seriously affected Huron culture, the goal of the Jesuits was to make fundamental changes in it. Their activities in Huronia created serious dissension between Indian Christians and traditionalists; that dissension weakened the Huron response to the Iroquois threat. And the Iroquois threat was partly the consequence of the competition between French and English fur-trading dominance.[55] In the background was the smallpox epidemic, which in the late 1630s had wiped out half of the Huron population. While the fur trade alone was not responsible for the smoke that rose from Saint-Marie-aux-Hurons in 1649, it was nevertheless a central part of the French-Huron relationship, and that relationship brought the final disaster.[56]

The destruction of Huronia and the depletion of fur-bearing animals in eastern North America pushed the explorer and the trader deeper into the interior of North America. The new networks that sprang up out of Fort Churchill, Montreal, and St. Louis followed many of the patterns already observed in the French-Huron trade. Nevertheless, on the western woodlands and Plains, where settlement pressure was slight until the middle of the nineteenth century, the partnership of Amerindian and European trader was fruitful. There, moreover, at least until the amalgamation of the Hudson's Bay Company and the North West Company in 1821, the tribal hunters often experienced the benefits of a seller's market. Once again the European traders found it necessary to operate in conformity with indigenous trading habits. Once again they found the Indians eager to trade. In 1730 La Vérendrye reported that a Cree spokesman "begged me to receive them all into the numbers of the children of our Father, to have pity on them and their families, that they were in a general condition of destitution, lacking axes, knives, kettles, guns, etc., that they hoped to get all these things from me if I would let them come to my fort."[57] But anxiety for European goods did not mean that substandard goods were acceptable. One Hudson's Bay Company trader, after a bad experience, reported home in 1728 that "never was any man so upbraided with our powder, kettles and hatchets, than we have been this summer by all the natives, especially by those that border near the French."[58] When Jean-Baptiste Truteau was advised to carry out some detailed market research in the early nineteenth century, the Company of Explorers of the Upper Missouri explicitly recognized that the Indian trade could not be taken for granted.[59] The western trading system, then, was again a meshing of European market economics and elements of the traditional exchange system, which was political as well as economic in nature. A careful and detailed examination of this trading system concludes that by the end of the eighteenth century market considerations had become dominant.[60]

No specific calculation of the comparative profits and losses of the European and Amerindian partners in the fur trade is even remotely possible. Even the standard of economic measurement would be almost impossible to establish. But that the European merchants and their companies found the business worthwhile goes almost without saying. They stayed in it and, in the case of the Hudson's Bay Company, for example, resisted the encroachments of settlement as long as possible.[61] On the Native American side the case is obviously more difficult to assess. When furs were plentiful, the prices high, and the Indians' bargaining power strong, the benefits were evident. On the Pacific coast the prosperity, the technological improvements, and the intellectual stimulus that came as part of the trade in the early years fostered an impressive cultural flowering.[62] Similar responses were doubtless witnessed elsewhere. But markets fluctuated as fashions changed and fur-bearing animals declined in the face of indiscriminate harvesting. And worse, the trade involved more than economic profits and losses. The same trade routes that brought buyer and seller together also brought epidemic diseases.[63]

IV

Although it was not recognized at the time, nor by historians in a systematic fashion until recently, the most significant consequence of early contact was biological. There is still much controversy over pre-Columbian demography, but there is substantial agreement that traditional, low-population estimates must be adjusted dramatically upward.[64] In the absence of a pre-Columbian census, there is, of course, a necessary tentativeness about all population estimates.[65] Nevertheless, the total population for North and South America at the time of Columbus's arrival would seem to have been in the area of 57 million. About four and one-half million of those Amerindians lived north of Mexico, of whom perhaps a million occupied present-day Canada, Alaska, and Greenland.[66] That figure had fallen to approximately 350,000 by the end of the nineteenth century. By 1890 the Indian population of the United

States stood at 250,000; in Canada, Alaska, and Greenland the figure for 1911 was 108,000.[67] That astonishing decline explains why, until recently, even sympathetic observers anticipated the total disappearance of Amerindian culture.[68]

While many factors led to the diminution of the Native populations, the "virulent disease frontier" is now generally recognized as the one of primary significance.[69] "The invasion of the New World populations by Old World pathogens," Henry Dobyns, a pioneer in this area of research, has written, "constituted one of the world's greatest biological disasters."[70] While Native Americans had suffered from such diseases as hepatitis, encephalitis, polio, and perhaps yellow fever, the Europeans introduced them to the contagions of smallpox, whooping cough, measles, chicken pox, bubonic plague, typhus, malaria, diphtheria, amoebic dysentery, influenza, and a number of helminthic infections. Wherever syphilis originated,[71] it was almost certainly brought to the people north of Mexico by Europeans.[72] The virulence of these diseases among indigenous North Americans is explained by the lack of previous contact. North America was virgin soil, its people lacking in both immunity and, despite a highly developed system of cures for indigenous diseases, medical treatment. The list of known epidemics is lengthy: between 1616 and 1619 a plague swept through New England that reduced the Indian population by 90 per cent. A decade later smallpox brought havoc to the St. Lawrence region, killing tens of thousands of Iroquois. A century later the same disease, perhaps the worst of the Indian killers, reduced the Cherokee population by half, while in 1837 six thousand Blackfoot, two-thirds of the total population, succumbed to the same infection. That same epidemic virtually exterminated the Mandans in the Dakotas. European-imported diseases were probably a major contributing factor in the extinction of the Beothuks of Newfoundland, whose last survivor died of tuberculosis in 1823. An 1862 smallpox epidemic, spreading north from Victoria, reduced the Native population from 60,000 to 20,000 in British Columbia.[73]

Knowing nothing of these mysterious diseases, Native Americans reacted with anger, fear, and panic. David Thompson, a western explorer, described the devastation of a smallpox epidemic:

> They had no idea of the disease and its dreadful nature . . . more men died in proportion than women and children, for unable to bear the heat of the fever they rushed into the Rivers and Lakes to cool

themselves, and the greater part thus perished. The countries were in a manner depopulated, the Natives allowed that far more than half had died, and from the number of tents which remained, it appeared that about three-fifths had perished. [74]

The most obvious consequence of epidemics was drastic population reduction. Though total figures, or even reliable approximations, are virtually impossible to calculate, a reasonable figure would certainly exceed 50 per cent. One estimate of the effect of disease on the population of the northern Plains between 1734 and 1850 indicates that in 1781-82 virtually every tribe – Arapaho, Arikara, Assiniboine, Blackfoot, Cheyenne, Cree, Crow, Flathead, Gros Ventre, Hidatsa, Kutenai, Mandan, Nez Percé, Shoshoni, and Sioux – suffered losses in excess of 25 per cent. Nearly half of these tribes were visited by an equally costly epidemic in 1837-38. [75] The Cree, it is interesting to note, escaped this 1837 ravage because of the effective action of William Todd, a Hudson's Bay Company employee, in carrying out a "massive vaccination." [76]

The importance of population loss, no matter how extensive, cannot be measured in numbers alone. Just as significant is the fact that many of the common epidemic diseases cut down men and women in their most productive years, a time when their services to their families and their communities were most critical. Edwin Denig, of the Western Fur Company, recognized this problem when he wrote of the 1837-38 epidemic among the Assiniboine that "generally very old or very young persons were the only ones who recovered. Most of the principal men having died, it took years to recover from the shock. Young men had to grow up, remnants of bands had to be collected, new leaders to be formed, property to be had." [77]

A second consequence of population shrinkage was territorial movement. Tribes most seriously weakened by loss through disease were easily driven from their traditional territories by their enemies. The decimated Mandan, for example, joined with the remnants of the Arikara and Hidatsi in an attempt to preserve fragments of their existence. In fact, their condition was so feeble that they became almost totally dependent on the assistance of the United States government. By 1862 further epidemics, combined with Sioux depredations, had reduced these three tribes to a single village. The devastating impact of smallpox on the Assiniboine in 1837 opened the prairie parklands to large-scale migrations of Woodland Cree who, having been immunized against the disease, became the numerically dominant group in the area.[78]

Finally, a major consequence of epidemic disease was a breakdown of traditional values and beliefs. It was easy enough for the Indians to hold the Europeans responsible for the frightening new diseases. As early as the 1640s the Hurons were remarking that "since we pray we see by experience that death carries us off everywhere."[79] But the fact remained that their own cures and their own medicine men were totally ineffective when faced with these foreign contagions. Perhaps the Europeans, and especially the missionaries, had already sown the seeds of doubt,[80] but the helplessness of the trusted shaman in the face of smallpox, measles, and cholera produced a more lasting scepticism, with consequences that may have led to serious questioning of traditional cosmology. David Thompson observed this reaction in the Saskatchewan country in 1780:

> About the tenth day we came to the "One Pine." This had been a fine stately tree of two fathoms girth, growing among a patch of Aspens, and being all alone without any other pines for more than a hundred miles, had been regarded with superstitious reverence. When the smallpox came . . . the master of one of the tents applied his prayers to it, to save the lives of him and his family, burned sweet grass and offered upon its roots three horses to be at its service, all he had, the next day the furniture of his horses with his Bow and Quiver of Arrows, and the third morning, having nothing more, a Bowl of Water. The disease was now on himself and he had to lie down. Of his large family, only himself, one of his wives and a Boy survived. As soon as he acquired strength he took his horses and all his other offerings from the "Pine Tree," then putting his little axe in his belt, he ascended the Pine Tree to about two-thirds of its height, and then cut it off, out of revenge for not having saved his family.[81]

Once the value system, already corroded by other aspects of contact, came into question, the final subversion was not far in the future, for the shaman was "a principal barrier to the eradication of Indian culture."[82]

The drastic decimation of the Native population through disease may well have produced another quite unforeseen result: a disturbance in nature's balance. That is one possible interpretation of a story that puzzled the observant David Thompson. He wrote:

A strange idea prevails among these Natives, and also of all the Indians to the Rocky Mountains, though unknown to each other, that when they were numerous, before they were destroyed by the Small Pox all the animals of every species were also very numerous and more so in comparison of the number of Natives than at present; and this was confirmed to me by old Scotchmen in the service of the Hudson's Bay Company, and by the Canadians from Canada; the knowledge of the latter extended over all the interior countries, yet no disorder was known among the animals, the fact was certain, and nothing they knew of could account for it.

In nature, both hunter – wolf or Indian – and hunted – deer or beaver – are necessary to maintain the equilibrium. The destruction of predators may temporarily cause the hunted to flourish. But rapid food depletion may then bring large population losses. So perhaps disease was the explanation of the observed decline of animals – disease among the Indians.[83]

The destructive effect of epidemic disease on the Native American populations cannot be taken as evidence of weakness or backwardness. Within the demands of their own environment, Amerindian medical knowledge and practice were not only adequate but in some ways superior to European knowledge. Their use of herbs was very sophisticated, their methods of childbirth and birth control effective and humane. Almost every European observer noted the generally sound health and physical condition of the inhabitants at the time of initial contact. The observation of Nicholas Denys in 1672 was fairly typical:

> They were not subject to disease, and knew nothing of fevers. If any accident happened to them . . . they did not need a physician. They had knowledge of herbs, of which they made use and straight away grew well. They were not subject to the gout, gravel, fevers or rheumatism. The general remedy was to make themselves sweat, something which they did every month and even oftener.[84]

The Iroquois understanding of psychology was attested to, often grudgingly, by such a writer as Père Charlevoix, who noted of the shaman that "what proves the power of imagination over men is that these physicians with all their absurdities cure to the full as often as our own." That opinion is emphatically seconded by modern experts. "Iroquois understanding of psycho-dynamics,"

Anthony Wallace has written, "was greatly superior to that of the most enlightened Europeans of the time."[85]

The Indian readily shared his medical cures with the European, as Cartier's scurvy-ridden crew learned. But the tragedy was that Indian medical knowledge proved largely ineffective against the virulent diseases planted in the virgin soil of the Americas by the European intruder.[86] Unconscious "germ warfare" was the most important single cause of the depopulation and demoralization of Native American societies.

Though disease was an unintended companion of the European trader, one destructive item in the trader's bag of goods was not: alcohol. From the time of the earliest contacts, Europeans discovered both the Indian's almost insatiable desire for liquor and his apparent inability to consume it in moderation. "These skins were bartered for brandy," Nicholas Denys wrote in 1672, "for which they ever since they first began to trade with fishermen are very greedy and they herewith fill themselves up to such an extent that they frequently fall over backwards, for they do not call it drinking unless they overload themselves with this strong drink in beastly fashion."[87] Given Amerindian proclivities, the temptation to use brandy, whisky, and other intoxicants in the trade was a virtually irresistible temptation. And as the traditional value system of the Amerindians disintegrated as a consequence of various elements of the contact relationship, the Indians lost confidence in themselves and turned more and more to the consolations of intoxication. It may be one of the great ironies of post-contact history that the missionaries, who opposed the brandy and whisky trade, actually contributed to the Native American's reliance on it through their corrosive impact on Native religious beliefs.[88]

But the fur trade cannot be exonerated from blame for the alcohol trade. Faced with price competition between companies and with the demands of the Native Americans for better prices, the European traders found that alcohol was the commodity best suited to satisfy demand and protect profits. Its advantages were twofold. Since it was one of the few trade items that the Indians desired in almost unlimited quantities, it could induce the trappers to increase their volume of furs as nothing else could.[89] Moreover, since the cost of alcohol could be controlled by the simple process of watering it down, it effectively protected margins of profit in a seller's market. As an item in gift-giving ceremonies, a practice increasingly used as an inducement to trade, alcohol assumed an enormous importance.[90]

The North West Company trader Duncan M'Gillivray cynically anticipated the economic historian's argument when he wrote in 1794 that "when a nation becomes addicted to drinking, it affords a strong presumption that they will soon become excellent traders."[91] Even after the Hudson's Bay Company's monopoly was established and the whisky trade officially suppressed, M'Gillivray's philosophy continued to animate the illegal trade out of such places as Fort Whoop Up and to contribute to the final disintegration of Amerindian culture on the western Plains. As much as 25 per cent of the Blackfoot population may have perished from the effects of alcohol in the years between 1869 and 1874 alone.[92] Alcohol, too, was an epidemic disease.

V

The onrush of settlement, shrinking markets, and the reduction – even extinction – of some species of fur-bearing animals all contributed to the fur trade's decline. In a sense, it died of its own success, for success brought the depletion of resources. The gun, the steel trap, and the horse were critical elements in that success and decline. Each played its part in ensuring a greater harvest of animals in the short run. Each played its part in increasing Native American dependence on the Europeans, first by expanding the importance of fur-gathering in the Indian economy, and then by contributing to the indiscriminate exploitation that led to exhaustion of the resource. In the end all the Indian had left was dependence. That was the essence of the tragedy of the single-crop staple economy.

The danger of the exhaustion of resources was foreseen by some at least as early as the mid-seventeenth century. Father Le Jeune recognized that the Indians were not conservationists when he observed that when the Montagnais "find a lodge they kill all, great and small, male and female. The danger is that they will exterminate the species in the region, as has happened among the Hurons."[93] If the valuable furs disappeared in the East, the supply on the northwest Plains seemed inexhaustible. But that optimistic assessment ignored the potential of the steel trap baited with castoreum when combined with the determination of trappers and traders alike to gather in the maximum harvest. David Thompson assumed that the Indian had invented the use of castoreum, though it, like the steel trap, was apparently a European innovation.[94] But Thompson's account of the fate of the beaver, and those who depended on it, as recounted to him by an elderly Indian in Swan River country, remains a classic:

> About two winters ago Weesaukejauk [the Flatterer] showed to our brethren, the Nepissings and Algonquins the secret of their destruction; that all of them were infatuated with the Castoreum of their own species, and more fond of it than we are of fire water. We are now killing the Beaver without any labour, we are now rich but soon [shall] be poor, for when the Beaver are destroyed we have nothing to depend on to purchase what we want for our families, strangers now ruin our country with their iron traps, and we, and they, will soon be poor.

That prediction of disaster took only four years to be fulfilled, Thompson noted in 1797, and drew an ecologically sound moral: "A worn out field can be manured and again made fertile; but the Beaver, once destroyed cannot be replaced; they were the gold coin of the country, with which the necessities of life were procured."[95] Attempts were made by the Hudson's Bay Company to prohibit the use of steel traps and control the slaughter of beaver, but the effort was unavailing. The trappers did not understand the need for conservation, some traders refused to accept any threat to profits, and no central authority existed to enforce compliance.[96]

The growing scarcity of beaver increased the importance of other animals, notably the buffalo. In 1805, Zebulon Pike had remarked on the critical importance of this huge beast when he wrote: "The Yanctongs and Titongs are the most independent Indians in the world; they follow the buffalo as chance directs, clothing themselves with the skins, and making their lodges, bridles and saddles of the same material, the flesh of the animal furnishing their food."[97] To that list of uses should be added pemmican as a trade item.[98] After 1821 the Indians no longer had the pemmican market to themselves, for many of the Métis, who had been released from the Company's staff with the reorganization, now turned to the buffalo hunt. When demand for buffalo robes developed, especially in the United States, Indian and Métis alike set out to reap the profits.[99]

While the buffalo hunt was by no means dependent on the rifle and the horse, both of these European additions to Native American life contributed to the near extinction of the buffalo.[100] By 1880 the buffalo joined the beaver (though it was only down, not out) and the passenger pigeon as victims of the contact between European technology and markets on the one hand, and the Indian hunting culture on the other.[101] And the disappearance of the buffalo left once proud, even arrogant, tribes like the Plains Cree starving and faced with little alternative but to beg the authorities for sustenance.[102] And the price of the sustenance, from both Canadian and United States governments, was submission to life on a reservation.

That final state of dependence developed only gradually, but it was perhaps inherent in the character of the trade. Furs provided the Indians with the currency to purchase European technology, utensils, and trinkets. Those commodities undoubtedly gave the Indians a higher standard of living, an easier way of life. But this change in lifestyle also meant that they discarded Native skills. A Montagnais is quoted as saying that "the Beaver does everything perfectly well; it makes kettles, hatchets, swords, knives, bread, in short it makes everything."[103] As the trade became all important, dependency increased because other sources of livelihood were neglected. By the middle of the eighteenth century, Peter Kalm realized that guns had become indispensable to the Indians of New France, for without them "they would starve to death."[104] The Europeans not only supplied guns and ammunition; only they could repair the often poor-quality weapons. "The old Indians, when speaking of their ancestors, wonder how they could live, as a Beaver was wiser, and the Bear stronger, than them," David Thompson recorded, "and they confess, that if they were deprived of the Gun, they could not live by the Bow and Arrow, and must soon perish."[105]

The horse and the gun went together as the most prized possessions of the Indians of the central Plains, where, by the middle of the eighteenth century, "the northeastward moving frontier of the horse met the southwestward moving frontier of the gun."[106] Together they radically altered life on the Plains. For one thing, they contributed to the increasing bloodiness of intertribal warfare. The Plains Cree, for example, quickly recognized the importance of the gun in their effort to defeat the Dakotas and take over their hunting territories. Later, when their woodlands hunting grounds were exhausted, the Cree turned their weapons against the Gros Ventres and Blackfoot in a struggle for control of the Plains.[107] As for the horse, it not only increased mobility, it also reduced the exhausting tasks of Plains Indian women by providing a new beast of burden. Moreover, it modified social structures, for the ownership of horses became the measure of wealth, allowing the rich to prosper and the horseless poor to grow poorer. [108] But neither increased mobility nor greater firepower could disguise the fact that the traditional foundations of the Plains hunting culture were vanishing. "We have been running wild on the prairie," Lame Bull told the treaty negotiators in 1855, "and now we want the white man's sons and daughters of our Great White Father to come to our country to tame us." [109] The pathetic plea was hardly necessary.

Drastic shifts in the social organization of Indian tribes, in response to the demands of the European trade, were evident among most Indian tribes. The Chippewas, who lived in the vast region around the Upper Great Lakes, gradually moved from pre-contact village organization to more centralized hunting bands in response to fur-trade imperatives. Moreover, here as elsewhere the trade encouraged neglect of other forms of livelihood, notably fishing. That meant that when winter arrived, food had to be purchased from the European traders. And the food the Chippewas bought back was often the same provisions they had earlier sold to the traders for whisky and trinkets. Thus, whatever equality had originally existed between hunters and traders disappeared. [110]

For the Cherokee, scattered through the southern Appalachians bordering the Carolinas, Georgia, Tennessee, and Virginia, trade with the British at Charleston also had profound effects on social and economic development. Despite their isolation and their tradition as a trading people, the attraction of European goods, especially the gun, was fatal. In the early eighteenth century the trade, composed of deerskins, dried plants, and slaves, was an exchange between equals. But it was, as John Phillip Reid has remarked, "an unequal equality." [111] While at the outset the British modified their trading patterns and regulations to conform to Cherokee practices, the Cherokee gradually came to need the British more than the reverse. Other factors, familiar elsewhere, also increased the disparity in the relationship. Population reduction through disease forced increasing use of European agricultural tools, which contributed to soil exhaustion. Moreover, the growing importance of the herb trade forced neglect of food production. Finally, the time and the energy necessary for the preparation of skins and herbs for market, combined with the decreased population, forced neglect of hunting grounds, where careful management was necessary to ensure the animal supply.[112]

By the 1730s Cherokee dependence on the British was nearly complete. A conservative group, advocating a return to the old isolation, found little response among the majority, who "did not wish to be without the better kind of hatchet," the European-supplied gun.[113] The assimilation of the Cherokee people was now almost unavoidable, and the trend was accepted and even encouraged. Acceptance of the white man's ways was demonstrated graphically by the gradual adoption of a centralized, coercive authority to replace the almost anarchic, traditional consensual organization.[114] And that new state set about abolishing many traditional practices, such as the clan right of retribution. But the tragic irony of the Cherokee was that they consciously chose acculturation and political organization as a means of protecting the territories they occupied only to discover that even that was not enough.[115] Despite the support of the Supreme Court in the famous case of the *Cherokee Nation v. the State of Georgia* (1831), the Georgians were successful in removing most of the Cherokee people to the Indian territory west of the Mississippi.[116] That better hatchet proved to be double-edged.

VI

It was certainly not the fur trader's intention to undermine Amerindian culture. His very livelihood depended on its preservation. Unlike the settler who followed in his path, the fur trader needed the Indian.[117] For the most part he tolerated the Indian way of life, sometimes he admired it, and frequently he became intimately involved in it through *mariage à la façon du pays*. From the outset of contact there had been intermarriage and the recognition that such arrangements could be mutually advantageous. In the marriage of Pocahontas and John Rolfe, both Europeans and Amerindians recognized a traditional method of cementing an alliance. At quite another level, intermarriage took place because Europeans – *coureurs de bois* and "white Indians" – were attracted to the Native American lifestyle. As Peter Kalm observed, many young men in New France "settle among the *Indians* far from *Canada*, marry *Indian* women, and never come back again."[118] Since the male-female ratio in New England was fairly well balanced, miscegenation was less common there.[119] And it is important to note that intermarriage seems to have virtually always taken place between European men and Amerindian or Métis women.

Mixed marriages produced many prominent offspring: Corn-planter, the half-brother of the Seneca prophet Handsome Lake; Sequoyah, inventor of the Cherokee syllabary; and Jean-Baptiste Charbonneau, born to the famous Shoshoni, Sacajaweah, and her voyageur husband on the Lewis and Clark expedition. In fact, mixed marriage was a fairly common phenomenon on the nine-teenth-century frontier. The 1825 United States census recorded 225 such marriages among the Cherokee alone; by mid-century, mixed marriages were common among the Blackfoot. One Scottish fur trader, his three Cree wives, and twenty-seven children estab-lished a distinct new tribe, the Willow Indians, on the Canadian Plains at the end of the eighteenth century. [120]

The pattern of these unions usually followed the Indian custom of what might be called common-law marriage. Apart from the mutual satisfactions of cohabitation, these marriages had obvious material advantages for both fur traders and Indians. An Indian wife provided a trader with a skilled travelling companion and inter-preter and a privileged relationship with a particular group of Indians. Daniel Harmon, a Nor'wester from Vermont who never lost his Puritan conscience, left a colourful account of his "country marriage." Two years after arriving in the Northwest, and already acquainted with traders who had Indian wives, he wrote:

> a Chief among the Crees came to the Fort accompanied by a number of his relations who appeared very desirous that I should take one of his Daughters to remain with me, but to put him off I told him that I could not then take a woman however in the fall perhaps I might for I added I had no dislike of her. But he pressed me to keep her at once as he said he was fond of me and he wished to have his Daughter with the white people and he almost persuaded me to accept her, for I was sure that while I had the Daughter I should not only have the Father's hunts but those of his relations also, and of course [this] would be much in the favour of the Company & perhaps in the end some advantage to me likewise – so that interest (and perhaps a little natural inclination also) I found was nigh making me commit another folly, if not a sin, – but thanks be to God alone if I have not been brought into a snare laid no doubt by the Devil himself.

Three years later, after "mature consideration," he succumbed to fourteen-year-old Elizabeth Duval, whose mother was a Cree. She bore him fourteen children. When Harmon returned to Vermont after sixteen years in Indian country, he took Elizabeth and the surviving children with him, and he made the marriage legal. "On the whole," he wrote, "I consider the course which I design to pursue as the only one which religion and humanity would justify."[121]

For the tribe from which the wife came, the marriage provided a guarantee of continued good relations and perhaps trading preferences. For the woman, whose wishes may not have been much taken into account, such a marriage may have provided a slightly easier way of life. Thus the practice of marriage according to the custom of the country reached the highest echelons of the trade in both the United States and British North America.[122] Alexander Culbertson, a leading bourgeois in the American Fur Company, took the daughter of a prominent Blood Indian for his wife. Edwin Denig had two Indian wives and was quite clear about the economic advantages that went along with these liaisons.[123] In Canada the most prominent of the numerous traders who took advantage of the custom of the country was no less a personage than George Simpson, the governor of the Honourable Company.[124]

Naturally, the treatment of these women and of their offspring varied. Some, including Medicine-Snake-Woman, Culbertson's wife, eventually returned to the tribal life. Others, like Simpson's Betsy, were found other husbands. Still others, probably a minority, returned with their husbands to the East for retirement. One woman, Suzanne-Pas-de-Nom, won an important legal case in which the Canadian courts established that her *mariage à la façon du pays* was legally binding.[125] The fate of offspring varied as well. Some were sent off to established schools, where they were provided with the manners and knowledge necessary for future careers in Canada and Great Britain.[126] Others were less fortunate, perhaps. Left to grow up in the West, they led a semi-nomadic, semi-agricultural life, in the trade, the buffalo hunt, and a little agriculture. French-language Métis and English-speaking "country-born" made up the majority of the inhabitants of Red River in 1869, when one of their number, Louis Riel, called them together to resist Canadian manifest destiny.[127]

It is difficult to make any sure assessment of the significance of miscegenation in the overall relationship between Europeans and Indians. Apart from the personal benefits and costs of intermarriage, the end result was probably disadvantageous to the Native Americans. It doubtless contributed to the breakdown of traditional family and kin relationships, introducing European patterns of male-female relationships. Within the structure of the fur trade, intermarriage worked well enough, apparently, but it declined rapidly with the arrival of settlement and European women. In short, it was a convenience the Europeans discarded once its usefulness was exhausted. In some settlement areas, the relatively happy country marriages seem to have been succeeded by prostitution and a much more unpleasant kind of concubinage.[128] While the offspring of the mixed marriages might have provided a bridge between the two cultures, that rarely happened. Acceptance by one or other of the two cultures apparently offered the most satisfactory life for most of these people. Certainly the fate of most Canadian Métis, since the final defeat of Louis Riel in 1885, has been a miserable one for most of these survivors of the fur trade's golden years.[129] In the last analysis, the fur trade failed to prepare the Indian or mixed blood for the world that arrived with large-scale settlement.

VII

The encroachment of white settlement, wholesale removal of long-established tribes, and finally confinement on reservations, in both Canada and the United States, marked the last stage in the closing of the "frontier." That process reduced once-dominant Amerindian societies to a status of marginality in North America. The relationship to the land had been fundamental to the shape, functioning, and much of the belief system of Amerindians. The making over of North American landholding patterns in the image of Europe therefore radically undermined the Native culture. At Tippecanoe, Tecumseh protested vainly against the apparently inexorable process:

> The Great Spirit gave this great Island to his red children; he placed the whites on the other side of the big water; they were not contented with their own, but came to take ours from us. They have driven us from the sea to the lakes; we can go no further.[130]

Placing the Native Americans on circumscribed territories and dividing the rest of North America into individually owned properties was the most conclusive sign of the Europeanization of North America. While Amerindian concepts of property varied from tribe to tribe, they all reflected the needs of societies whose existence depended on the products of nature. Usufruct, not registered legal land title, was fundamental, and common ownership was frequent.[131] European contact brought profound changes. The fur trade had already led to some important alterations in property relations. Among the Montagnais, who had traditionally practised common ownership of hunting grounds, the competition of the trade led to the establishment of "family hunting territories," though changes in available food sources may also have encouraged this development.[132] Moreover, the traditional Montagnais family organization, which was bicentred, became predominantly patrilocal in response to the demands of the trade.[133]

Similar changes were experienced by other tribes. In the process of land purchase, whether by fair means or otherwise, patrilineal laws of property were gradually forced on such groups as the Iroquois, who had traditionally followed matrilineal lines of inheritance.[134] This change transformed the status of both men and women in Iroquois society. Traditionally, the Iroquois and other Amerindian women had worked the soil, a custom that revealed not their subordination but rather their ownership of the land. The pattern of the European way of life, where men assumed the farming role, may have eased the woman's physical burdens, but it similarly reduced her to a status "more like her white sisters."[135] For the male the change was not less crucial. Now the landowner, the male also found himself relegated to doing "women's work" and being more dependent on his wife and children for help than he had ever been in his hunting and warring roles.[136] Those traditional concepts of property and the division of labour were probably major reasons for the resistance of Indians to confinement on reserves and acceptance of European agricultural practices.[137] The white man's "lazy Indian" was a man whose occupation had disappeared.

European settlement, even on a limited scale, challenged the Amerindian understanding of land ownership. The Indian did not "own" the land in the European sense of holding a legally enforceable title. Nevertheless, there was recognition, both tribal and intertribal, that defined areas – village sites, agricultural plots, fishing places, hunting territories, and berry patches – belonged to specified groups.[138] Alden T. Vaughan's claim that "the disparity between English and Indian concepts of land tenure was actually rather slight"[139] is accurate enough if one ignores, for the moment, the European legal system.

But the arrival of European immigrants, European governments, and European laws brought customary Indian title into jeopardy.

Europeans now laid claim to the lands either through proprietary right, various forms of purchase, or by simple occupancy. To continue to hold land legally, Native Americans were forced to recognize the validity and authority of the newly installed system. In short, European law came to define Amerindian property rights. Given that dominant fact, the question of whether Amerindians received a fair return for their property becomes an interesting but distinctly subordinate consideration. [140]

Yet even acceptance of the new system did not guarantee inalienable claims to property. Large tracts of land that were not exploited according to European prescriptions could be considered vacant, and then be occupied. A report of a committee of the Canadian legislature examining Indian policy in 1844 approvingly quoted a passage from Emmerich de Vattel's *Le Droit des gens* (1758):

> The earth . . . belongs to mankind in general, and was designed to furnish them with subsistence. If each nation had from the beginning resolved to appropriate to itself a vast country that the people might live only by hunting, fishing and wild fruits, our globe would not be sufficient to maintain a tenth part of its present inhabitants. We do not, therefore, deviate from nature, in confining the Indians within narrower limits. [141]

Natural philosophy thus aided land hunger as Indians throughout the continent felt growing pressure to surrender or sell their lands. As the Six Nations, who had stood by the British in the American Revolution, learned to their sorrow, even solemn agreements could be modified at the will of the dominant partner. The reward for their loyalty in 1783 had been more than one-half million acres of productive land along the Grand River in Canada. By 1841, a series of complicated transfers and controversial sales had reduced that tract by more than 50 per cent. [142] Indians in British Columbia learned that the size of a reservation could vary according to government response to settler pressures. [143] In the United States, the removal of Cherokee, Choctaw, Chickasaw, and Creek, under various forms of persuasion, gave full meaning to Chief Justice John Marshall's apt description of the Cherokee (and by inference, Amerindians generally) as a "domestic, dependent, nation." [144]

The American West, in the post-Civil War decades, was the scene of a series of bloody wars against the Sioux, the Cheyenne, and most of the other Plains tribes. As a result, the Indians were forced to accept reservation life, and the last unsettled lands were opened to whites. To the north the pressure of settlement was less intense and the process much more peaceful, but the end result was remarkably similar. After the abortive Métis rebellion in Red River in 1869, Canada acquired the Hudson's Bay Company territories. To prepare the way for settlement a quasi-military constabulary, the North-West Mounted Police, was organized to oversee the signing of treaties and the establishment of reservations for increasingly destitute Indians. [145]

The Amerindians, through land sales, treaties, and wars, were to be moved, confined, and eventually "civilized" to make way for the inflow of Europeans. An instruction to the lieutenant-governor of the North-West Territories stated the policy frankly enough:

> while assuring the Indians of your desire to establish friendly relations with them, you will ascertain and report to His Excellency the course you may think the most advisable to pursue, whether by Treaty or otherwise, for the removal of any obstructions that might be presented to the flow of population into the fertile lands that lie between Manitoba and the Rocky Mountains. [146]

As elsewhere across the continent, the "obstructions" were systematically removed. What the Indians received in exchange for "fertile lands" evoked this description from a Canadian missionary at the end of the nineteenth century: "The new mode of life on a Reserve, dwelling in filthy houses, badly ventilated, has induced disease; the idle manner of living, being fed by the Government, and having little to do; the poor clothing worn in the winter; badly cooked food, the consciousness that as a race they are fading away." [147]

VIII

When Frederick Jackson Turner, speaking *ex cathedra*, proclaimed the closing of the American "frontier" in 1893, he was right in at least one sense. The frontier that Columbus, Verrazzano, Cabot, Cartier, and Hudson had opened, and on which the drama of European-Amerindian contact had commenced, was closed by the end of the nineteenth century. If all the world had once been America, then by 1890 most of North America was Europe. [148] Cartier's traffic sign had pointed the way for explorers, missionaries, traders, and settlers who had gradually changed, dispersed, and enclosed the Native populations. In the mythical struggle between Aataentsic's children, Tawiscaron and Iouskara, for control over the world on the turtle's back, Tawiscaron the Creator had won the day. In the post-Columbian world, the Amerindian must often have concluded that the victory had gone to his destructive brother.[149]

The Indians who joined Louis Riel for his last stand at Batoche in 1885 were the brothers of those who marked "the symbolic end of Indian freedom" at Wounded Knee five years later.[150] What had begun in fragile sailing ships had been completed by the railways, the Northern Pacific and the Canadian Pacific. They brought soldiers to pacify and settlers to occupy. They bound the new European-sponsored nations together and reminded the old Amerindian nations that the new technology had triumphed. Unexpected consequences had flowed from small beginnings. "Simple people, with simple trades and simple goods," V.S. Naipaul wrote of Africa, though it might have been of America, "but agents of Europe."[151]

THREE

Making a Garden
out of a Wilderness

*"The Land is a Garden of Eden before them, and behind them a
desolate wilderness."*

Joel 2:3

"Is not america," Fernand Braudel asks in *The Perspective of the
World*, the third volume of his magisterial *Civilization and Capitalism*, "perhaps the true explanation of Europe's greatness? Did not
Europe discover or indeed 'invent' America, and has Europe not
always celebrated Columbus's voyages as the greatest event in history 'since the creation'?" And then the great French historian concludes that "America was . . . the achievement by which Europe
most truly revealed her own nature."[1] Braudel wrote without any
intended irony, but that final remark about Europe truly revealing
"her own nature" is perhaps what is really at issue in the current
reassessment of the implications of Columbus's landfall at
Guanahari, or San Salvador, as he named it in his first act of semi-
otic imperialism. ("Each received a new name from me,"[2] he
recorded.)

That "nature" is captured by Marc Lescarbot in a sentence from
his remarkable *History of New France*, published in 1609, which goes
right to the heart of what we have apparently decided to call the
"encounter" between the Old World and the New that Columbus
symbolizes. Acadia, he wrote, "having two kinds of soil that God
has given unto man as his possession, who can doubt that when it
shall be cultivated it will be a land of promise?"[3] I hardly need
to explain why I think that sentence is so revealing of the European
"nature," but I will. It forthrightly articulates the renaissance

European's conviction that man was chosen by the Creator to possess and dominate the rest of creation. And it further assumes that, for the land to be fully possessed, it must be cultivated: tilled, improved, developed. The result: a promised land, a paradise, a garden of delights. Lescarbot's observations seemed so axiomatic then, and for nearly five centuries afterward, that almost no one questioned his vision of a promised land – at least almost no European. But that has begun to change. Contemporary Europe, as much in its western as in its eastern portions, struggles to redefine itself. Consequently Europe overseas, as J.G.A. Pocock recently argued in a brilliant essay,[4] is being forced to look again at the meaning of what Gómara in his *General History of the Indies* (1552) called "the greatest event since the creation of the world"[5] – the meaning of the "discovery of America."

The general shape of that reassessment has been emerging for more than a decade. Indeed, the seminal work, Alfred W. Crosby's powerful study, *The Columbian Exchange: Biological and Cultural Consequences of 1492*, is two decades old. In that book Crosby argued that most of the histories of European expansion had missed the real point. It was not principalities and powers but rather organisms, seeds, and animals that wrought the most fundamental changes in post-Columbian America. "Pandemic disease and biological revolution," not European technology and Christian culture, allowed Europeans "to transform as much of the New World as possible into the Old World."[6]

If Crosby offered a startling new explanation for the ease with which Europeans conquered the Americas, it remained for a Bulgarian cultural critic, living in Paris, to dissect the language and ideology of Columbian imperialism. In his brilliant if sometimes infuriatingly undocumented *The Conquest of America*, Tzvetan Todorov argued that sixteenth-century Europeans adopted two equally destructive attitudes toward the inhabitants of the New World. On the one hand, Amerindians were viewed as "savages," radically different and inferior to Europeans. Consequently, they could be enslaved. On the other hand, the Native peoples were seen "not only as equal but as identical." Consequently, they could be assimilated. Whether "noble savage" or just "savage," Amerindians were never accepted on their own terms – different but equal. "Difference," Todorov wrote, "is corrupted into inequality, equality into identity."[7] *The Conquest of America* is, in essence, a subtle questioning of Eurocentricity, an assertion that the conventional story of 1492 had for too long been a monologue in which only European voices and values had been heard. Together, Crosby and Todorov – not just them, though they have been essential – have argued that to understand the coming together of Europe and America the ecological and intellectual worlds of both sides of the encounter must be brought into dialogue. If Europe discovered America in the centuries following 1492, it is equally true that America discovered Europe – and each revealed its "own nature."

What began as a trickle with Crosby and Todorov has since become a near flood. Its most extreme and popularized form is found in Kirkpatrick Sale's recent *Conquest of Paradise*, a book that has received far more attention, even from serious reviewers, than it warranted. Sale is not just critical of the Admiral of the Ocean Sea, though he certainly is that, but his principal point is an indictment of "the essential unsuitability of European culture for the task on which it was embarking."[8] In Sale's view, pre-Columbian America was a continent whose people lived in such harmony with each other, and with nature, as to approximate paradise. The European quest for gold, inspired by greed and God, destroyed that Edenic life. Exaggerated as his claims are, and driven as they are by a kind of moral certainty unbecoming to an historian, Sale's book nevertheless does raise some matters that will increasingly be part of the historian's agenda in examining the early period of the European entry into the Americas.

And that brings me back to Marc Lescarbot and the issues that might be considered in an ecological approach to the early history of Acadia. The history of the environment and the people who lived in pre-contact and especially proto-historical Acadia is not a new subject. Though his name is rarely mentioned in books about Canadian historical writing, the pioneer in environmental history in the Maritime region was an extraordinary scholar named William Francis Ganong. A graduate of the University of New Brunswick, Harvard, and Munich, Ganong taught natural science – botany was his specialty – at Smith College, Massachusetts, throughout his scholarly life. But he devoted most of his research to the natural history, geography, and general history of Acadia. His maps of early explorations, his editions of Nicolas Denys's *Description and Natural History of Acadia* and Chrestien Le Clercq's *New Relation of Gaspesia*, and his hundreds of articles in a variety of journals represent a contribution to early Canadian history that has yet to be properly recognized – at least by historians. When I set out on my current research work on the natural and anthropological history of early Canada one of my ambitions was to compile an historical bird watcher's guide – a chronology of the discovery of the birds of Canada. I quickly found that Ganong had been there well before me: in 1909 he published in the *Transactions of the Royal Society of Canada* "The Identity of Plants and Animals mentioned by the Early Voyages to Eastern Canada and Newfoundland."

The second Maritime scholar for whom the environment was a necessary component of history was Alfred G. Bailey. His work is more generally known because of the reissue in 1969 of his seminal *Conflict of European and Eastern Algonkian Cultures 1504-1700*, which had first appeared in a small edition in 1937 and then dropped from sight. Professor Bruce Trigger has argued persuasively that Bailey was the first practitioner of what has come to be known as ethnohistory, the synthesis of historical and anthropological techniques. It is also true that Bailey had a profound sense of that symbiosis of environment and culture that made North American societies what they were, and an understanding that, when European social, religious, and economic practices altered that environment, Native culture could hardly remain unchanged.

Finally, there is the well-known work of the historical geographer Andrew Hill Clark. His *Acadia*, published in 1968, is a model of environmental history, though his emphasis is upon the impact of the newcomers on "the face of the earth" and the modification of European culture in the face of the demands of a new environment.

Obviously, then, the foundations of Acadian ecological history have been well laid. A new approach, based on a wider conception of ecology, is William Cronon's *Changes in the Land Indians: Colonists and the Ecology of New England*. This excellent book has, I think, demonstrated that the early history of North America can be profitably recast. Cronon looks at the manner in which the interaction between Natives and newcomers in New England led to alterations in the landscape, the introduction of new crops and diseases, the reduction of animal populations, the clearing of the forest, and the establishment of a "world of fields and fences" legally enforced by a system that established rights of private ownership. Moreover, Cronon makes the crucial point that in this encounter the contrast was not, as Europeans usually argued, between wilderness and civilization, but rather "between two human ways of living, two ways of belonging to an ecology."[9] That this approach might be adapted to the history of Acadia is immediately obvious, especially since

Cronon himself often resorted to the evidence of those conscientious French record-keepers whose works are so familiar to historians of the French empire in North America.

The process whereby a way of life – the European one – triumphed over the Amerindian one was fairly rapid in New England, being virtually completed by 1800, as Cronon demonstrates. Since the colonization of Acadia, a vast area that included present-day Nova Scotia, New Brunswick, Prince Edward Island, part of Quebec (Gaspesia), and a portion of Maine, advanced at a slower pace, the two ways of life existed side by side, interacting with one another, for a longer period of time. Leslie Upton's study, *Micmacs and Colonists*, noted that at the beginning of his period, the Treaty of Utrecht of 1713, the number of Micmac people of Acadia still roughly equalled European settlers even though the Native population had declined drastically. In the seventeenth century Acadia had been the scene of imperial competition and war between France and Britain and that had hardly been conducive to extensive settlement. By 1650 there were some fifty households at Port Royal and Le Have; that population had grown to about 900 souls by the 1680s. So, too, population was spreading from Port Royal to the Minas Basin, to Beaubassin and scattered along the north shore of the Bay of Fundy. "When the British took control for the third and last time," Upton writes, "capturing Port Royal in 1710, there were just over 1,500 native born Acadians with roots going back from two to four generations. The Micmac population stood at about the same number having declined from 3,000 or so at the beginning of the seventeenth century. In one hundred years the French had been able to establish a white population only half the size of the Micmacs' at their first arrival."[10] It is the very slowness of the process, and the richness of the documentation for the seventeenth century, that makes the study of the ecology of contact in Acadia so fascinating.

Between 1604 and 1708 six major writers – of varied background – composed accounts of what Nicolas Denys called "the natural history" of Acadia (and this leaves out Jacques Cartier's sixteenth-century account). Now I think it is highly significant that Denys believed that "natural history" included not just geography, geology, climate, and the flora and fauna, but also the inhabitants of the new land. The model, of course, was Pliny's *Natural History*, a work that played such a large part in determining what was discovered in America that the Roman almost deserves to be ranked with

Columbus.[11] Nor was Denys in anyway unique: Champlain, Lescarbot, Biard, Le Clercq, and Dièreville, the authors of the other five major contemporary accounts of seventeenth-century Acadia, all followed a similar recipe though varying the amounts of the ingredients somewhat. Each of these writers approached Acadia from an ecological perspective, setting people squarely in their environment and noting the contrast between European and Amerindian ways of living in, and belonging to, their environment.

Each of these seventeenth-century writers devoted a substantial portion of his book to descriptions of the natural world. There was a certain awesomeness about this wilderness and its abundance of birds, beasts, fish, and flowers. In 1604, at Seal Island, Champlain's keen eye identified firs, pines, larches, and poplars, and more than a dozen species of birds, not all of which he recognized. At nearly every landing he made similar observations.[12] He identified the skimmer with its extended lower bill, while Denys described the majestic bald eagle carrying off a rabbit in its talons. Marc Lescarbot provided comparable descriptions. His famous poem "Adieu à la Nouvelle France" is a versified catalogue of the environment, including that indigenous marvel, *"un oiselet semblable au papillon,"* the hummingbird. This ornithological marvel, sometimes called the Bird of Heaven, provoked the same sense of admiration in early visitors to North America that the flamboyant parrot produced in explorers of South America, beginning with Columbus. The parrot, captured and transported, quickly became the symbol of America in post-Columbian art. The hummingbird, impossible to rear in captivity, remained in the Americas. Among insects the firefly was highly appealing, the mosquito detested.[13]

Of the creatures of the animal world none attracted more curiosity than the beaver. It became an animal more marvellous in the Plinean imaginations of Le Clercq and Denys than in reality. It performed as architect, mason, carpenter, even hod carrier, walking upright with a load of mud piled on its broad tail. A natural rear end loader! "Its flesh is delicate," Father Le Clercq reported, "and very much like that of mutton. The kidneys are sought by apothecaries, and are used with effect in easing women in childbirth, and in mitigating hysterics."[14] The value of beaver pelts hardly needed comment.

Then there was the moose that cured itself of epilepsy by scratching its ear with its own cloven hoof. At least the flying squirrel was the real thing. Denys's description of the cod fishery, not surprisingly since he was a merchant, was accurate and detailed. On the southeast coast of St. Mary's Bay, when the tide dropped, Champlain found mussels, clams, and sea snails, while elsewhere oysters abounded. The swarms of fish that swam in the waterways filled these men with excitement. On the Miramichi, Denys claimed that he had been kept awake all night by the loud sounds of salmon splashing. The fertility and agricultural potential of the new land were naturally a constant preoccupation. "The entire country is covered with very dense forests," Champlain wrote of the site that would become Annapolis Royal, ". . . except a point a league and a half up the river, where there are some oaks which are very scattered and a number of wild vines. These could be easily cleared and the place brought under cultivation." Nor did Champlain miss the minerals and metals – silver at Mink Cove, iron further north on Digby Neck.[15]

Moreover, it is from these writers that at least a partial sketch of the lives and customs of the Northeastern Algonquian peoples can be reconstructed. Champlain recorded the practice of swidden agriculture among the Abenaki – corn, beans, and squash – and even noted the use of horseshoe crab shells, probably as fertilizer.[16] Hunting and fishing methods were remarked upon, though the lack of detail is somewhat surprising, particularly when contrasted with the lengthy accounts of religious beliefs – or supposed lack of them – of the various inhabitants of Acadia. "Jugglery," or shamanism, and also medical practices were of particular interest – indeed, Dièreville even convinced himself of the efficacy of some shamanistic cures. So, too, dress, hairstyles, courtship and marriage customs, and ceremonies surrounding childbirth and death were carefully recorded and sometimes compared to classical and contemporary European practices. Lescarbot, for example, concluded that the Jesuits were quite mistaken in attempting to force Christian monogamy on the Micmacs, arguing that indigenous marriage customs would best be "left in the state in which they were found." In contrast to some Jesuit writers – and Brian Moore – Lescarbot judged the Aboriginal people very modest in sexual matters. This he attributed partly to their familiarity with nakedness but chiefly "to their keeping bare the head, where lies the fountain of the spirits which excite to procreation, partly to the lack of salt, of hot spices, of wine, of meats which provoke desire, and partly to their frequent use of tobacco, the smoke of which dulls the senses, and mounting up to the brain hinders the functions of Venus." On the other hand, he believed that one romantic innovation introduced by the French actually contributed to the improvement of Aboriginal life: the kiss. Though Professor Karen Anderson has followed up Lescarbot's insight about the impact of the missionaries on marriage among the Native people of New France, no one, as far as I know, has advanced our knowledge of the relationship between civilization and osculation. [17]

Virtually all male European visitors to Acadia were struck by the division of labour in Aboriginal communities. Women, it was agreed, "work harder than the men, who play the gentleman, and care only for hunting or for war." Despite this, Lescarbot wrote approvingly, "they love their husbands more than women of our parts." It is interesting that in his discussion of the ease with which Micmac marriages could be dissolved, Father Le Clercq remained detached and uncensorious. "In a word," he remarked laconically, "they hold it as a maxim that each one is free; that one can do whatever he wishes: and that it is not sensible to put constraint upon men." And the priest understood that the maxim applied to both men and women. [18]

Games and the Native peoples' apparent penchant for gambling were described though not always understood. Then there were science and technology. Father Le Clercq, perhaps the most ethnologically astute of seventeenth-century observers, provided an intriguing account of the ways the Gaspesians read the natural world: their interpretation of the stars and the winds, how they reckoned distance and recognized the changing seasons. The usefulness and limitations of indigenous technology were also commented upon. The efficiency of the birchbark canoe won widespread admiration. "The Savages of Port Royal can go to Kebec in ten or twelve days by means of the rivers which they navigate almost up to their sources," Lescarbot discovered, "and thence carrying their little bark canoes through the woods they reach another stream which flows into the river of Canada and thus greatly expedite their long voyages." While household utensils, manufactured from bark, roots, and stumps, were ingenious, the French realized that the Aboriginals were happy to replace them with metal wares. War and its weaponry drew the somewhat surprised comment that "neither profit nor the desire to extend boundaries, but rather vengeance, caused fairly frequent hostilities between native groups." Torture was graphically described, and condemned, though it was recognized – and judged a sign of savagery – that "to die in this manner is, among the savages, to die as a great captain and as a man of great courage."[19]

Much else also caught the attention of these ethnologists: the commonality of property, the importance of gift exchange, the practice of setting aside weapons before entering into discussions with strangers, and the expectation that strangers should do the same. And even though the Natives were "crafty, thievish and treacherous," Lescarbot admitted somewhat superciliously that "they do not lack wit, and might come to something if they were civilized, and knew the various trades."[20]

Though observations and judgements were made with great confidence, indeed, often rather cavalierly, these Europeans were aware that there often existed an unbridgeable communications chasm between the observers and the observed. Like every explorer before them, the French in Acadia attempted to resolve the problem in two ways. The first was to take young Natives back to France for an immersion course in French. ("We had on board a savage," Lescarbot noted in 1608, "who was much astonished to see the buildings, spires and windmills of France, but more the women, whom he had never seen dressed after our manner.") While these interpreters were doubtless helpful in breaking down the "effects of the confusion of Babel," it was hardly a permanent resolution to what Father Biard realized was a fundamental problem. Yet for the French to learn the local languages was time-consuming and the results often frustrating. Learning words was not the same as learning to communicate. "As these Savages have no formulated Religion, government, towns, nor trade," Biard recorded in exasperation, "so the words and proper phrases for all of these things are lacking." The confusion of words with things, of the sign with the referent, was, as Todorov has brilliantly shown, endemic to the European attempt to comprehend America. Acadia was no exception, though I have, unfortunately, not found any example quite so delicious as the linguistic dilemma encountered by Protestant missionaries in Hawaii. There the Islanders reportedly practised some twenty forms of sexual activity judged illicit – perhaps better, non-missionary. Each had a separate name in the native language, thus making translation of the Seventh Commandment virtually impossible without condoning the other nineteen forms of the joy of sex! The Native peoples of Acadia were apparently much less resourceful – or the celibate Jesuits less well trained as participant-observers. [21]

The natural, ethnographic, and linguistic accounts were not, of course, the work of biological scientists or cultural anthropologists – even taking into account our contemporary scepticism about the objectivity of anthropologists. Rather, they were the observations of seventeenth-century Frenchmen taking inventory of a new land they intended to explore, settle, develop, and Christianize – in brief, to colonize. It is in their works that much of what Braudel called Europe's "own nature" is "most truly revealed." In differing ways it is made emphatically plain by each of these authors that the French objective in Acadia, in the words of Father Biard, was "to make a Garden out of the wilderness." Nor should this be read narrowly as simply meaning the evangelization of the people who lived in Acadia. [22]

In the revealing introduction to his rich and thoughtful *Relation* of 1616, Biard wrote: "For verily all of this region, though capable of the same prosperity as ours, nevertheless through Satan's malevolence, which reigns there, is a horrible wilderness, scarcely less miserable on account of the scarcity of bodily comforts than for that which renders man absolutely miserable, the complete lack of the ornaments and riches of the soul." The missionary continues, offering his scientific conviction that "neither the sun, nor malice of the soil, neither the air nor the water, neither the men nor their caprices, are to be blamed for this. We are all created by and dependent upon the same principles: We breathe under the same sky; the same constellations influence us; and I do not believe that the land, which produces trees as tall and beautiful as ours, will not produce as fine harvests, *if it be cultivated*." Wilderness the expanses of Acadia might be, but a garden it could become, if cultivated. For Father Biard and his contemporaries, "subjugating Satanic monsters" and establishing "the order and discipline of heaven upon earth" [23] combined spiritual and worldly dimensions. Champlain, for whom the Devil and his agents were as real as for Biard, expressed the same objective in a more secular way when he told the local people he met in the region of the Penobscot River that the French "desired to settle in their country and show them how to cultivate it, in order that they might no longer live so miserable an existence as they are doing." The comment is made the more striking when we remember that Champlain knew that some of the inhabitants of

Acadia did practise agriculture – though he never suggested that they "cultivated" the land.[24]

It is perhaps not too much to suggest that "cultivation" was a distinctly European concept. "For before everything else," Marc Lescarbot maintained, "one must set before oneself the tillage of the soil." At the first French settlement at Ste. Croix gardens were sown and some wheat "came up very fine and ripened." The poor quality of the soil was one reason for the move across the Bay of Fundy to establish Port Royal, "where the soil was ample to produce the necessaries of life." But there was more to cultivation than the production of simple foodstuffs. For Lescarbot, at least, the powerful symbolism of planting a European garden in what had been a wilderness was manifest. He wrote on his departure from Port Royal to return to France in July, 1607:

> I have cause to rejoice that I was one of the party, and among the first tillers of this land. And herein I took the more pleasure in that I put before my eyes our ancient Father Noah, a great king, a great priest and a great prophet whose vocation was the plough and the vineyard; and the old Roman captain Serranus, who was found sowing his field when he was sent to lead the Roman army, and Quintus Cincinnatus, who, all crowned with dust, bareheaded and ungirt, was ploughing four acres of land when the herald of the Senate brought him the letters of dictatorship. . . . Inasmuch as I took pleasure in this work, God blessed my poor labour, and I had in my garden as good wheat as could be grown in France.

While Lescarbot might be dismissed as suffering from an overdose of renaissance humanism, it seems more sensible to take him seriously. His florid rhetoric should be seen for what it really was: the ideology of what Alfred J. Crosby has called "ecological imperialism" – the biological expansion of Europe. What Lescarbot, and less literary Europeans, brought to bear on the Acadian landscape was the heavy freight of the European agricultural tradition with its long-established distinction between garden and wilderness. In that tradition God's "garden of delight" contrasted with the "desolate wilderness" of Satan. Though the concept of "garden" varies widely, as Hugh Johnson notes in his *Principles of Gardening*, "control of nature by man" is the single common denominator.[25]

The transformation of the wilderness into a garden is a constant theme in the early writings about Acadia. Father Biard had brought European seeds with him when he arrived in 1611 and at St. Saveur "in the middle of June, we planted some grains [wheat and barley], fruit, seeds, peas, beans and all kinds of garden plants." On Miscou Island (Shippegan Island) Denys discovered that although the soil was sandy, herbs of all sorts as well as "Peaches, Nectarines, Cling-stones" and what the French always called "the Vine" – grapes – could be grown. But, as so often is the case, Lescarbot provides the most striking account of what gardening meant. At Port Royal, he "took pleasure in laying out and cultivating my gardens, in enclosing them to keep out the pigs, in making flower beds, staking out alleys, building summer houses, sowing wheat, rye, barley, oats, beans, peas and garden plants, and in watering them." European seeds, domestic animals – chickens and pigeons, too – fences – mine and thine.[26]

Of course, before a garden could be planted, the land had to be cleared. Denys described that work – and its by-product: squared oak timber that could fill the holds of vessels that would otherwise have returned empty to France. If clearing the land did not produce enough space for the garden, then the sea could be tamed, too. In the Minas Basin, where the settlers apparently found cultivating the land too difficult, Dièreville recounted the construction of a remarkable piece of European technology:

> Five or six rows of large logs are driven whole into the ground at the points where the Tide enters the Marsh, & between each row, other logs are laid, one on top of the other, & all the spaces between them are so carefully filled with well pounded clay, that the water can no longer get through. In the centre of this construction a Sluice is contrived in such a manner that the water on the Marshes flows out of its own accord, while that of the Sea is prevented from coming in.

Thus the tidal marshes were dyked for cultivation.[27]

Pushing back the forest, holding back the water, fencing a garden in the wilderness. The rewards would be great – "better worth than the treasures of Atahulpa," Lescarbot claimed. Was the symbolism intentional? Atahualpa, the defeated ruler of Peru, offered his Spanish captors led by Francisco Pizarro a room full of gold and silver in return for his freedom. The Spaniards accepted the ransom and then garrotted the Inca. Hardly a scene from a garden of delights.[28]

The French in Acadia were certainly not the Spanish in Peru. Still, the garden they planned was intended to produce a greater harvest than just sustenance for anticipated settlers. It was to be a garden for the civilization of the indigenous peoples. "In the course of time," Champlain observed on his initial meeting with the people he called Etechemins (Maliseet), "we hope to pacify them, and put an end to the wars which they wage against each other, in order that in the future we might derive service from them, and convert them to the Christian faith." The words were almost exactly those attributed to Columbus at his first sighting of the people of the "Indies": "they would be good servants . . . [and] would easily be made Christians." Even the most sympathetic observers of the Native peoples of Acadia were appalled by their apparent failure to make for themselves a better life, a failing that was often attributed to their unwillingness to plan for the future. For Father Biard, Christianity and husbandry obviously went hand in hand. Living the nomadic life of hunters, fishers, and gatherers resulted in permanent material and spiritual backwardness. "For in truth, this people," he claimed, "who, through the progress and experience of centuries, ought to have come to some perfection in the arts, sciences and philosophy, is like a great field of stunted and ill-begotten wild plants . . . [they] ought to be already prepared for the completeness of the Holy Gospel . . . Yet behold [them] wretched and dispersed, given up to ravens, owls and infernal cuckoos, and to be the cursed prey of spiritual foxes, bears, boars and dragons." In Father Le Clercq's view the "wandering and vagabond life" had to be ended and a place "suitable for the cultivation of the soil" found so that he could "render the savages sedentary, settle them down, and civilize them among us." Though Lescarbot's outlook was more secular, he shared these sentiments completely and expressed them in verse:

> This people are neither brutal, barbarous nor savage,
> If you do not describe men of old that way,
> He is subtle, capable, and full of good sense,
> And not known to lack judgement,
> All he asks is a father to teach him
> To cultivate the earth, to work the grape vines,
> And to live by laws, to be thrifty,
> And under the sturdy roofs hereafter to shelter.

The leitmotif of this rhetoric is obvious: the images of the Christian garden and the satanic wilderness, summed up in the verse from the Book of Joel, quoted by Father Biard: "The Land is a Garden of Eden before them, and behind them a desolate wilderness."[29]

Yet it would be quite wrong to assume that these seventeenth-century French visitors to the New World were blind to the potential costs of gardening in the Acadian wilderness. Indeed, there is considerable evidence of nagging suspicions that the very abundance of nature provoked reckless exploitation. Denys witnessed an assault on a bird colony that is reminiscent of the profligacy of Cartier's crew among the birds at Funk Island in 1534. Denys's men "clubbed so great a number, as well of young as of their fathers and mothers . . . that we were unable to carry them all away." And Dièreville captured all too accurately the spirit of the uncontrolled hunt when he wrote that:

> . . . . , Wild Geese
> And Cormorants, aroused in me
> The wish to war on them. . . .

He used the same militant language in his admiring account of the "Bloody Deeds" of the seal hunt, and also provided a sketch of another common pursuit: the theft of massive quantities of birds' eggs. "They collect all they can find," he remarked, "fill their canoes & take them away." Scenes like these presaged the fate of the Great Auk, the passenger pigeon, and many other species. [30]

These were the actions of men whose attitude toward the bounty of nature contrasted markedly with that of the indigenous inhabitants of North America. In Europe the slaughter of birds and animals was commonplace, indeed it was often encouraged by law. As Keith Thomas remarks in his study of *Man in the Natural World* – which is largely restricted to Great Britain – "It is easy to forget just how much human effort went into warring against species which competed with man for the earth's resources." Without succumbing to the temptation to romanticize the attitude of North American Native people toward their environment – they hunted, they fished, some practised slash and burn agriculture – there is no doubt that their sense of the natural world was based on a distinctive set of beliefs, a cosmology that placed them in nature rather than dominant over it. Animistic religion – "everything is animated," Father Le Clercq discovered – a simple technology, a relatively small population, and what Marshall Sahlins has termed "stone age economics" made "war" on nature unnecessary, even unacceptable. "They did not lack animals," Nicolas Denys noted, "which they killed only in proportion as they had need of them." By contrast, the Europeans who arrived in Acadia at the beginning of the seventeenth century belonged to a culture where, in Clarence Glacken's words, "roughly from the end of the fifteenth to the end of the seventeenth century one sees ideas of men as controllers of nature beginning to crystalize." Or, as Marc Lescarbot put it, articulating as he so often did the unstated assumptions of his fellow Frenchmen, "Man was placed in this world to command all that's here below."[31]

The distinction between the "wilderness" and the "garden," between "savagery" and "civilization," between "wandering about" and commanding "all that is here below," is more than a philosophical one, important as that is. It is also, both implicitly and explicitly, a question of ownership and possession. In what has been called "enlightenment anthropology" – though I think that places the development too late – the function of the term "savage" was to assert the existence of a state of nature where neither "heavy-plough agriculture nor monetarized exchange" was practised and from which, therefore, civil government was absent. Moreover, civil government, agriculture, and commerce were assumed to exist only where land had been appropriated, where "possessive individualism" had taken root. Thus the wilderness was inhabited by nomadic savages, without agriculture or laws, where the land had never been appropriated. Consequently, when Europeans set about transforming the wilderness into a garden, they were engaged in taking possession of the land. "The ideology of agriculture and savagery," in the words of J.G.A. Pocock, "was formed to justify this expropriation."[32]

As European gardeners began slowly to transform the wilderness of Acadia, so, too, as was their intent, they began the remaking of its indigenous inhabitants. And once again, though they rarely expressed doubts about the ultimate value of the enterprise, some Europeans did recognize that a price was being exacted. First there was the puzzling evidence of population decline. In a letter to his superior in Paris in 1611, Father Biard wrote that the Micmac leader Membertou (who himself claimed to be old enough to remember Cartier's 1534 visit) had informed him that in his youth people were "as thickly planted there as the hairs upon his head." The priest continued, making a remarkably revealing comparison:

It is maintained that they have thus diminished since the French have begun to frequent their country; for, since they do nothing all summer but eat; and the result is that, adopting an entirely different custom and thus breeding new diseases, they pay for their indulgence during the autumn and winter by pleurisy, quinsy and dysentery which kills them off. During this year alone sixty have died at Cape de la Hève, which is the greater part of those who lived there; yet not one of all of M. de Poutrincourt's little colony has ever been sick, notwithstanding all the privations they have suffered; which has caused the Savages to apprehend that God protects and defends us as his favorite and well-beloved people.[33]

The reality, of course, was more complex than this assertion that God was on the side of the immunized. Though the French were unaware of it, Acadia, like the rest of the Americas, was a "virgin land" for European pathogens. Denys hinted at this when he wrote that "in old times . . . they [the Natives] were not subject to diseases, and knew nothing of fevers." Certainly they had not been exposed to the common European maladies – measles, chickenpox, influenza, tuberculosis, and, worst of all, smallpox. (The "pox" – syphilis – Lescarbot believed was God's punishment of European men for their promiscuous sexual behaviour in the Indies.) The immune systems of the indigenous peoples of Acadia were unprepared for the introduction of these new diseases, which were consequently lethal in their impact. Father Le Clercq, at the end of the century, reported that "the gaspesian nation . . . has been wholly destroyed . . . in three or four visitations" of unidentified "Maladies." Marc Lescarbot probably identified one important carrier of European infections when he stated that "the savages had no knowledge of [rats] before our coming; but in our time they have been beset by them, since from our fort they went over to their lodges."[34]

Disease, radical alterations in diet – the substitution of dried peas and beans and hardtack for moosemeat and other country foods – and perhaps even the replacement of polygamy by monogamy with a consequent reduction in the birth rate all contributed to population decline. Then there was the debilitating scourge of alcohol, another European import for which Native people had little, if any, tolerance. Just as they sometimes gorged themselves during "eat all" feasts, so they seemed to drink like undergraduates with the simple goal of getting drunk. Even discounting Father Le Clercq's pious outlook, his description of the impact of brandy on the Gaspesians was probably not exaggerated. The fur traders, he charged, "make them drunk quite on purpose, in order to deprive

these poor barbarians of the use of reason." That meant quick profits for the merchants, debauchery, destruction, murder, and, eventually, addiction for the Amerindians. Though less censorious, or
less concerned, than the priest, Dièreville remarked that the Micmacs "drank Brandy with relish & less moderation than we do; they
have a craving for it."[35]

Estimating population declines among Native peoples is at best
controversial, at worst impossible. Nevertheless, there seems no
reason to doubt that Acadia, like the rest of the Americas,
underwent substantial reduction in numbers of inhabitants as a
result of European contact. Jacques Cartier and his successors, who
fished and traded along the coasts of Acadia, likely introduced
many of the influences that undermined the health of the local
people. Therefore Pierre Biard's 1616 estimate of a population of
about 3,500 Micmacs is doubtless well below pre-contact numbers,
as Membertou claimed. Since it has been estimated that neigh-
bouring Maliseet, Pasamaquoddy, and Abenaki communities
experienced reductions ranging from 67 to 98 per cent during the
epidemics of 1616 and 1633 alone, Virginia Miller's calculation that
the pre-contact Micmac population stood somewhere between
26,000 and 35,000 seems reasonable.[36] That was one of the costs of
transforming the wilderness into a garden.

If the effects of disease and alcohol were apparent, though
misunderstood, then another aspect of the civilizing process was
more subtle. That process combined Christian proselytizing, which
eroded traditional beliefs, with the fur trade, which undermined
many aspects of the Native peoples' way of life. There is among
contemporary historians of European-Amerindian relations a tendency to view the trading relationship, which was so central to the
early years of contact, as almost benign, a relation between equals.
Missionaries, politicians, and land-hungry settlers are credited with
upsetting the balance that once existed between "Natives and newcomers" in the fur trade. There can be no doubt that recent scholar-
ship has demonstrated that the Natives were certainly not passive
participants in the trade. Far from being naive innocents who gave
up valuable furs for a few baubles, they traded shrewdly and
demanded good measure.[37]

Nevertheless, it is impossible to read seventeenth-century
accounts of the trade and still accept the whole of this revisionist
account. These were eyewitness testimonies to the devastating
impact of alcohol on the Native traders and their families: murder

of fellow Natives, maiming of women and abuse of children, the destruction of canoes and household goods. Beyond this, brandy, often adulterated with water, was used by Europeans "in order to abuse the savage women, who yield themselves readily during drunkenness to all kinds of indecency, although at other times . . . they would be more like to give a box on the ears rather than a kiss to whomsoever wished to engage them in evil, if they were in their right minds." The words come from the priest, Father Le Clercq, but the merchant, Nicolas Denys, concurred. That, too, was part of the fur trade. [38]

Moreover, the trade cannot be separated from other aspects of contact that contributed to the weakening of Micmac culture. Fur traders carrying disease and trade goods unintentionally contributed to the decline of both traditional skills and indigenous religious belief. Nicolas Denys's discussion of Micmac burial customs illustrates this point neatly. Like other Native people, the Micmacs buried many personal articles in graves so that the deceased would have use of them when they disembarked in the Land of the Dead. The French judged this practice both superstitious and wasteful – especially when the burial goods included thousands of pounds of valuable furs. They attempted to disabuse the Native of the efficacy of this practice by demonstrating that the goods did not leave the grave but rather remained in the ground, rotting. To this the Natives replied that it was the "souls" of these goods that accompanied the "souls" of the dead, not the material goods themselves. Despite this failure Denys was able to report that the practice was in decline. The reason is significant and it was only marginally the result of conversion to Christianity. As trade between the French and the Micmacs developed, European goods – metal pots, knives, axes, firearms – gradually replaced traditional utensils and weapons that had once been included in burial pits. The use of European commodities as burial goods proved prohibitively expensive. Denys wrote that "since they cannot obtain from us with such ease as they had in retaining robes of Marten, of Otter, of Beaver, [or] bows and arrows, and since they have realized that guns and other things were not found in their woods or their rivers, *they have become less devout*." Technological change brought religious change. It also led to dependence. [39]

No doubt the exchange of light, transportable copper pots for awkward, stationary wooden pots was a convenient, even revolutionary change in the lives of Micmacs. But convenience was purchased at a price, and the Native people knew it. Father Le Clercq was vastly amused when an old man told him that "the Beaver does everything to perfection. He makes us kettles, axes, swords, knives and gives us drink and food without the trouble of cultivating the ground." It was no laughing matter. If, at the outset of European contact, the Native people of Acadia had adapted to the trade with Europeans rather successfully, they gradually lost ground, their role of middlemen undermined by overseas traders who came to stay. While Nicolas Denys deplored the destructive impact of itinerant traders and fishermen on the Native people, his only solution was to advocate European settlement and the enforcement of French authority. "Above all," he concluded his assessment of the changes that had taken place in Native society during his time, "I hope that God may inspire in those who have part in the government of the State, all the discretion which can lead them to the consummation of an enterprise as glorious for the King as it can be useful and advantageous to those who will take interest therein." In that scheme, when it eventually came to pass, the Micmacs and their neighbours found themselves on the margin. [40]

To these signs that the work of cultivation produced ugly, unanticipated side effects must be added the evidence of near crop failure in the spiritual garden of Acadia. In 1613 a disgusted Father Biard reported meeting a St. John River sagamore (Cacagous) who, despite being "baptized in Bayonne," France, remained a "shrewd and cunning" polygamist. "There is scarcely any change in them after baptism," he admitted. Their traditional "vices" had not been replaced by Christian "virtues." Even Membertou, often held up as the exemplary convert, had difficulty grasping the subtleties of the new religion. He surely revealed something more than a quick wit in an exchange that amused the Jesuit. Attempting to teach him the Pater Noster, Biard asked Membertou to repeat in his own language, "Give us this day our daily bread." The old sagamore replied: "If I did not ask him for anything but bread, I would be without moose-meat or fish." Near the end of the century, Father Le Clercq's reflections on the results of his Gaspé mission were no more optimistic. Only a small number of the people lived liked Christians; most "fell back into the irregularities of a brutal and wild life." Such, the somewhat depressed Recollect missionary concluded, was the meagre harvest among "the most docile of all the Savages of New France . . . the most susceptible to the instruction of Christianity." [41]

It was not just these weeds – disease, alcohol, dependence, and spiritual backsliding – in the European garden in Acadia that occasionally led the gardeners to pause and reflect. Possibly there was a more basic question: was the wilderness truly the Devil's domain? The Northeastern Algonquian people were admittedly "superstitious," even "barbarian," but certainly not the "wild men" of medieval imaginings, indistinguishable from the beasts. If they enjoyed "neither faith, nor king, nor laws," living out "their unhappy Destiny," there was something distinctly noble about them, too. Despite the steady, evangelical light that burned in Biard's soul, he could not help wondering if the Micmac resistance to the proffered European garden of delights was not without foundation. "If we come to sum up the whole and compare their good and ill with ours," he mused briefly in the middle of his *Relation* of 1616, "I do not know but that they, in truth, have some reason to prefer (as they do) their own kind of happiness to ours, at least if we speak of the temporal happiness, which the rich and worldly seek in this life." Of course, these doubts quickly passed as he turned to consider "the means available to aid these nations to their eternal salvation."

Marc Lescarbot, for whom classicism and Christianity seemed to have reached their apogee in the France of his day, and whose fervour for cultivating the wilderness was unlimited, found much to admire in the peoples of Acadia. They lived "after the ancient fashion, without display": uncompetitive, unimpressed by material goods, temperate, free of corruption and of lawyers! "They have not that ambition, which in these parts gnaws men's minds, and fills them with cares, bringing blinded men to the grave in the very flower of their age and sometimes to the shameful spectacle of a public death." Here surely was "the noble savage," a Frenchman without warts – "a European dream," as J.H. Elliott remarks of the humanists' image of the New World, "which had little to do with American reality."[42]

There was yet another reason for self-doubts about the superiority of European ways over Amerindian ways; the Native people struggled to preserve their wilderness, refusing the supposed superiority of the garden. Even those who had become "philosophers and pretty good theologians," one missionary concluded, preferred "on the basis of foolish reasoning, the savage to the French life." And Father Le Clercq found that some of the people of Gaspesia stubbornly preferred their movable wigwams to stationary European houses. And that was not all. "Thou reproachest us, very inappropriately," their leader told a group of visiting Frenchmen, "that our country is a very little hell in contrast with France, which thou comparest to a terrestrial paradise, inasmuch as it yields thee, so thou sayest, every provision in abundance . . . I beg thee to believe, all miserable as we may seem in thine eyes, we consider ourselves nevertheless much happier than thou in this, that we are contented with the little that we have." Thus having demonstrated, 300 years before its discovery by modern anthropology, that having only a few possessions is not the same as being poor, the Algonquian leader then posed a devastating question: "If France, as thou sayest, is a little terrestrial paradise, are thou sensible to leave it?" No reply is recorded.[43]

It is simple enough to imagine one. Even those who could describe as "truly noble" the Aboriginal people of Acadia remained convinced that civilization meant cultivation. "In New France," Lescarbot proclaimed, "the golden age must be brought in again, the ancient crowns of ears of corn must be renewed, and the highest glory made that which the ancient Romans called *gloria adorea*, a glory of wheat, in order to invite everyone to till well his field, seeing that the land presents itself liberally to them that have none." The state of nature, a Hobbesian state of nature without laws or kings or religion, would be tamed, "civilized," when men "formed commonwealths to live under certain laws, rule, and police." Here, in Braudel's phrase, Europe's "own nature" was revealed.[44]

Perhaps such thoughts as these filled the heads of the Frenchmen who, according to Micmac tradition, gathered to enjoy one of the "curious adventures" of Silmoodawa, an Aboriginal hunter carried off to France "as a curiosity" by Champlain or some other "discoverer." On this occasion the Micmac was to give a command performance of hunting and curing techniques. The "savage" was placed in a ring with "a fat ox or deer . . . brought in from a beautiful park." (One definition of "paradise," the *OED* reports, is "an Oriental park or pleasure ground, especially one enclosing wild beasts for the chase.") The story, collected in 1870 by the Reverend Silas Tertius Rand, a Baptist missionary and amateur ethnologist, continues: "He shot the animal with a bow, bled him, skinned and dressed him, sliced up the meat and spread it out on flakes to dry; he then cooked a portion and ate it, and in order to exhibit the whole process, and to take a mischievous revenge upon them for making an exhibition of him, he went into a corner of the yard and eased himself before them all."[45]

If, as Lescarbot's contemporaries believed, the wilderness could be made into a garden, then the unscripted denouement of Silmoodawa's performance revealed that a garden could also become a wilderness. Or was he merely acting out the Micmac version of Michel de Montaigne's often quoted remark about barbarians: we all call wilderness anything that is not *our* idea of a garden?

FOUR

Sauvaiges, Indians, Aboriginals, Amerindians, Native Peoples, First Nations

"In the beginning the white man came to speak to the Indian, who was sitting on the end of a log. 'Sit over!' said the white man. So the Indian allowed the stranger to sit on the log. But the other fellow kept on pushing him and repeating, 'Sit over! sit over!' until the Indian found himself at the other end of the log. And then the white man said, 'Now this log is mine!'"

C.M. Barbeau, *Huron and Wyandot Mythology* (1915)

THE FRENCH "DISCOVERERS" pronounced the people of North America "*sauvaiges*," the English, following the Spaniards, preferred "Indian," though it meant the same thing: uncivilized. Later they were variously labelled "Aboriginals," "Amerindians," and "Native peoples." Today they call themselves "the First Nations." Each of these names disguises the complexity of the people it is intended to encompass, but each also reveals an historical attitude. "*Sauvaiges*" were uncivilized, lacking religion, laws, and government. "Indians" were wards of the newly established European societies in North America, isolated on lands reserved for them once the newcomers had taken what they wanted, requiring Christian beliefs, education, and agriculture in preparation for full integration into Canadian society. "Native peoples," and more obviously "First Nations," implies rejection of the savage/civilization dichotomy and demands recognition of an "inherent" right to self-determination. In North America, as in so many other places touched by European expansion and imperialism, nationalism, that most European of ideologies, rather than assimilation, has taken root in Amerindian society. Ironically, that, too, is a form of assimilation. Language, spirituality, and a special relationship to the land, once claimed as the unique characteristics of French-Canadian nationalism, have now been thoroughly appropriated by the First Nations![1]

Today, Canada's Native people, defined by section 35(1) of our constitution as "the Indian, Inuit and Métis people," number some 800,000: 467,000 status Indians, 20,000 Inuit, with the remainder belonging to the complicated categories of non-status Indians and Métis. These are the surviving descendants of the approximately one million people who inhabited present-day Canada, Alaska, and Greenland at the time of European intrusion into North America. Since that number had fallen to approximately 110,000 by the first decade of this century, it is obvious that a quite remarkable recovery has been made in the past twenty-five years, due largely to improved medical care.[2] In 1500 these people belonged to a dozen language families often as different from one another as Swedish and Italian or perhaps even Chinese, and they spoke more than fifty variations of these language families. Huron and Mohawk, for example, both Iroquoian peoples, spoke languages as different as French and Spanish. Most of these language groups, with the exception of the extinct Beothuk, continue to exist, sometimes precariously, sometimes vigorously.

In pre-contact times, and for varying periods afterwards down to the present, these peoples developed socio-economic systems that ranged from hunting, fishing, and gathering, mainly along the Atlantic coast, on the Prairies, and in the North, to the corn-based agriculture of the St. Lawrence region and the rich sea-going, rainforest cultures of the Northwest Coast. Their socio-political organizations differed greatly, though the clan system was widespread. Their animistic religious beliefs were expressed in many forms: for the Iroquois the world was an island resting on the back of a turtle, while the Northwest Coast peoples knew that Raven had released the first men from their confinement in a clam shell. Art forms varied according to region and beliefs, reaching their apogee in the ceremonial carvings of the Northwest Coast, which, in the view of Claude Lévi-Strauss, compared favourably with the achievements of Greece and Egypt.[3]

As European expansion, beginning in the sixteenth century, spread across the continent, Native peoples were gradually reduced to a state of abject dependency, in body if not always in spirit. European diseases, against which the North Americans had developed no immunities, reduced populations by 50 per cent or more. The fur trade, in which Native people at first participated almost as equals, eventually led to severe reduction in resources, modified traditional economies, and introduced alcohol, for which Native people had unquenchable thirst. Christianity undermined traditional belief systems and Native self-confidence. Then came the settlers and developers hungry for land that they convinced themselves was either vacant or unused. European people, animals, plants, machines, and, perhaps above all, laws and police led to the gradual dispossession and marginalization of the original inhabitants of contemporary Canada. Sometimes treaties were signed, sometimes not, but the result was the same: Native people were pushed onto limited territories where they became meagrely supported wards of the Canadian Department of Indian Affairs established in 1876. Nor were these "reserves" guaranteed, for incoming settlers often successfully pressed for further reductions. In southern Saskatchewan alone, reserve lands shrank by a quarter of a million acres by 1928.[4] In British Columbia, where only a few treaties had been signed, Indian lands were subject to almost constant modification.[5]

Jacques Cartier, Canada's Christopher Columbus, unwittingly revealed the assumptions that would govern Canadian policy toward Native people for 450 years when he first landed on the Gaspé coast on July 8, 1534. "We perceived that they are a people who would be easy to convert,"[6] he wrote. A little later he broadened the objective: these people could readily be *"dompter"* – a verb that means to subdue, tame, subjugate, or "mould," as the standard English translation puts it. Four hundred years later, in 1920, Duncan Campbell Scott, a distinguished poet who earned his living as a public servant in the Department of Indian Affairs, echoed Cartier when he stated that "our object is to continue until there is not a single Indian in Canada that has not been absorbed into the body politic, and there is no Indian question, and no Indian Department."[7] The spirit of Jacques Cartier, dressed up in the liberal language of equality, still inspired the Trudeau government's 1969 White Paper (*Statement of the Government of Canada on Indian Policy, 1969*), the term appropriately unfortunate in the circumstances, whose goal was to abolish wardship and make Native peoples citizens like everyone else – Canadians without reservations, one might say!

Each of these policy statements rested on what, to a greater or lesser degree, was the benevolent, if misguided, belief that Native peoples had to be raised up, transformed, civilized, in order that they could enjoy the fullness of Canadian life. Making Native peoples *equal* to Europeans meant making them *the same* as Europeans. As Tzvetan Todorov argues in *The Conquest of America*,[8] the idea that peoples could be equal *and* different was inconceivable during the centuries of European expansion and dominance. Only decades of brutal experience, and finally recognition of failure, forced a revision of that harsh philosophy.

Christianity, education, and agriculture were the chosen instruments of the policy of equality through assimilation. It is easy, even popular, to condemn the missionaries, from the seventeenth-century Jesuits, through the nineteenth-century Society for the Propagation of the Gospel, to the twentieth-century Methodists and Presbyterians, who attempted, with varying degrees of success, to convert the Native pagans to the self-evident truths of Christianity. But it needs also to be remembered that it was often missionaries who sought to protect the Natives from the worst depredations of merchants, settlers, and politicians. And, in the early years of the Native political renaissance, it was often Christianized Natives who led in the demands for justice.[9] But the missionaries were also responsible for an educational system whose purpose was to separate children from parents in residential schools, suppress Native languages, and make "the Red Man White in all but colour," as a Saskatchewan newspaper put it in 1888.[10] The purpose of these schools was stated clearly in a departmental report in 1889: "The boarding school dissociates the Indian child from the deleterious home influences to which he would otherwise be subjected. It reclaims him from the otherwise uncivilized state in which he has been brought up. It brings him into contact from day to day with all that tends to effect a change in his views and habits of life. By precept and example he is taught to endeavour to excel in what will be most useful to him."[11] The effort was almost entirely misdirected; the results, if one could measure the unmeasurable, were an enormous addition to human misery and little to human enlightenment. That the schools were also one of the major centres for the spread of tuberculosis, a deadly Indian killer until recent decades, will also have to be added into the final sum.[12]

Attempts to eradicate Aboriginal culture included prohibition of traditional religious practices. Plains Indian ceremonies such as the

Thirst Dance and the Sun Dance were forbidden by law. The potlach, a Northwest Coast gift-giving celebration marking various rites of passage, came under a similar ban. It was judged both pagan and profligate. Confiscated masks, rattles, and headgear were shipped off to Canadian museums – at least what was left after United States and European museums had skimmed off the cream. Though the prohibitions were never successfully enforced, by the 1940s the carving skills of the Northwest peoples were in critical decline. But the revival, encouraged by anthropologists in the 1950s, marked a new birth for Native culture soon evident on the organizational and land claims fronts.[13]

Efforts to transform Plains Indians into farmers during the later years of the nineteenth century also produced meagre results. It has often been argued that Native people, some of whose ancestors practised agriculture successfully well before the arrival of Europeans, simply could not adapt to farming – they were either culturally unsuited to settled agricultural life or too lazy, too stupid, too uncivilized. Recent research has suggested a rather different explanation: the Department of Indian Affairs did not really want the Native people to succeed in agriculture, especially if that success made competition too keen for European settlers. How could a policy based on the following directive be expected to win the enthusiasm of Native people? ". . . restrict the area cultivated by each Indian to within such limits as will enable him to carry on his operations by the application of his own personal labour and the employment of such simple implements as he would likely be able to command if entirely thrown upon his own resources, rather than to encourage farming on a scale to necessitate the employment of expensive labour-saving machinery."[14] Indians were supposed to learn "peasant" farming just at the time when Clifford Sifton's "peasants in sheepskin coats" and other European immigrants were turning their backs on exactly that type of agriculture in the Canadian West. Naturally, the poorly devised policy failed. Cattle raising, ineptly promoted by the Department of Indian Affairs, prospered no better.[15]

It is, of course, easy to criticize these policies and easy to generalize about their results: alienation, short life expectancy, poverty, substandard housing, low levels of education, high levels of alcohol consumption, excessive rates of incarceration. These conditions naturally varied from band to band, province to province – worst in

the Prairie provinces, least bad in Quebec, is probably a fair generalization. Here is the picture recently painted by the *Report of the
Aboriginal Justice Inquiry of Manitoba*:

> Aboriginal people living on Manitoba reserves experience the most
> crowded housing conditions in Canada. The majority of homes on
> reserves are heated by cook stoves and space heaters. Less than one
> half on-reserve homes in Manitoba have indoor plumbing. . . .
>
> Indians are twice as likely as other Manitobans to have less than a
> grade nine education, three times less likely to complete high-
> school, and six times less likely to receive a university degree. The
> unemployment rate for Indian people is four times higher than for
> non-Indian people. These statistics greatly underestimate the true
> state of Aboriginal unemployment, since they only consider those
> people actively looking for work. . . . Manitoba's Indian population
> has among the highest rates of welfare dependency in Canada, at
> close to 80% for reserve residents. . . .
>
> The Indian death rate for persons between 25 and 44 years of age
> is five times the non-Indian rate. The average age of death for Indian
> men is 25 years younger than for non-Indian men. Tuberculosis,
> known as the disease of poverty, occurs seven times more frequently
> in Manitoba's Indian population. . . .
>
> . . . a similar picture is presented when one examines the prov-
> ince's prison population. In 1965, 22% of prisoners at Stony Moun-
> tain federal penitentiary were Aboriginal. In 1984, this proportion
> was 33%. In 1989 the superintendent of the institution told our
> Inquiry the figure was now 40%. [16]

In 1989 in Manitoba, 55 per cent of provincial jail prisoners were
Native people, while 67 per cent of admissions to women's prison
were Aboriginal and approximately 70 per cent of admissions to
youth detention centres were drawn from the Native population.
Alcoholism, substance abuse, prostitution, and family violence levels can be measured in similar percentages. And, as the Manitoba
inquiry demonstrated in its detailed examination of the brutal murder of Helen Betty Osborne in northern Manitoba in 1971 and the
police shooting of J.J. Harper in Winnipeg in 1988, the treatment of
Native people by the police and justice systems is far from neutral in
matters of race. [17]

The unvarnished truth about Canadian policy toward the Native
people is that it has been a disastrous failure. That failure is best

summarized in the words of a recently published document entitled
To the Source prepared by the Assembly of First Nations. It reads:

> [Our] ancestors never gave the land up – that was impossible, for to
> our people land, like air or water, cannot be bought or sold. They
> signed treaties with the incomers in a spirit of trust and honour, tak-
> ing their responsibilities very seriously and expecting the Europeans
> to respect their own words. And what did the Europeans give in
> return? Small sums of money – tiny sums compared to the value of
> the land and its resources. Promises that haven't been kept. Patches
> of land too small to support traditional hunting, so isolated that
> almost no one has a job. 'Education,' which meant beating their lan-
> guage and religion out of whole generations of small children, or
> shipping them off to white schools full of racism, often miles from
> home and family. 'Social services' that snatched thousands of chil-
> dren from their homes, but that can never be stretched far enough to
> help those who need it. Housing – often substandard houses, and
> nowhere near enough of them.
>
> They also offered white culture and values, which our people did
> not want. The struggle for cultural supremacy started as soon as the
> Europeans landed. Since then, the federal and provincial gov-
> ernments, churches, social agencies – virtually every authority and
> institution in Canada – has done everything in its power to turn
> Aboriginal peoples into Eurocanadians. These institutions have
> used force, bribery, co-option, coercion, conversion, persuasion,
> persecution, trickery, neglect, forcible adoption, and sheer indiffer-
> ence. They have employed the courts, the schools, social services,
> the prisons, the churches, the police, even the army, and legions of
> federal and provincial bureaucrats. They have taken our land, our
> rights, and our children. They had, as natural allies, smallpox, mea-
> sles, diphtheria, and influenza, which killed and demoralized our
> foreparents, and our vulnerability to alcohol, which is still killing and
> demoralizing our people.
>
> They have left an ungodly mess, one that our people spoke about
> in pain and anger: the poorest, most traumatized, and most troubled
> single population in Canada, with rates of unemployment, welfare
> dependence, substance abuse, family violence, imprisonment, and
> suicide far beyond the levels in any other group. Too many of our
> people have drowned in self-hatred, or have victimized others
> because they were victims themselves.
>
> But they didn't break us. We survived. [18]

The language of that indictment is powerful – but essentially accurate in its description both of the policy and of its outcome. Against formidable odds, Canada's Native peoples have survived. Indeed, in the twenty-six years since the 1969 White Paper they have finally forced an almost total reversal of the policy first announced by Jacques Cartier in 1534.

The protest mounted by the organizations formed by Native peoples against the 1969 White Paper was so powerful that by 1973 the Trudeau government was forced to withdraw it. Gradually government policy, encouraged by court decisions that recognized Aboriginal rights once thought to have been extinguished, has come to accept that land claims based on treaties and more generally on Aboriginal title must be settled through negotiation.[19] Moreover, as the new constitution of 1982 stated, "Indians, Inuit and Métis" have been accepted not as peoples to be assimilated, but rather as peoples whose distinct status is enshrined as a positive, indeed as a fundamental, feature of Canadian life. Nor is that fundamental feature to be recognized as just one more ethnic group in Canada's multicultural mosaic. Beginning at least as early as 1983 the Trudeau government, in giving general approval to the recommendations of the report of a parliamentary committee known, after its chair, as the Penner Committee,[20] accepted that Native peoples should increasingly govern themselves. Since then, and particularly since 1990 when the Meech Lake Accord, designed to amend the constitution in a manner that aimed to satisfy certain Quebec stipulations but that ignored the concerns of Native people, was defeated by the vote of Elijah Harper, the lone Aboriginal member of the Manitoba legislature, the issue of Aboriginal self-government has become a central issue in Canadian constitutional debate. The Oka crisis during the summer of 1990 intensified the debate.[21]

The principal Aboriginal organizations – the Assembly of First Nations, the Native Council of Canada, the Métis National Council, and the Inuit Tapirisat – have all elaborated claims to a measure of self-government. This demand is founded on the assertion that the right to self-government is "inherent," one that existed prior to the arrival of the Europeans, not one that can be granted to them by the descendants of Columbus, Cartier, and Cook.

These claims are set out most explicitly, and in considerable detail, in *To the Source*, which enumerates and explains the constitutional claims of the Assembly of First Nations. Grand chief Ovide

Mercredi was himself denied official status as an "Indian" because both his mother and grandmother were Europeans until the Canadian Charter of Rights declared gender discrimination unconstitutional. Since becoming grand chief this Manitoba Cree lawyer has demonstrated great skill in advancing his people's cause and winning support in the non-Native community. He seems equally at home in full Plains Indian regalia and in a three-piece suit. Underlying the constitutional position of the Assembly is a form of pan-Indian nationalism that almost seems to mimic Quebec nationalism, a fact that explains the sometimes bitter exchanges between Mercredi and other Native leaders and Quebec nationalist politicians.

> Quebecers will never agree to have their destiny decided by the rest of Canada. In the same way, the First Nations will never agree that their destiny is anything but their own choice. On this point, as on many others, no one is in a better position than us to understand the traditional aspirations of Quebecers. But understand us, too. You have not allowed yourselves to be assimilated, you have not allowed your collective identity as a people, as a nation, to be undermined. We are no less distinct than you. We deserve to survive just as much as you do. If it belongs to Quebecers and no one else to decide what powers to grant themselves to ensure their full flowering, then it is the same for us. [22]

Mercredi, appearing before a committee of the Quebec National Assembly in February, 1992, argued that the ethnic and cultural diversity of Quebec undermined its claim to the right of national self-determination. The angry responses of Quebec nationalists, already infuriated by the highly successful campaign of the Mistassini Cree to defeat plans for hydro development in the James Bay area and aware that Native land claims in the province cover about 85 per cent of Quebec's territory, replied that Mercredi's idea of a "nation" was racist. [23]

Native leaders have been reluctant to spell out the details of self-government for several reasons. The first is that the varying socio-economic conditions under which Native people currently live mean that there is no consensus on how much self-government is desired. Second, the presence of a large number of Native people in Canada's cities – the largest number, some 65,000 in Toronto, for example – makes any uniform concept of self-government almost impossible to conceive. And finally, for strategic reasons Native leaders have preferred to remain at the level of principle, fearing that some of their non-Native support will collapse once the extent of their claims is particularized. That danger seems very real if one looks at even part of the lengthy shopping list set out in the Assembly of First Nations constitutional statement:

That the Constitution recognize First Nations' inherent right to self-government

That First Nations be recognized as separate and distinct societies

That First Nations self-government be implemented in a way and at a pace to be determined by each First Nation

That new fiscal relations between First Nations and the federal government will be necessary in order to answer the needs of First Nations governments, but that the fiduciary responsibility of the federal government must remain until such new arrangements have been satisfactorily completed

That these new fiscal arrangements should be built on the basis of resource sharing

That the Canada Clause acknowledge First Nations governments as being on equal terms with the federal and provincial governments

That the Canada Clause should refer to our ongoing contribution to this country and our presence in this land before either of the 'two founding peoples'

That past injustices to First Nations and their members be acknowledged and admitted

That First Nations languages be recognized as official languages of Canada, with the same status as French and English

That First Nations have exclusive jurisdiction for First Nations for taxation, including tax immunity

That First Nations justice systems be established to apply Aboriginal principles and practices of justice to our own people, since the current application of Canadian justice to Aboriginal peoples has resulted in miscarriages of justice and the legal expression of racism

That federal and provincial governments take steps to appoint qualified First Nations lawyers to the Bench, up to and including the Supreme Court of Canada, in order to rectify bias against Native people in the courts of Canada

That First Nations language and culture be recognized, protected, and promoted throughout Canada

That the uniqueness of our cultures, traditions, and languages be
specifically recognized in the Constitution and by the governments
and people of Canada

That the Canadian Constitution be amended to reflect the original relationship of treaty federalism with First Nations.[24]

To this already formidable list several other highly controversial
items can be added from the same document:

That Quebec and the other provinces recognize the territorial
integrity of First Nations

That First Nations reclaim full jurisdiction over resources on
reserves and shared jurisdiction on resources off-reserves, not
excluding the option for full jurisdiction over off-reserve resources,
and that First Nations consent is required for any and all resource
development

That the Canadian Charter of Rights and Freedoms shall not
override First Nations law, but that gender equality be formally
established in formal Aboriginal Charters of Rights and Freedoms.[25]

This latter demand, which amounts to a claim for a notwithstanding clause similar to the one that allows provinces to set aside
certain sections of the Charter, is based on the argument that
Native "nations" do not share the "liberal" values enshrined in the
Canadian Charter – an argument sometimes advanced by Quebec
nationalists.[26] Some Native women, represented by the Native
Women's Association of Canada, utterly reject this position, con-
tending that "male dominated aboriginal governments" need to be
restrained by the gender equality provisions of the Canadian
Charter.[27]

Resolving the problems and even contradictions contained in
these extensive claims for distinct constitutional status will doubtless require many years of negotiation, followed by numerous court
decisions. Most obviously, the potential clash between Quebec's
insistence on its "distinct society" and territorial integrity and the
parallel demands of the Native people could prove profoundly
disruptive. But people in other parts of Canada, too, may find that
the somewhat romantic view of Native people that has recently

developed – symbolized by the image of Elijah Harper with his white eagle feather – will require revision once the extent and cost of Native claims is fully understood. But one point is clear: relations between First Nations and other Canadians are now set on a new course. Al Hunter, a member of the Rainy River First Nation, explained this change metaphorically:

> First, they told us that we no longer needed a canoe. Then, they told us that we no longer know how to build a canoe anyway. They will offer a new, shiny, better canoe, but it comes with one of their navigators and they will own the canoe – maybe it will be a motorboat. All we have to do is step ashore, return to the land, pick a fine cedar tree, trim the bark from a tall-standing birch, gather the sap from spruce, and build a new canoe – carve new paddles, our own paddles. If we don't know how, we can ask our Elders.[28]

The journey is certain to be arduous.

FIVE

The Evolution of Nationalism in Quebec

"The nation, it is a little like liberty, the liberty of Madame Roland and of some others, . . . what interests can be served in its name!"
André J. Bélanger

H UBERT AQUIN, the brilliant Quebec novelist, was also a political writer of great talent, and perhaps the only nationalist intellectual capable of meeting Pierre Trudeau on his own ground – the logic of historical development. Aquin almost always went to the heart of the matter, even if that meant a certain amount of simplification. In a 1962 analysis of nationalism in Quebec he wrote:

> Throughout our history we have confused nationalism and the defence of rights when there is, in my view, opposition between these two attitudes. The defender of our rights is someone resigned to a minority status, while the nationalist wants first of all a nation, wishes the minority condition to be ended. True nationalists want separation and independence, not the perpetuation of a provincial or minority position.

For Aquin a "nation," defined as a culturally homogeneous community, should become a state; for Trudeau, there was no need – indeed, it was undesirable – for cultural nations and political sovereignty to coincide. Each understood the other's logic in a way that was rare in the rather confused debates about Quebec's place in Canada during the 1960s and 1970s. [1]

Yet the confusion of that debate is readily explained: Aquin's logic too easily brushed aside a great deal of French Canada's history. In making the thrust toward political independence the

determining criterion of a true nationalist, he cast several generations of cultural and even economic nationalists into outer dark-
ness. Nationalist politics in these terms flickered briefly during the
abortive rebellions of 1837-38, then was virtually extinguished until
the founding of the small separatist parties, particularly Le Rassemblement pour l'Indépendance Nationale, in the early 1960s, leading
to the foundation of the Parti Québécois in 1968. In fact, however,
nationalism defined as the collective will of a distinctive community
to survive and grow according to its own cultural imperatives
existed, at least among the leadership classes of French Canadians,
from the early decades of the nineteenth century. Only occasionally, and even then only in the case of a minority of nationalists, was
political sovereignty viewed as the essential means to the end of cultural survival. More often other forms of what might be called
"autonomy" were judged realistic and sufficient. Indeed, it can be
argued that, with some important differences in detail and especially in timing, nationalism among French Canadians paralleled
similar movements in Europe and exhibited the same "mutations"
that E.J. Hobsbawm noted in his account of *The Age of Empire*. That
is especially true of what Hobsbawm calls the "growing tendency to
assume that 'national self-determination' could not be satisfied by
any form of autonomy less than full state independence" and the
"novel tendency to define a nation in terms of ethnicity and especially in terms of language."[2] Yet, it must be emphatically added
that in Quebec those mutations remain, even today, only one tendency among those committed to the survival and growth of the
French-speaking culture in Canada.

New France was a child of the *ancien régime*, "a supplement to
Europe," in the words of the eighteenth-century geographer Guil-
laume Delisle.[3] Nevertheless, by the middle of that century, French
settlers in North America had developed a sense of distinctiveness
from their homeland: they were *habitants*, not *hivernants*, calling
themselves *canadiens*. But it was the British Conquest and its aftermath that emphasized that distinctiveness – 65,000 or so French-
speaking *colons* separated from their Roman Catholic mother
country, part of an English-speaking Protestant empire. But a sense
of difference was not nationalism, nor could it be in a society where
popular participation in politics was largely unknown and unsought
after. It was only during the years of the French Revolution that the
first, modest stirrings of liberal and popular unrest were felt. The
constitution of 1791 (granted three months before the new French

constitution of 1791), which included a representative assembly, drew that discontent into constitutional channels but also, unwittingly, provided the context for the birth of nationalism and nationalist politics. That constitution institutionalized ethnic conflict: the *canadien* majority dominated the elected assembly; the English-speaking minority controlled the appointive legislative and executive councils. And the assembly and other, limited, British freedoms produced political groupings, campaigns, and a relatively free press. If, as many historians contend, modern nationalism was a child of the French Revolution, then French Canadians were among those who witnessed that birth. Yet the revolutionary doctrines of 1789 attracted the interest and sympathy of only a handful of what might be called political intellectuals. It also, of course, attracted the interest and hostility of the leaders of the Catholic Church who were at pains to point out to their flocks the benefits of membership in a Protestant empire, something that had resulted from what the future bishop, abbé J.-O. Plessis, called the *"providentiel"* conquest. "Be faithful," he warned, "or renounce your title as a Christian."[4] By the mid-nineteenth century this theme of the *providentiel* separation of the *canadiens* from France became a dominant note in French-Canadian political thought. Some, like Thomas Chapais, a leading historian and conservative politician, distinguished between "radical France, conservative France, free-thinking France and Catholic France, France which blasphemes and France which prays," and even most Liberals would have agreed it was that second France, "the France that prays," that was "the true fatherland of our intelligence, as the Catholic Church is the fatherland of our souls."[5]

As the nationalist movement developed in Lower Canada in the 1820s and 1830s it drew on some liberal ideas then current both in France and in the English-speaking world. But it drew even more on the social, economic, and political grievances of French Canadians who increasingly resented the economic and political domination of an English-speaking minority. By the 1830s Louis-Joseph Papineau's *patriote* party claimed to represent *la nation canadienne*, and in 1837-38 a pathetic armed revolt against British domination – a revolt duplicated in English-speaking Upper Canada – was crushed. Papineau's nationalism was founded on a belief that the French-speaking agricultural society, whose members were overwhelmingly Roman Catholic (though Papineau himself was a mild sceptic), was threatened by the English-speaking, commercial

Protestant minority backed by the British Colonial Office. The rebellion failed miserably, suggesting, not for the last time, that the concerns of the nationalist elite had made only a superficial impact on the rapidly growing, economically unprogressive rural population.[6] Yet the *patriote* ideology, with one notable revision, established the essential outlines of French-Canadian nationalism for a century.

During the 1840s, when L.-H. LaFontaine was working out the political strategy necessary to avoid Lord Durham's recommendation that French Canadians be assimilated, the first systematic statement of French-Canadian nationalism appeared. It was the work of an historian, François-Xavier Garneau. In his *Histoire du Canada*, Garneau hoped to follow the principles of what he called "the modern school of history"; men like Jules Michelet, "who regards the nation as the source of all power." In four large volumes Garneau set out an account of his people that provided them with the essential components of any nationalist ideology: a meaningful past, one with lessons for the present and hopes for the future. It was the story of an heroic struggle by *un petit peuple* for survival – against the Amerindians, the elements, and, finally, the British. Out of that *lutte des races* a nation had been forged, French, North American, agricultural, one where Catholicism was an important, though not a dominant, factor.

Garneau was a nineteenth-century liberal nationalist. He believed in representative government and was thankful that the British had brought it, he disapproved of clericalism and regretted that the Huguenots had been excluded from New France, and he viewed the nation as an essentially secular community. "There is something touching and noble at the same time in the defence of a nationality, a sacred heritage that no people, no matter how degraded, has ever repudiated. Never has a greater and more sacred cause inspired a rightly disposed heart and deserved the sympathy of generous spirits."[7] Implicit in that nationalism was a conservative mood: the need, he emphasized, was defence and preservation, and he urged caution on his compatriots, for change might mean loss of those very characteristics that defined their national being. It was these conservative seeds in Garneau's nationalist garden that bore the most abundant fruit after 1850.

Throughout the European world, and in North America, the failures of the liberal-nationalist thrust of the early decades of the nineteenth century were followed by the triumph of a conservative nationalism. Indeed, as Sir Lewis Namier argued in his *1848: The Revolution of the Intellectuals* (1946), that outcome was almost foreordained. Quebec fell into that familiar pattern. After 1840, the Church, led by the energetic ultramontane prelate, Mgr. Ignace Bourget of Montreal, began a recruitment and re-organization drive that would gradually give the Church dominant place in Quebec society. As the Church extended and consolidated its control over education and other social institutions in Quebec,[8] so, too, it redefined that society's ideology. Where Garneau had recognized religion as a component of nationalism and the Church as one of the institutions of collective survival, clerical ideologists made religion integral to nationalism and awarded the Church the central role in the defence of the nation. Abbé Laflèche, the most brilliant theoretician of ultramontanism and soon to be Bishop of Trois-Rivières, wrote in 1866: "The providential mission of the [French] Canadian people is essentially religious: it is the conversion to Catholicism of the poor faithless people who inhabit this country, and the extension of the Kingdom of God by the formation of a nationality that is above all Catholic." And if the implications were not obvious, Mgr. Bourget of Montreal made them so in an 1868 pastoral letter: "the true patriot," his priests were to tell their flocks, "is a sincere Catholic. Religion inspires love of country, and the love of country causes love of religion. . . . Without religion, the national interests are sacrificed; and without the fatherland, religious interests are forgotten and set aside."[9]

When Frenchmen, and others, were celebrating the centennial of the Revolution in 1889, French Canadians, for the most part, recalled other events drawn from their own history. The national holiday of French Canada was not July 14, or for that matter, July 1, the date of Canadian Confederation. Rather it was – and is – June 24, St. Jean Baptiste Day. On that day in 1889 a celebration was held just north of Quebec City at the place where the explorer Jacques Cartier had wintered 355 years earlier, a place that conveniently coincided with the first residence established in 1625 by the Jesuit fathers, including the future martyrs Jean Brébeuf and Gabriel Lalement. That the date marked the 240th anniversary of the destruction of the Jesuit mission to the Hurons was not lost on the celebrating crowds. One of the orators of the day – a day attended by all of the important political and religious leaders of Quebec – summed up the meaning of the Cartier-Brébeuf monument in these words: "Cartier-Brébeuf! It is France and the Church taking possession of the New World."[10] With such ancient and sacred events to commemorate, a mere centennial was hardly worthy of special note!

The changes rung on the theme of this French-speaking, Catholic nation with its rural foundation and spiritual mission in North America – the eldest daughter of the Church, apostate France having abdicated – were infinite in the years before 1960. And, of course, by making religion so central to national identity these clerical ideologists provided themselves and the Church with the principal leadership role in the struggle for survival. "If there is a ruling class here," Henri Bourassa, a leading nationalist spokesman in the early twentieth century, noted approvingly in 1902, "it is certainly the clergy." It should also be observed that having nominated themselves the leaders in the struggle for national survival, churchmen also made themselves a prime target for those who, in the years after World War Two, began to fear that the battle had been lost.[11]

There are, perhaps, two important points that need emphasis about the dominant clerico-nationalist ideology that permeated Quebec's traditional elites before the Quiet Revolution. The first is that it was nationalist in a religious and cultural sense, but rarely in a political or economic manner. Abbé Laflèche's book was written partly as a defence of the Confederation scheme then debated. Bourget had his doubts about Confederation, but he kept them quiet. Only a rare ultramontane journalist like Jules-Paul Tardivel expressed separatist sentiments and he, like his better-known successor, abbé Lionel Groulx, nationalist historian and activist, postponed independence to a date well into a utopian future.[12] More typical was Henri Bourassa, whose speeches in Parliament and on the public platform, and whose editorials in his nationalist newspaper, *Le Devoir*, all combined an ardent cultural nationalism with a powerful defence of a Canada founded on a federation of autonomous provinces and a compact of two distinct "races" living on terms of equality from Halifax to Vancouver.[13] The nation, being defined culturally, included not only the Quebec Francophones who made up 80 per cent of the population, but also that 20 per cent of the Francophone population that lived elsewhere in Canada. (Indeed, it sometimes also included those hundreds of thousands of Quebecers who had emigrated to the United States.) Moreover, since this definition of nationalism was so deeply infused with religion, its primary focus was on the Church rather than the state.

Indeed, the state was sometimes viewed as an instrument of the Church. The French-Canadian nation was, thus, an *église-nation*.

The second and equally important observation to be made is that what clerico-nationalists described was an ideal, not a real nation. This is particularly obvious in economic matters and the persistent description of the French-Canadian nation as having *une vocation rurale*. If Quebec remained predominantly rural through most of the nineteenth century, growing numbers of French Canadians did not. First, there were those hundreds of thousands who emigrated from rural poverty in Quebec to low-paid urban work in the United States – perhaps 900,000 between 1840 and 1930. Then after about 1900, when the industrialization of Quebec began to take off, the movement toward the cities intensified so that by 1921 a slight majority of Francophone Quebecers lived in urban areas. The process had taken place with the encouragement of successive provincial governments more influenced by the need to create jobs and to collect revenues than by the preachments of clerical nationalists. And, indeed, the Church had never been unanimous about the rural virtues and at least some of the clergy recognized the virtues of industrialization – it kept their flocks from emigrating.[14] While the call for increased support for colonization – rural settlement of surplus population – continued to make its impact on Quebec governments until after World War Two, the urban-industrial order had become irrevocable. The rural myth, however, lingered on.

Whatever consensus there was about the nature of the French-Canadian nation – and it was never unanimous – began to be shattered in the interwar years. During the 1920s abbé Groulx's *Action française* kept the light of clerico-nationalism aflame, a beacon against the dangers of industrial-urban life. "We need to hold onto the land," the priest-historian wrote in 1924, "attach ourselves to the healthy life which created the vigour of our forefathers, and we crowd insanely into cities where we are decimated by infant mortality and where the level of morality falls sharply."[15] At the end of the decade came the depression – and a paradoxical result. Most obviously, the limitations of clerico-nationalist ideology were harshly revealed; many individuals and groups began to call for a full acceptance of the new industrial order and a re-evaluation of social thought.[16] A collection of dissident young Liberals calling themselves the Action libérale nationale was one such group. Yet it was swallowed up in a new political party, the Union Nationale, which effectively re-imposed traditional nationalist ideas on the province for the next twenty-five years, while presiding over the accelerated industrialization of Quebec society. Appropriately, just at the end of the Duplessis years, a *Royal Commission of Enquiry on Constitutional Problems*, the Tremblay Commission, provided a systematic statement of the ideology that had played so dominant a role in Quebec's intellectual life, one that insisted that the Church "had supplied French Canada with its thought, its way of life and the majority of its social institutions."[17] But that ideology was now under siege.

While the events of World War Two, especially the divisive debate over conscription for overseas service, turned Quebecers in on themselves, the war-induced economic growth had a much more permanent impact. Iron ore, aluminum, pulp and paper, and hydroelectricity together produced the final demise of clerico-nationalism. Out of this new economic order grew a new secular elite that saw its worldly ambitions constrained by an ideology that undervalued economic success and scientific learning, condemned state involvement in social and educational affairs, rejected birth control, and sanctified patriarchy. Gradually these new elites insisted that social and economic problems be subjected to the scrutiny of empirical social science rather than the *a priori* moralizing of Catholic social teachings. Two groups in particular – though they were not alone – characterized this new outlook.[18]

In a society where historical interpretation had always been at the heart of nationalist ideology, it is hardly surprising that a major assault on the old nationalism came in the form of historical revisionism. Abbé Groulx's successors at the Université de Montréal – Professors Maurice Séguin, Guy Frégault, and Michel Brunet – were secular men, two of them trained in the United States. Together they challenged the view that the Church had dominated New France and remained to save the French Canadians after the Conquest. Instead, they argued that New France, like New England, had been a colony led by a thriving *bourgeoisie* that the Conquest had destroyed, turning the economy over to British merchants. That left the French Canadians excluded from commerce, forced into the rural life. After the Conquest it was not the Church but rather the seigneurial system and a soaring birth rate that had prevented assimilation. The Church, by contrast, in singing the virtues of ruralism, condemning commerce and state intervention, had left the field free for occupancy by the British. Lacking a middle class, the neo-nationalists contended, French Canadians had lost control of the economy even in the one province where they were a majority. The result was a profound crisis: French-Canadian culture was unprotected and often poverty stricken in an urban-industrial order controlled by foreigners. Canadians dominated *canadiens*.[19]

The implications of the Montreal historians' teachings were explicit: French Canadians should set about using the state to promote a new entrepreneurial class in order to regain control over their economic life. Only in this way could they build a modern nation, one that eschewed messianic appeals. This meant concentrating on Quebec as the national state of French Canadians, forgetting the minorities whose fate was assimilation, and unmasking the myth of national unity that merely disguised French-Canadian subordination to the English-speaking majority. Gradually, Canadian federalism would be reformed to reflect the existence of two equal nations. "The government charged with defending and promoting the common good of the French-Canadian nationality is that of the province where the immense majority of the French Canadians live. That is why Quebec cannot be considered simply as one of ten provinces. It has the right to claim a special status."[20] How special became the central issue in the constitutional debates of the 1960s.

Though Brunet and his colleagues never explicitly connected their nationalism with the cause of independence, the implications were there. A second influential historian, Maurice Séguin, in a little book entitled *L'idée de l'indépendance au Québec* (1968), first broadcast over Radio-Canada and then published in the separatist journal *Laurentie*, left little to the imagination. Brunet, himself, developed a theory of so-called "associate states," which was a forerunner of René Lévesque's sovereignty-association – political sovereignty combined with a Canadian common market. With the Montreal historians the concept of *état nation* replaced that of *église-nation*; nationalism was once again viewed as a secular phenomenon.[21]

A second group of thinkers in the 1950s articulated an even more radical criticism of traditional nationalism. This was a loose association of social scientists, lawyers, journalists, and labour leaders who, in 1950, founded a little magazine called *Cité libre*. Pierre Elliott Trudeau became the best known of this group, but he was not alone in his advocacy of a "functionalist" approach to Quebec's problems. His long, documented, and brilliantly polemical introduction to a study of one of Quebec's major post-war labour conflicts, *La Gréve de l'amiante* (1956), dissected traditional clerical and nationalist dogma that, he argued, ignored the realities of French-Canadian life. "Alas," he concluded, "it was the very idealism of the nationalists that most hurt them. *They loved not wisely but too well*; and in their anxiety to obtain nothing but the best for French Canadians, they developed a social thought impossible to put into practice and which to all intents and purposes left the people without intellectual guidance."[22] While this may seem to have been an affirmation of the Montreal historians' viewpoint, Trudeauites did not call for a revised and modernized nationalism. That, they believed, would only substitute old myths with new. Seeing themselves as spokesmen for the working people of Quebec, the *citélibristes* viewed nationalism as a bourgeois ideology; the Montreal historians' formulation was thus merely an ideology for a new business class. Nor did they believe that Quebec needed to construct a nation-state or acquire a special status. Quebec's powers in the Canadian federal system were sufficient; the problem was not the lack of power but rather the failure to use it imaginatively and effectively. While the Montreal historians called for a modernized nationalism and increased provincial autonomy, the *citélibristes* worked toward a modernized social thought and a fully utilized federalism.[23] But each group was preoccupied with the future of French Canada.

The death of Premier Duplessis in 1959 probably removed the cap from the growing frustrations felt by Quebecers, though it is unlikely that even he could have prevented the explosion indefinitely. But with *le chef* gone the "quiet revolution" that had been under way since the end of the war now manifested itself in reforms in education, labour laws, the civil service, the construction of a welfare state, and a pronounced *dirigiste* thrust in economic matters. The state replaced the Church as the principal institution in the collective lives of Quebecers. As the Church had formerly hoped to formulate an ideology to justify its role as the ruling class, so the new bureaucratic ruling class redefined that ideology. The state of Quebec, the national homeland of French Canadians, or as they now increasingly called themselves, Québécois, could no longer accept a status of one province among many. Instead, it must be accepted as a nation, perhaps as not a fully independent one, though that was a future possibility, but at least as *une province pas comme les autres. Egalité ou indépendance* became the cry of even so conservative a politician as the Union Nationale's Daniel Johnson. In Quebec, as elsewhere in the post-colonial world, the process of modernization was a strong stimulus to nationalism, perhaps because change made citizens uneasy about their identities, perhaps because modernizers discovered that nationalist appeals could mobilize the people to support change. In Quebec, as elsewhere, reform, *le rattrapage*, was expensive and nationalist arguments, even threats, proved effective in pushing the central government out of lucrative tax areas in favour of *l'état du Quebec*.[24]

Increasingly, then, the post-1960 Lesage government found Brunet-like arguments appealing and useful. For René Lévesque, the most nationalist of Lesage's ministers and later the leader of the Parti Québécois, Quebec was vulnerable, like "a lobster during shedding season,"[25] its old values and institutions gone and a new shell yet to be grown. That shell would be the state, the Quebec state. Only the state that French Canadians controlled could be expected to assume the task of making Quebecers *maîtres chez nous*: increasing their control over the economy and making their language the dominant one in public and private institutions. If those goals were frustrated by the Canadian constitution, the constitution should be jettisoned and a new one, recognizing Quebec's national status, devised.

During the early 1960s a number of small, often feuding, separatist-nationalist groups were founded. But it was only in 1968 that René Lévesque left the provincial Liberal Party and set about forming the first serious party of national independence since Papineau's disaster. *"Nous sommes des Québécois"* his party statement began, and with astonishing speed he created a movement ready to take power. That was achieved on November 15, 1976. Between then and May 20, 1980, when his party was defeated in a referendum asking for a mandate to negotiate sovereignty-association with the rest of Canada, there was a flurry of activity attempting to legitimize the national project. The Minister of Finance, Jacques Parizeau, *un bon bourgeois* with a Ph.D. from the University of London, provided financial and economic management of a quality that almost quieted the fears of the business community and brought social peace to an unsettled labour scene. Rules concerning party financing were reformed and the problems of the depressed rural economy addressed. Most important of all was Bill 101, the Charter of the French language. This legislation, designed to end a controversy over language that had grown angrier for a decade, made French the only official language of the province and required its use in both public and private business. Limited language and educational rights were recognized for the Anglophone minority, but not for new immigrants, including "immigrants" from Canada. Though the Anglophones objected, as did leaders of other ethnic groups, and many of those with mobility due to professional skills departed for other parts of Canada, the law was widely accepted as a satisfactory solution to a pressing problem.

Yet the very success of the PQ's language legislation and its overall capacity to provide good government may well have been the cause of its failure to achieve its principal goal: political sovereignty accompanied by economic association with Canada. Of course, the Lévesque government knew that at no time since polls had been conducted on the topic had anything like a majority of Quebecers favoured independence. For that reason the PQ had promised never to act without a referendum. The party had calculated that, once in power, it could convince more people that independence was practical if the new government acted responsibly. In fact, the opposite seems to have happened. The effective promotion of Francophone interests by the provincial government seemed to demonstrate that independence, which would be disruptive, was unnecessary. The fruits of the educational reforms of the sixties came in the shape of a new generation willing and anxious to occupy managerial posts in the private sector – especially since the public sector was full, even bloated. The application of the new language laws to business greatly increased opportunities of this new business-school educated elite. So, too, did the departure of significant numbers of unilingual Anglophones: "the accelerated Frenchification of the Quebec economy," in Dominique Clift's words. [26] With education and social mobility came rising incomes for Francophones. In 1961 Francophones in Quebec had been near the bottom of the province's salary scale. By 1980 French-Canadian ownership of the economy was increasing while Francophone salaries had caught up and even passed those of Anglophones. A confident, new bourgeoisie had emerged, as Michel Brunet had hoped. [27] But its goals were not what he had predicted or hoped for.

Having achieved a status of importance, if not complete dominance, in the new Quebec, this bourgeoisie was not anxious to destabilize the ship by supporting radical constitutional change. Unlike the bureaucratic middle class that had spearheaded the state-building reforms of the 1960s, this new private-sector middle class saw no benefit, and perhaps even some threat, in the further growth of the state. When asked to approve a referendum calling for negotiations on sovereignty-association these people demurred – though the outcome was close enough. Sixty per cent of Quebecers voted *"non,"* 40 per cent said *"oui,"* but the Francophone population divided almost equally. Nevertheless, it was a devastating defeat for Lévesque's *état-nation* dream. Though his party won re-election in 1981 it was rudderless, and finding it necessary to pay the bills it had run up in the pre-referendum years the government adopted increasingly unpopular policies, especially unpopular with the very people – civil servants and teachers – who formed its most loyal support. And so Quebec's first *indépendantiste* government collapsed, its mission unfulfilled.[28] The new nationalism, then, was a victim of its own success.

Yet if yuppies – or as the French say, *bon chic, bon genre* – are no longer statist-nationalists, that should not be taken to mean that nationalism in Quebec is finally interred. The French-Canadian collective consciousness has roots that are deep and a *vouloir-vivre* too resilient to be destroyed even if the distinctive characteristics of contemporary Quebec are less definite, more North American, than ever before. The ticking time bomb that may set off yet another nationalist upsurge is the threateningly low birth rate that is part of Quebec's modernization.[29] Once French Canada had the highest birth rate in the Western industrial world; today it has the lowest. Quebec is a society where traditional family structures and gender relations, to say nothing of birth control practices, have undergone a radical change. That has resulted in a demographic revolution whose implications are only now being assessed and the "national" consequences contemplated.[30] That is for the future.

For now, then, let me conclude. Nationalism has proven a durable and malleable ideology in French Canada's history. Its content evolved as the society it sought to describe underwent change. But its goal remained consistent: the defence and legitimation of a French-speaking culture in North America. *La survivance* and *l'épanouissement* have been the historic rallying cries of nationalists in Quebec. And that is likely to remain so even in a modern Quebec where *Liberté, égalité et fraternité* are more highly valued than at any time in the past.[31]

SIX

The Paradox of Quebec

*"What will finally become of French Canada? To tell the truth, no one
really knows, especially not French Canadians, whose ambivalence on
this topic is typical: they want simultaneously to give in to cultural
fatigue and to overcome it, calling for renunciation and determination
in the same breath. "*

Hubert Aquin, *"The Cultural Fatigue of French Canada"*
(1962)

I

"CANADA IS NOT a country," the Quebec poet Jean-Guy Pilon
wrote as he crossed the Prairies heading for Vancouver in 1968, "it's
a continent washed by three oceans where twenty million people
live, about one third of them French. . . . In these vast stretches of
the Anglo-Saxon West I feel the difference inside me. I am definitely
not at home and I realize how true it is to say that Quebec is an
entity unto itself with its own culture, language, way of life."[1] But
having affirmed his distinctiveness Pilon went on to wonder if, and
for how long, that difference could be preserved. "What will
become of it?" he queried, and suggested that the answer be postponed for another ten years. Twenty-five years and more have
passed, but the ambiguity remains.

That very ambiguity about the future has long characterized
Quebec and makes French Canadians a paradox for most of us.
The same electorate that gave René Lévesque, an avowed
souverainiste, provincial power on November 15, 1976, gave Pierre
Elliott Trudeau, an avowed federalist, even stronger support on
February 18, 1980. One of Quebec's greatest artists, Paul-Emile

Borduas, declared about twenty years ago, "I hate all national-isms."[2] Today most Quebec artists and writers would probably insist that nationalism was what inspired their work. Yet even in a society where many of the leading intellectuals are proclaimed *indépendantistes*, two young philosophers recently published a book, *Le Territoire imaginaire de la Culture*,[3] rejecting the nationalist identi-fication of state and nation on which the policies of the Lévesque government rested. That the paradox, the ambiguity, is there is readily demonstrated. It has been the most striking result of opinion surveys on the independence question and Parti Québécois sup-port.[4] One nationalist insists that "It is necessary to resolve it now or to resign ourselves to perish."[5] Another, quite accurately seeing sovereignty-association as part of the ambiguity, recently wondered out loud "if the national movement is not irreversibly on the way to disappearance."[6]

In the face of this paradox how can an English Canadian be expected to decipher the riddle on the face of the French-speaking sphinx? For over forty years I have been trying, and I must confess that some of the message still eludes me. Recently several writers have tried to extract the secret by the use of codes supplied by Karl Marx, Albert Memmi, Jurgen Habermas, Nicos Poulantzas, Louis Althusser, among others.[7] The results, to say the least, are confus-ing. Is the sphinx bourgeois or merely petit bourgeois? Is the class struggle nationalist or anti-nationalist? These are intriguing ques-tions, but until they are settled perhaps there is still some value in an approach that tries to understand what is on Quebecers' minds by listening to what they have had to say over time. Let me begin at a period of severe crisis in French Canada's history.

II

The year 1840 was grim for French Canadians. Papineau's abortive rebellion and its aftermath left the *canadiens* profoundly pessimis-tic. Durham's *Report*, recommending assimilation, had an air of finality about it. Union with Upper Canada, as the essential first step, was about to be forced on Lower Canada. So bleak was the future that Etienne Parent, the most brilliant political writer of his generation and editor of the nationalist *Le Canadien*, declared his acceptance of assimilation if that was the price necessary to gain responsible government.[8]

In that depressed atmosphere of 1840, two *canadien* artists set down, one in poetry, the other in paint, their convictions and feelings about the future. In doing so they provided two enduring clues to the wellsprings of nationalism among French Canadians. The poet was François-Xavier Garneau, later to become famous as an historian. In 1840 he published "Le Dernier Huron" ("The Last Huron"), a poem about a people who had been defeated, dispersed, and assimilated.

> Their names, their eyes, their festivals, their history,
> Are buried with them forever
> And I remain alone to speak their memorial
> To the people of our day![9]

The Hurons, of course, stood as symbols for *canadiens* who, Garneau feared, would share the fate of that once proud and powerful Indian nation.

An Indian also served as a symbol of French Canada in Joseph Légaré's 1840 painting entitled *Paysage au Monument à Wolfe*. Here we see the Indian apparently offering to surrender his bow to the statue of the conqueror, General James Wolfe. Yet nearby, hidden behind a tree trunk, is a canoe waiting to carry the Indian away to his freedom. The critics seem agreed that the Indian (a Mercury figure) is more cunning than submissive, and that he is really preparing to escape to the freedom and independence of the forest.[10]

Taken together these two works of art symbolize the psychological dimension of nationalism among French Canadians. The Last Huron syndrome is the nightmare of ultimate extinction. Légaré's deceptively submissive Indian represents the dream of complete freedom. After nearly a century and a half, neither the nightmare nor the dream has come true. But they remain part of the French-Canadian nationalist psyche, as the psychiatrist-turned-politician, Dr. Camille Laurin, has often noted.[11]

Fear of the future, fear of extinction can be traced to at least two sources. The first is historical. Defeat, something shared by Amerindians and *canadiens*, is a central part of the French-Canadian historical experience. In the beginning was the Conquest. Each generation of French Canadians studies, reinterprets, and tries to come to terms with this central fact of their history – and of all Canadian history. Yet it never goes away. Here is a passage from the Quebec government's 1978 statement of policy on Quebec cultural development. It is a lengthy passage but it is a perfect summary of the currently dominant view of the Conquest among Quebec nationalists.

> Then the Conquest came. A small population having had at its disposal a relatively brief time to implant itself firmly on its territory, the original Canadians had to turn in on themselves and assure themselves of the foundations of their survival and of their development in a country firmly taken in hand by another people whose language, religion, laws, political institutions and genius were foreign to them. A conquered group, politically and economically dominated, the Canadians little by little developed the sentiments of a minority and became progressively marginalized in a country which was formerly theirs, but whose commanding heights had quickly escaped them. Regrouping themselves, chiefly in the rural areas, they clung to the soil, to their language, to their religion, to their way of life. As a result of the Conquest, they became isolated as businessmen from the great North American trade and have thus been rendered rather impermeable to the great revolutions of the Western world; they have been satisfied to endure, anchored in the solid realities which form the basis of peasant life.[12]

Each of the Parti Québécois's major public documents takes that sense of defeat symbolized by 1759 as its point of departure, once again demonstrating the centrality of the Conquest to nationalist thought.[13]

Consciousness of a second defeat has assumed an increasingly prominent place in the ideology of contemporary Quebec nationalism: the failure of Papineau's rebellion in 1837-38. In the past, Papineau's anti-clerical side lessened his attraction to clerical nationalist writers. But today, in a secular Quebec, he has been rehabilitated and the *patriotes*, even though they failed, have gained a new respectability. "One hundred and thirty years ago," Robert Lionel Séguin has written, "the Patriots at Saint Denis showed us the road to dignity and liberty. Fertile seeds from which we are gathering the fruit now."[14]

To the Conquest and the abortive rebellion of 1837, other familiar defeats are often added: Riel's hanging, Manitoba schools, Regulation 17 in Ontario, conscription in two world wars, even the air traffic controllers' crisis of 1976 when the use of French in the air space over Quebec was prohibited. Victories, when they come, are always too late: the Supreme Court of Canada rejected some restrictions on English in Quebec in less than three years after enactment; a Manitoba law abolishing French waited ninety years for the same result. A history filled with defeats and humiliations must surely stimulate pessimism. "The only issue – a more or less long-term issue," a Montreal historian wrote in the 1950s, "is the assimilation of the weaker culture by the stronger." And yet that pessimistic nationalism was closely linked with the rise of separatism in the 1960s, and its historical interpretation has been part of the official ideology of the Parti Québécois.[15]

Fear of the future has a second underlying cause: numbers. Throughout their history French Canadians have been preoccupied with their minority position. That is hardly surprising. New France was a tiny colony, outnumbered even by its Huron allies in the seventeenth century and constantly overshadowed by the more heavily populated English colonies to the south. While the French outnumbered the English in the Canadas until the 1850s, the pressure of English-speaking immigration was a major influence in the growth of the *parti patriote* in the 1830s.[16] One of the themes that runs constantly through Garneau's *Histoire* is his fear for a future in which the *canadiens* will be a minority. Again and again he refers to *"un peuple peu nombreux," "un peuple si faible en nombre,"* and so on. "But a people of small numbers," he observed in explaining the French Canadians' attitude during the American Revolution, "cannot control its own destiny, is obliged to act with much care and prudence."[17]

Throughout the latter half of the nineteenth century French-Canadian leaders were extremely conscious of two demographic facts. The first was *la revanche des berceaux*, "the revenge of the cradle." An extraordinarily high birth rate meant that French Canadians fulfilled the Malthusian law: population doubled every twenty-five years. "During the last two centuries," a Quebec demographer wrote in 1957, "world population has been multiplied by three, European population by four, and French Canadian population by eighty, in spite of net emigration which can be estimated at roughly 800,000."[18] Given those figures even Sir John A. Macdonald's view that the solution to the French-Canadian problem lay in immigration and copulation sounds futile.

But the other half of the demographic picture for French Canadians was emigration, chiefly to the United States. That "national haemorrhage" quite understandably obsessed French-Canadian leaders from the 1840s to the early twentieth century.[19] While some optimists thought that these southbound waves of Roman

Catholics would one day restore puritan New England to the true faith,[20] the more frequent reaction was fear – fear that Quebec's population losses would be English Canada's political gain. Abbé J.-B. Chartier put the issue very bluntly when he declared that only "traitors" rejoiced at the sight of Quebecers moving to the United States; keeping them at home was "a question of life or death for the French-Canadian race."[21] The campaigns of Curé Labelle, Arthur Buies, and others to colonize northern Quebec, and Canada, were conducted in the fulsome rhetoric of providential mission, but the goal was a very worldly one: to keep French Canadians at home where their heads could be counted by census takers and vote gatherers.

That preoccupation with numbers has not declined in the slightest. Nowhere in Canada is the decennial census scrutinized more thoroughly than in Quebec. In the last thirty-five years Quebec Francophones have fully absorbed the values and aspirations of urban-industrial people everywhere. That has been accompanied by a dramatic decline in the birth rate. In 1961 Quebec's leading demographer, Jacques Henripin, speculated about population trends in Canada. If existing immigration and birth rates remained constant and French Canadians continued to adopt English at the 1961 rate, he predicted that by 1981 only 23.5 per cent of the Canadian population would be French-speaking, and that percentage would fall to 17 per cent by the year 2011. In 1951 the percentage was 29 per cent.[22] That statement, cautious and careful as it was, set off a chain reaction that led directly to Bill 101, the Charter of the French Language, in 1977. But before that stopping place had been reached the language issue had proven its potency: in St. Leonard something near communal strife erupted between Francophones and immigrants anxious that their children learn English. Both the Union Nationale government of Jean-Jacques Bertrand and the Liberal administration of Robert Bourassa fumbled the issue. And that played a significant part in the election victory of the Parti Québécois in 1976. In the midst of these events a commission, known as the Gendron Commission, produced a massive report in which a convincing case was made for making French the working language of the province. Here was that commission's conclusion:

> This policy does not represent a false concern with the problem of numbers. It is clear the falling birth rate of French speakers, together with the slight attraction that the French language exercises on the

non-French-speaking constitutes a subject of legitimate concern for French-speaking Quebecers. The fear that French-speaking people will become a minority, if it is unfounded inside Quebec, is much more valid on the Canadian level.[23]

"The fear of becoming a minority": there is the heart of the matter. It is, in fact, the leitmotif of much Quebec nationalist writing from Garneau through to successive policy statements of the Lévesque government. It was central to the White Paper on language policy, where one bold-faced subheading summed up the issue: "If the demographic evolution of Quebec continues, French-speaking Quebecers will be less and less numerous." The same point is underlined in the opening pages of the cultural policy statement and, inevitably, formed a central part of the argument for sovereignty-association. In the PQ government's White Paper *La Nouvelle Entente Quebec-Canada* two large graphic illustrations dramatize the following information: in 1851, 36 per cent of Canadians were Francophone; in 1971 that figure was 28 per cent and by 2001 it will drop to 23 per cent. That in turn means that Quebec, which in 1867 held more than one-third of the seats in the Canadian House of Commons, will by 2000 hold less than one-quarter. "Under these circumstances," the authors of the White Paper argue, "it would be an illusion to believe that, in future, Francophones can play a determining role in the government of Canada. On the contrary, they will be more and more a minority and English Canada will find it increasingly easy to govern without them. In that respect, far from being an anomaly, the Clark government is a sign of things to come."[24]

By appealing to "the fear of becoming a minority," to the Last Huron syndrome, the Lévesque government hoped to convince Quebecers that the time had come to choose independence, to fulfil Joseph Légaré's vision of freedom. That theme, too, runs deeply in Quebec history. From the resort to arms in 1837 to Lévesque's proposed New Deal in 1979, the hope for independence always remained alive among small groups of Quebecers. For the most part it has never been much more than a dream to be achieved some day. After Papineau's defeat the dream of separate nationhood lived on in a segment of *le parti rouge*, which opposed Confederation in 1865 (as did a few *bleus*, including the young Honoré Mercier). What the *rouge* favoured in 1865 was not complete independence but a loose form of federalism in which the member states would remain sovereign. When the Quebec Resolutions passed the Canadian Assembly (twenty-seven French Canadians in favour, twenty-two opposed), a newspaper of *rouge* persuasion fulminated: "On this memorable night has been committed the most iniquitous and degrading act which the parliamentary system has witnessed since the Irish deputies sold their country to England for positions, honours and gold."[25]

Like much else in Quebec in the latter part of the nineteenth century, the idea of independence acquired a clerical and conservative tone though its origins with the *rouges* had been secular and liberal.[26] Its chief exponent, Jules-Paul Tardivel (his enemies called him Jules-Paul Torquemada after the head of the Spanish Inquisition), edited a newspaper characteristically called *La Vérité*. In the 1880s, Riel's execution and Macdonald's centralizing policies convinced him that only independence would save Quebec from Anglo-Saxon Protestant domination. In his utopian novel, *Pour la Patrie*, published in 1895, he described the events that, with God's help, led to independence in 1945. One passage, explaining the nationalist goal, is especially interesting:

> Our geographical position, our natural resources and the homogeneity of our population enable us to aspire to be ranked among the nations of the earth. It is possible that Confederation offers certain material advantages, but from the religious and national point of view it is filled with dangers for us, for our enemies will certainly manage to wear it away until it is a legislative union in everything but name. Moreover the chief material advantages that are derived from Confederation could be obtained equally well through a simple postal and customs union.[27]

In addition to the obvious similarities to sovereignty-association as devised by the Parti Québécois, Tardivel's projected République de la Nouvelle-France contains some other revealing details. Most notable was the assumed peaceful manner of its achievement – no revolution, no civil war, just a rather heated parliamentary debate, in which a sympathetic English-Canadian Catholic played a crucial role. René Lévesque's plans were postulated on a similar assumption. Canadians, he believed, are sufficiently civilized to be able to work out a division of their country in a federal-provincial conference, presumably carried on prime-time television with suitable commentary.

Those who kept the light of Quebec independence alive during the generations that followed Tardivel were equally reasonable in their expectations. In 1922 Canon Lionel Groulx and his friends in l'Action française published an inquiry in *Notre Avenir Politique* that concluded the future was unfolding, as expected, toward independence. But it would come as a natural evolution "as soon as Providence wishes it."[28] French Canadians were called on to prepare themselves, but the timetable was unspecified. So, too, the young separatists who joined with André Laurendeau in Jeune Canada in the late thirties spoke only in terms of an undefined future when, by undefined means, "one day a country will be born."[29]

Until the 1960s, then, when Le Rassemblement pour l'Indépendance Nationale and later the Parti Québécois were born, the ideal of independence was simply that, an ideal, more perhaps a state of mind than a concrete political project. Yet it is impossible not to be struck by the degree to which the Parti Québécois fits into this tradition of ambiguity and caution. Independence by steps: *étapisme*. Not even Mackenzie King, that Canadian master of ambiguity, of never doing things by halves that could be done by quarters, could have improved on the Lévesque-Morin strategy. First the removal of the independence issue from the 1976 election by the promise of a referendum. Then a definition of independence that is not independence but sovereignty-association. Next a referendum asking not for approval of sovereignty-association, but merely a mandate to negotiate. Finally a promise of yet another referendum on the outcome of the negotiations. Everything is hedged. Is it any wonder that a muscular separatist like Pierre Vallières, in frustration, pronounced the PQ strategy "as ineffective in liberating Quebec as the improvised result of the Patriots of 1837-38"?[30]

Why is nationalism in Quebec so cautious in tactics, so modest in its demands? Légaré's Indian may be preparing to escape into freedom, for the canoe lies ready. Yet he is also in the act of surrendering his bow to the statue of Wolfe. Perhaps it is not Mercury after all but rather, as the playwright Robert Gurik once contended, Hamlet who is *Prince de Québec*.[31] If, as I have been arguing, French-Canadian nationalism is driven by a fear of extinction, on the one hand, and the dream of absolute freedom, on the other, then it is driven in contradictory directions. Fear of the future and hope for the future combine to create indecision, ambiguity, paradox. Is that not Papineau, brilliantly characterized by Fernand Ouellet as *Un Etre Divisé*, and by Garneau as *"l'image de notre nation"*? Caught between the desire to preserve and the desire to liberate, between nationalism and liberalism, he was paralysed, a Franklin without being a Washington.[32]

Garneau himself expressed that same tension, which is at the heart of French-Canadian nationalism. At the conclusion of his great *Histoire*, having surveyed the struggles of his people from the first arrival of the explorers to the union of 1840, he drew one last lesson. It is often quoted, and rightly so, for it catches, as nothing else does, the essential character of nationalism in Quebec:

> Let the Canadians be faithful to themselves; let them be wise and persevering, let them not be seduced by the brilliance of social and political novelty. They are not strong enough to follow a career of that sort. It is for great nations to test new theories: they can move freely in their spacious orbits. For us, part of our strength comes from our traditions; we must not stray far from them and alter them only gradually.[33]

That sense of prudence, that belief in the need to tread carefully and to be guided by past traditions, has continued to characterize French Canadians throughout their history. And it is against the background of modest, but persistent, nationalism that the goals of Quebecers can best be understood, whether expressed in the demand for equality of linguistic rights, special powers for the province of Quebec, or sovereignty-association.

Put simply, the goal of French Canadians has always been security, and the strategy for its achievement is the recognition of equality. For a self-conscious minority, both the goal and the means of achieving it are perfectly understandable. By definition a minority is potentially at the mercy of the majority. It lacks security. It must discover a way to maximize its position, to find a mechanism that will allow it to act as an equal or near equal. Consciously, or otherwise, this has always been the strategy of French Canadians anxious to preserve their national distinctiveness. And that includes virtually all French Canadians for, though they have often been divided on means, they have never been divided on ends.

What strategies are possible and available? Papineau tried one route: equality established through independence. That is the tradition of *d'égal à égal*, the Parti Québécois call to arms. But the lesson that many of Papineau's followers drew from the rebellion's failure was that equality would have to be achieved within a political system that they shared with other Canadians. Such equality might never be perfect, but it would be attainable. That was the central

message of L.-H. LaFontaine's Address to the Electors of Terre-
bonne in 1840. He demanded, and received, an equal share of the
power within the Union: that was what the Rebellion Losses Bill
demonstrated. But the primary symbol of his success was the
repeal of the prohibition against the use of French that had been
part of the original union constitution. He practised what Canon
Groulx admiringly called *"une politique nationale"*[34] by convincing
French Canadians to stand united behind him and thus to maximize their strength. This is the strategy of "French power" practised by every successful French-Canadian federal politician since
Cartier: by the concentration of the minority's votes in one party it
becomes a near equal.

It is not a perfect strategy and, since it has resulted in defeats as
well as victories, critics have devised alternatives. The primary one,
historically, might be called "fortress Quebec." It stands between
"French power" and separation, taking something from each. It
argues that since French Canadians will always be a minority in the
federal system, they should concentrate their talents at the provincial level where they are a majority. Quebec, as the homeland of
French Canadians, should thus be recognized as a province *pas
comme les autres* with powers, at least in some areas, equal to those of
the federal government or of all the other provinces combined. This
strategy was practised in a limited manner by Mercier in the 1880s,
and by Duplessis and Lesage in more recent times. The report of
the Tremblay Commission on Constitutional Problems in the late
1950s worked this theory out most completely. And variations on
the theme of "fortress Quebec" – though offering fortress status to
other provinces, too – can be found in Claude Ryan's 1980 proposal
for *A New Canadian Federation.*[35]

Underlying each of these strategies is a conception of French
Canada and/or Quebec as a distinctive society, a nation in one of
several senses, deserving equality with other nations and particularly with its partner, English Canada. That equality is seen as a
necessary condition for the security that alone will banish the Last
Huron nightmare, and fulfil, at least in part, Légaré's dream.

III

Discovering the formula that will guarantee Francophones security
through equality has been the persistent quest of Quebecers for
nearly two centuries. The very vitality of Francophone culture

today is testimony, surely, to the degree of success that French Canadians have achieved. Neither Garneau's fears nor Légaré's hopes have been fulfilled. Both possibilities remain, and so does the riddle on the face of the French-speaking sphinx.

The ambiguity remains because it is an accurate reflection of the reality of Quebec society, its hopes and its fears. But it is more than that. It also reflects the shrewdness of a small, determined people who have discovered over the centuries that in the end survival depends on themselves, and that no single strategy is perfect. Where some see ambiguity as a sign of weakness – "cultural fatigue," [36] the brilliant novelist, Hubert Aquin, called it – others, and I think correctly, judge it more sympathetically. "The French Canadians' frequent duality of allegiances whereby they elect federal and provincial governments," Michel Morin and Guy Bertrand concluded their dissection of the public philosophy of Quebec, "is sufficient testimony to the natural intelligence of the people, of individuals anxious to guarantee their liberty and their rights by setting the princes who govern them against each other." [37]

SEVEN

The Coming of the Quiet Revolution

On JUNE 20, 1956, Maurice Duplessis's Union Nationale party was returned to power for the third consecutive time since 1944. The victory was a bitter blow for the growing forces of emancipation in Quebec, and especially for the provincial Liberal Party. Georges-Emile Lapalme, who had stepped out of federal politics to assume the provincial leadership in 1950, had worked vigorously to rebuild his party after the defeat of 1952.[1] He had established an independent provincial organization, the Quebec Liberal Federation, and attempted to introduce democratic practices within the party. A newspaper, *La Réforme*, edited by Jean-Louis Gagnon, carried the party's message to a growing list of party faithful and provided a forum for the discussion of a variety of proposals for reform in the political, educational, social, and economic structure of Quebec society. The party's program in 1956 reflected this new philosophy: it proposed increased agricultural subsidies, extensive educational reform, liberalized labour legislation, and more stringent controls over foreign capital in the development of natural resources. Yet, when the votes were counted on the night of June 20, the Union Nationale had actually increased its standing in the legislature, while the Liberals' total dropped from twenty-three at dissolution to twenty in the new house.[2] It looked as though the age of Duplessis would never end.

The 1956 election suggested two general conclusions to Quebecers who opposed the Duplessis regime. The first was that the Union Nationale machine was more powerful even than anyone had suspected. The second conclusion drawn by an increasingly large group of people was that as long as the opposition remained fragmented – there had been candidates from the provincial CCF or PSD, from the Labour Progressive Party, two independent nationalists, and a host of other independents in the 1956 election – there could be no certainty of defeating the Duplessis party. These conclusions were obvious. But what was more difficult was to devise ways both of cracking the power of the Union Nationale machine and of formulating a basis for coalition among disparate opposition groups.

The power of the Duplessis machine lay, at least superficially, in its unlimited use of patronage and its willingness to practise corruption and intimidation during elections. Shortly after the 1956 election two priests, abbé Gérard Dion and abbé Louis O'Neill, both of Laval University, published a stinging condemnation of what they called "political immorality in the province of Quebec" in a little known clerical publication, *Ad Usum Sacerdotum.* The article, soon picked up by *Le Devoir* and broadcast across the province and the country, zeroed in on two kinds of political tactic: intellectual blackmail and plain vote-buying. The first took the form of building the myth of the Communist menace and the Ottawa menace, sometimes linked together. The second included patronage, violence on election day, telegraphing votes, and numerous other carefully devised methods of ensuring the desired outcome at the ballot box. But what was worse than the practices themselves, Dion and O'Neill insisted, was that they were accepted, almost without a whisper of criticism, by large numbers of Quebecers. "The danger is all the greater," they wrote, "because a great deal of evidence shows that the consciences of the faithful and even those of members of religious orders no longer experience any feeling of scandal when confronted with such corruption."[3]

But why was a people so easily corruptible and so readily intimidated? Four years later, early in 1960, a teaching brother soon to be famous as Frère Untel, attempted an answer to the question: "We are afraid of authority; we live in a climate of magic, where under penalty of death we must infringe no taboo, where we must respect all of the formulae, all of the conformities."[4] The faithful French-Canadian Catholic's obedience to his Church had transferred his unquestioning loyalty to matters of politics. And politicians, traditionally, had found this a useful condition to encourage. It made their main objective – holding office – much simpler. Since Quebec was the only province in which the French Canadians were a majority, skilful politicians could play upon Quebecers' fears that their culture and language would be threatened by the majority unless unquestioning support was given a party that represented the national needs. Maurice Duplessis was a master of appealing to his people's insecurities and of intertwining religious and cultural concerns. In 1948 he had asserted a theme he repeated consistently as the justification for his policies. "The legislature of Quebec is a fortress," he wrote, "that we must defend without failing. It is that which permits us to construct the schools which suit us, to speak our language, to practise our religion and to make laws applicable to our population."[5] Here was an appeal to a state-of-siege mentality.

But there was more than this insecurity at the root of the French Canadians' apparent acceptance of immorality in politics. Historically, many French Canadians had developed an attitude toward government that combined the concept of the paternalistic provider with an opposition to state intervention in society's affairs. Thus the government, or rather the party in power, was expected to provide jobs at least for its supporters and dole out contracts and local improvements to loyal constituencies. But that same state was warned constantly to keep its nose out of the matters like education and social security, which were, after all, religious not political duties.

Each of these apparently contradictory attitudes stemmed from a view of government and the state as something external to, even foreign to, French-Canadian society. The French Canadians' traditional concept of authority was hierarchical, from the top down, not egalitarian or democratic. Monsignor L.-A. Pâquet, a distinguished French-Canadian theologian, summed up this view very well when he wrote that "all authority other than God's own comes from divine authority. . . . The idea of authority born of the free will of man, and constituted according to human calculations alone, has thrown into the world a social conception which is only a cause of trouble and a source of instability. . . . What must not be admitted, is that the people itself is sovereign, and that, in choosing the members of a legislative assembly, it delegates to them the power to govern."[6]

This conception of authority, more than anything else, allowed corrupt electoral habits to develop in Quebec. Since authority came from on high rather than from the people themselves, its actions were hardly matters of individual responsibility. And so, as Gérard Filion wrote after the 1956 election, "Most of the people in Quebec seem to have two consciences, one for their private lives, the other for their public life. . . . Lying, cheating, stealing is hateful when one is engaged personally but when done in the name of a Party, a Deputy, or one's Government, it is innocent, in fact almost considered as an act of virtue."[7]

If this attitude toward authority explained on the philosophical level Duplessis's apparently unbreakable hold on power, the divisions within the opposition were nearly as important on the strategic level. Quebec was certainly not monolithic in its support of the Union Nationale; even in 1956 that party had obtained only 51 per cent of the popular vote, which was more than it had received in any post-war election. The Liberals were the largest opposition group, ensured of at least 40 per cent of the voters' support. The PSD, or Quebec wing of the CCF, had made a significant impact on a small circle of intellectuals but had failed to penetrate the masses. This did not mean that the labour unions were happy with the existing political situation. Duplessis's restrictive labour laws and obvious favouritism toward big business made the unions, especially the Catholic unions, potential supporters of political change. There was also an important wing of the Roman Catholic Church, epitomized by Father Georges-Henri Lévesque and the School of Social Sciences at Laval, that was more than ready to reject the religious conservatism that lay at the base of the traditional French-Canadian nationalism. Then there was that group loosely termed "intellectuals." Some were nationalists, but of a new school. At *Le Devoir* the leadership of André Laurendeau and Gérard Filion was designed to turn the paper's nationalism in a leftward direction: to take up the cause of the labour unions, to demand educational reform, to support plans for better social welfare programs, and above all, to denounce the corruption of the Duplessis administration. ("*Le Devoir* is a bolshevik newspaper," Duplessis remarked in 1954.)[8] Less nationalist, even anti-nationalist, but more liberal, even socialist, was the group of intellectuals that expressed themselves through the little magazine, *Cité libre*.

The central figure in the *Cité libre* group was Pierre Elliott Trudeau. Since the beginning of the 1950s he and his friends had been propounding one basic idea about the fundamental weakness of Quebec society. That idea was the lack of democracy in Quebec. By the mid-fifties, and most notably after Duplessis's victory in 1956, the *citélibristes*, and especially Trudeau, began seriously to develop a strategy to unite the opposition forces in order to defeat the Union Nationale and launch Quebec on a course of democratic reform.

Perhaps the *citélibristes* could be called the "philosophers" of the "Quiet Revolution." Their function was to de-mystify traditional beliefs and institutions, to unmask the authoritarianism, clericalism, and corruption of the *ancien régime*, and to prepare the way, intellectually, for its overthrow. Pierre Juneau, Gérard Pelletier, Charles Lussier, and the others who helped start *Cité libre* would all have agreed with Pierre Trudeau's exhortation in the first issue of the magazine.

> We wish to testify to the Christian and French fact in North America. So be it: but let us make a *tabula rasa* of all the rest. It is necessary to submit to methodical doubt all of the political categories that the previous generation bequeathed to us: the strategy of resistance is no longer useful for the full flowering of the city. The time has come to borrow from the architect that discipline called "functional," to cast into the nettles the thousand prejudices with which the past encumbers the present, and build for the new man. Let us overthrow the totems, break the taboos. Or better, let us consider them cancelled. Coldly, let us be intelligent. [9]

Through the pages of *Cité libre*, at the sessions of the newly founded *institut canadien des affairs publiques* – Quebec's Couchiching, founded in the fifties – over Radio-Canada, and wherever else the opportunity offered, Trudeau and his friends preached a consistent message: the great need of Quebec was a large infusion of democratic thinking. The old concept of authority, from on high, had to be replaced with a new philosophy: the doctrine of popular sovereignty. If democracy could be achieved, all else would follow: educational reform and social and economic planning could begin, and corruption could be ended. The spirit of Duplessis and the spirit of democracy were sworn enemies. "Democracy first" became Trudeau's rallying cry and one behind which he hoped he could help to unite all of the forces opposed to the Union Nationale in Quebec.

The obvious step for Trudeau and his friends would have been to unite with the Liberal Party. But that was not possible. For all that they admired Lapalme's efforts to democratize the party and give it a modern program, Trudeau and his friends suspected that a large segment of the party was as traditionalist as the Union Nationale and, if in power, far from immune to anti-democratic and corrupt proceedings. "I cannot help admiring the tenacity of the small group of men who set out to infuse some democratic blood into the veins of a party which has never been anything more than a syndicate of the private interests," was the way that Trudeau expressed his somewhat sceptical attitude to the Liberals in 1956. [10]

Instead, the effort was made, in September, 1956, to launch Le Rassemblement, an organization whose somewhat vague objective was "to build a movement of education and democratic action." Pierre Dansereau, of the Université de Montréal, was its first president, Trudeau vice-president. Its constitution and declaration of purpose were lengthy and detailed. But its first principle was an explicit statement of the doctrine of popular sovereignty and its clear implication: "Men live in society in order that each individual can realize himself to the maximum. The only justification for political authority is to permit the establishment and development of an order which will favour this realization." And the last of its general principles underlined the point again. "A true political conscience will be born only at the instigation of a vast political education movement which will make the people conscious of their powers and put them in a well-established position to exercise them."[11]

There was something rather too academic about Le Rassemblement. It held its meetings, argued over ideology and strategy, but it lacked a power base. Gérard Bergeron, who sympathized with the aims of the group, described a typical member this way: "Politically, he is a worried, bitter, aimless man. The social force which he represents has no political expression. It operates in a vacuum." Trudeau was not prepared to accept this assessment.[12] In October of 1958 he prepared a long manifesto – "A Democratic Manifesto" – that was a call for all the divided opposition forces to come together to fight for democracy. "Democracy first," he declared. "After that it will be up to the sovereign people to opt freely for the choices they prefer."[13]

Nothing better expresses the philosophy of Le Rassemblement than the series of articles Trudeau wrote for Jacques Hébert's journal *Le Vrai* during 1958 under the title "Les Cheminements de la Politique." *Le Vrai* was the organ of the Civic Action League, which had been organized to cleanse the notably corrupt politics of Montreal. The movement was closely allied with the social nationalists of *Le Devoir* and its first leader, like the editor of *Le Devoir*, was a one-time member of the Bloc populaire. This was Jean Drapeau, who was elected mayor of Montreal in 1954. Three years later, Drapeau was defeated when the Union Nationale openly supported his opponent. *Le Vrai*, founded in 1956, was a sparkling and pugnacious newspaper. It could not have been otherwise under the editorship of Jacques Hébert. The journal's style was polemical, its cause the underdog. Though occasionally spiced with polemic, Trudeau's almost professorial articles on the true source of political authority and the virtues of democracy struck a somewhat calmer note than was usual for the paper. But what is most impressive about these journalistic pieces is the ease with which obvious erudition is transformed into clear, simple statements of fundamental political philosophy. He stated the essence of his argument early in the series in a paragraph that illustrates the style and logic of his mind.

> Human societies differ therefore from beehives because men always remain free to decide what form of authority they will give themselves and who will exercise it. There are many men who have the responsibility to take these decisions, and not God, Providence, or Nature. In the last analysis a given political authority exists only because men accept to obey it. In this sense it is not so much authority which exists; it is obedience. [14]

This series, like "A Democratic Manifesto," was the platform upon which Trudeau hoped to launch a political coalition strong enough to defeat the Union Nationale. At the end of 1958 Le Rassemblement, with Trudeau as president, resolved to open discussions with other political and educational groups that shared the goal of "democracy first." The time seemed ripe, for the two labour organizations, the Canadian Congress of Labour and the Quebec Federation of Labour, had indicated their intention to join in the establishment of a "new party," while the Quebec Liberals had recently passed a resolution calling for the union of all democratic organizations. Thus, Le Rassemblement was prepared to join these forces and to enter directly into political action. [15] Three months later a group of twenty-one well-known Quebec intellectuals representing the Liberals, the PSD, the Civic Action League, the unions, and the universities launched an appeal for unity among the opposition parties. [16] Trudeau was among them.

This *union des forces démocratiques*, despite its promising beginning, ultimately came to nothing. Within the group ideological quarrelling and the unwillingness of some of the constituent parts to sink their identity in the common cause proved enfeebling. Outside political events were moving too quickly. The ice jam, created by sixteen years of Union Nationale rule, was breaking up. In 1957 the federal Liberal Party had suffered defeat at the hands of John Diefenbaker. Maurice Duplessis could no longer tar the provincial

Liberals with the federal centralist brush. More particularly, Jean Lesage was freed from his Ottawa duties to assume the leadership of the Quebec Liberals. Then in September, 1959, Maurice Duplessis died while touring northern Quebec. At once the regime began to crumble though at first it was held together, and even showed signs of renewal, under Paul Sauvé. But within three months Sauvé suffered a fatal heart attack. When the party faced the electorate, divided and tired, under the leadership of Antonio Barrette in June, 1960, its great days were over. "The Union Nationale is a man without a party," Gérard Bergeron had written in 1958. "That is its strength and its weakness. The provincial Liberals constitute a party without a man. That is their weakness without being a strength."[17] In two short years, two elections and two deaths had changed all of that.

In 1960 the Liberals had united all the opposition forces. The PSD ran no one. Pierre Laporte, once an independent nationalist of the *Le Devoir* variety, had joined the Liberal camp, as had René Lévesque, who was both more left and more nationalist than traditional Liberals. Yet one group was notably absent, though no one commented on it at the time. These were the men of *Cité libre* and Le Rassemblement. Their political force had never been great. Their writings remained as proof of a major contribution to the coming of the Quiet Revolution. But after 1960 Trudeau and his friends seemed fated for the calm life of the university, the editorial chair, the trade union central, the law firm, or the civil service. Or so it appeared.

For Trudeau, at least, the years of the fifties were of fundamental importance. They were the years when he thought through and elaborated his political philosophy: the nature of authority, the strength of democracy, the value of federalism, the role of the state in economic life, the function of trade unions, the place of the Church, and the fundamental importance of individual liberty. But he learned also about the mechanics of politics. Le Rassemblement and the *union des forces démocratiques* failed in the short run. But the experience probably taught Trudeau that founding a new party was far more difficult than assuming control of an old one. It was a lesson he remembered when he once again set out on *Les Cheminements de la Politique*.

EIGHT

"Au Diable avec le Goupillon et la Tuque": The Quiet Revolution and the New Nationalism

"Borduas was the first to break radically. . . . He risked everything. Modern French Canada begins with him. He taught us the lesson which had been lacking. He let loose the liberty on us. "

Pierre Vadeboncoeur, *La Ligne du Risque* (1963)

I

"LA RÉVOLUTION SILENCIEUSE," the Quiet Revolution, is a phrase that conjures up nothing so much as contradiction. Can a revolution occur silently? Did Quebec experience a revolution in the 1960s? Was Quebec quiet in the 1960s? Only the last question can be answered unambiguously – and negatively. Quebec was a tumultuous and noisy place in the 1960s. Much of the noise was the sound of steam escaping an overheated society: nationalists, students, workers, peace activists, even ecologists. Much the same as elsewhere in the industrialized world. But some of the noise in Quebec was the sound of builders renovating, if not wholly reconstructing, a society. The rhetoric of these renovators was, in many ways, familiar. It was nationalism, a central doctrine of Quebec intellectual and emotional life since the early nineteenth century. But it was not merely the same old nationalism, though it had identifiable roots in the past. Indeed, it was perhaps even more radically new than its exponents realized.

What made the nationalism of the 1960s new and different, even radically different, were the socio-economic changes that had overtaken Quebec and Quebecers since about 1940. A profound change in both the social order and the value system of Quebec was well begun by the early 1950s, moved into a turbulent phase in the 1960s, and gradually settled into the accepted consensus. Out of these changes came a new self-image formulated in a nationalism that, while related to the past, was the expression of a new set of social values, a new public philosophy.

The transformation that Quebec experienced after 1940 can be reduced to the shorthand abstractions, urban and industrial growth. What they meant in human terms can best be seen in Gabrielle Roy's classic *Bonheur d'Occasion* (1945), the tale of Maria Chapdelaine in the city. From the 1880s, when 73 per cent of French-speaking Quebecers lived in the countryside, until 1951, when 67 per cent resided in an urban setting, an inexorable transformation had been taking place. But after 1940 the process accelerated to a rate exceeded only by British Columbia and Alberta, and Quebec rapidly became the most urbanized province in Canada. By 1951, 34 per cent of all Quebecers lived in Montreal. The 1971 census classified the 4,759,000 French-speaking Quebecers as follows: rural farm: 6 per cent; rural non-farm: 16 per cent; urban: 78 per cent. [1]

Despite the continuous character of this socio-economic transformation, neither public authorities nor most of those who defined the society's values willingly accepted the new reality. Or, even if they did, only minimum steps were taken to adjust public policies to new needs – perhaps because some thought the new reality only temporary, or capable of being reversed. In 1927, when more than 60 per cent of Quebecers were already urbanites, Henri Bourassa, still an important nationalist leader and politician, could express the hope that changes in Canadian tariff policy would "put a brake on the orgy of industrialism which disturbs the country and re-establish the preponderance of the rural life, the only guarantee of the health and the *sanity* of peoples."[2]

But in the post-war years the new reality could no longer be ignored, though there was much disagreement about the kind of response required. The nature of the problem was dramatically highlighted in a strike by some 5,000 miners in the asbestos industry lasting for three months in the spring of 1949. There, Quebec workers found themselves arrayed against an American corporation, a provincial government that called itself nationalist, and most of the important voices in a Church that had always claimed to be the front-line defender of French-Canadian interests. The support of Monsignor Charbonneau, Bishop of Montreal, the nationalist daily *Le Devoir*, and a small but important group of younger intellectuals was not enough. The workers lost the battle, though the war was to last much longer, and the outcome was far more complicated. Monsignor Charbonneau's reward was exile in Victoria, British Columbia.[3]

If the Asbestos strike marked the rite of passage of a union movement growing up, it was also a revelation that the old values defended by traditional politicians, traditional churchmen, and traditional nationalists were, at best, ill-suited to the needs of an industrial society and, at worst, merely justification for a reactionary and repressive elite in both state and church. A new society was emerging, one whose size and shape ensured that the old institutions and ideologies could neither define nor confine it.

Even before the workers, the middle class, or for that matter the social scientists, social critics, or politicians realized fully what was transpiring, there was at least one visionary who did. His name was Paul-Emile Borduas, Quebec's most imaginative and radical artist. Because he was a visionary and an artist he was easily dismissed. So he departed first for New York and finally to Paris, never to return to his beloved Sainte Hilaire. But Borduas's life and work epitomize better than any other example what was happening to Quebec: he was the avant-garde, not just as an artist. Borduas, his biographer tells us, was a young French-Canadian painter who, during his youth in the 1920s, deviated in no way from orthodoxy. He wanted to follow a career as a church decorator. His talents were recognized by Monsignor Olivier Maurault, who sent him to study at les Ateliers d'Art sacrés in Paris in 1928. When the economic crisis struck he was forced to give up his studies and return home, where he hoped that his friend, the church artist Ozias Leduc, would help him find work. But the churches, like the economy, were in financial trouble and could not afford new religious art. Eventually Borduas found employment as a teacher in a state-supported art school. Thus, unconsciously, he took the first step along the road to secularism, to a view of the world that led to the creation of his magnificent *automatiste* paintings from which all conventional religious significance disappeared.[4] It led also, in 1948, to his famous manifesto, *Réfus globale*. That revolutionary document, signed by Borduas and fifteen young associates, attacked the values of Quebec society uncompromisingly. Beginning with a capsule history of this *petit peuple* – the rural settlements, the Conquest, the Church, the story of *la survivance*, the fear of modern ideas, of *les poétes maudits* – the manifesto rose to a crescendo first as a challenge – "the frontiers of our dreams are no longer what they were," then denunciation –

"to hell with the holy-water-sprinkler and the tuque," and finally aspiration – "we will follow our primitive need for liberation."[5] *Le goupillon et la tuque* – the holy-water-sprinkler and the tuque, the symbols of traditional culture, the centrepieces of traditional nationalist ideology, these had to be unmasked and rejected. Quebec had to become a modern society like the others – the United States, France, English Canada – just as Borduas and his followers would shift their talents away from crucifixes, stations of the cross, rural landscapes, and habitant families, toward modern, abstract, international art.

To concentrate on one individual, however talented, and to insist that his career symbolizes the transformation of a whole society may seem perverse. But the symbolism is there, one that provides an invaluable insight into what has happened in Quebec and the new self-image, the new nationalism that developed during the years of the Quiet Revolution. Let me explain what I mean.

II

Traditional French-Canadian nationalism was the dominant ideology of Quebec's leading classes from the second quarter of the nineteenth century until the 1950s. Though its exponents varied somewhat in their outlook, and there were significant challenges to its dominance at least from the 1930s onwards, certain fundamental ideas had a remarkable capacity to endure. Together these ideas and values described an idealized nation, one that had existed in the past, was often threatened in the present, but which, given inspired leadership and correct doctrine, would again materialize in the future. This nation was French in culture (though that meant the culture of pre-revolutionary France, the France *"qui prie,"* not the one *"qui blasphéme"*), Catholic in religion, and agricultural in socioeconomic organization. The Church, the parish, and the family were its essential institutions. The state, the very idea of which implied secularism, played only a marginal role in this conception of the nation, for the society's civilizing mission was much more intimately related to the religious state: the Church.[6] Here was *l'église-nation*, advocated, praised, blessed, and only rarely and softly cursed – in the speeches and writings of nationalist clergy, politicians, journalists, novelists, poets, and educators. It can be found fully and systematically formulated in Monsignor L.-F. Laflèche's *Quelques considérations sur les rapports de la société civile avec la réligion et la famille* (1866), most fantastically in Jules-Paul Tardivel's *Pour la Patrie* (1895), oratorically in Monsignor L.-A. Pâquet's frequently reprinted "Sermon sur la Vocation de la Race française en Amérique" (1902), and in the voluminous historical and polemical writings of abbé Lionel Groulx, of which *L'Appel de la Race* (1922) and the essays collected in *Dix Ans d'action française* (1926) serve as the best examples. Even those organs of opinion like the mass circulation daily, *La Presse*, which favoured the industrial development of Quebec, can be found expressing similar stereotypes. On the occasion of the sixtieth anniversary of Confederation in 1927, *La Presse* pointed to Place d'Armes in Montreal as exemplifying Canadian virtues. On one side stood the Church of Notre Dame facing the Bank of Montreal with a statue of de Maisonneuve, the city's founder, in the centre. "It is the image of the Fatherland, with all that signifies. On the one hand, the contribution of the first Canadians, of those who were the first and who have guarded their faith, their virtues and everything which explains their survival and can contribute to the greatness of the nation. On the other hand, the material contribution of our English-speaking compatriots with their eminent practical qualities."[7] Here was a convenient ethnic division of labour that gave spirituality and virtue to the French Canadians, leaving to the English materialism, practicality, and, of course, control of the economy.

This traditional nationalism forged in the crucible of the Catholic religion focused not on politics and economics, but on culture and religion. Usually it was most clearly articulated when cultural and religious rights were threatened: when French-language, Roman Catholic schools were abolished by the provinces of Manitoba or Ontario and when the English-speaking majority attempted to drag French Canadians into the defence of the British Empire.[8] Only occasionally, and ineffectually, did these nationalists concern themselves with the problems created by burgeoning industrialism, which produced the conditions Lord Durham had predicted in the 1840s: the French Canadians were becoming a proletariat in an Anglo-Saxon capitalist world.[9]

This traditional nationalism was expressed lucidly, if somewhat nervously, in the *Rapport de la Commission royale d'enquête sur les problèmes constitutionels*, or Tremblay Commission, which reported to the Quebec government in 1956. It is the philosophical rather than the constitutional portions of the Report that are relevant here. The definition it gave to French-Canadian culture was traditional

– "Christian inspiration and French genius," as was its insistence on the fundamental differences between the French and English "confronting cultures." So, too, its account of the perilous historical conditions through which French Canadians had lived drew on the standard nationalist history as expounded from F.-X. Garneau to abbé Groulx. French and English, the Report observed, "since 1760, live in competition in Canada; with one desiring despite military defeat and political subjection, to preserve its particularism and, with that end in view, seeking to take back into its own hands, and as extensively as possible, the conduct of its own life; the other, resolved to install its institutions and to organize the country according to its ideas and its interests and to have its culture everywhere predominate."[10]

But the Tremblay Report was more than just a systematic statement of conventional wisdom. It recognized that something new had been added to the old French-English equation: industrialism. "If the Conquest put the French Canadians out of tune with the political institutions," the Commission concluded, "the industrial revolution put them out of harmony with the social institutions." Here was a threat of the most demanding character. Now the Commission harked back to earlier nationalists who had warned against urban-industrial society and sang the praises of agriculture. Industrial capitalism, the commissioners warned, "is in complete disaccord with the Catholic French Canadian culture": materialist rather than spiritual, scientific and technical rather than humanist, individualistic rather than communal. Here was the basic challenge: "We have to choose between the Christian concept and materialism, either in its pragmatic or philosophic form" – by which the commissioners meant that both North American capitalism and Marxian communism were antithetical to Christianity.[11]

Having identified the threat of secularism, though the Commission preferred the term "materialism," it could only urge a renewed defence of Quebec's autonomy as a province that, because of its Francophone and Catholic majority, had to be recognized as a province "*pas comme les autres.*" But it only hinted at new strategies that might be required to defend the values that made French Canada a distinct "nation." "The whole institutional system which, up to now has been the broadest and most sympathetic expression of French Canada's special culture, must be completely remade along new lines."[12] The authors of that prophetic sentence little realized how extensive the remaking would prove to be. Nor could they have foreseen how the remaking of institutions would hasten the acceptance of the secular values that were so inimical to the traditional conception of the nation.

III

During the 1950s Premier Maurice Duplessis's conservative, even reactionary, Union Nationale government managed to dominate Quebec political life through a combination of nationalist rhetoric, a corrupt political machine, a gerrymandered electoral map, and good economic times. But in these same years a vigorous debate about Quebec's past and future developed. In this debate the validity of traditional nationalism was questioned from at least four fairly distinct perspectives. First there were the members of Père Georges-Henri Lévesque's recently founded school of social sciences at Laval University who, having adopted an empirical approach to social analysis, questioned the *a priori* character of social thought in Quebec. These sociologists, economists, and industrial relations experts urged a more inductive, social science approach to the province's social problems. Whether they were professors like Maurice Lamontagne and Maurice Tremblay, or trade union activists like Jean Marchand, they agreed that social thought and social action had to begin by accepting Quebec's urban-industrial condition. Nationalism, at least as traditionally preached, was condemned as an obstacle to a clear perception of Quebec realities.[13]

That view was taken a long step further by the young social scientists, lawyers, journalists, and trade unionists who founded the magazine *citélibre* in 1950. Led by Pierre E. Trudeau and Gérard Pelletier, both of whom had supported the workers at Asbestos, they developed a forceful and well-documented polemic against traditional nationalists and nationalism generally, arguing for what they called a "functional" analysis of social problems and social reform. Like the Laval social scientists, the *citélibristes* argued that nationalism – all nationalism – was unacceptable for it was merely the rhetoric of vested interests who opposed social change. Nationalists identified imaginary enemies outside the fortress walls, when the real enemies were within. Home rule was less important than who ruled at home. Nationalist thought, in Trudeau's words, "can only be a timid and reactionary thought." In this critique of traditional ideology, Trudeau and his friends were often sharply anti-clerical, though never anti-Catholic. But their anti-clericalism, or liberalism, and their concern for a more equitably ordered, industrial society led them to insist that the state had to accept a positive role in social and industrial development, for "some state planning has become an absolute necessity . . . ."[14]

The re-evaluation of the role that the state should play in Quebec was one of the main themes in Quebec social thought in the 1950s. For most, though by no means all,[15] that meant the provincial state. *Le Devoir*, the most important nationalist newspaper, began to advocate a more positive role for the state after Gérard Filion and André Laurendeau took charge of the newspaper in the 1950s. These two modern nationalists began to transform the old message preached by Henri Bourassa and his disciples into a new social doctrine that accepted industrial society without any hint of nostalgia for the old agrarianism. *Le Devoir* expounded liberal Catholic social views and argued that the state had responsibility both for social justice and as the defender of French-Canadian society. In 1959 Filion wrote that "French Canadians will remain drawers of water and hewers of wood, small storekeepers and small investors, with a few millionaires here and there, as long as they will not make the only government they have under their control serve in the elaboration and realization of a large-scale economic policy."[16]

More nationalist, focusing almost exclusively on Quebec as the one place where French Canadians had a chance, more controversial than *Le Devoir*, were the views of a new school of historians who came into prominence at the Université de Montréal in the 1950s. The most visible and audible of these young scholar-polemicists was Professor Michel Brunet, son of a small businessman whose post-graduate training had been in the United States, where he was attracted to the economic interpretation of history. In a series of speeches and essays, in which he developed a thesis originated by his colleague, Professor Maurice Seguin, Brunet argued that traditional Quebec nationalism was nothing more than a rationalization of French-Canadian economic inferiority and a justification for clerical power. It was not the Church that had ensured French-Canadian survival but rather a high birth rate and isolation in the seigneurial system, away from the Conqueror. The society was nevertheless feeble because its entrepreneurial middle class had been decapitated by the Conquest, leaving the economy in the hands of the British. Whatever the validity of the Seguin-Brunet thesis as history, its contemporary implications were clear. The old clerical nationalism with its emphasis on agriculture, its illusions about French Canada's civilizing mission, and its fear of the state had to be banished. In its place Quebecers should concentrate on building a new entrepreneurial class, make use of the state to defend Francophone interests, and forget about the minorities living outside the province. For Brunet there were Canadians and *canadiens*; the latter group, the minority, being under constant threat of assimilation, had only one, fleeting hope, and that lay in building a strong provincial state into a national state. [17]

Like *Le Devoir*, and utterly unlike *Cité libre*, the Montreal historians were nationalist. But they, like all the other groups considered here, shared the conviction that the old, religion-centred, rural, anti-statist nationalism had outlived its usefulness, if it had ever had any. In its place Quebec needed a new value system, a public philosophy that welcomed the industrial order, assimilated the new social sciences as a replacement for moral exhortation, and willingly used the state for economic and social development, including educational reform. Implicitly or explicitly, each of these groups – and others – were advocating a secular social philosophy, nationalist or non-nationalist. [18] Some attacked the Church for its historic role; others merely concluded that its role in the new society would have to be a diminished one. The Church recognized the threat of these developments. In 1953 the Church hierarchy noted that "a wind of bad-quality liberation seems at present to blow on certain groups. According to these people, it is necessary to free the people from the hold of the Church. . . . It is, in a new form, pure and simple Protestantism." [19]

The fact is, as Jean Hamelin's recent history of the Church in Quebec demonstrates brilliantly, the Church was already in retreat in the 1950s, though it engaged in a strenuous rearguard action. New recruits declined in number and, of those who entered, fewer stayed the course. The deconfessionalization of some institutions, most notably the Catholic trade unions, was under way. Church attendance declined notably, and by the sixties a declining birth rate demonstrated the ineffectiveness of the Church's teaching about birth control. In 1956 a Church commission concluded that "our people no longer have a Christian life, they have not even the natural virtues. . . . Our Christians ignore their religion and the Bible." The urban-industrial order was having exactly the impact on the Catholic population of Quebec that the clerical nationalists had long prophesied. By 1970 a Church-appointed inquiry described the Church as *"en crise"* and documented the claim with statistics such as these: where 2,000 young Quebecers had taken up religious vocations in 1946, only about 100 followed that path in 1970.[20]

The mighty army of the Church, once more numerous in proportion to population than in any country outside of Latin America, had fallen into irreversible decline. It could no longer defend the ramparts against an advancing secularism promoted by a new elite connected with the universities, the mass media, and such social organizations as the trade unions. These were the people who, in Quebec as elsewhere, led the "ethnic revival" that touched many parts of the world by the 1970s. These "secular intellectuals," as Anthony Smith calls them, espoused an "enlightened" rationalism of the sort found in Pierre Trudeau's writings advocating a secular, pluralistic, democratic society in place of the *ancien régime*. In Quebec the growing acceptance of these new ideas, and the socio-economic changes they reflected, opened the way for the collapse of Maurice Duplessis's Union Nationale government and the election of Jean Lesage's Liberals with their promise of reform and modernization. That new regime, the product of the socio-economic and intellectual evolution that had preceded it, gradually brought Quebec's public institutions more fully into conformity with social and intellectual reality. In short, it built a Quebec welfare state accompanied by a new nationalist ideology that defined the society's changed self-image.[21]

IV

Though the Lesage Liberals were elected on a platform that promised both to defend Quebec's autonomy in the Canadian federal system and to make fuller use of provincial powers than Duplessis had done, the party was not explicitly nationalist. Lesage himself had begun his political career in Ottawa and returned to Quebec only after the federal Liberals lost power in 1957. Moreover, the Duplessis regime had given nationalism such a bad name that many of its opponents – except perhaps *Le Devoir* – identified nationalism with reaction. What the Liberals were committed to – reforming education, the public service, the labour laws, and, more generally, the promotion of economic development – had, at least superficially, little to do with nationalism. In the process of implementing these policies, the politicians and their allies among the new elites

found that nationalism was a useful weapon in the battle to overcome some of the obstacles that stood in the path of change. Yet it
was not the old nationalist rhetoric of Duplessis but rather a new
ideology that focused on, and legitimized, state action. Three
examples, among many, will illustrate this argument: educational
reform, the expansion of state control over hydroelectricity, and the
establishment of the Quebec Pension Plan. [22]

The new ideology and its goals are very clearly revealed in the
Report of the royal commission the Lesage government appointed
to examine the province's educational system. Despite its chair-
manship – Monsignor Alphonse-Marie Parent – the thrust of the
Report was unambiguously secular. This is to say that the commissioners argued that the function of education in a democratic,
industrial society was to equip citizens with the knowledge and
skills necessary to achieve worldly success: "to afford everyone the
opportunity to learn; to make available to each the type of education best suited to his aptitudes and interests; to prepare the individual for life in society." While the commissioners were aware of it,
in failing to include among the goals the orthodox Catholic claim
that education and religion cannot be separated, they simply
skirted the issue. Moreover, and this was the main point of the
Report's first volume, they contended that while education had
once been the preserve of private organizations and churches, "now
the state has become the principal agent for organizing, co-ordinat-
ing and financing all education." Though the nationalist note was
very muted, the Report did remark that an effective educational
system was "a condition of progress and survival of any country." [23]

From these propositions flowed logically the Commission's first,
and perhaps most important, recommendation: the appointment
of a Minister of Education. Since the last Minister of Education had
been abolished in 1875 the absence of a political head of the educational system had always been viewed as a recognition of the
Church's primacy in the field. As the leaders of the Church perceived instantly, the state was now being called upon to terminate
that primacy. The struggle over Bill 60, which the government
introduced in 1963 to implement the Parent Commission's first
recommendation, was, on the whole, a decorous one conducted for
the most part behind closed doors. The Church asserted its traditional position but rather than challenging the principle of the new
proposal merely demanded, and obtained, a guarantee that confes-
sional schools would still be allowed under the proposed scheme. A

new "concordat" was established between church and state, in Professor Léon Dion's view, but it was one under which the state's supremacy in education was recognized as a fact. The secular goals of education would soon be dominant. By 1980 even the Catholic school committee admitted that schools operated "according to a pedagogical and administrative rationality that is clearly not to be found in the gospel."[24]

At least two conclusions can be drawn from the education reforms implemented during the 1960s. The first is that, since control of education has always been regarded as fundamental to the defence of Quebec's distinctive culture, after 1963 the state, and not the Church, obviously had assumed that onerous responsibility. As the aims of education would now be defined more in relation to the needs of the state than the needs of the Church so, too, the definition of the nature of Quebec's distinctiveness would be altered inevitably. The educational system, and this is the second conclusion, as defined by successive volumes of the Parent Report, was to be centred, bureaucratized, and, essentially, secular, one designed to prepare young Quebecers for life in the urban-industrial world. As such it would differ only in detail – and language – from the educational systems of New York, California, Ontario, or British Columbia. Insofar as the educational reforms reflected the spirit of the Quiet Revolution and the new nationalism that accompanied it, one of its paradoxical consequences was the replacement of a distinctive educational system by one that was essentially North American in spirit and function.

In the debate over educational reform the nationalist argument was more implicit than explicit. In the almost concurrent debate over a proposal to bring the remaining privately owned power companies under the publicly owned Hydro-Québec system established in 1944, the nationalist theme was utterly explicit. While the economic and administrative advantages of a unified hydroelectric system and the costs and benefits of the heavy expenditures required to complete the takeover were debated, the decisive political issue was expressed in the campaign slogan: *Maîtres chez nous.* René Lévesque, Minister of Natural Resources and chief architect of the nationalization plan, put the case in this manner: "The state must not be absent from the economic scene, for in our particular case that would be equivalent to pure and simple abandonment of the most effective instrument of economic liberation that we possess." And he continued explaining that while it was not desirable for the state to control the whole economy, it was necessary to "ally the dynamism of private enterprise with the advantages of concerted action by the whole nation." Here, then, the conflict was presented as one between the Quebec state, representing "*la nation entière*," and the Anglo-Canadians who were majority owners of the private power companies. Nothing more graphically reveals the outcome of that struggle than a photograph in Clarence Hogue's celebratory study of Hydro-Québec depicting the strained faces of Shawinigan Water and Power Company employees "attending a French lesson in 1964." Hydro was now completely in the hands of what one of its propagandists called "the national state of French Canada," where the operational language was, quite naturally, French. [25]

Whether the costs and benefits of hydro nationalization were shared equitably by the members of "*la nation entière*" is a controversial question. [26] What is obvious, however, is that the new nationalism used to legitimize the hydro policy emphasized the issue of French-Canadian economic inferiority as the source of cultural weakness. Both hydro nationalization and educational reform were based on that assumption and were designed, in part, to correct it. Moreover, the new nationalism accepted without hesitation the urban-industrial society. Hydro-Québec, and especially the new developments carried out by Francophone engineers, technicians, and workers at places like Manicouagan, came to symbolize the new industrial man who stood at the heart of the new Quebec. The chansonnier Gilles Vigneault turned a prosaic industrial achievement – and ecological calamity[27] – into a popular, nationalist folksong. Where once politicians dreamed that perhaps a school or a bridge would carry their names into posterity, after the 1960s only a power dam sufficed!

The third, and most important, observation is that in this new nationalist ideology the state was again the leading actor. If Church and Nation had once been natural partners, the campaigns for educational reform and hydro nationalization had forged a new partnership of State and Nation, revealed in the growing usage of the phrase "*L'État du Québec*." And state policy in hydro, as in education, meant the centralization and standardization of a system that had once been decentralized and somewhat chaotic. Quebec would now have a hydro system very like that which existed in other Canadian provinces and American states. It would have it because it was necessary, or at least desirable, for the promotion of an industrial economy of the sort found in New York and Ontario.

If the Lesage government's policies in education and hydroelectricity can be seen as an extension of state power where once the Church reigned and over the economy into areas traditionally dominated by Anglo-Canadians, the conflict over pensions brings the struggle to the inter-state level. Since the 1940s the federal government had been developing policies in the social security field that sometimes infringed on provincial jurisdiction or, at least, touched on disputed areas of jurisdiction. The Duplessis government had regularly protested these policies both on grounds of jurisdiction and because the Church in Quebec, viewing social security as a form of charity, opposed state intervention in this area.[28] The Lesage government intended not only to defend provincial jurisdiction but also to devise social security measures that would be run by the state. Consequently, in 1963, when the federal government announced its intention to establish a universal, portable, contributory pension scheme, the Quebec government objected that it intended to implement its own plan. One reason for the Quebec government's decision, in addition to the jurisdictional question, was the scheme devised by a group of talented, nationalistic technocrats to use pension-plan funds for public investments that would assist Francophone participation in the economy. *Maîtres chez nous* had many dimensions.

The struggle between Quebec and Ottawa was dramatic and very public, and both politicians and the media presented it as involving stakes high enough to destroy Confederation. And it is at least arguable that during this conflict Quebec was as close to moving toward independence as it has been at any subsequent time. In the end the crisis was surmounted. Quebec had a demonstrably superior plan, and a government that was far more determined and clear-minded than Ottawa. Quebec won the battle and thus gained control over its plan and its vast financial resources together with an alteration in federal-provincial tax-sharing agreements that significantly increased Quebec's tax room and revenues. Lesage had insisted that since Quebec was the homeland of the majority of French Canadians it needed a pension plan tailored to its needs. He had used the nationalist argument effectively, flexed the muscles of the Quebec state, and won an impressive, if not total, victory.[29]

From this abbreviated account of a complex issue, a few conclusions may be drawn. First, what might have been a slightly sordid haggle over the division of public funds was converted into a nationalist cause. It was the national homeland of Francophones against Ottawa, where Francophones, always a minority, were hardly visible between 1957 and 1965. Second, the Lesage Liberals had taken a traditional Quebec position and transformed it into a modern cause: it was not the right of the Church in the social field that was being defended, but rather the determination of the Quebec state to move into an area once claimed by the Church and the federal government. Finally, again as in the examples of education and electricity, the new welfare state, of which the pension plan was only one piece, would provide centralized, rationalized, and standardized services to replace the patchwork of haphazardly organized, often patronage-ridden institutions. In this the Quebec government was taking a course already marked out in other industrial societies, though, as the Caisse de Dépôt et Placement illustrated, Quebecers were willing to make important innovations.

v

The essence of the new nationalism was invoked to justify the developments that have come to be known as the Quiet Revolution. Where traditionally the Quebecer's self-image, his nationalism, focused on language, religion, and the land, the new ideology was articulated by a society for which rural life was only a memory, often a bad one. For members of an urban-industrial society, the concern was with new questions that traditional religious and social teachings seemed incapable of answering. And if traditional socio-religious answers were inadequate, then the Church as an institution was less and less relevant. As new ideas, founded on economics and sociology more than theology and moral philosophy, were explored, so, too, a new institution had to be found or created to implement these ideas. That institution already existed: the provincial state provided by Canadian federalism. An *église-nation* became an *état-nation* with the only question being the degree of autonomy that the new *état* might want.

The principal remaining similarity between the old and the new nationalism was language. Yet on closer examination even that similarity is limited. Like the old nationalists, the new were determined to defend the French language as a sheet anchor of Quebec's distinctiveness. But traditional nationalists invariably identified language with religion: *la langue gardienne de la foi, la foi guardienne de la langue.*[30] Language questions often meant purity of language, language as a vehicle of a literary culture, and perhaps above all, language as a medium of education for French and Catholic students everywhere in Canada. Language was protected and preserved by the Church and the educational system and, of course, the two were actually one.

For the new nationalists language came to have a different or at least an additional significance. Indeed, language became even more important than in the past for the simple reason that, as Quebec became more like the rest of North America socio-economically, language became its principal distinguishing characteristic. Thus, during the Quiet Revolution language became a growing preoccupation and a source of increasing tensions as the cry for French unilingualism developed.[31] But the issue was almost totally divorced from religious concerns. Nor was it predominantly a literary or narrowly cultural one. Instead it was socio-economic. Quebecers had come to the conclusion that it was the language of the economy, not the language of the Church, that determined both individual and collective destinies – at least in this world. An economy where corporate managers operated in English was an economy where French Canadians rarely became corporate managers. How could this be changed? The response to this, as to so many other questions, was state intervention. It began, haltingly, with the Lesage government's establishment of a Department of Cultural Affairs. It continued wherever the state moved into the economy and French was made the operational language. It reached its culmination in the work of the Gendron Commission on the situation of the French language in Quebec[32] and in legislation by the Bourassa and Lévesque governments designed to make French the dominant or exclusive language in all sectors of Quebec life. What lay behind these acts, and the surrounding controversy, was expressed very forthrightly in the White Paper on language policy that preceded Bill 101 in 1977. It stated:

> The Quebec that we wish to build will be essentially French. The fact that the majority of the population is French will be distinctly visible: at work, in communications, in the country. *It is also a country where the traditional division of powers, especially in matters concerning the economy, will be modified*: the use of French will not be generalized

simply to hide the predominance of foreign powers over Franco-phones; this usage will accompany, will symbolize a reconquest by the Francophone majority of Quebec of the hold which returns to it on the levers of the economy.[33]

Once again, then, the principal characteristics of the new nationalism are crystal clear. In language policy as elsewhere, the state replaced the Church; the values served are secular rather than sacred; the outcome is centralization and homogenization. Though the appeal to traditional values is evident, the thrust is toward the present and future, even at the expense of past distinctiveness.[34]

VI

The rapidity of change in Quebec in the 1960s, and the vigour with which Quebecers asserted their desire for new social and constitutional arrangements, was often startling, especially to English-speaking Canadians and to outsiders. Yet what was happening in that society was far from unique. There has been an "ethnic revival" in almost every part of the world during the last quarter-century. Punjabis, Ibos, Catalans, Basques, Serbs, Croats, Walloons, Occitanians, Bretons, perhaps even Bavarians have, with varying degrees of assertiveness, joined with Québécois in their determination to retain their distinctiveness in an homogenizing world. A variety of hypotheses have been advanced in an attempt to understand this phenomenon. The British social philosopher Ernest Gellner has contended that nationalism is the product of an industrializing society, the glue that holds the society together when old loyalties and obligations based on regions, families, and religion are eroded by socio-economic change. Nationalism imposes a common literacy, what he calls a "high culture," on a society in order to unify it and fit its citizens for the needs of industrial activities. "It means the generalized diffusion of a school mediated, academy supervised idiom, codified for the requirements of reasonably precise bureaucratic and technological communication." While nationalist rhetoric is advanced as an appeal to preserve a society's uniqueness, it is in reality a justification for profound change. "It preaches and defends continuity, but owes everything to a decisive and utterly profound break in human history."[35]

There is much to be said for this hypothesis when applied to Quebec. As I have argued, the new nationalism of the Quiet

Revolution, while appealing to certain historic hopes and fears, was in fact the ideological component of a qualitatively different society. [36] So, too, this nationalism legitimated policies whose thrust was toward a more homogeneous, bureaucratized, and centralized society, drawn together by a new educational system, a more centralized economy, and a common welfare and social security system. [37] Thus, Gellner's contention that nationalism propels the transition from a "culture-religion" to a "culture-state" is appealing.

In Quebec in the 1960s there were certainly those who suspected that their nation was being destroyed consciously by the very people who claimed to be saving it. In 1964 abbé Groulx published what he thought would be his last book. Entitled *Chemin de l'Avenir,* this was a long lament for a nation suffering "the social sickness of a disruptive industrialism." [38] He pointed to youthful unbelief and moral laxity, a creeping secularism nourished by American materialism, and the anti-clericalism of *Cité libre* and Radio-Canada. For him the Quiet Revolution was a "denial of history, of traditions, a turning of the back on the past; an attack more than cunning against all of the elements that constitute the French-Canadian man, even of the foundations which had until now formed the basis of his life." [39] No wonder he was astonished to receive a letter of congratulations from Premier Lesage, who, evidently not being a very careful reader, was following a quite contrary road to the future.

Yet Lesage's instinct may not have been entirely misguided for he, or his advisers, recognized that not everything about the Quiet Revolution was new. It had connections with the past. Gellner's exclusive emphasis on the relationship between industrialization and nationalism fails to account for nationalism's earlier history in Quebec and elsewhere. Anthony Smith offers a more balanced perspective, one that can fit abbé Groulx and Premier Lesage on the same continuum. The ethnic revival, he writes, is "at one and the same time an attempt to preserve the past, and to transform it into something new, to create a new type upon ancient foundations, to create a new man and society through the revival of old identities and the preservation of the 'links in the chain' of generations." [40] Nationalism, then, is more than outward symbols; it is also the articulated will of a community to preserve its distinctiveness. That will has a long history in Quebec; it has been persistent and moderate. It has never completely disappeared, though it has changed with the changing needs of society, and especially the changing aspirations of Quebec's leading classes. "Imagined by successive petites bourgeoisies – the liberal professions, the clergy, the new middle class – the nation, as a concept, offers this ideological plasticity that allows it to be associated with the most varied projects," André-J. Bélanger has written. "The nation, like liberty, that of Mme. Roland and others . . . what interests can be served in its name!"[41]

During the Quiet Revolution, then, a new nationalism evolved that, like the old, expressed the aspirations of Quebec's leading classes. A transformed society required a new self-image: modern, urban, industrial, and secular. Paul-Emile Borduas's angry challenge had been met: the holy-water-sprinklers and the tuques, those relics of traditional Quebec, almost vanished, replaced by micro-computers and hard hats. Borduas might have judged the change a mixed blessing.

"I never thought I could be as proud . . .": The Trudeau-Lévesque Debate

"It is not the idea of nation that is retrograde; it is the idea that the nation must necessarily be sovereign. "
Pierre Elliott Trudeau, "New Treason of the Intellectuals," *Federalism and the French Canadians* (Toronto, 1968)

"What does this French Quebec want? Sometime during the next few years, the question will be answered. And there are growing possibilities that the answer could very well be – independence. "
René Lévesque, "For an Independent Quebec," *Foreign Affairs* (October, 1976)

". . . only two positions seem logical to me: that of Mr. Trudeau, who won the referendum of 1980, and that which preaches the independence of Quebec. The rest look like a kind of constitutional embroidery. "
Marcel Rioux, *Une Saison à la Renardière* (Montreal, 1988) [translation]

MANY CANADIANS, AND doubtless foreigners, too, found the Canadian constitutional debate of the 1970s something of a puzzle. Quite apart from the confusion created by arcane constitutional details best left to lawyers and other addicts, there was the dominant role played by two Francophone Quebecers: Pierre Elliott Trudeau and René Lévesque. If this was a Canadian drama, surely central casting had been mischievous in failing to assign one starring role to an English-Canadian thespian. And the theatre analogy could be carried further: the particularly obtuse Premier of Newfoundland, Brian Peckford, once described the debate as "The

René and Pierre Show." That suggested it was just a soap opera in which two middle-aged matinée idols made increasingly melodramatic gestures in a personal competition for the hearts of their sentimental viewers. Sunset Boulevard North. Or, if another simplifying analogy were needed, there was always sport. Now Lévesque and Trudeau could become aspiring champions lurching round after round from corners marked "Quebec" and "Canada," urged on by their seconds to deliver the final knockout blow. Muhammad Alis in the federal-provincial ring. In the age of television, personality simplifies, ideas confuse. Or so we are told.

But reducing the debates of the 1970s to mere personality clashes, however dramatic, banishes confusion at the risk of introducing obfuscation. Trudeau and Lévesque *were* powerful personalities and ambitious men. One had been a television star, the other an accomplished athlete. Each, doubtless, wanted to finish first in his chosen sport: politics. But each was also a politician with fixed conclusions on an issue that went to the very essence of the history and existence of the community in which they were both deeply rooted. Neither Trudeau nor Lévesque created an issue that divided them: it existed before they came on the scene and lives after them. It can be simply stated: "All we need to know is this: is it in the interests of French-speaking Canadians to be a majority in a pluralist Quebec state, or a minority in a pluralist Canadian state? That is what the whole debate is about." [1]

Those are Trudeau's words, but Lévesque could easily have uttered them. They agreed on the question; they disputed the answer. Yet both were champions of the community Trudeau called *francophones canadiens*, though Lévesque would have used the term "French Quebecers." The debate turned on that nuance. It measured the gap between the federalist and the nationalist and made it appropriate, though not necessary, that both gladiators should be Francophone Quebecers. But the nuance also created confusion for those who would have preferred a simpler dichotomy: French against English, Quebec against Canada. That Trudeau and Lévesque were both Francophone Quebecers made that simplification impossible. The confusion can be dispelled only by examining the ideas they expounded.

As Canada's centennial celebrations drew to a close in 1967, two Quebec politicians published books setting out proposed courses for the future of Canada, French Canada, and Quebec. *Le Fédéralisme et la Société canadienne-française* appeared just as Expo '67 was closing its doors on Ile Ste-Hélène in Montreal. Its author, Pierre Elliott Trudeau, was the federal Minister of Justice, a post that included responsibility for tending Canada's constitution. A politician of only two years' experience, he was just beginning to develop a public profile. Long known among Quebec intellectuals – and by a few in English Canada – as a brilliant lawyer, political writer, and one of the founders of the little magazine *Cité libre*, he seemed always out of step with the dominant views of his province's leaders, and, by 1967, increasingly so. In English Canada he was hardly known at all except as something of a non-conformist bachelor who had coined the aphorism that the state had no place in the bedrooms of the nation.

Trudeau's book, a series of essays and documented polemics, had been written over a period stretching from 1957 to 1964. The essays were devoted to analysing Canadian federalism and the place of French Canadians in that system. The focus was on Quebec. The earliest articles were critical of the centralizing tendencies of Ottawa and of those French Canadians – usually on the left – who supported that tendency. The later essays were sharp, even shrill, assaults on those French Quebecers who, by the early 1960s, had taken up various versions of the slogan, *Québec d'abord*. A book of this sort, with chapter headings like "De libro, tributo . . . et quibusdam aliis" and "Federalism, Nationalism and Reason," was hardly, at least in normal times, expected to hit the bestseller list. But in fact the book, and the English version that appeared early in 1968, was soon on that list (though not all buyers were readers), and Trudeau was launched on a trajectory that would make him Prime Minister of Canada for over a decade and a half.

The author of the second book, this one entitled *Option Québec*, whose sales in French and English were also brisk, was much better known both inside and outside Quebec. René Lévesque, former journalist and television *vedette*, had joined Jean Lesage's *équipe du tonnerre* in 1960 and played a leading part in launching the Quiet Revolution. As Minister of Natural Resources in the Lesage government, he had led a successful campaign in 1962 to bring the last eleven privately owned power companies into the publicly owned Hydro-Québec. Later, as Minister of Family and Social Affairs, he had continued the building of the Quebec *état-providence*. But he also acquired the reputation of being a loose cannon on the deck of the Quebec ship of state. And as that ship heaved through the sometimes heavy waves aroused by fundamental reforms in education, the economy, labour laws, the civil service, and social policy, Lévesque became increasingly, if unsystematically, critical of the federal system. He also became more openly nationalist in his outlook and discovered that nationalist rhetoric was effective in mobilizing popular support for government measures. In 1963 he defined "nation" as "a group of men of the same cultural family with a place on the map," and went on to say that "nationalism" had to be used to overcome the "economic sickness" of Quebec. "The question," he said, "is to use it as much as possible, because no one is ever sure of controlling it, no one can actually control this force."[2] Hydro nationalization, in Lévesque's hands, was not merely an economic measure; rather, it was a step toward French Quebecers becoming masters in their own house.[3]

While Lévesque's frequent jabs at Ottawa and at the "Rhodesians of Westmount" (the English-Canadian establishment in Quebec) made him something of a hero among French Canadians, especially with the student populations among whom nationalism had witnessed a new birth,[4] they also jarred English-Canadian complacency. In 1963 he bluntly told an English-Canadian television audience that "I am a Quebecer first, a French Canadian second . . . and I really have . . . well, no sense at all of being a Canadian."[5] His use of terms revealed a lot – being a "French Canadian" apparently meant being a French-speaking Quebecer, not a French-speaking Canadian. But those implications, and others, were only gradually becoming clear.

Lévesque's remarks – he rarely used prepared texts – were those of a man who, in contrast to the more academic approach of Pierre Trudeau, thought as he acted, or better, talked as he thought. As a radio and television journalist by trade, Lévesque was more at home with the spoken word than the written word. (At one of their early meetings Trudeau, waiting for Lévesque to finish a promised article for *Cité libre*, had snapped, "Say, Lévesque, you talk damn well, but I'm beginning to wonder if you can write at all." "Write . . . write . . .," Lévesque replied, "first I've got to have the time. . . ." And Trudeau shot back, "And something to say."[6]) Of course, Lévesque would prove to have lots to say, but he reacted more than he analysed. He was always a man of action, where Trudeau, at least until 1965, was an intellectual, one whose critics claimed was nothing but a dilettante in a Mercedes. Lévesque's book, *Option Québec*, was characteristic: it was not really a book at all, but rather a compilation of newspaper articles, government documents, snippets of speeches written and spoken by a variety of people. Lévesque's *imprimatur* was on it, since he had led the group of former Liberals and bureaucrats out of Lesage's Liberal Party in the fall of 1967. He made the founding of the Mouvement souveraineté-association possible. He would be the leader of the Parti Québécois when it was established in 1968.

During the 1950s Trudeau and Lévesque had become casual acquaintances. Lévesque's work and interests had concentrated on international affairs – his program *Point de Mire* had brought the world's events into hundreds of thousands of Quebec living rooms. Trudeau, whose wealth made permanent employment unnecessary and whose liberal views kept him out of regular academic life, concentrated his attention on Quebec, though foreign travel and international affairs also appealed to him. But Quebec politics and the trade union movement absorbed much of his time.

The events of the 1960s drew Lévesque and Trudeau into closer touch. Trudeau was part of a small group of intellectuals who met fairly regularly with Lévesque, now a minister, who used them as a sounding board for ideas he hoped to advance in cabinet. Obviously, the two men were fascinated by each other, but each had reservations. In his marvellous memoir, *Les Années d'impatience 1950-1960*, Gérard Pelletier provides a revealing glimpse of the two men. Trudeau, he writes, admired

> René's vitality, his lively intelligence, his aptly chosen words, his unexpected turns of thought, his imagination, the quirkiness of his learning, his extensive knowledge of history and astonishing memory for the smallest items of news – all this left Trudeau breathless. . . . I suspected him at the time of thinking privately that a journalist's background, combined with a star temperament, could only produce a tainted or at least dubious political philosophy.

As for Lévesque, he

> could not help having a deep respect for the other's intelligence. . . . Trudeau's political erudition clearly impressed him. . . . For Lévesque, Trudeau embodied the scholar type, whose profound, authoritative knowledge he envied, but also the ivory tower intellectual, insensitive to certain realities, whose facetious brand of humour irritated him exceedingly.[7]

These attitudes, doubtless hardened and occasionally touched with anger, remained constant after Trudeau entered federal politics in

1965 intending to defend the federal system (Lévesque, interestingly, had urged Jean Marchand not to go alone to Ottawa but to take his two "*copains*" with him)[8] – and after Lévesque moved to establish a political party whose goal was to destroy that system. At that point in 1968, Trudeau and Lévesque agreed on at least two fundamental propositions. The first was that Quebec's future had to be settled democratically. Each man believed profoundly in the sovereignty of the people. Second, they agreed that the time of choice, individual and collective, was fast arriving. What that meant was that each had concluded that the fuzzy, rhetorical debates about Quebec's place in Canada, which had consumed so much energy for the previous decade, were futile. The proposed panaceas – *une province pas comme les autres*, a particular status, a special status (today we call it "distinct society") – all missed the point. French Canadians would either be equal partners in a federal system that gave full guarantees to their rights throughout Canada or they would achieve equality through the establishment of a sovereign state. Special status, Trudeau and Lévesque agreed, was neither fish nor fowl.

By 1968 Trudeau's option had been worked out systematically and tested in numerous intellectual jousts. The essence of his position was contained in a paragraph that formed part of a bitingly sarcastic attack on the early proponents of separatism. In "La Nouvelle Trahison des clercs," published in 1962, he declared:

> The die is cast in Canada: there are two main ethnic and linguistic groups; each is too strongly and too deeply rooted in the past, too firmly bound to a mother culture, to be able to engulf the other. But if the two will collaborate at the hub of a truly pluralistic state, Canada will become the envied seat of a form of federalism that belongs to tomorrow's world. Better than the American melting pot, Canada could offer an example to all those new Asian and African states . . . who must discover how to govern their polyethnic populations with proper regard for justice and liberty. What better reason for cold-shouldering the lure of annexation to the United States?[9]

If Trudeau's option was intellectually elegant and idealistic, Lévesque's option carried a powerful emotional resonance. His book began, "*Nous sommes des Québécois*," and went on to explain:

> What that means first and foremost – if need be, all that it means – is that we are attached to this one corner of the earth where we can be

completely ourselves; this Quebec where we have the unmistakable feeling that here we can really be at home. . . .

At the core of this personality is the fact that we speak French. Everything else depends on this essential element and follows from it or leads infallibly back to it.[10]

Where Lévesque had once described himself as a *Quebecer* and a *French Canadian*, the second designation had now disappeared: he was a *Québécois*. Early in 1969 he told a reporter that "I've never had any feeling of being Canadian, but I've always had an incredibly strong sense of being North American. The place where I'm most at home outside Quebec is the United States."[11] Trudeau and Lévesque differed not only about Canada; they felt quite differently about the United States.

The origins of Lévesque's nationalism and his gradual transition into an *indépendantiste* are difficult to trace in detail. Nor do his published memoirs help much. But like many young French Canadians, he was introduced to nationalist sentiments at school, and living side-by-side with the English in New Carlisle may have made him a ready subject. At seventeen he wrote in the student newspaper at the Collège des Jésuites in Quebec City that "French Canada will be what French Canadians deserve,"[12] sentiments remarkably like those held by Pierre Trudeau. He learned some Canadian history, and like all Quebec nationalists came to see the Conquest of 1759 as both the source of Quebec's inferiority and the historical event that needed undoing. In later years he recalled his admiration for abbé Groulx's novel, *L'Appel de la race*, the story of the breakup of a mixed marriage that symbolized Confederation.[13] But action, not theory, always attracted Lévesque, and he drew his general conclusions from personal experience. As a journalist who had devoted most of his attention to international events, his mind was turned to Canadian affairs by a strike of French-language Radio-Canada producers in 1959. He joined that strike as a sympathizer and soon came to share the frustration of the producers at the failure of the federal government to step in and settle the dispute in the publicly owned network. Lévesque concluded that nothing of the kind would have been allowed to happen in the English network. "Of such signal advantages," he told the Montreal *Gazette*, "is the privilege of being French made up in this country. And even at the risk of being termed 'horrid nationalists,' we feel that at least once before the conflict is over, we have to make plain our deep appreciation of

such an enviable place in the great bilingual, bicultural and frater-
nal Canadian sun."[14] Here was an expression of that minority
sensitivity that would lead to the idea of independence.

Lévesque's years in the Lesage government made him increasingly impatient with what he believed to be the intransigence of the
English-speaking business elite in Quebec and the rigidity of the
Canadian federal system. In these years, when French-Canadian
representation at Ottawa under John Diefenbaker's Conservatives
and in the early Pearson years was ineffective, Lévesque became
convinced that Quebecers were ready to run their own affairs.
"Now that our new generations are bringing us more and more pro-
ficiency every year," he observed in 1967, "there is no reason which
can, which should prevent Quebec from realizing that thing that's
been kicking around in our collective back room for the last two
hundred years, which is to get our chance to make our own way as a
society."[15]

The term Lévesque preferred to use to describe the option he
chose by 1967 and that he would defend so ably and determinedly
until his departure from office in 1985, was not "nationalist" or
"separatist." Even *indépendantiste*, though he used it, was less preferred than *souverainiste*. And that was important. Though
Lévesque never felt "Canadian," he never proposed complete separation from English Canada. Instead, he favoured a continuing economic association within a structure where each "nation" would be
equal, despite differences of size. He once called it "sovereignty-
cum-association," and that position revealed his moderation, even
conservatism. For all his rhetoric about "colonialism" and "Westmount Rhodesians," Lévesque knew that Quebec and Quebecers
neither were oppressed in the manner known in the colonial world
nor did Francophones hate Anglophones in any systematic way. As
he wrote in 1976, "undoubtedly French Quebec was (and remains
to this day) the least ill-treated of all colonies in the world."[16]
Hardly the language of a firebrand nationalist. Moreover, it should
be added that René Lévesque, for all of his suspicions of the Anglophone minority in Quebec, consistently defended that minority's
right to the use of its language, though not as an equal right with
French. This was not always a popular view in his party.

The Lévesque vision of Canada, if he can be said to have had one,
was based on a view of what was convenient, necessary, and practical. For him, that had to be a relationship between equal nations. In
that vision Quebec was central, Quebec was first. In preparation for

the 1980 referendum, the Parti Québécois issued a program whose title summed up the objective: *D'égal à égal.*

For Trudeau, too, Quebec was central. Though perhaps the most clear-headed defender of federalism in our history, Pierre Trudeau was French Canadian from Quebec. Before he entered politics, his writings were almost exclusively about Quebec. His goal was to help rid his province of the reactionary, paternalistic, nationalist regime of Maurice Duplessis, and the road to that goal, as he saw it, was to educate Quebecers in the values and uses of democracy. To those who cried *"Québec d'abord!,"* he replied *"Démocratie d'abord!"* His brilliant essay entitled "Some Obstacles to Democracy in Quebec" and the popular articles published in *Vrai* and collected later in *Les Cheminements de la politique* (1970) were passionate pleas for democratization and attacks on the nationalism he thought stood in its way. For him, the checks and balances of federalism provided desirable guarantees for pluralism and freedom.

In his youth Pierre Trudeau may have been attracted to French-Canadian nationalism. He campaigned in 1942 on behalf of a nationalist candidate named Jean Drapeau, who was an opponent of conscription for overseas service. And in 1944, at age twenty-four, after a long canoe trip in the Canadian North, he wrote a lyrical essay entitled "L'ascéticisme en canot" ("Asceticism in a Canoe"), which concluded: ". . . I know a man who had never learned 'nationalism' in school, but who contracted this virtue when he felt the immensity of his country in his bones, and saw how great his country's creators had been."[17]

This "nationalism" was not connected with ethnicity, but rather with a sense of place and pride in ancestral achievement. That perhaps explains why he altered the word to "patriotism" when it was translated into English a quarter of a century later.[18]

If René Lévesque's political baptism during the 1959 Radio-Canada producers' strike led him to a nationalist conclusion, Pierre Trudeau's first association with the Quebec working class resulted in a quite different analysis. In the spring of 1949 Trudeau travelled to Thetford Mines with his friend, the labour journalist Gérard Pelletier. There he met Jean Marchand, the secretary-general of the Confédération des travailleurs catholiques du Canada, who was leading an illegal strike in the asbestos industry. Trudeau addressed the workers, joined the pickets, and concluded that the union movement represented the best hope for the future of democracy in

Quebec. In that strike he witnessed an alliance between an American-owned corporation and the nationalist government of Quebec, an alliance sanctioned by many of the leaders of the Roman Catholic Church that was devoted to crushing a French-Canadian workers' organization. This reactionary provincial government promoted a narrow ideology founded on "clericalism, agriculturalism and paternalism toward the workers,"[19] an ideology utterly out of tune with the dominant industrial order of Quebec. That ideology and the institutions that promoted it, Trudeau concluded, had to be undermined.

In the years after the Asbestos strike, when Trudeau worked as a legal adviser to various union movements, his conviction that nationalism was a primary obstacle to French-Canadian progress hardened into an unshakable conviction he would never change. In his lengthy polemical introduction to a collection of essays entitled *La Grève de l'amiante*, he set out to dismantle traditional social and nationalist thought and to call upon his contemporaries to replace *a priori* nationalist idealism with a hard-headed empirical approach to Quebec's social realities. He concluded: "An entire generation is hesitating at the brink of commitment. May this book provide elements to enlighten its choice."[20] Thus he was dubbed an "anti-nationalist" and, unlike some of his comrades in the fight against Duplessis who later found the "reform" nationalism of the 1960s appealing, Trudeau maintained that stance, and, if anything, intensified and clarified it in the battle against the so-called "new nationalism." In 1964 he and six other intellectuals – all younger than Trudeau – set out their answer to the "national question" that was once more consuming so much energy. In their "Manifeste pour une politique fonctionnelle," published in *Cité libre* and *Canadian Forum*, they proclaimed:

> In the present political context, what matters is to put the emphasis back on the individual, regardless of what his ethnicity, geography or religion happens to be. The social and political order must be founded primarily on the universal attributes of man, not on what makes him different. A set of political and social priorities based on the individual is totally incompatible with an order of priorities based on race, religion or nationality.[21]

Thus, by the time he chose to plunge into federal politics in 1965, he had become a fierce critic of nationalism – though he never denied the existence or value of nations. He had also become a proponent of Actonian ethnic pluralism as the soundest basis for a liberal democracy. By working to strengthen federal representation from Quebec in Ottawa, the balance could be restored to a situation in which Quebec, under Lesage's Liberals, appeared to be pulling itself, step by step, out of Confederation. Moreover, since he and his friends believed that nationalism in Quebec was the product of the failure of Canadian federalism to provide enough space for French Canadians to exercise their rights, that space would have to be made by reforming federalism, not by seceding from Canada. "The most effective way to cure nationalist alienation would probably be to put in a better kind of government," he explained to his somewhat unhappy readers of *Cité libre*. As Dorval Brunelle has put it so exactly, the goal was twofold: "against both French Canadian nationalism and passive federalism."[22]

Separation, independence, sovereignty – all these, in Trudeau's view, meant the identification of state and nation, an inward-turning by French Canadians and, at least in the worst-case scenarios implied in some of the early separatist writings, a return to the reactionary society of pre-1960. This was counter-revolution, a return to what he disdainfully called "the wigwam complex."[23] Where Lévesque accepted nationalism as a positive sentiment that could energize reform, Trudeau believed that nationalism based on ethnic homogeneity was negative, bound in the end to stifle reform. Actonian pluralism, a state in which ethnic distinctions balanced each other and were accepted as positive virtues, guarantees of liberty, was Trudeau's ideal; that stood at the heart of his political ideas and was the basis of his vision of Canada. And it was the point on which he and René Lévesque differed irreconcilably.

Well before the *trois colombes* – the labour leader Jean Marchand, the journalist Gérard Pelletier, and Trudeau – set off for Ottawa, Trudeau had set out explicitly the conditions necessary if his gamble was to succeed. There were two conditions for successful federalism:

> First, French Canadians must really want it; that is to say, they must abandon their role of oppressed nation and decide to participate boldly and intelligently in the Canadian experience. . . . The second condition is that the dice not be loaded against French Canadians in the "Confederation game." This means that if French Canadians

abandon their concept of a national state, English Canadians must do the same. We must not find Toronto, or Fredericton, or above all, Ottawa exalting the *English* Canadian nation. . . . [24]

Thirty months after his decision to join the Liberals – they were not sure they wanted him at first – and work in Ottawa, Pierre Trudeau was Prime Minister of Canada. At about that same time his old associate, René Lévesque, no longer a cabinet minister, began to build a new political party devoted to his ideas and his leadership. His ascent to power was almost as spectacular as that of Trudeau: on November 15, 1976, his party was elected on its third attempt. ("We're not a minor people," he told his joyous supporters that night, "we're maybe something like a great people.") [25] The road to sovereignty-association had opened up. The stage was set for what seemed to be the final act in the great debate about Quebec's future and Canada's future. It would last six years, and would include the defeat and resurrection of Pierre Trudeau and then the referendum. On May 20, 1980, Quebec voters, by a sixty/forty split, rejected Lévesque's request for permission to begin negotiations on the sovereignty-association question. Trudeau now moved to patriate the Canadian constitution, complete with a new Charter of Rights and Freedoms and an amending formula. Lévesque, on behalf of his province, rejected that constitution, demonstrating that the referendum had not ended the debate.

When Pierre Trudeau left office in 1984, he knew that while Lévesque had lost, he himself had not won – at least not unconditionally. Speaking at Laval University in the spring of 1984 he once again defended his conception of Canadian federalism. In closing, he admitted that there was still much work to be done to harmonize the several "little homelands" with "the bigger homeland." He continued:

Our Canadian attachment will probably always be more distant, less deeply rooted in the soil than our attachments as Quebecers, Newfoundlanders or Albertans. But, exactly for this reason, we must make sure our institutions can embody our collective will to live and instill it in the minds of all Canadians, and in the minds of foreigners wishing to do business and build a better world with us. [26]

In 1962, Hubert Aquin, who would soon be recognized as one of Quebec's finest novelists, explained to his fellow Quebec nationalists that while hostility to English Canadians was at the root of the quest for independence, the English were not the essential problem. "It's the French Canadians we have to fight," he explained. [27] That was a shrewd judgement. Indeed, it is the key to understanding the history of Quebec and of Canada between 1960 and 1980.

Pierre Trudeau and René Lévesque: two Quebecers devoted to the survival and full flowering of a modern French-speaking society. In Lévesque's view that could be achieved only if his "minor people" became a "great people": sovereignty for Quebec. Trudeau believed that the future of his "little homeland" would best be guaranteed through participation in the "bigger homeland," a federal system built on equality between French- and English-speaking Canadians throughout Canada. For the *francophone canadien*, Trudeau, Canada was central; for the *Québécois*, Lévesque, Canada was marginal – at best. Nevertheless, both leaders, Trudeau and Lévesque, were, in Gérard Bergeron's happy phrase, "our two-sided mirror" – both reflections of the same community. [28]

On the evening of November 15, 1976, following the Parti Québécois's stunning victory in that day's election, René Lévesque, in a state of barely controlled emotion, told his supporters: "I never thought I could be as proud to be a Quebecer as I am tonight."

On the evening of May 20, 1980, following the victory of the federalist option in the Quebec referendum, Pierre Elliott Trudeau, his reason only just controlling his passion, confessed: "I never thought I could be as proud to be a Quebecer and a Canadian as I am tonight . . . ." [29]

The parallel was intentional; the summary perfect.

TEN

Language Policy and the Glossophagic State

T HE SUPREME COURT of Canada, in the *Reference re Manitoba Language Rights*, stated:

> the importance of language rights is grounded in the essential role that language plays in human existence, development and dignity. It is through language that we are able to form concepts; to structure and order the world around us. Language bridges the gap between isolation and community, allowing humans to delineate the rights and duties they hold in respect of one another, and thus to live in society. [1]

If one were to apply that principle as a measuring stick against which to test the historical development of language policy in Canada the shortfall would be more than a little embarrassing. Yet to measure the past by that principle would be an unhistorical exercise, for it represents a philosophy of language and language policy that is the product of the very evolution that is the focus of this discussion. Indeed, what I want to suggest in my survey of this broad subject is that insofar as there has been anything systematic enough in the language to be worthy of the label "policy" it has, until recently, been founded on a rather different understanding of the role of language in society. Even today, I will conclude, the implications of this new philosophy have barely been considered.

Language policy in Canada has been an attempt to answer the question: who has the right to use what language, when, and where? That question has been posed, and reposed, because Canada has never been a linguistically uniform community. Language policy, then, has had as its goal the definition of relations between language groups or, to put that another way, to define group rights. Consequently, the need to define a language policy was first faced when New France was ceded to Great Britain in 1763. Prior to that date no policy was needed: the state spoke French, the Church used

Latin and French, the world of work and play was French, and there was no decided policy about the linguistic basis for relations with the Native peoples – though it is striking that many missionaries and traders acquired some command of one of the local languages. Having conquered New France the British first assumed that assimilation would naturally follow. But as every schoolgirl knows, that policy had to be abandoned when English-speaking settlement failed to materialize. In 1774 Quebec was accepted as a "distinct colony" within an English-speaking Empire, one where the religion and legal system, though not the language, of the majority were given legal recognition. When that "catastrophe shocking to think of" – the American Revolution – erupted, a new constitution became necessary due to the sudden arrival of large numbers of English-speaking settlers. The 1791 constitution, establishing Lower and Upper Canada, represented a return to the policy of 1763: Canada was to be an English-speaking colony in which French Canadians were to be gradually, and voluntarily, assimilated. English was established as the language of public affairs and an attempt was made to establish it as the language of education. The policy failed. From the outset Francophone members of the Legislative Assembly spoke in their own language and made it evident that they would use these new institutions to defend their culture. The Royal Institution of Education found no favour with Francophones, who preferred to leave education with their French-speaking Church. Numbers, in Lower Canada, proved more effective than policy.

That situation obtained for fifty years until, in the wake of the failed rebellions of 1837-38, Lord Durham's famous *Report* vigorously reasserted the policy of assimilation in order to establish peace between the "two nations warring in the bosom of a single state." Durham's *Report* might well be called the first systematic statement of language policy in Canada, one that had no legitimate successor until the 1960s and 1970s produced the *Report of the Royal Commission on Bilingualism and Biculturalism* (1965-71), the *rapport de la Commission d'enquête sur la situation de la langue française et sur les droits linguistiques au Québec* (1972) (the Gendron Commission), the Quebec White Paper on language,[2] and its federal counterpart, *Towards a National Understanding* (1977).

On language, as on all other matters, Durham's *Report* is a very impressive, carefully conceived document, a point recently reaffirmed by Janet Ajzenstat in *The Political Thought of Lord Durham*.[3]

Durham's assumptions about language policy remained at the heart of most subsequent language debate in Canada. The first of those assumptions was that language policy was fundamental to nation-building. Durham subscribed to the nineteenth-century liberal view – one shared by John Stuart Mill, for example, but rejected by Lord Acton – that linguistic homogeneity was a requirement of the nation-state, even the colonial nation-state. The conclusion he drew about British North America, as everyone knows, was that if it was to remain British its inhabitants would have to speak English. Francophones would have to accept assimilation. The claim that linguistic and cultural homogeneity is a requirement of nationhood resurfaced repeatedly in both English and French Canada during the language controversies of the century following Durham's mission.

Less commonly heard, at least until the 1960s, but no less important, was Durham's contention that language policy and social policy are intimately connected. It was Durham's view that social mobility in an English-dominated North American economic system depended on a thorough knowledge of English. If French Canadians were to avoid the status of a permanent underclass, they would have to acquire the language of the economy. "I desire to give the Canadians our English character," he wrote, "for the sake of the educated classes, whom the distinction of language and manners keeps apart from the great Empire to which they belong." And he continued that he was even more anxious that the "humbler classes" be "amalgamated" because "their present state of rude and equal plenty is fast deteriorating."[4] The great liberal principle of equality of opportunity, whether in imperial politics or in the workplace, demanded the removal of those linguistic distinctions that, in Durham's view, placed French Canadians in an unequal starting position.

Not until the 1960s and 1970s did the important issue of the language of work return to the centre of the stage in the language debate in Canada. First came the Bilingualism and Biculturalism studies demonstrating that French Canadians occupied a shockingly low position on the economic ladder, especially in Quebec.[5] These were followed by debate and studies in Quebec confirming the earlier conclusions and proposed responses.[6] All of these later studies confirmed Durham's prognosis, but most of them also turned him on his head. Where Durham had recommended that French Canadians be anglicized to fit the economy, later studies made the more sensible and humane suggestion that the world of work be francicized to fit Francophones. Durham would have understood the argument, though he would surely have rejected the goal, presented by Camille Laurin in the Quebec White Paper on language this way:

> The Québec we wish to build will be essentially French. The fact that the majority of its population is French will be clearly visible – at work, in communications, and in the countryside. It will also be a country where the traditional division of powers, *especially in matters concerning the economy,* will be modified.[7]

For Laurin, as for Lord Durham, language was much more about power than about poetry. Each believed in what Jean Laponce in *Languages and their Territories* has called, in neither of our official languages, "a glossophagic state."[8]

The Union of 1841, though not the federal union Durham had recommended, had assimilation – glossophagia – as one of its goals, for English alone was recognized as an official language. But political reality – French power – defeated ideology, and in 1849 Lord Elgin dramatized that reality by reading the Speech from the Throne in both French and English. That pragmatic acceptance was translated into the British North America Act of 1867, which, for the first time since the Conquest, gave constitutional recognition to French as one of the two official languages of "the new nationality." Bilingualism was accepted in the federal Parliament and its courts and in the government of the newly created province of Quebec. Moreover, the BNA Act made provision for a denominational school system in Quebec that, in practice, gave institutional support to linguistic duality. Roughly similar arrangements were made in Manitoba in 1870 and in the Northwest Territories in 1874, though these became victims of the cultural wars of the 1890s.

The debates about language policy in the century following Confederation centred to a large extent on the issue of minority educational rights outside of Quebec. The abolition of French as an official language in Manitoba, for example, attracted far less controversy and litigation than the abolition of state support for denominational schools, schools that were Catholic and, in many instances, Francophone. The argument about separate schools was both religious and linguistic, and, although the two issues cannot really be divided, I will do so for purposes of my analysis of language policy. Four particular concerns dominated this debate.

First, there was the contention that if Canada was to become a "nation," then cultural and linguistic homogeneity was necessary at least outside of Quebec. That was D'Alton McCarthy's contention in the 1890s in his campaign in Manitoba and the Northwest, and it would resurface in the debate over the 1905 Autonomy Bills establishing Alberta and Saskatchewan and in the school controversies in Ontario, Manitoba, and Saskatchewan between 1912 and 1919. On the whole that argument carried the day. In defending French language and Roman Catholic rights, most nationalists made exactly the same equation between language and culture or "race," and added religion. Henri Bourassa's famous speech at the 1910 Eucharistic Congress entitled *Religion, Langue, Nationalité*[9] is only one of a multiplicity of possible examples.

Second, the contention and counter-contention about the nature of the Confederation settlement of 1867 is summed up in the old query: act or compact? Those, chiefly English Canadians, who insisted on the "act" thesis contended that the BNA Act, insofar as language was concerned, meant exactly what it said: English was the language of Canada outside of Quebec with limited recognition for French in federal institutions and a fuller bilingualism in Quebec. That was what Henri Bourassa called the "reservation" theory of Confederation: French Canadians, *comme les sauvages*, could only exercise their rights when they remained on the Quebec reservation. To that theory he opposed the idea of a "compact" or *entente* between cultures that implied equality of French and English Canadians from coast to coast, an equality of communities. Until the 1960s Bourassa's theory remained exactly that – a theory supported by a large number of French Canadians and rejected by most English Canadians.

Third, the language debate was complicated by immigration, which brought, particularly to the Canadian West, a number of additional languages sometimes spoken by people more numerous than those who spoke French. What claims could these groups make, on grounds of right or practicality, that their languages should be recognized at least as languages of education? The Manitoba answer in the so-called Laurier-Greenway settlement of 1897 was that those languages had as much right to recognition as French – restricted but significant use as a language of instruction. By 1916 the Manitoba government decided – and the other Prairie provinces followed suit – that a mistake had been made. Educational reforms in the Prairie provinces placed all non-English languages on an equal footing: they were prohibited as languages of education, though they could be taught as subjects. (In rural areas, where non-English groups were concentrated, these requirements were often ignored except when the provincial inspector paid his visits!) [10]

The fourth issue, one I will merely mention, was cost. How much could developing provinces, or even a developing country, afford to spend supporting education in languages other than English? The answer was, almost always, not much. Quebec, of course, was an exception because there the minority language was English, which was supported by constitutionally guaranteed Protestant schools and the financial resources of an economically powerful community.

Lord Durham's argument about cultural uniformity and nation-building was not the only one at work in this debate. It would be quite inaccurate to leave the impression that the insistence that English be accepted as the only official language of education outside of Quebec was simply a matter of Anglo-Saxon prejudice or racism – though there was enough, more than enough, of that. Durham's second argument also was a factor. Men such as J.S. Woodsworth and J.W. Dafoe, for example, believed that getting ahead in an English-speaking country and continent required a knowledge of the dominant language and an immersion in the dominant culture. Non-English speakers were open to exploitation both economically and politically because they were not integrated into the system, and integration required, as the first necessity, a command of English. Those progressive educational reforms that resulted almost invariably in the reduction, even erasure, of minority language rights were based not so much on bigotry as on paternalism: the conviction that the reformers knew what was best for the objects of reform, namely, the "foreigners," a term that could include French Canadians. The well-known argument presented in John Porter's *The Vertical Mosaic*, [11] that the price of the cultural mosaic is a class system in which the English, and to a lesser degree the French, are dominant would have won approval from early twentieth-century educational reformers. It was also Durham's concern.

Without simplifying the record too drastically, then, it can be said that prior to 1960 disputes about language and language policy focused largely on educational rights, to a lesser extent on the language of government, and almost not at all on the language of the private sector, except in the sense that education was designed to prepare students for work in the private sector where English predominated at all but the unskilled level. There were minor exceptions, such as the campaign by La Ligue des Droits français, supported by *Le Devoir*, to force Eaton's to issue its catalogue in French. If we believe Roch Carrier's wonderful story "The Hockey Sweater," we must conclude that the campaign failed!

What eventually changed the emphasis of this debate, bringing the language of work to the forefront, was the growth of the welfare state, at all levels of government. And that was accompanied by the gradual but insistent blurring of the line that once, at least theoretically, divided the private from the public sector, whether in economics, social security, health care, or that vague area called "culture." The growth of government and government services meant that employment opportunities in the public sector multiplied rapidly. Consequently, the language of work became an important criterion for employment, and one subject to political pressure. Though Francophones had long been dissatisfied with their under-representation in the federal public service, especially at the upper levels, it was no accident that that discontent became more pronounced with the rise of the welfare bureaucracy. Nor was it an accident that once the Quebec state, after 1960, moved to improve and expand its public service, the federal government had to pay more attention to the demands of its Francophone employees. Otherwise they could and often did seek careers in Quebec. The second consequence of increased government activity was, of course, a rising demand from those to be served in their own language. The Royal Commission on Bilingualism and Biculturalism and the Official Languages Act[12] were responses to these concerns, among others.

In Quebec the issue soon moved beyond public-sector concerns. By 1960 it had become widely recognized that the state must play a role in preserving and promoting the French language in an urban-industrial society. The stages leading from the Lesage government's tentative efforts in the language promotion area through the controversies of the Bertrand and first Bourassa administrations to the enactment of Bill 101 in 1977 cannot be discussed in detail. But the point of all of the recent language legislation in Quebec has been to ensure that Francophone Quebecers will be able to live their lives, at work as well as at home, in French. It has also been designed to ensure that new immigrants will be assimilated into the French rather than the English stream in Quebec, a goal whose urgency is increased with every drop in the Francophone birth rate. These concerns form the essence of the report of the Gendron Commission.

Increasing state intervention in language matters has raised in a dramatic fashion the old question of the relation of language and culture. Are they distinct or inseparable entities? Part of the problem is that the definition of "culture" is almost infinitely expandable – at last count there were about 300 different definitions of the word. Successive attempts by both government and intellectuals in Quebec to give the term acceptable content have been less than convincing.[13] But differing theories of the relation of language to culture have underpinned contemporary language policies. In a bilingual state it is logical to designate language as a simple means of communication. That is the assumption of the Official Languages Act. By contrast, the authors of Quebec language policy have argued that language, culture, and identity are inseparable, and that is stated in the preamble to the Charter of the French Language.[14]

If those contrasting views of language policy seem straightforward, then a look at the arguments in the recent Supreme Court case over the language of signs in Quebec – the *Brown Shoes*[15] case – suggests that the ground is more slippery than first appearances might suggest. In that case the Quebec government lawyers, in defending the prohibition of English signs, argued that there was no connection between language and culture despite Bill 101's assertion to the contrary. In their decision, the Supreme Court justices reaffirmed their opinion in the *Reference re Manitoba Language Rights* and stated:

> Language is so intimately related to the form and content of expression that there cannot be true freedom of expression by means of language if one is prohibited from using the language of one's choice. Language is not merely a means or medium of expression; it colours the content and meaning of expression. It is, as the preamble of the *Charter of the French Language* indicates, a means by which a people may express its cultural identity. It is also the means by which the individual expresses his or her personal identity and sense of individuality.[16]

Thus Joshua Fishman's *Sociology of Language*,[17] controversial though it may be among language theorists, has become a central principle of Canadian jurisprudence on language policy. And, it should be noted in passing, language is made the key to both collective and individual identity as if neither claim were open to controversy. What would James Joyce or Joseph Conrad have thought?

Though the defenders of Bill 101's regulations respecting commercial signage were thus hoisted on their own petard, the full implications of enshrining the Fishman doctrine in our jurisprudence are far from having been explored. How, for example, does it apply to French-language minorities in Alberta? Or, for that matter, to those whose mother tongue is neither French nor English? Could the doctrine be used to justify the claim of Canada's Native peoples to official recognition of some or all of their numerous languages? These, and other questions, remain for the future.

Let me conclude this rapid and sometimes simplified survey by noting, first, that language policy has moved from being a relatively minor item on the public agenda in the years prior to 1960 – relatively minor, but always volatile – to one of central importance. Second, as it has evolved, policies based on two distinct philosophies and designed to achieve different goals have been implemented. There is a federal policy of official bilingualism formulated in the Official Languages Act and enshrined in sections 16-22 of the Charter of Rights and Freedoms. It has been adopted by New Brunswick and to a lesser extent Ontario and Manitoba. Then there is the Quebec policy of modified unilingualism followed by or, more accurately, preceded by the other six provinces. To that mix is added a commitment, stated in both the Charter of Rights and the Charter of the French Language,[18] to multiculturalism, a commitment that has a whole range of largely unexamined implications for language policy, especially in education. How compatible these philosophies, goals, and commitments are, no one would dare predict.

That said, the issues involved in language policy – those of nation-building, of cultural pluralism or uniformity, of economic opportunity and social harmony – are no different than they were when Durham laid them out in 1840. What we should have learned from Durham, I would argue, is that an impressive analysis does not automatically lead to a just, or even a workable, solution.

ELEVEN

Alice in Meechland or The Concept of Quebec as a "Distinct Society"

*"If the recognition of Quebec as a distinct society turns out not to mean
anything, Quebeckers will realize it and begin fighting again."*
Claude Morin, in *Globe and Mail*, November 3, 1987

NO DISCUSSION OF constitutional matters in Canada should
take place without ready access to a copy of Lewis Carroll's standard reference work, *Through the Looking Glass and What Alice
Found There*. Certainly that is true of the 1987 Constitutional
Accord and especially of section 2, which refers to "a fundamental
characteristic of Canada" and describes Quebec as "a distinct society." A moment's thought about those seemingly innocent phrases
should remind us of Alice's first discussion with Humpty Dumpty.

"Don't stand there chattering to yourself like that," Humpty
Dumpty said, looking at her for the first time, "but tell me your
name and your business."

"My name is Alice, but –"

"It's a stupid name enough!" Humpty Dumpty interrupted
impatiently. "What does it mean?"

"*Must* a name mean something?" Alice asked doubtfully.

"Of course it must," Humpty Dumpty said, with a short laugh:
"*my* name means the shape I am – and a good handsome shape it is,
too. With a name like yours, you might be any shape, almost."

The difficulty with the terms "fundamental characteristic" and
"distinct society," as they are used in the 1987 Constitutional
Accord, is that they describe something that rather than being "a
good handsome shape . . . might be any shape, almost." Like

Humpty Dumpty, I think that names should have understood meanings. In section 2 of the Accord they do not.

Historically, at least since the early nineteenth century, Francophones in British North America/Canada, developed a consciousness of their distinctiveness both individually and collectively. The most obvious badge of that distinctiveness was language, while the Civil Code provided a legal foundation for difference. And, at least until recent decades, Catholicism and the Church were linked to that identity. Also, it was long insisted by many nationalists – even when the facts contradicted them – that French Canadians were naturally an agricultural people.[1] Finally, and most important, French-Canadian distinctiveness was founded on an interpretation of the past that made the collectivity unique: the struggle for survival in North America made this *petit peuple* North American but not Anglo-Saxon, French-speaking but not French. From that sense of uniqueness grew a sense of mission that assigned French Canadians the task of continuing their quest for survival and fulfilment as a distinct "race," "people," or "nation."[2]

Until the 1960s that "people" or "nation" usually included Francophones wherever they lived in Canada and even, sometimes, included those who had emigrated to the United States. Moreover, whatever term was used to describe the collectivity – "race," "nation," "people" – it was intended to describe a cultural and sociological entity rather than a political or constitutional one – except perhaps in the case of those who followed Louis-Joseph Papineau.[3] Of course, within that cultural and sociological definition, those Francophones who lived in the St. Lawrence Valley, "the homeland," were central. After 1867, when the province of Quebec was created, that territorial definition was strengthened since it was the one province with a Francophone majority. Even so, that distinctiveness was called French Canadian more than Québécois. (This confusion of French Canadian and Québécois often irritated members of the diaspora, Acadians and Franco-Manitobans, who insisted that their way of being French Canadian was as valid as that of the Québécois.)

In the period stretching roughly from the Second World War to 1960 the concept of distinctiveness changed, as did the focus of that distinctiveness. Once the obvious facts of industrialization and urbanization were accepted, the myth of "ruralism" was rejected. As the outlook and ambitions of Francophones grew more secular, the centrality of the Church and religion in the definition of distinctiveness was questioned. In some ways French Canadians seemed to be becoming less "distinctive." Soon it came to be recognized that the dangers and challenges of industrial society made the state a necessary instrument not only of modernization but also as a means of preserving and promoting cultural and sociological distinctiveness.[4] And that, in turn, further reinforced the territorial definition of Francophone distinctiveness. Without entirely losing sight of the diaspora, Quebec French Canadians were becoming Québécois. This term, of course, was not entirely satisfactory, since about 20 per cent of Québécois were non-Francophones and thus not members of what had traditionally been thought of as the distinct "people" or "nation." That remains a somewhat confused issue. But what does seem clear is that the contemporary sense of distinctiveness retains from the past an emphasis on language, a sense of a common history (though there is less agreement about its meaning than there once was), and a conviction that Quebec, both geographically and constitutionally, is the focus of that distinctiveness.[5] But it should also be added that language in the new context means something more than an instrument of a culture in a literary or philosophical sense. In the debate over Bill 101 the issue was clearly one of power and social mobility, though the matters of culture, purity of language, and other traditional preoccupations were not wholly absent. Professor Fernand Dumont summed up the new situation aptly when he observed that "language is not only poetry. It is also power."[6]

The idea that the distinctiveness of Quebec should be recognized constitutionally is far from new. Indeed the very act of creating that province in 1867 was, implicitly, a recognition of distinctiveness. But the British North America Act also included several explicit recognitions of that fact. For example, section 94 recognized the civil law of Quebec as distinct and, if the intent expressed in that provision had been fulfilled ("uniformity of all and any laws relative to Property and Civil Rights" in all provinces except Quebec), Quebec would have had a "special status" in that area. In addition, the special character of Quebec was recognized in section 133, which not only made French, for the first time, an official language of Canada, but also made Quebec, alone among the original provinces, bilingual. In this, and in some other ways, Quebec has never been a province exactly like the others for its historic characteristics made some constitutional variations desirable.

It was not until the 1950s, perhaps because some Quebecers had begun to realize that Quebec's traditional distinctiveness was disappearing under the impact of urban and industrial growth, that arguments began to be devised to justify demands for a wider recognition of Quebec's power to defend its distinctiveness. These arguments were given systematic form in the *Rapport de la Commission royale d'enquête sur les problèmes constitutionels* (1956), commonly known as the Tremblay Commission. Though that Commission's definition of Quebec's distinctiveness was remarkably traditional – a French-speaking Roman Catholic society, spiritual rather than material in its values and goals – it made a powerful argument for provincial autonomy in areas into which the new federal welfare state was moving, and it insisted that Quebec was not a province like the others. [7]

During the 1960s a new political and bureaucratic elite transformed the familiar process of constructing a provincial welfare state into an exercise in nation-building. A new nationalist ideology both legitimized that process and redefined the concept of "distinctiveness" into a Quebec-centred, secular doctrine. [8] Like French-Canadian nationalists in the past, the neo-nationalists of the 1960s were both moderate and persistent. Only a small fringe group demanded outright independence and linguistic uniformity in the manner of nineteenth-century nationalists in Europe and post-1945 nationalists in the colonial world. Instead, their demands were for a recognition of the priority of the French language in Quebec and the recognition of Quebec as a *province pas comme les autres,* with, according to the intensity of the theorist's nationalism, a "different status," a "particular status," a "special status," "associate states," or "sovereignty" accompanied by "association." For various reasons – lack of definition, unworkability, federal opposition, lack of popular support, among others – none of these proposed constitutional methods of recognizing Quebec's distinctiveness was realized. [9] But the thrust behind the demand, and the rhetoric supporting it, never totally dissipated even though the "mood" of Quebec altered radically, leaving the nationalist movement, at least temporarily, in disarray and even exhaustion. [10]

Perhaps a rough measure of that new "mood" is the new phrase that has been adopted in the latest attempt to capture Quebec's special character. That, of course, is "distinct society" or, alternatively, "distinct identity," phrases that seem to avoid the implication of "national" or "quasi-national" status. And that, at long last, brings us to the 1987 Constitutional Accord that enshrines these phrases.

The point of this introduction has merely been to demonstrate that the idea of French-Canadian/Quebec distinctiveness is not new either historically or in terms of constitutional practice. It is a reality. Therefore, to criticize the concept of a "distinct society" as it appears in the Accord is not to reject the fact of that distinctiveness. It is to criticize the Accord for its inadequate reflection of the reality.

Though the term "distinct society" has a familiar ring it only assumed a central place in constitutional discussions after the Quebec referendum of May, 1980, and especially after the proclamation, without Quebec's formal adherence, of the constitution of 1982. The Quebec provincial Liberal Party, in its 1985 program, set out as one of its conditions for accepting the new constitution "inscription, in *the preamble of the new constitution,* of a statement explicitly recognizing Quebec as the hearth of a distinct society and the cornerstone of the French-speaking element of the Canadian duality."[11] Other conditions, designed to give meaning to that concept, included a veto on constitutional amendments, limitations on the federal spending power, constitutional recognition of the Cullen-Couture agreement on immigration, and the right of the Quebec government to participate in the nomination of Supreme Court justices from that province.

In his now often cited, but perhaps less frequently read, speech at Mont Gabriel on May 9, 1986, Gil Rémillard, as a minister in the Bourassa government, repeated these conditions, stating that the recognition of Quebec as a "distinct society" should include increased powers in immigration, limitations on the spending power, a veto on constitutional amendments, and the right to "participate in the selection and nomination of judges." This latter condition was especially important, he argued, because the court's rulings touched values "that are essential parts of Quebec's distinctiveness such as the Civil Code and, in certain aspects, of fundamental rights and freedoms."

In that speech the Quebec minister made two additional points of importance in light of the subsequent Meech Lake agreement. The first concerned the new Quebec government's view of the Canadian Charter of Rights. After four years of interpretation, he said, the Charter was "a document that we can be proud of as Quebecers and Canadians." Consequently, the new government would no longer use the *non obstante* clause in relation to articles 2 and 7 to 15. "We wish that the fundamental rights of Quebecers be as well protected as those of other Canadians."

Second, though not listing it as one of his specific conditions, Rémillard expressed a profound concern about the inadequate protection provided for Francophone groups outside Quebec, especially in the matter of control over schools and the issue of "sufficient numbers" required to warrant minority language schools. These matters, he thought, should be part of a new constitutional package. [12] These, then, were the general propositions advanced by the Liberal government of Quebec as a negotiating position in the discussions leading up to the signing of the Meech Lake–Langevin Block Accord.

Before I turn to an examination of section 2 of that Accord, the one dealing with Quebec as a "distinct society," two observations seem in order. The first is that the description of Quebec as a "distinct society" is not part of the preamble, as the Liberal government had demanded, but is rather a substantive interpretive clause covering the constitution and the Charter. Second, all those areas that Rémillard outlined at Mont Gabriel are dealt with separately, meeting Quebec's conditions almost to the letter: a Quebec veto (though now given to all provinces) on an extended list of constitutional changes (including Senate reform and the admission of new provinces), guarantees respecting Quebec's role in the appointment of Supreme Court justices (again, other provinces receive similar rights), and a limitation on the spending power. Whatever one may think of these provisions, they certainly seem congruent with those conditions set out by the Quebec government. To that, however, the Accord adds the interpretive clause, leaving the concept of "distinct society" undefined. Thus the task of giving meaning to that sociological and psychological phrase will be left to the courts. It is not, as is normal, interpreting the application of a defined constitutional term but the definition of the term itself that our elected representatives have turned over to the judiciary. Moreover, it is not just the definition of *any* term that is given the courts. It is the definition of what has always been a primordial aspect of Canadian history and constitutional concern: the relations between French- and English-speaking Canadians and the place of Quebec in the Canadian constitution. What are the problems raised by this decision?

Any careful reading of section 2 of the Accord will demonstrate that it is shot through with contradiction, confusion, and ambiguity. Section 2(a) recognizes "the existence of French-speaking Canadians, concentrated inside Quebec but also present elsewhere in

Canada." That, presumably, refers to an ethnic group whose mother tongue is French and whose roots extend back to the beginning of the European part of our history. In addition, section 2(a) recognizes "English-speaking Canadians, concentrated outside Quebec but also present in Quebec." That, presumably, *does not* refer to an ethnic group but rather to the fact that English is the *lingua franca* of those of many mother tongues other than French. To put this another way, French is both a defining characteristic of an ethnic group and one of Canada's two official languages; English is simply one of the two official languages. These two entities are not, therefore, equivalents, though the Accord leaves the unwary with the impression that they are.

Or are they equivalents? Here we come to the question of defining the term "distinct society." To what does that phrase refer? Is it to "Quebec" or to "the French-speaking Canadians centred in Quebec"? Those, of course, are not the same. Many Francophone Quebecers, especially among those who have joined the debate over the Accord, believe or hope that the term "distinct society" refers to the Francophone majority. English-speaking Quebecers, naturally, fear and reject that conclusion and hope that "distinct society" refers to a bilingual, multicultural society. Rémillard, the Quebec Minister of Intergovernmental Affairs, appears to accept the first interpretation; those who speak for Alliance Québec defend the latter. [13]

In the debate in the Quebec National Assembly in June, 1987, Premier Robert Bourassa offered what is presumably the official view of his government in this matter. He stated: "The French language is a fundamental characteristic of our uniqueness, but there are other aspects, such as our culture and our institutions, whether political, economic or judicial." These were not defined, he said, because definition "would confine and hamper the National Assembly in promoting this uniqueness." Then, he added:

It must be noted that Quebec's distinct identity will be protected and promoted by the National Assembly and government, and its duality preserved by our legislators. *It cannot be stressed too strongly that the entire constitution, including the Charter, will be interpreted and applied in the light of the section proclaiming our distinctiveness as a society.* As a result, in the exercise of our legislative jurisdictions we will be able to consolidate what has already been achieved, and gain new ground.

Finally, after a reference to the safeguard clause confirming existing powers over language, he added: "we have for the first time in 120 years of federalism managed to provide constitutional underpinnings for the preservation and promotion of the *French character of Quebec*."[14]

Here, then, is a crystal clear statement of the view that "distinct society" and "French character" are interchangeable concepts. But elsewhere only confusion reigns.

Senator Lowell Murray, one of the architects of the Accord, nicely – I refrain from saying intentionally – expressed this confusion when he explained the lack of definition:

> We decided not to define Quebec's distinct society more clearly. If, in the 1930's, anyone had tried to define Quebec's specificity, it might have been said that Quebec was Catholic and French-speaking. I don't think today's politicians would use these kinds of terms to define Quebec's specificity.

Here the reference is exclusively to the Francophone majority. But the learned Senator then continued:

> We all know that we can quickly draw up a list of those characteristics that describe Quebec. There is the obvious fact that Quebec is the only province to have a French-speaking majority and an English-speaking minority. There is also the fact that it uses the civil code and that it evolved under a different Crown for 150 years before the 1763 Royal Proclamation. There are also the cultural and social institutions. As you can see it would be easy to draw up a list, but that list might unduly limit the concept itself.[15]

There are two interesting aspects to this part of the statement. The first is that the "distinct society" now includes both French- and English-speaking people. Second, and equally revealing, is the fact that Senator Murray's list contains *nothing* that is not already guaranteed in the 1867 version of our constitution: the Civil Code, control over education presumably being the "social and cultural institutions" referred to, and official bilingualism, which is what seems to follow from his description of the population's ethnicity. Does that mean that the concept of a "distinct society" is merely a description of the status quo as established in 1867? That would surely surprise many Quebecers.

Another witness before the Joint Committee, Yves Fortier, a leader of the Quebec bar, appeared to agree with Senator Murray's second definition but to go a step further. "Quebec society within Canada is not defined solely by the characteristics of the Francophone majority, and clause 2 states this specifically," Fortier contended. "Quebec's distinctive society is composed of English-speaking Canadians, native people, and people from ethnic groups."[16] Now, I find no reference to "native people" and "ethnic groups" in section 2. It may be that section 16, the so-called non-derogatory clause, adds these groups to Quebec's distinctive identity. If so, are the Quebec government and legislature responsible for the preservation and promotion of French, English, Aboriginal, and multicultural rights? Again, I think that might be an unwelcome surprise to some Quebecers. "Preservation," maybe. But anyone familiar with the last twenty years of debate over language and culture in Quebec could be forgiven any amount of scepticism about "promotion."

Nor does the Report of the Joint Committee add any light to this obscurity; indeed, on this, as on much else, it only obfuscates the matter further. When Zebedee Nungak of the Inuit Committee on National Issues, himself a Quebecer, expressed the fear that his people might be "out-distincted by a distinct Quebec," the Committee's majority replied that: "The members of the Joint Committee have no doubt that other communities within Canada might also be defined as 'distinct societies' and the fact that they are not referred to in Section 2 does not mean that these other characteristics or other cultural groups have been rejected or given second class status."[17]

Whether or not Nungak was satisfied with the Joint Committee's evident reluctance to extend "distinct" status to other groups, he may have thought of an Inuit version of Gilbert and Sullivan's insistence that where everybody is "distinct," nobody is "distinct." Or perhaps he was moved to turn to Alice:

> "When *I* use a word," Humpty Dumpty said in rather a scornful tone, "it means just what I chose it to mean – neither more nor less."
>
> "The question is," said Alice, "whether you *can* make words mean so many different things."
>
> "The question is," said Humpty Dumpty, "which is to be master – that's all."

As so often, Humpty Dumpty was right: that is the question. Section 2 is not merely a description of some supposed sociological construct. It is an interpretive clause concerned with the allocation of power. And that is where the issue of who is "master" must be confronted. Let me illustrate.

The "Legislature and Government of Quebec" is given the "role . . . to preserve and promote the distinct identity of Quebec." It obviously matters very much, in language policy, for example, which of Senator Murray's "distinct societies" is referred to – "the French-speaking Canadians centred in Quebec" or a bilingual Quebec? The history of Quebec since 1968 suggests that it cannot be both. Who will be master?

The "Parliament of Canada and the provincial legislatures" have the "role . . . to preserve the fundamental characteristic of Canada" and, apparently, the existing geographical distribution of that characteristic. Does that, for example, mean preservation of a situation in Alberta where it is evidently unacceptable to ask a question in French in the provincial legislature? Distinction seems to come in varying fundamental hues. And does preservation include policies devised by the federal government and applicable to the inhabitants of the distinct society of Quebec? When the Canada Council and the Social Sciences and Humanities Research Council make grants to Quebecers to study the French language in that province, or to compose Quebec music and poetry, is that merely preserving or is it promoting? The same question might be raised about the CBC/Radio-Canada and the NFB/ONF. Under the "distinct society" clause a future Quebec government will be able to challenge federal "promotion" of Francophone culture – and perhaps even Anglophone or allophone culture – in Quebec on the ground that Quebec, not Ottawa, has the role of "promoting" that society's "distinct identity." It is even possible that "reasonable compensation" may be demanded by Quebec when it opts out of federal programs in this area.[18]

Yet it is surely absurd, given the proposition that the existence of French- and English-speaking Canadians represents "a fundamental characteristic of Canada," that the federal government and Parliament should not have an explicitly recognized role to "promote" as well as "preserve" that characteristic. The term "preserve" conjures up the image of an endangered species. Under the new Accord that is surely the potential fate of linguistic minorities unless governments as well as legislatures are mandated to promote as well as preserve their languages.

The second area of concern turns on the relationship between the "distinct society" (and "fundamental characteristic") interpretive clause and the Canadian Charter of Rights and Freedoms. Section 16 of the Accord, in exempting sections 25 and 27 of the Charter, section 35 of the 1982 Constitution Act, and class 24 of section 19 of the British North America Act from interpretation "in a manner consistent with" section 2 of the Accord, obviously leaves the rest of the Charter subject to section 2. That means, at least potentially, that those rights and freedoms, which are the foundation of Canadian citizenship, may vary from one part of Canada to another if, in some way, "preserving" our "fundamental characteristic" or "preserving and promoting" Quebec's distinct identity appears to require it. Attention has frequently, and rightly, been drawn to the impact that this interpretive requirement may have on the "sexual equality" provisions. But that concern should not be allowed to disguise the possibility that "fundamental freedoms," "democratic rights," "legal rights," and "language and educational rights" also fall under this rule of interpretation.

This potential problem is troubling for at least two reasons. First, the Accord's architects, especially Senator Lowell Murray, have claimed on the one hand that rights such as "sexual equality rights" are not subject to this rule of interpretation ("they are not subject to any interpretive disposition"). But at the same time Senator Murray has insisted that the Charter cannot be exempt from the interpretive clause because that "would empty virtually all sense from the distinct society disposition." [19] Are both arguments possible? Surely not.

Second, if we return to Rémillard's moderate set of conditions we note that he not only indicated the Quebec government's willingness to accept the full application of the Charter, "a document that we can be proud of as Quebecers and Canadians," but he never once suggested that the concept of "distinct society" should be applied to its interpretation, since his party's platform had asked only that the phrase be included in the constitution's preamble. The shift in positions at Meech Lake has never been explained.

To the extent that the interpretive clause (section 2) could potentially vary the character of Canadian citizenship rights, it is unacceptable. Mr. Justice Lucien Cannon's judgement in the *Alberta Press* case (1937) remains as convincing now as it was nearly sixty years ago. He stated:

Every inhabitant of Alberta is a citizen of the Dominion. The province may deal with the property and civil rights of a local and private nature within the province, but the province cannot interfere with his status as a Canadian citizen and his fundamental right to express freely his untrammelled opinion about government policies and discussion of matters of public concern.[20]

It is, of course, easier to identify the problems created by the lack of definition in the "distinct society" clause than it is to arrive at a formula that would both clarify the clause and win the consent necessary for the Accord's approval. The Accord's supporters have concluded that the only acceptable solution is to leave the matter to the courts. That seems nothing less than an abdication of responsibility. Terms like "fundamental characteristic," "distinct society," and "distinct identity" are not legal terms; rather, they are sociological and psychological. They are, presumably, statements about the shape and values of a community. Those statements require definition by the elected representatives of a democratic society. As Professor Léon Dion has written: "Rather than leave to the courts the responsibility of deciding all of these judicial issues on the basis of particular cases, let us rather ask our legislators to have the courage to define the objectives of this society before Quebec and the whole of Canada."[21] To do less than that almost certainly assures continuing controversy over precisely the issue the Meech Lake Accord claims to settle, namely, the status of Quebec and of the Francophone community within Canada.

But what alternatives exist? One possible approach would be to amend section 16 to exempt the whole of the Charter from the vague conditions described in section 2. Having done so, a more specific constitutional provision dealing with Quebec's powers in the language field should be devised to increase the province's control in that sensitive area. Such a clause would fulfil Rémillard's Mont Gabriel goal: "We wish to assure English-speaking Quebecers of the linguistic rights to which they have rights. These rights obviously must be situated in the context of the French-speaking character of Quebec society and the strong desire of the government to assure its full flowering."[22]

The adoption of this strategy would remove some of the objections to the Accord that have been heard in Quebec and elsewhere, for it would clarify some of the ambiguity of the "distinct society" clause. And by increasing Quebec's power over language policy it would go a step beyond the original conditions set by the current Quebec government.

In conclusion, I would simply reiterate my essential concern. As it stands in the Constitutional Accord of 1987 the "distinct society" clause may mean much or nothing. If it means much, we need to know how much. If it means nothing, we should think again. Otherwise Professor Daniel Latouche may be right that "in 50 years time the only thing which will distinguish Quebec will be a clause affirming that difference."[23] Or to return to Alice, we might recall Humpty Dumpty's complaint that he would not recognize Alice at a future meeting since her face was just like everyone else's. He continued:

"Now if you had two eyes on the same side of the nose, for instance, or the mouth at the top – that would be *some* help."

"It wouldn't look nice," Alice objected. But Humpty Dumpty only shut his eyes and said "Wait till you've tried."

Once defined, the "distinct society" may not "look nice," but it will be recognizable. And that, in my view, would make the constitution understandable without the aid of a looking glass.

TWELVE

Cultural Nationalism in Canada

"Have we survived?
"If so, what happens after Survival?
Margaret Atwood, *Survival*

"What in heaven's name do we have to do in Canada to prove to the
world that we are not hick nationalists? We are in the vanguard of
internationalism and have been for some time. . . . We stand next to no
one in the wholesale abandonment of a national culture and far from
lamenting the loss, no one even waved good-bye because we were so
busy saying hello to its replacement. . . . Canada in the throes of
nationalism? Don't make me laugh. It is in the throes of nothing.
As usual."
John Fraser in *The Globe and Mail*, June 19, 1976

"Continentalism is treason."
S.M. Crean, *Who's Afraid of Canadian Culture?*

I

"THE VERY WORD Americanization is a challenge to us; for though
we are Canadians, we also live in America," a leading Canadian
novelist remarked in 1929. "Are we going to allow ourselves to be
identified with that tendency of our neighbours to the south which
bids fair to recast the established values of life? The fight is on
between the ancient ideals of Europe and those of this new America
which is asserting itself from day to day."[1] Frederick Philip Grove
expressed here a dilemma that has never ceased to puzzle both
Canadians and foreigners who have attempted to make sense of
Canadian culture. What values, those inherited from Europe or
those developed in response to North American conditions, should

characterize Canadian life? And would either of these alternatives assure the growth of an indigenous Canadian culture, one dominated by neither the standards of Europe nor those of the United States?

In the almost unending discussion of this dilemma the meaning of the word "culture" has never been entirely clear. Not surprisingly perhaps, for, as Raymond Williams has observed, culture "is one of the two or three most complicated words in the English language."[2] For some it has quite obviously meant "high culture" – music, art, literature, and philosophy. But more frequently it has meant something broader, vaguer, and more emotional: a set of social values or a way of life. That latter sense of culture is the one intended by nationalists at least since Herder at the end of the eighteenth century developed the idea of separate cultures rather than one culture or civilization. In contemporary Canada there can be no doubt that cultural nationalists, whether discussing education, broadcasting, painting, or literature, are using the term "culture" in a very broad sense. Evidence of this contention is close at hand. Margaret Atwood's *Survival*, though presented as a thematic guide to Canadian literature, is in fact a quest for the meaning of the entire Canadian experience.[3] In that, she is following in a track set out by many Canadian historians over several generations.[4] The debate about foreign professors in Canadian universities or the impact of American social science methodology has always been couched in terms of Canadian values as contrasted with "internationalist" or "imperialist" values.[5] A similar anxiety runs through a recent socio-economic study of the corporate structure of the Canadian economy,[6] as it does in a rather clumsy nationalist-Marxist attempt to reinterpret the history of Canadian art.[7] Even some Canadian writers on sport, especially the national sport of hockey, discuss their subject in the context of a Canadian culture. ("If we cannot save hockey we cannot save Canada," Bruce Kidd and John Macfarlane claim dramatically.)[8] Finally, and in a somewhat confused fashion, a book entitled *Who's Afraid of Canadian Culture?*, while focusing on cultural institutions, is preoccupied with the value system, the way of life, that those institutions allegedly fail to reflect and sustain.[9]

The fact is, then, that Canadian cultural nationalists are rarely concerned with simple or specific questions such as the percentage of foreign art gallery curators in Canada, the amount of advertising revenue scooped up by the Canadian edition of *Reader's Digest*, or the volume of American-produced cable TV that is beamed into

Canada. These things are symbols of what is more basic – the challenge of Americanization. Or in a more positive sense, Canadian cultural nationalists want to preserve, or develop, a set of Canadian social or cultural values that will guarantee our distinctiveness from the United States. Once that is understood, it is not difficult to comprehend the cultural nationalist's conviction that state intervention, direction, and even ownership must be seen as fundamental to the whole process of differentiating Canada from the United States. It is not merely that the state alone has the resources necessary to finance cultural survival, though that is important, it is also that a statist or socialist approach to culture would in itself be evidence that Canadian culture is different from the free-enterprise culture of the United States. Though expressed more frequently in recent years than in the past, this view is hardly a new one. Indeed, its clearest expression came in 1932 when Graham Spry, a leading supporter of a publicly owned broadcasting system in Canada, told a parliamentary committee:

> Why are the American interests so interested in the Canadian situation? The reason is clear. In the first place, the American chains have regarded Canada as part of their field and consider Canada as in a state of radio tutelage, without talent, resources or capacity to establish a third chain on this continent. . . . In the second place, if such a Canadian non-commercial chain were constructed, it would seriously weaken the whole advertising basis of Canadian broadcasting. The question before this Committee is whether Canada is to establish a chain that is owned and operated and controlled by Canadians, or whether it is to be owned and operated by commercial organizations associated with or controlled by American interests. *The question is, the State or the United States?*[10]

The history of Canada for the last century or more has, in part, been an attempt to nurture a distinctive culture, in the broad sense of that term. Indeed, it has probably been believed by people concerned about such questions that only when Canada had developed a distinctive way of life, or culture in a broad sense, would it produce culture in the more restricted sense of works of imagination and intellect. In view of this fact, it is perhaps useful to take a brief historical look at the discussion of the nature of the Canadian culture or identity. Until fairly recently that discussion turned on the not always very precise distinction that Frederick Philip Grove was attempting to draw when he counterpoised "Europe" and "America." Was Canada's true culture to be found in preserving inherited "Europeanness" or in developing its "North Americanness"?

II

There was a time, not so many years ago, when to speak of Canada as a North American nation was viewed, at least in some quarters, as a heresy. In 1933 John W. Dafoe, editor of the *Winnipeg Free Press*, delivered a series of lectures at Columbia University in New York, which were subsequently published under the title, *Canada: An American Nation.* He worried somewhat about the problem of a title for reasons he explained in a letter to a friend. "As a general title," he wrote, "I have had from such thought as I have been able to give to it, no luck. If I thought Mexico would not regard it as a *casus belli*, I might suggest 'North America's Other Democracy.' 'America's Other Democracy' is more accurate but very flat. 'Canada – A North American Democracy' might earn me a lambasting from my imperialistic friends, but I am hardened to this usage."[11]

Dafoe was here engaged in a polemical practice with a long and honoured tradition among nationalists in Canada: branding people whose conception of Canada differed from his with a pejorative tag. The dirtiest word in his vocabulary was "imperialist," a description Dafoe applied to virtually anyone who did not wish to see Canada's relations with Great Britain defined in exactly the fashion that he did. These people, usually loyal Canadian nationalists themselves, would, of course, have replied in kind, denying to those who thought like Dafoe the worthy title of "nationalist" and branding him a "continentalist." These three terms "nationalist," "imperialist," and "continentalist" have a fairly long history in Canadian political usage. Sometimes they have been used as terms of abuse, but at others they have been uttered as compliments. If the word "internationalist" is added to them, and it, too, has been a term of both denigration and approbation, a good deal of Canadian political discourse could be analysed. I do not wish to enter into a long analysis of historical semantics at this point, but some discussion of the past is necessary if any serious attempt is to be made to assess the concept of Canada as a North American nation.

Dafoe's term, "Canada: An American Nation," was a minor heresy in the 1930s and would still be to some Canadians today because of their conviction that an earlier term, one enshrined in our constitution, was more proper and accurate. That term was

"British North America." Throughout most of the nineteenth century, and probably down to the end of the Great War, most English-speaking Canadians would have unhesitatingly asserted that their country, while North American in geography and in many of its material characteristics, was nevertheless British in its cultural and political traditions. There can be no doubt that by the time of Confederation, and certainly in the three or four decades afterwards, a national consciousness was developing among English-speaking Canadians. It expressed itself in, among other ways, a desire for Canada to achieve a status of greater equality with Great Britain, but within a united British Empire. It was this determination to achieve nationhood without rupturing the sacred unity of the Empire that caused later generations of Canadian nationalists to condemn these British North American nationalists as "imperialists." The Grants and Parkins and Denisons and Leacocks who wrote and spoke so eloquently about Canada's national aspirations within the British Empire in the thirty years before Versailles were, as Professor Carl Berger has so effectively shown, a variety of Canadian nationalist.[12] Both Sir John A. Macdonald and Sir Robert Borden understood what these men were talking about and, to some degree, shaped their policies in keeping with similar assumptions.

Nor were these men mere sentimentalists yearning for a piece of the action in an age of the British Empire's ascendancy. No doubt, of course, there was something of this. But more important was their assessment both of the meaning of Canada's historical experience and of her strategic position in North America. First of all, nineteenth-century Canadians were convinced that what differentiated them from the United States was that they had preserved British political institutions and adapted them to the needs of the North American environment. They believed that their evolutionary history was superior to the revolutionary experience of their southern neighbours. They further believed that the evolutionary and conservative record of the past was a good guide to the future. By preserving those British traditions they could move toward nationhood gradually, modifying but never rejecting Canada's relationship with Great Britain. Thus Canada could avoid many of the problems they felt characterized the turbulent republic to the south.

Moreover, the preservation of the imperial tie had important strategic implications. A small country like Canada, standing in such close proximity to the United States, always lived under the threat of absorption. It must always be remembered that the nine-teenth-century experience of Canadians included several bitter memories of relations with the United States: the War of 1812, a long series of border disputes, the ruptured relations of the Civil War years, and the inflated claims of the United States at the Washington Conference in 1871. In the nineteenth century that famous undefended frontier had yet to be discovered. [13] The very existence of Canada, most nineteenth-century Canadians realized, was an anti-American fact. And for the preservation of that fact the association with Great Britain obviously had to be maintained. The British garrisons in Canada and the British Navy on the seas provided Canada's major military defence. These, of course, were defences of last resort; Canadians already believed that their best defence lay in Anglo-American amity.

Finally, it should never be forgotten that until the First World War Canada relied heavily on British capital, technology, and markets in developing her industrial and agricultural economy. Many of the largest developmental projects in Canada – the CPR, for example – were financed with the aid of British capital. In 1914, 75 cent of all foreign capital in Canada came from British sources. Nor should one ignore the fact that the greatest source of immigration to Canada during the nineteenth century was the British Isles. Thus, the close relationship with Britain that was implied in the concept of Canada as a "British North American nation" was based on strategic and material factors as well as historic and sentimental reasons.

By the end of the century, however, perceptible changes were already beginning to take place. Indeed, even during the nineteenth century, it seems almost unnecessary to remark, a significant element in the Canadian population already thought of itself as essentially North American and displayed a rather detached attitude toward Great Britain. These, of course, were the French-speaking Canadians who were British subjects neither by birth or political tradition nor to any great extent by economic interest. They were British subjects by conquest. This is not to suggest that they were anti-British. Indeed, they tended to look on the British as generous conquerors who had, after a struggle, permitted them to remain themselves. Their tradition was strongly monarchist and they saw the value of British support in preserving Canada's separate status in North America. Though it was not always so, the French Canadians' loyalty to the British Empire should have been unquestioned provided it was understood that their responsibilities to that

Empire related exclusively to the defence and development of that part of the Empire in which they lived.

Those who did not understand this fact should have learned it from the Boer War experience, though most did not. While English Canadians like Principal Grant of Queen's University or John Willison of the Toronto *Globe* could, from their assumptions, logically argue that Canadian participation in South Africa was a Canadian national responsibility, few French Canadians could have agreed. Neither Henri Bourassa nor Sir Wilfrid Laurier saw it that way, though Laurier was eventually forced to find a middle position – "limited participation in the Boer War, but not necessarily participation in all Imperial Wars." What the French Canadian, who had no ties with France comparable to those of English Canadians with Britain, was really saying in 1899 was that Canada, despite membership in the Empire, was a North American nation. While many English-speaking Canadians wished to see Canada's national status affirmed by the assumption of greater responsibility within the Empire, for the French Canadian, Canada gained national status by rejecting those responsibilities and affirming her autonomous status as a nation in North America. Armand Lavergne, a rising officer in Henri Bourassa's nationalist army, spoke for a long and well-established tradition when he told the Canadian Military Institute in 1910: "Now I wish you to understand that although the French Canadians may differ with you in many ways and means on the subject of 'National Defence', there is one thing you must not forget, and that is, that the spirit of the French Canadians is the same today as in 1775 and 1812. The Nationalists of Quebec today are willing and ready to give their last drop of blood for the defence of the British flag and British institutions in this country." And he concluded, in case any of his enthusiastic audience had missed the point about "in this country," by asserting that, "We are loyal just as you are, but we understand that our duty as Canadians, and as part of the Empire is to build up a strong Canada by preparing in Canada a strong national defence."[14]

After 1900 several new factors entered the equation on what might be called the North American side. In the first place it had never been true that all English Canadians accepted British North American assumptions about Canada. Some, notably such Liberals as Edward Blake and Richard Cartwright, had begun to argue in the 1880s for closer relations with the United States, hoping to renegotiate the reciprocal trade agreement the United States had abrogated in 1866. Even Sir John A. Macdonald, a British North American always, had never shown any enthusiasm for the formal schemes of imperial federation that were frequently discussed. Then the decision of the Alaska Boundary Dispute in 1903 was interpreted by many Canadians as a betrayal of Canada's interests by Britain – and that only a few years after Canada had responded so gallantly to Britain's call for aid in South Africa.

To this was added the weight of a vast new immigrant population that arrived in Canada between 1900 and 1914. Only about one-third of these people came from the British Isles, with the majority moving from the United States or Europe. It could not be expected that many of these newcomers would have any powerful sentimental attachment to Great Britain – many may have had the opposite feeling, wanting to leave Europe behind them. In any event, these people, who formed a large segment of the newly opened Canadian West, became a sympathetic audience for those who argued for the affirmation of Canada's North American character. That explains why some leading British-Canadian nationalists, including Stephen Leacock, were immigration restrictionists.

A further factor, which before 1914 was only beginning to be felt, was the changing character of the Canadian economy. While British investment, largely in the form of bonds and loans, remained dominant,[15] American investment was growing. Moreover, as several observers noted at the time, U.S. investment was different: it was not in the form of bonds and loans, it was direct investment that carried ownership and control with it, and these investments frequently took place in sectors of the Canadian economy – natural resources, in particular – where major markets were to be found most frequently in the United States. It is one of the unfortunate ironies of Canadian economic policy in the years between Confederation and the Great War that many of the measures designed to develop and protect a Canadian national economy, and to create jobs at home for Canadians, had the effect of encouraging U.S. investors to move directly into Canada either to escape the effects of the Canadian tariff against the United States or to gain the advantages of the British preference.[16] While the shift from an economy oriented toward Britain and Europe to one oriented toward U.S. markets and capital was not completed until the 1920s, the trend was already becoming evident by 1914.[17]

As U.S. capital moved into Canada, so, too, did American labour organizations, specifically the AFL. These unions came, frequently on the invitation of Canadian workers, to help in the formation of unions and to win better wages and working conditions for Canadians. Their contribution was substantial. But it is also true that they brought with them the Gompers pattern and philosophy of union organization and gradually took control of the Trades and Labour Congress of Canada. After 1902 with the triumph of the AFL unions in the TLC, the Canadian union movement became, from the perspective of AFL headquarters in Washington, just another "state federation of labour." Here was the beginning of the fragmentation of the Canadian labour movement, which might have developed along an east-west axis but was, like the Canadian economy itself, shifting in a continentalist direction.[18] In the 1930s the story was repeated, with some variations in the field of industrial unions. The CIO union organizers, who had plenty to keep them busy in the United States, came to Canada with considerable reluctance. But once they came they rapidly established their dominance. By 1950, in the words of Pat Conroy, the secretary-treasurer of the Canadian Congress of Labour, the CCL had been reduced "to the status of a satellite organization."[19] Thus, a major institution of a modern industrial society – the trade union movement – had become very much North American and indeed continentalist in its orientation. One consequence of this development, though it is also attributable to other causes, was the emergence of a separate union movement among a large number of French-Canadian workers – the Catholic syndicate, now known as the CSN or CNTU.[20] From the viewpoint of the workers, of course, these developments may have been a necessary response to their most immediate needs. But from the perspective of the trade union movement as an institution of national integration the implications are obvious enough.

It is interesting to note that the story of farmers' organizations in Canada is a rather different one. There has, of course, been fragmentation here between the Canadian Council of Agriculture, for example, with its provincial sections, and the Union Catholique des Cultivateurs. So, too, the influence of American ideas on Canadian agricultural movements, from the Grange to co-operativism, has been extensive.[21] But Canadian farmers, while willing to learn from their American counterparts, have always preserved their independence. Perhaps the reason is that Canadian agriculture developed in competition with United States agricultural products, while the industrial and natural resources component of the Canadian economy has developed more as an adjunct to its southern counterpart.

Beyond agricultural and labour organizations every democratic society spawns a multiplicity of voluntary organizations: professional, social, intellectual, and athletic. Whether these are organizations of medical doctors, Kiwanians, political scientists, or hockey players, they can play a role in national integration. There are very few studies of such organizations in Canada but a necessarily superficial observation suggests that many of these organizations have become continental in direction rather than simply Canada-wide. Kinsmen and Rotary Clubs are examples; the Canadian Clubs are not. The Canadian Historical Association is independent, but many historians in Canada do not belong to it or, for a variety of reasons, also belong to, say, the American Historical Association. The same is probably true of political scientists, physicists, architects, and teachers of language and literature. In any final assessment of continental influence in Canada a full study of these voluntary organizations would have to be made. Such associations could conceivably be as significant as, for example, the direction in which the Canadian economy or foreign affairs outlook has developed. My guess would be, and it is only a guess, that these informal associations between Canada and the United States have rapidly grown since 1914 while similar contacts with Britain and Europe have probably declined.

Even before World War One there was already considerable concern about the Americanization process that was perceived to be taking place. The periodicals of the time carried numerous articles with such titles as "The Effect of the American Invasion," "Our Industrial Invasion of Canada," and "The Americanization of the Canadian Northwest."[22] J. Castell Hopkins, a prolific writer and ardent exponent of closer imperial unity, described the situation in this way in 1908:

If the bosom of the future should hold a destiny of Canada apart from the British Empire, if the cherished ideal of loyal British peoples around the globe should never be realized and separation rather than closer union become a fact, it will be due in no small measure to the present day Americanization of Canadian thought, Canadian habits, Canadian literature and the Canadian press. By this I do not mean the creation of an annexation sentiment. Indeed, the process I referred to is going on side by side with the growth of still more vigorous opposition to continental union. It is rather the gradual but steady development of a non-British view of things; a situation in

which public opinion here regarding the heart of the Empire and
Imperial policy is formed along the lines of United States opinion,
and, therefore of an alien viewpoint.[23]

Most English Canadians would probably have agreed that Canada was a British country in the years before 1914, but that assertion
of Canadian Britishness sometimes had a curious twist. Howard
Ferguson, whose logic was by no means his strongest suit, used this
interesting argument in attacking French-language schools in
Ontario in a speech in 1911. "This is a British country and we must
maintain it as such if we are to maintain the high destiny that Providence intended for Canada," he told his constituents. "The bilingual system encourages the isolation of races. It impresses the mind
of youth with the idea of race distinction and militates against the
fusion of the various elements that make up our population. . . . The
experience of the United States where their national school system
recognizes but one language simply proves the wisdom of the system."[24] Was Ferguson saying that the best way to remain British
was to adopt American educational policies? (Lord Durham had
once warned of this element in English-Canadian thinking. "Lower
Canada must be *English* at the expense, if necessary, of not being
British," he reported an informant as having told him.[25]) That was
what Henri Bourassa detected: "thanks to the campaign against the
French language the English provinces are becoming Americanized rapidly," he claimed in 1916. "Toronto the loyal, Toronto the
royal. Yankee Toronto, Yankee in its tastes, Yankee in its habits –
those who protest their loyalty loudest are least loyal at heart."[26]

During the age of Laurier much of the political controversy in
both domestic and external affairs had turned on the highly emotional question of the essential character of Canada: British or
North American. The inconclusive debate over imperial defence
was fundamentally a discussion of that issue. So, too, was the
perennial question of some form of reciprocal trade agreement with
the United States. In English Canada, the British Canadians were
doubtless predominant intellectually: the Grants, Parkins,
Leacocks, and Macphails. But their position of pre-eminence was
increasingly challenged by the Ewarts, Dafoes, and Skeltons of the
North American school. And French Canadians had long since
opted for North America. It took that perceptive Frenchman André
Siegfried to raise the fundamental question just at the time that
Europe was collapsing into war in the autumn of 1914. "American

habits, British loyalty!" Siegfried wrote. "The entire problem of Canada's future seems to me to be summarized in these two terms. Is it possible that a Dominion which is American in its way of life can remain attached to Britain?"[27]

The Great War, 1914-18, in which Canada participated with such effectiveness, at such enormous cost, is the pivotal event in the transformation of Canada from a British North American to an American nation. There is no doubt that in September, 1914, the British North Americans carried the day. Just as the American nation to the south had few reasons to doubt that its interests were best served by remaining isolated from the European war, the British North American nation in the north was equally convinced that its responsibility was best expressed in Laurier's "Ready, Aye Ready." J.W. Dafoe, a westerner with an increasingly North American outlook, favoured unlimited participation. Henri Bourassa, a consistent critic of Canadian involvement in imperial affairs, was prepared to go along, though not in an unlimited fashion. Yet as the war dragged on, bringing increasingly high casualty rates, profound internal divisions, and frequent irritations with British conduct of the war, a growing number of Canadians appeared to have had serious doubts about too intimate relations with the Empire and Europe. Moreover, once the United States entered the war, old animosities, which had already been disappearing, seemed to vanish. It was Sir Robert Borden, for instance, who is often viewed as an "imperialist" working for closer imperial ties, who moved unsuccessfully to establish the first Canadian diplomatic representation at Washington. It was also Borden who expressed himself before the Imperial War Cabinet in 1918 in a profoundly North American fashion. "Future good relations between ourselves and the United States were, as he had said before, the best asset we could bring home from the war. . . . He wished . . . to make it clear that if the future policy of the British Empire meant working in co-operation with some European nation as against the United States, that policy could not reckon on the approval or support of Canada."[28] Borden was here expressing a sentiment that perhaps most Canadians, irrespective of party or ethnic background, would have accepted. Certainly it was the underlying assumption of Canadian foreign policy between the wars, whether that policy was set by Arthur Meighen on the matter of the Anglo-Japanese Alliance in 1921, by R.B. Bennett during the Manchurian crisis of 1931, or by Mackenzie King from Chanak in 1922 to Munich in 1938. And of their critics, those who preached internationalism, like J.W. Dafoe, were probably less influential than those who, like J.S. Woodsworth and Henri Bourassa, called for a more thoroughgoing isolationism.

North American isolationism, which meant drawing closer to the United States, aroused few fears among Canadians. The United States had been our ally during the Great War and that seemed to erase all the lingering fears of "manifest destiny" and the "big stick." Sir William Peterson, principal of McGill University and a long-time imperialist, expressed the new spirit when the Americans entered the war in 1917. "It has also done something," he wrote in that confident rhetoric so characteristic of university presidents, "to consolidate the interests of the English-speaking peoples, and to hasten the day when a mutual understanding between Britain and America will bring with it an effectual guarantee for the peace and prosperity of all mankind."[29] That sentiment was to prevail after the war. Few Canadians would have taken seriously Archibald MacMechan's article in an early number of the *Canadian Historical Review* in 1920, entitled "Canada as a Vassal State." In seven pages he summed up all the ways in which Canada had become bound to the United States – everything from investment and sport to chewing gum and Mother's Day was attributed to American influence. And here is what he said about Canadian universities at a date when hardly an American professor had yet stepped across the border. "The curriculum, text-books, methods of teaching, oversight of students, 'credits' are borrowed from the United States. Organization and administration are on the American Model. Among the students, American ideas prevail."[30] If MacMechan was right, most Canadians probably would have responded by asking for more. And that is what they got, whether they asked for it or not.

Canada's withdrawal from the Empire-Commonwealth – for that in fact was what it was – into fortress North America was partly the result of revulsion against Europe and its bloody battlefields. It was also the consequence of the conviction that Canada's internal problems, both developmental policies and the restoration of national unity, had to be given first priority. And finally, it reflected the further evolution of those trends in the Canadian economy that had already been evident before 1914. If a symbolic date is needed to mark the change, the year 1926 would be better than most.

There are many reasons for choosing this date, most of them well known. But there is a reason less often remarked upon, but which is very deserving of consideration. An important cultural event revealed with great clarity the temper of the times: in 1926 a journalist named F.B. Housser published a book entitled *A Canadian Art Movement: The Story of the Group of Seven*. Housser's book is a vibrant expression of Canadian cultural nationalism, and it marks the apotheosis of the Group of Seven. In 1926 the Group was still basking in the warmth of its reception at the famous Wembley Exhibition of 1924. That had been a dual triumph. Not only had the Group's work received lavish praise from the English critics, but their very presence at the Exhibition marked the triumph of the new artists over the traditionalist and European-oriented painters of the Royal Canadian Academy.[31] Housser's task was to delineate the elements of the nationalism the Group so consciously sought to create. The job was not too difficult, for several of the painters, notably A.Y. Jackson, Arthur Lismer, and Lawren Harris, had frequently explained their conception of Canadian nationalism. But Housser succeeded perhaps better than any of them had ever done:

> Our British and European connection in fact, so far as creative expression in Canada is concerned, has been a millstone about our neck. . . . As long as Canada regarded herself artistically as a mere outpost of Europe; so long as her painters elected for voluntary mediocrity by the mental admission that Canadians possessed no potentialities with which to create a culture as good or better than Europe's; so long was our 20th Century born spirit of independence voiceless. . . . For Canada to find a complete racial expression of herself through art, a complete break with European traditions was necessary; a new type of artist was required, a type with sufficient creative equipment to initiate of its own through handling new materials by new methods and what was required more than technique was a deep-rooted love of the country's natural environment. . . . The message that the Group of Seven art movement gives to this age is the message that here in the North has arisen a young nation with faith in its own creative genius.[32]

Housser quite accurately saw that the Group of Seven was a painters' movement that had turned its back on Europe. Canadian painting had to be about Canada. Both form and content had to be distinctive. And so the "Hot Mush School" was born. The school's triumph over adversity was certainly much easier than Housser allowed, and it was complete by 1926. Indeed, it might be argued that the Group's triumph at Wembley in 1924 was at least as revealing of what was happening to Canada as was Mackenzie King's success in 1923 at the Imperial Conference. The message of the Group was simply that culturally Canada was a North American nation. These new painters had come, in Lawren Harris's words, "to realize how far this country of Canada was different in character, atmosphere, moods, and spirit from Europe and the old land."[33] What F.B. Housser did was to provide the Group with one of the elements necessary to any nationalist movement: a history.

Since politics imitates art, it is not surprising that 1926 is better known as the date marking some events of a more prosaic character than the triumph of the Group of Seven. The first of these is the Balfour Declaration, which provided the theoretical explanation for the autonomy of the dominions within the British Commonwealth. The dominions were now recognized as nations in the traditional sense of having the right to control fully both internal and external policies. For Canada, however, the date has another perhaps more profound, though frequently ignored, significance. After 1926 American investment in Canada exceeded British investment, and Canada's major economic axis was moving increasingly in a north-south direction.[34]

The shift in the source and kind of foreign investment did not pass unobserved in 1926. Bank publications and the *Financial Post* took note of the change. *Canadian Forum*, which in the inter-war years was the intellectual organ of the North American trend in Canadian nationalism, published a sober analysis entitled "The Penetration of American Capital in Canada." The author, J. Margorie Van derHoek, was interested not only in the economic aspects of this development but also in the potential political consequences. Though fully aware of Scott Nearing's arguments for the view that the flag follows investment, Van derHoek rejected them:

> In the first place the Dominion is not a backward country peopled by a race indifferent to the development of their country; but, on the contrary, an energetic nation of ambitious thrifty people. The government is stable, the people politically minded and not the dupes or blind followers of vain leaders. In the second place, although Canada is not a power of the first rank itself, yet it is part of the British Empire and thus enjoys the prestige and strength of Great Britain. This nullifies any idea of annexation of Canada by force. There is still the possibility that American capital may secretly buy up the newspapers, endow the churches and universities, and begin a careful education of the public to the idea that annexation to the United

States would be the course for best development. . . . But the loyalty to the British connection, which is so striking and refreshing a feature of Canadian history, would act as an effective counter weight to such propaganda unless this country was in the midst of severe economic distress.[35]

Three months after these lines were published, in November, 1926, the first Canadian minister was appointed to Washington, something that those who thought of themselves as British North Americans had long resisted.[36]

Given these developments it is perhaps not too unfair to suggest that another event during these years was more than a mere coincidence. This concerns a radical alteration in military strategic thought. Since the military establishment was small, the importance of this development should not be exaggerated. But it is of interest. In 1920, Colonel J. Sutherland Brown was appointed Director of Military Operations and Intelligence. "Buster" Brown may be taken as an illustration of the adage that military men are always fighting the last war – in this instance, the War of 1812. In any case, as Professor Eayrs has pointed out, Brown's Defence Scheme No. 1 argued that strategic planning should be based on the assumption that the major military threat to Canadian security came from the United States. Whatever significance was attached to Defence Scheme No. 1, it lapsed into obsolescence with Brown's transfer to another post in 1927 and was officially cancelled in 1931.[37] Here was a clear sign of the times, and one that revealed some important assumptions about the "fireproof house" theory of Canadian security that prevailed in the inter-war years.

Another university president, this time from Toronto, perhaps best summed up the spirit abroad in Canada by the mid-twenties. Sir Robert Falconer, in a series of lectures delivered in England in 1925 under the title of *The United States as a Neighbour*, explained effectively the basis of the close relations that existed between Canada and the United States. Canada, in effect, had become a northern extension of the Republic, and that seemed a happy enough circumstance to Falconer. After all, "Americans of Anglo-Saxon origin and English-speaking Canadians are more alike than any other separate people." That, of course, left out a lot of Americans, to say nothing at all of nearly 50 per cent of Canadians! Economics, geography, and communications had drawn the two nations together, and American education, especially graduate education, was enormously important to Canada: "It is from the American university chiefly," the Toronto president remarked, "that this health giving influence is coming in like a refreshing breeze." Nor could his series end without a rhetorical flourish about the mission of Canada. Once more Canada's special place in cementing the moral unity of the English-speaking world was trotted out. It may sound platitudinous now, but once that was a mission that made Canadians proud, for it was the essence of their nationalism: it gave Canada a uniqueness that, at the same time, could serve all mankind:

> A review of the history of the relations between the United States and Canada affords encouragement to those who believe that a better day will come for the world when all the branches of the English-speaking peoples work in sympathy with one another. . . . If ever a new order is to be ushered in, the day will certainly begin with the creation of sympathy between them. For the hastening of such a day Canada, in her history, her character and her position holds a unique privilege and, if she takes advantage of it, the world of the future will judge that she will have played a part given to few nations in the progress of humanity. [38]

No book of Canadian humour should be without a section devoted to the predictions of Canadian nationalists!

Men who thought like Falconer shaped Canadian policy in the inter-war years. Their first assumption was that increasingly the interests of Canada and those of the United States were the same, and that these differed from those of Britain and Europe. The second assumption, one that F.D. Roosevelt and W.L.M. King expressed in speeches at Kingston and Woodbridge, Ontario, in August of 1938, was that the United States would defend Canada against external aggression. Here, then, are the roots of a common North American defence policy.

There is, however, more to the story. As Europe lapsed into war again in the late 1930s Canada was placed in a particularly difficult position. Despite the isolationist mood of the country, many Canadians were prepared to go to war again to fight the Nazis or to aid Britain. This sentiment not only threatened the internal unity of the country but also threatened to disrupt Canadian-American relations, for, as a popular book of the time put it, "Canada compromises America's isolation." [39] These factors, plus a third one, provided the rationale for the heavy Canadian involvement in the North American defence system that has been a foundation of Canadian policy since the Second World War – the Permanent Joint Board on Defence, the Defence Production Sharing Agreements, and NORAD. That third factor, sometimes ignored by critics of the wartime agreements, was that after 1939 both Britain and Canada became convinced that the Axis powers could only be defeated if the United States was brought into the war. Thus, Canada's involvement with the United States must be seen as part of an effort to nudge its southern neighbour into fuller support for the Allied cause. This is what underlay persistent platitudes of Mackenzie King and other Canadians about Canada's role as a "lynchpin" or "bridge" between Britain and the United States. Here the whole theory of the "North Atlantic Triangle" and the "moral unity of the English-speaking world," so dear to Canadians since at least the 1890s, was being worked out in practice.[40] At the end of the war King recorded in his diary words that simply echoed Sir Robert Borden's sentiments of 1918. Returning from England in November, 1945, King observed in his sanctimonious way "that it is hard to believe it is not part of some larger design to help keep the English-speaking peoples together and of furthering international good will at a time when that would seem to be more necessary even than before the beginning of the last Great War."[41]

This Canadian role of bridge has, of course, always been partly a myth. It is true that as long as the United States remained neutral it was possible to act as something of a go-between. But that did not last long and King was probably more realistic when he described his role at the Quebec Conference some years later: "I was, as you recall, not so much a participant in any of the discussions as a sort of general host, whose task at the Citadel was similar to that of the General Manager of the Chateau Frontenac."[42] The fact surely is that the North Atlantic Triangle was never an isosceles – Canada was always a minor leg and by 1945 the British side was also rapidly shrinking. As has frequently been observed, after 1940 Canada, which for twenty years had been affirming its North American character, found itself alone in North America alongside a gigantic American partner that was about to assume the role of policeman in a world passing rapidly from hot to cold war.

The Cold War ensured that the alliance system established during World War Two would be maintained and strengthened. NATO was a multilateral arrangement that helped redress the balance against American might. But in North America multilateralism gave way to bilateralism, with NORAD being added to the earlier arrangements in 1958. Once again Canada set out into a period of massive internal development heavily financed by American direct investment: in 1945 $4.9 billion of American capital were invested in Canada, and that had increased nearly fourfold by 1963. While statistics do not tell the whole story, the Task Force on Foreign Ownership and the Structure of Canadian Industry reported in 1968 that U.S. investors controlled 97 per cent of the capital in the automobile industry, 90 per cent in rubber, 54 per cent in electrical equipment. Foreign, largely U.S. ownership and control reached 62 per cent in mining and smelting and 74 per cent in oil and natural gas.[43] If all business assets are considered, only about 27 per cent were foreign controlled in 1968 and it is at least possible that by the 1970s the percentage had levelled off and may even have been declining.[44]

But investment figures do not tell the whole story. Increasingly, the United States had become the major market for Canadian products, particularly the new mineral and oil staples. And some sections of the Canadian economy, such as the automobile industry, had become fully integrated into a continental system. This, plus the pegged relationship of the Canadian and U.S. dollar, ensured that the Canadian economy became highly sensitive to economic fluctuations within the United States. So close had this relationship become that in 1965 one perceptive, if gloomy, Canadian, Professor George Grant, was prepared to pronounce a lament on the death of Canada gobbled up in continentalism.[45] Three years later, George Ball, one-time Undersecretary in the U.S. State Department, offered a somewhat similar prognostication. He wrote:

Sooner or later, commercial imperatives will bring about the free movement of all goods back and forth across our long border. When that occurs, or even before it does, it will become unmistakably clear that countries with economies inextricably intertwined must also have free movement of the other vital factors of production – capital, services, labour. The result will inevitably be substantial economic integration, which will require for its full realization a progressively expanding area of common political decision.[46]

Nor was this problem an economic one alone. In 1950, the *Report of the Royal Commission on the Arts, Letters and Sciences* warned of the growing impact of American culture on Canada. A similar concern was expressed by the 1957 Royal Commission on Broadcasting. In 1961 the O'Leary Commission on Publications observed that

> . . . the tremendous expansion of communications in the United States has given that nation the world's most penetrating and effective apparatus for the transmission of ideas. Canada, more than any other country is naked to that force, exposed unceasingly to a vast network of communications which reaches to every corner of our land; American words, images and print – the good, the bad, the indifferent – batter unrelentingly at our eyes and ears. [47]

Added to this concern with cultural continentalism have been expressions of anxiety about the substantial percentage of United States citizens who have been employed in Canadian universities, the expanding sector of the Canadian publishing industry taken over by U.S. firms, and American domination of the Canadian sporting scene. [48] By 1970, a growing number of Canadians were prepared to admit that there was a large element of truth in Harold Innis's 1948 remark that Canada had "moved from colony to nation to colony." [49]

The causes of this condition of dependence – some would call it colonialism – are numerous and complex. The easiest attitude is to attribute it to an amorphous, undefined state called "colonial-mindedness." This manifests itself in the belief that others can always do things better than we can and therefore that we Canadians should either copy the initiatives of others, or let them do our tasks for us. That this condition exists cannot be denied, though it is not as widespread as is sometimes suggested in the rhetoric of the most ardent critics of our national inferiority complex. But even to the extent that it does exist, it is less a cause than an effect of our condition.

One of the most obvious reasons for Canadian dependence is simply size and geography: 27.5 million people living beside 255.5 million can hardly expect to be equals, especially when the larger community is as technologically advanced and economically powerful as the United States. Nor is it surprising, given the example of American affluence and power at their doorstep, that many Canadians should both aspire to a similar standard of life and become convinced that the way to achieve it is through adopting American techniques. There is a large element of truth, and irony, in Professor Mel Watkins's argument that even Macdonald's National Policy was copied from an American patent.[50] The difficulty was that without some serious and determined effort to stimulate and develop Canadian capital formation, technological innovation, and entrepreneurship, the adoption of the United States model almost inevitably brought with it the need for American and other foreign parts to make the model work. "High tariffs and lavish railway subsidies expressed the limits of political action," Professor Watkins once remarked, "while, significantly, education, particularly business schools, and freer banking – which might have facilitated the rise of new domestic entrepreneurs – were neglected."[51]

The same proposition might be tested in the context of many other aspects of Canadian life: the military establishment where American weaponry, sometimes of a somewhat obsolete kind, is dominant; the mass media where Disneyland, *Sesame Street*, and *Dallas* make Canadian as well as American cash registers ring; and in Canadian education, where everyone from John Dewey to Jerry Rubin has made an impact. The theme runs through much of John Porter's controversial but penetrating study, *The Vertical Mosaic*. Porter placed special emphasis on the failure of our educational system to keep pace with the "kind of society that has been emerging during the century."[52] Too frequently, when Canadians lacked the skills demanded by modern industrial society, governments have relied upon skilled immigrants, who were relatively cheap, rather than entering into the expensive business of upgrading Canadians through education. Skilled immigrants from the United States have frequently been among the most readily available. (An ironic twist to Porter's argument might be noted in passing. His contention is that the very conservative and status-conscious character that has distinguished us from the upwardly mobile melting pot to the south has forced Canadians to rely on outside initiatives for many of its dynamic developments. In other words, Canada has fallen under American domination because it has not adopted American values!)[53]

The controversy during the 1970s over the large number of foreign citizens who teach in Canadian universities[54] can partly be explained in Porter's terms. The large-scale expansion of higher education in Canada since the 1950s, made necessary by population growth, rising aspirations, and economic demand, was made possible to a considerable extent by the availability of well-trained scholars and teachers from other countries, particularly the United States, where the importance of expensive post-graduate education had long been recognized. The Canadian alternative would have been a massive, and costly, crash program to educate Canadians, and even this would have necessitated sending many Canadians abroad for specialized education. Instead, the undergraduate bulge came first, followed only later by a modest expansion of graduate education. To fill the gap Canadian universities employed a large number of foreign professors. Today we have relatively large graduate programs educating qualified Canadians at a time when undergraduate numbers are levelling off or declining, and when educational expenditures are increasingly resented by the taxpayer. The result is a growing number of frustrated, underemployed Canadians unable to find university positions. This has been followed by cutbacks in expenditures in graduate education. When, and if, the next bulge comes in higher education we will doubtless again be found frantically searching abroad for more professors. [55]

Whatever side one took in the controversy over foreign professors in our universities, it is difficult to escape two conclusions. First, the situation was one of our own making, and it was made for reasons that appeared good, or at least necessary, at the time. Second, what has happened in our universities illustrates, in microcosm, a process that has taken place in many segments of Canadian society. The desire to keep up with our affluent neighbour, combined with the unwillingness or inability to pay the price, has meant increased dependence on the United States. There is, after all, no such thing as a free lunch.

There are obviously many other reasons for the growing continental influence on Canada. Many economists, including those who composed the Report of the Watkins Task Force, have criticized the structure of Canadian industry and public policies governing the industrial sector of the economy. Tariffs, anti-trust policies, and certain features of our tax laws have reduced competitive performance and encouraged foreign takeovers. Then, too, there is the difficulty Canadian businessmen sometimes experience in obtaining funds for expansion – funds more readily available to prospective United States buyers who have the strong backing of giant multinational assets. [56] Finally, there is the often decried, but never fully explained, conservatism of Canadian investors who apparently favour blue-chip stocks in the United States to riskier Canadian ventures.

Canadians have worried about this drift toward continentalism for many years: the concern is almost as old as the country itself.[57] Royal commission has followed royal commission, and these in turn have been followed by task forces, parliamentary investigations, and endless debate. But whether for ideological reasons, lack of will, conflicting vested interests, varying regional needs, or just plain lack of imagination, only a few definite policies have emerged out of the clouds of rhetoric. A CBC, a CRTC, a Canada Council, and even a Canada Development Corporation have been put in place. The impact of these institutions, though important, is hardly the equal to the vast and apparently attractive power of continental drift. In a society like Canada, which is still gripped by an ideology of developmentalism and growthmanship, perhaps the drift is inevitable – especially when significant segments of our population have yet to experience the advantages of the affluent society.

All that being said, and perhaps even partly explained in the calm manner that becomes an historian, one pertinent fact remains: with Canada having become a North American nation, a large number of Canadians are unhappy or at least uneasy. They now realize that simply casting off European encumbrances has not resulted in the emergence of a distinctly Canadian culture. Indeed, there is more than a suspicion that becoming North American has meant becoming American – or almost. Canadian Senate committees are rarely alarmist, yet one such committee studying the mass media concluded in 1970 that: "Cultural survival is perhaps the most critical problem our generation of Canadians will have to face, and it may be it can be achieved by using all the means at our command."[58]

Many Canadians, though it is impossible to say how many, share that opinion, though there are differences about the nature and disposition of "the means at our command." Yet one thing seems fairly certain: Canadians are anxious to make their own decisions about the future development of their culture and polity. Making your own decisions, after all, is itself an evidence of a distinctive national culture. And that explains why many Canadians resented the assumption underlying the comment, doubtless made with friendly intent, by Thomas Enders, the then U.S. ambassador to Canada, to the effect that "Canadians want to be less dependent, less focused upon the U.S. *We* encourage them in that. But *we want them* to do it in a positive way– by building new ties with other countries rather than just loosening their ties with us."[59]

The wellspring of cultural nationalism in Canada has always been the desire to make our own judgements about what is best for us, about what policies are negative or positive. Today, as in the nineteenth century, in a world of nations, it remains true that self-government is always preferable to what someone else believes may be good government.

THIRTEEN

Imagining a North American Garden: Some Parallels and Differences in Canadian and American Culture

In the beginning (he said) God created me and you and put us in a
second English garden   Victoria   where to prove his love primrose
and hawthorn bloomed in the wilderness

And why (I asked) did you leave the first English garden?

England (he said) being perfect required looking at from a distance and
proved more perfect from Victoria than from London my ship rounded
the Horn   I heard whales with mermaids' heads singing I touched a
Gold Rush   the whales turned into seagulls and crows who flew
impudently said raucous fascinating things about this new England

I see no other England (I said) I see trees bigger than the tallest English
mountain   wider than the British Isles   I see myself   now trunk
shaped settled like a tree   my hands long branches that feather a sky
with iridescent paint   I have rolled out a new map giving names to
unknown indentations I am Canadian

Florence McNeil, "*Conversations with my*
Father   Establishing place," Emily.

"CROSSING THE BORDER" is one of those claustrophobic stories
so characteristic of the American writer, Joyce Carol Oates. It is the
story of a failing marriage in a failing country, of a young American
couple heading north into exile, to Canada, looking for "a new life,
a new country." From Florida, Canada looked like a northerly
country "with fresh air, chilled from the arctic, a ceaseless cleansing
wind. But from Detroit, Canada only three minutes away, the view
was different – it would be sweltering there, too. Indeed, you
travelled south from Detroit to enter Canada." Momentarily

Canada was south, the United States north. But that was merely geography. "The border between two nations," the young woman in the story mused as she looked at the road map, "is always indicated by broken but definite lines, to indicate that it is not quite real in any physical sense but very real in a metaphysical sense. . . ."[1]

Though she lived in Canada for several years, Joyce Carol Oates seems never to have attempted to specify the metaphysical nature of Canada, except perhaps to hint that its best writers were still trying to cast off the yoke of the nineteenth-century British tradition.[2] If that perception is a bit outdated, it is nevertheless true that in looking for cultural comparisons between Canada and the United States, it is the metaphysical rather than the physical that must be examined. Well, not quite. Both Canadians and Americans have a lot of geography and it is the fashion in which that geography has been interpreted that provides each of these two nations with a culture – what Joyce Carol Oates meant by "metaphysical." As Northrop Frye once remarked, "The countries men live in feed their minds as much as their bodies: the bodily food they provide is absorbed in farms and cities; the mental in religion and the arts. In all countries this process of material and imaginative *digestion* goes on."[3] The manner and speed of imaginative digestion offers a clue to parallels and differences between nations like Canada and the United States.

Let me begin at the beginning with a few simple, obvious, but important historical observations. First there was Europe, which from the sixteenth to the twentieth centuries spread out through much of the world. In that process North America was Europeanized, its indigenous populations pressed to the margins as European peoples, institutions, and beliefs became dominant.[4] But a second process was also taking place: European peoples, institutions, and beliefs were being Americanized. By that I mean that Europeans in North America came, at various rates, to think of themselves as distinctive, as people no longer of Europe, but rather as people of North America.

In the case of the United States, that process of Americanizing European culture was completed before the end of the nineteenth century. The decision to enter into that process was taken quite explicitly in 1776 with the Declaration of Independence. By approximately the centenary of independence the process of nationalizing the community – a process that included a bloody civil war – was virtually complete. In Canada the process was far slower, for reasons that are commonplace. The country was founded on two distinct European cultures. One, the French, had been separated from Europe not by choice, but by conquest. The other, the English, was composed to a large extent of people, the United Empire Loyalists, who had come to Canada to avoid separation from Europe. Together these communities were small and divided in almost everything that counted: language, religion, and culture. They were united, mainly, in the conviction that they did not wish to become part of the United States. To both communities that appeared to mean retention of European ties: military, political, economic, and, at least for the English Canadians, cultural ties. Unlike the people of the United States, whose decision to Americanize European culture was being fulfilled in the nineteenth century, Canadians believed that an Americanized culture, one cut loose from its European roots, would destroy the distinction between Canada and the United States. Canada, then, was to be British North America, the name that remained on its constitution when it became the Dominion of Canada.

The United States was a revolutionary society that had a Declaration of Independence and a belief in self-evident truths about man's inalienable rights to "life, liberty, and the pursuit of happiness." Canada was a conservative society with a British North America Act committed to "peace, order, and good government." The United States was a society that had negated history and looked to the future; Canada was a society that had evolved from history and took its self-image from the past. For Canada, borders were important – they defined her separateness from the United States. Greg Curnoe's "Close the 49th Parallel, etc." could have been painted in the 1850s as easily as in the 1960s, though the style would have been British imperial rather than American Pop! For Americans, not borders but "frontiers" were what was important. Frontiers were not boundaries but places to go, to expand. Above all, they were places to go to become American – further away from European influence. Frederick Jackson Turner, exponent of the frontier interpretation of history, summed up a century of American thought when he wrote in 1893:

> the frontier is the line of most rapid and effective Americanization. The wilderness masters the colonist. It finds him in a European dress, industries, tools, modes of travel, and thought. It takes him from the railroad car and puts him in the birch canoe. It strips off the

garments of civilization, and arrays him in the hunting shirt and the moccasin. . . . Little by little he transforms the wilderness, but the outcome is not the old Europe. . . . The fact is that here is a new product that is American . . . the advance of the frontier has meant a steady movement away from the influence of Europe, a steady growth of independence on American lines.

"Me imperturbed, standing at ease in Nature," was Walt Whitman's way of expressing his attitude to nature whose frontiers encompassed "the Mexican Sea and Kanada." [5]

Canada expanded, too. Economic imperatives and population pressures were present by the mid-nineteenth century, as they were earlier in the United States. But the ideology – the rationalization for expansion – was revealingly different. Americans wanted to "Americanize" the West; Canadians were engaged in laying the basis for "the Britain of the West." The Canadian frontier would provide a place to "reproduce the British constitution with its marvellous heritage of balanced power and liberty; and to do this across the whole breadth of a continent – these are objects which are worth some labour, some sacrifice to obtain." [6] What that magazine writer of 1874 made explicit was clearly implicit in Ralph Connor's novel, *The Foreigner* (1909): the frontier was not an escape from Europe, but an extension of Europe. [7] In the United States, nature made man; in Canada, man civilized nature.

During much of the nineteenth century Canadians, especially English Canadians, expressed an attitude toward nature that was markedly different from their United States contemporaries. A painter like Thomas Cole, or a writer like Ralph Waldo Emerson, looked at nature and found God. In his 1835 "Essay on American Scenery" Cole wrote that from nature could be learned the "laws by which the Eternal doth sublime and sanctify his works, that we may see the hidden glory veiled from vulgar eyes." In 1836 Cole painted a series of five pictures entitled "The Course of Empire." They were individually entitled "Savage State," "Pastoral State," "Consummation," "Destruction," and finally "Desolation." In each painting a lofty mountain symbolizes nature. But only in the second panel, "Pastoral State," does a second, sublime peak reach high above the first. That was the perfect state. Here was a visual version of Emerson's essay on "Nature," published in the same year. "There I feel nothing can befall me in life – no disgrace, no calamity (leaving me with my eyes) which Nature cannot repair. . . . I become a transparent eyeball; I am nothing; I see all; the currents of the Universal Being circulate through me; I am part or parcel of God."[8]

These views contrast starkly with the fashion in which nature and civilization are presented, for example, in John Richardson's novel *Wacousta*. There civilization and morality are found within the military garrison, while chaos and terror lie outside, in nature. Here is the central image:

> When the eye turned woodward it fell heavily and without interest upon a dim and dusky point known to enter upon savage scenes and unexplored countries, whereas whenever it reposed upon the lake it was with an eagerness and energy that embraced the most vivid recollections of the past, and led the imagination buoyantly over every well remembered scene that had previously been traversed, and which must be traversed again before the land of the European could be pressed once more. The forest, in a word, formed the gloomy and impenetrable walls of a prison house, and the bright lake that lay before it the only portal through which happiness and liberty could again be secured.[9]

Where James Fenimore Cooper's Natty Bumppo might "light out to the west" in search of life, liberty, and happiness, Colonel de Haldimar obviously preferred the peace, order, and good government of Europe. And as has often enough been remarked, Mrs. Moodie, while *Roughing it in the Bush*, also had Richardson's sense of being surrounded – by the Irish, by "the ultra-republican spirit," by rampant disrespect for authority. Some might say, by North America, where wilderness was a "prison-house."[10]

It was not merely the belief that moral order lay in European civilization and moral chaos in nature that prevented Mrs. Moodie and other nineteenth-century Canadian writers from leaving their garrison. It was also a conviction that they would find nothing outside to stimulate their imaginations. Emerson and Thoreau urged their countrymen to look to nature, rather than to history, to find imaginative inspiration – "the landscape," Thoreau wrote, ". . . is earth's eye; looking into which the beholder measures the depth of his own nature."[11] Catharine Parr Traill, for all that she recognized and painted the beauties of Canadian nature, found nothing there for the imagination – largely because she was looking for something that was not there. "As to ghosts or spirits they appear totally banished from Canada," she wrote in *The Backwoods of Canada*. "This is too matter-of-fact a country for such supernaturals to visit. Here there are no historical associations, no legendary tales of those that came before us. Fancy would starve for lack of marvellous food to keep her alive in the backwoods." [12]

Where Mrs. Moodie and Mrs. Traill looked to Europe to discover the mythologies necessary to feed their fancies, Thomas Cole, his biographer tells us, had concluded that "remoteness from the old world is not a disadvantage as many may suppose, but decidedly beneficial. . . . Nature is the foundation on which to build and not past art." [13] Cole's Canadian contemporary, Joseph Legaré, used nature to depict historical themes and yearnings, for history was close to him. He was always conscious of his people's defeat in 1759, and of the need to struggle to preserve a distinctive identity. If American romantic historians – Bancroft and Parkman, for example – extolled the making of a new nation in America, the French-Canadian historian F.-X. Garneau called upon his people to preserve their Frenchness, which was made not on the frontier but in Europe. Where Walt Whitman turned to nature as an inspiration for his songs about America's glorious achievements and unbounded future, Louis Frechette and Charles Mair each turned to a version of Canadian history – not the same one – to inspire their nationalistic verses. Whitman wrote of "Democratic Vistas"; Frechette of "Le Legende d'un Peuple," the struggle to conserve its identity, Mair of "Tecumseh" and the struggle for the border.

Almost every European visitor to North America – Alexis de Tocqueville, Lord Bryce, André Siegfried – who bothered to visit Canada was struck by the contrast between the two nations. Tocqueville thought he found the *ancien régime* alive and well in Quebec; Bryce and Siegfried were both struck by the continuance of European institutions in an American context. Friedrich Engels, in 1888, wrote that "It is a strange transition from the States to Canada. First one imagines one is in Europe again, and one thinks one is in a positively retrogressing and decaying country." [14] This, of course, was a perceptive but limited observation. There was much about Canada that was un-European. Goldwin Smith, that pessimistic polemicist of the Grange, was totally convinced that Canada was, in reality, a North American nation by the 1890s and that the British connection and British institutions only shallowly disguised reality.

Whatever the truth of Goldwin Smith's claim, the Canadian "metaphysic" remained distinct from that of the United States. That was demonstrated by the Canadians' unwillingness to accept

the logic of Smith's argument, which was simply that since Canadians and Americans had a common environment, and a geography
that united them, nature in the form of annexation should be
allowed to run its course.[15] But acceptance of nature and rejection
of tradition were exactly what Canada's whole history had refused
to do. Americans had founded their identity on nature; they had
nationalized nature. Canadians, on the other hand, had founded
their identity on history and, as Carl Berger has demonstrated brilliantly in *The Sense of Power*,[16] they had nationalized that history.
This is simply another way of stating what Ann Davis says in her
splendid catalogue, *A Distant Harmony*, when she concludes her
analysis of parallels in Canadian and American art with the observation that differing approaches to man and nature "encouraged an
American concentration on the present and future and a Canadian
interest in the past."[17]

If Americans during the nineteenth century "imaginatively
digested" North America, Canadians were certainly beginning the
same process. Even Mrs. Traill, for all of her sympathy with the
poet's lament for the lack of a mythology, recognized another
source of at least "amusement and interest." "If its [Canada's] volume of history is yet blank," she observed, "that of Nature is open,
and eloquently marked by the finger of God . . . ."[18] Before the end
of the century Archibald Lampman had grasped the full potential of
this romantic theme. In a poem entitled "Freedom," he declared:

Out of the heart of the city begotten
Of the labour of men and their manifold hands,
Whose souls, that were sprung from the earth in her morning,
No longer regard or remember her warning,
Whose hearts in the furnace of care have forgotten
Forever the scent and the hue of her lands;
. . .
Into the arms of our mother we come,
Our broad strong mother, the innocent earth,
Mother of all things beautiful blameless.
Mother of hopes that her strength makes tameless,
*   Where the voices of grief and of battle are dumb,*
*   And the whole world laughs with the light of her mirth.*

Lampman also wrote a poem entitled "The City at the End of
Things,"[19] which might have been composed after a viewing of
Thomas Cole's "Destruction," for it is a bitterly apocalyptic

denunciation of industrial society's destruction of nature. That poem may offer a key to the drift of the Canadian imagination. As Canada became an increasingly industrial and urban society – a development that followed not far behind the United States – a new view of nature's meaning emerged, a view not dissimilar from one widely held in the United States.[20] At its most elementary this new view presented nature as a physically and morally healthy alternative to the city, manifested itself in hiking clubs, summer camps and cottages, Boy Scouts and Alpine Clubs, and produced national parks and conservation. It can also be seen in the popularity of the animal stories of Ernest Thompson Seton and in the life and writings of Grey Owl. In 1910 a young Canadian painter named A.Y. Jackson expressed the unease that he shared with many other Canadians about the spread of machine civilization and its effects on the artistic sensibility. As he told his cousin,

> Someday the farm hand will go to work, start the day by punching a clock in the Farm Products Co. Ltd., and then set about turning levers and pressing buttons. Even now the romantic milk maid has faded away, and cows are being milked by machinery. The ploughman weary homeward plods his way no more – it's nine furrows at once and run by gasoline. And how on earth the artist is to find any sentiment in that kind of thing beats me. The big round cumulous clouds that pile around the horizon in the summer time and look so majestic and calm – just imagine when the aeroplanes and dirigibles get busy at 90 miles an hour; won't we see the poor old cumulous stirred up like custard, and flung all over the sky.[21]

It was out of that sense of unease about the way of the Canadian world that the philosophy of the Group of Seven was born.

That story has been told often enough, and well.[22] But four aspects of it deserve repeating with emphasis: the rejection of Europe; the discovery of the North; the influence of nineteenth-century American writing; and its relation to Canadian writing. Let me look at these aspects separately and briefly.

Over and over again members of the Group insisted that what needed to be done, and what they were doing, was emancipating Canadian painting and Canadian culture, from Europe. F.B. Housser made the point most emphatically when he wrote:

> Our British and European connection, in fact, so far as creative expression is concerned, has been a millstone about our neck. . . .

For Canada to find a complete expression of herself through art, a complete break with European traditions was necessary; a new type of artist was required, a type with sufficient creative equipment to initiate of its own through handling new materials by new methods and what was required more than technique was a deep rooted love of the country's natural environment.

If Canada wanted to discover what was distinctive about its culture, its artists would have to desert the cities, "Which are like all cities the world over," Arthur Lismer claimed, and get out into the natural environment. [23]

For the Group, especially for its most articulate spokesman, Lawren Harris, the natural environment was the North. The discovery that Canadian nationality was connected with the North was hardly new. [24] But Harris's North had a special, even a religious, meaning. Writing in 1926, Harris declared:

We in Canada are in different circumstances than the people in the United States. Our population is sparse, the psychic atmosphere comparatively clean, whereas the States fill up and the massed crowd a heavy psychic blanket over nearly all the land. We are on the fringe of the great North, and its living whiteness, its loneliness and replenishment, its resignations and release, its call and answers – its cleansing rhythms. It seems that the top of the continent will ever shed clarity into the growing race of America, and we Canadians being closest to this source seem destined to produce an art somewhat different from our southern fellows – an art more spacious, of greater living quiet, perhaps of more certain conviction of eternal values. We were not placed between the Southern teeming of men and the ample replenishing of North for nothing. [25]

Since Doug and Bob McKenzie have taught us that the "comparatively clean psychic atmosphere" of the Great White North has long since been polluted by beer and back bacon, we now find Harris's messianic rhetoric rather naive, to say the least. But in a twentieth-century theosophical way, characteristic enough of Canadian culture of the time, [26] Harris was nationalizing nature, the North in particular, for Canadians, as American artists and writers had done a century earlier.

By the time that Harris was writing, the mid-1920s, American writers had already developed an attitude toward nature that rejected the pantheism of Lampman and the theosophy of Harris.

In a poem published as early as 1890 Emily Dickinson had written of a Darwinian nature:

Apparently with no surprise
To any happy flower,
The Frost beheads it at its play –
In accidental power –
The blonde assassin passes on –
The Sun proceeds unmoved
To measure off another Day
For an approving God.

Thirty years later, in 1919, Wallace Stevens published a poem, "Anecdote to a Jar," in which a jar symbolizes civilization on a mountaintop surrounded by "slovenly nature." At the end of the poem, in direct contrast to Thomas Cole's "Course of Empire," the jar, civilization, "took dominion everywhere."[27]

American poets like Dickinson and Stevens did not impress the painters who dominated Canadian art in the 1920s. Rather, it was American writers of an earlier period. While Walt Whitman had always had a following in Canada – Richard Maurice Bucke, the London, Ontario, psychologist and mystic, had been his biographer and literary executor – it was not until the twentieth century, when European traditions were being discarded and nature discovered, that he came into his own. Searching to find a way to describe Tom Thomson, whom he mythologized as a man who "had nothing to do with Europe," Arthur Lismer described him as "a sort of Walt Whitman, a more rugged Thoreau." Emily Carr read Whitman and "learned heaps of him by heart," and also carefully perused Emerson's essay "Nature" – all at the urging of members of the Group of Seven. Though engaged in a rather different artistic enterprise than the Group, David Milne also took inspiration in nineteenth-century American writing, specifically Thoreau's *Walden*, which he once described as producing "an explosion in my mind."[28] What these American writers provided for some of Canada's artists was something they had already provided for their American contemporaries: they turned attention away from Europe and inherited culture toward nature as the source of an indigenous culture.

By the 1920s, then, an aesthetic revolution was under way. That revolution brought modernism in culture and a North American perspective. The European tradition, according to Harris, "was totally inappropriate to the expression of the character, the power and clarity and rugged elemental beauty of Canada."[29] And that same discovery was being made by a new generation of Canadian poets. Where Mrs. Traill with her European way of seeing could find no mythology in Canada to sustain her imagination, F.R. Scott concluded that she had looked in the wrong place. He wrote:

> *Who could read old myths*
> *By this lake*
> *Where the wild ducks paddle forth*
> *At daybreak?*

For this new generation of painters and poets and writers, Canada had to seek its metaphysic in nature rather than in history. "Geological time," Scott wrote, "made ancient civilization but yesterday's picnic."[30]

Yet Scott realized, as perhaps the Group of Seven did not, that nature alone was no answer for Canadians in search of a culture in the modern world. Indeed, Scott knew very well that while nature had to be assimilated in culture, it alone could not make a culture. That, in part, was the meaning of his wonderfully satiric poem ironically entitled "The Call of the Wild," doubtlessly taken from the he-man American writer, Jack London. Scott wrote:

> *Make me over, Mother Nature,*
> *Take the knowledge from my eyes,*
> *Put me back among the pine trees*
> *Where the simple are the wise.*
>
> *Clear away all evil influence,*
> *That can hurt me from the States,*
> *Keep me pure among the beaver*
> *With un-Freudian loves and hates*
>
> *Where my Conrads are not Aiken,*
> *And John Bishop's Peales don't sound*
> *Where the Ransom's are not Crowing*
> *And the Ezras do not Pound.*[31]

Scott, and those who thought like him, knew that the Canadian imagination could not reject history any more than it could reject the modernism of Ezra Pound, at least if it wished to have a living culture. But the history that would inform Canadian culture would be of Canada's own making. That is essentially the meaning of

Scott's well-known poem, first published in 1946, entitled
"Laurentian Shield." It brings together nature and history in a way
that finally nationalizes nature in Canada. The story begins with the
new land:

> *Inarticulate, arctic*
> *Not written on by history, empty as paper.*

But the land searches for an appropriate voice, a way of expressing
itself. From the "prewords of prehistory" it moves to the words of
history: the story of the exploitation of Canadian resources by fur
trade, gold seeker, and monopolistic mining companies.

> *But a deeper note is sounding, heard in the mines,*
> *The scattered camps and mills, a language of life,*
> *And what will be written in the full culture of occupation,*
> *Will come, presently, tomorrow,*
> *From millions whose hands can turn this rock into children.* [32]

"The full culture of occupation," man and the land, history and
nature. Perhaps this is what we find in the paintings of Carl
Schaefer and Charles Burchfield, in whom civilization and nature
seem to unite in harmony. Here are two artists whom Ann Davis has
described as painters of the rural mood. But her perceptive text
makes evident that something more is needed to capture the way of
seeing that is found in these paintings. Neither strains to present
nationalist claims, a theme that runs through many of the earlier
paintings, more persistently in the insecure Canadian ones than in
the confident American works. Those issues seem settled. Burchfield had no time for nationalist art: "the American scene is no better or worse than other scenes, and the worthwhile artist doesn't
care about a subject for its national character," he maintained.
Though he moved from place to place, he had a powerful sense of
locality, a conviction that real roots, roots that nurtured the imagination, drew on a specific locale. That was a conviction he shared
with his Canadian friend, Carl Schaefer. "Returning to Hanover in
the summers and Christmas time, in the early thirties," Schaefer
remembered, "where I discovered my own heritage, the land, man
in harmony with nature." [33]

Here are two artists who, like their predecessors, needed to
belong to an identifiable community. In the United States in the
nineteenth century and in Canada well into the twentieth, they
called that community a "nation." In reality, however, each painter

interpreted not a nation, but a part of a nation. Even the Group of Seven was as regional as the Laurentian Shield. Quebec art, for example, had few affinities with the Group's version of nationalism. [34] Burchfield and Schaefer knew that locality fed their imaginations. In that they demonstrated – as a novelist like William Faulkner or a poet like Robert Lowell in the United States, a W.O. Mitchell or an Al Purdy, to say nothing of an Ann Hébert or a Roch Carrier, in Canada – that imagination and identity, as Northrop Frye claims, are rooted in locality. [35] William Kurelek understood that his best work flowed from a "feeling of communion" with the rural locale where he had grown up. [36] David Milne at Boston Corners or Palgrave felt that same sense of communion. So did Emily Carr who, as Doris Shadbolt has shown, through "her prolonged contact and empathy with one segment of the world's skin has led her to touch the pulse that animates the whole." [37] Even an automatist like Paul-Emile Borduas, who had wandered from Sainte-Hilaire to Montreal, then on to New York and finally Paris, recognized the source of his imaginative nourishment. Depressed and ill in 1958, he wrote that "a little hunting and fishing, a little affection in my luminously beautiful country would be the correct treatment." [38] Even in his most abstract work Borduas remained close to the mountain at Sainte-Hilaire.

What Burchfield and especially Schaefer also demonstrate is the reintegration of Europe into North American art. Having come to terms with North America and nature, they no longer found it necessary to reject Europe and history. That tension, which sometimes made spokesmen for the Group of Seven sound shrill and even silly, was resolved by a painter like Schaefer who readily recognized his indebtedness not only to Arthur Lismer and J.E.H. MacDonald but also to Dürer, Hirschvogel, and Altdorfer. [39] He realized, as Jacques de Tonnancour observed, that "art is not made after nature, but after art and with nature." [40]

The realization that nature and history together provided nourishment for the imagination allowed American and Canadian artists more fully to digest their countries. Through their imaginations, and in the different ways that their separate histories drew them, they were making North America their own. "An art must grow and flower in a land," Lawren Harris wrote in the 1920s, "before the country will be a real home for its people." [41] And making a home meant creating that metaphysical border that Joyce

Carol Oates knew was more real than the physical one. Artists – poets, painters, novelists, even historians – provide new maps, new ways of seeing north and south. As Al Purdy put it:

> *A. Y. Jackson for instance*
> *83 years old*
> *half way up a mountain*
> *standing in a patch of snow*
> *to paint a picture that says*
> *"Look here*
> *You've never seen this country*
> *it's not the way you thought it was*
> *Look again."*[42]

Or Paul-Emile Borduas in his *Refus globale*: "*Les frontières de nos rêves ne sont plus le même*" – "The frontiers of our dreams are no longer what they were."[43]

FOURTEEN

Nationalist Ideologies in Canada

We had fed the heart on fantasies,
The heart's grown brutal on the fare;
More substance in our enmities
Than in our love; O honey bees,
Come build in the empty house of the stare.
W.B. Yeats, *"Meditations in Time of Civil War"* (1923).

"THE HISTORY OF the recent past, as well as the last century, is far from teaching the necessary identity of the political state and the nation. . . . The attempt to make the culturally united nation-state the one and only basis of legitimate political organization has proved untenable in practise. It was never tenable in theory."[1] Writing at the end of the Second World War, historian Alfred Cobban drew these conclusions from his analysis of nationalism and national self-determination in European history. Cobban, and many who thought like him, believed that the Hitler War had conclusively demonstrated the evil of that type of nationalism that, in different ways, both Woodrow Wilson and Adolf Hitler had sanctioned: a nationalism based on the identification of the political and the cultural nation. They hoped that the era of nationalism was over.

The five decades that have elapsed since 1945 have, at the very least, shown that the critics of nationalism were too optimistic. Some would say that they were just plain wrong in viewing that doctrine in a wholly negative light. The reasons for this changed attitude, quite apart from the considerable factor of intellectual fashion, are quite numerous and fairly well known. In an era of decolonization in Asia and Africa dozens of new nations have emerged, though fewer have flourished. On the whole, the breakup of empires and the rise of new nations have won the approval of Western scholars and journalists, even when some of the new nations have proven unstable, corrupt, and authoritarian.[2] After all, our liberal heritage assures us that national self-government is preferable even to good government. "The brutal and destructive side of modern nationalism needs no stressing in a world torn by its excesses," Sir Isaiah Berlin remarked in speaking for the revisionists. "Yet it must be recognized for what it is – a worldwide response to a profound and natural need on the part of newly liberated slaves – 'the decolonized' – a phenomenon unpredicted in the Europe-centred society of the nineteenth century."[3]

Moreover, at the end of the Second World War nationalism was generally judged a conservative, even reactionary, phenomenon. By the 1960s, however, the wheel had turned full circle, with nationalism once again viewed as it had been by nineteenth-century liberals – as a force for progress and reform. Indeed, in a spate of polemical and also scholarly books, nationalism came frequently to be presented as a necessary engine of political and economic "modernization."[4] Here was a spirit that could unify backward, tribal societies and galvanize their inhabitants into the effort necessary to drag themselves into the twentieth century.[5]

Yet nationalist ideology is nothing if not malleable. Not only could it be evoked as a stimulus to "modernization" in the so-called "underdeveloped" countries, but it was apparently also found to be useful in another, contrasting role in the so-called "developed" countries. In some of these countries "modernization," often seen as a euphemism for "Americanization" with its giant, computerized government, business, educational, and labour bureaucracies, and the resulting homogenized sameness, created a new search for distinctive roots.

This is a recognizable phenomenon in Canada. It is the underlying theme of George Grant's elegant polemic, *Lament for a Nation*, which, in announcing the defeat of Canadian nationalism by the forces of modern technology, became a major stimulant to the now not-so-new nationalism of English Canada.[6] A similar theme, though presented without Grant's relentless pessimism, also informs Marcel Rioux's nationalist critique of the so-called "functionalism" of Quebec federalists.[7] "While national feeling formerly tended to unite various ethnic groups by focussing their political sentiments on the nation as a whole," Hannah Arendt observed, "we now watch how an ethnic nationalism begins to threaten with dissolution the oldest and best established nation-states."[8]

The late Professor Arendt was thinking of Great Britain and France, where the Scots, the Welsh, the Bretons, and the Provençals were displaying varying degrees of nationalist resurgence. She might just as well have been speaking of Canada, not least of all because she used the term "nation" in the two different ways in which it has constantly, and confusingly, been used in this country. The revival of nationalism in various parts of the world in the last twenty-five years has been paralleled by similar developments in Canada. But that nationalist revival has taken more than one form, has been derived from different concepts of the meaning of "nation," and has aimed at the achievement of conflicting goals. This is so for historical reasons that must be briefly recounted if the nature of nationalist ideologies in Canada is to be understood. Like most other ideological currents in Canada, our nationalist ideologies have European roots and can best be understood in that context.

Nineteenth-century Europe gave birth to the doctrine of nationalism that maintained that "humanity is naturally divided into nations, that nations are known by certain characteristics which can be ascertained, and that the only legitimate type of government is national self-government."[9] Much ink, rhetoric, and blood were spilled in an effort to ascertain with precision those "characteristics" that supposedly gave a nation "uniqueness." There were those, chiefly in Britain and France, who argued that a nation must be defined politically, that it developed within the boundaries of sovereign states, and that loyalty to that state, or nationalism, transcended cultural differences. The French historian Ernest Renan and his English contemporary, Lord Acton, in different ways, expounded this political concept of nationhood. The second concept of nation, found mainly in Germany and eastern Europe, was based on the idea of ethnic and cultural unity out of which a state should grow. The eighteenth-century German philologist, J.G. Herder, formulated the concept of ethnic nations most fully, though many nineteenth-century liberal nationalists, including John Stuart Mill and Guiseppe Mazzini, subscribed to variations of it.[10] The German historian, Friedrich Meinicke, made the distinction, and his preference was evident when he responded to Renan's well-known claim that "the existence of a nation is a plebiscite of all the people every day." Meinicke insisted: "The principle is not: whoever wants to be a nation is a nation. It is just the opposite: a nation simply is whether the individuals of which it is composed want to belong to that nation or not. A nation is not based on self-determination but on predetermination." [11]

The intellectual history of European nationalism turned on the debate between those who believed that nations were self-determined political-constitutional units and their opponents who insisted that linguistic and ethnic characteristics predetermined membership in nations. Unfortunately, much of the diplomatic and military history of Europe between 1789 and 1945 focused on the same question. The result, as one historian has observed, was almost inevitably "dissension and violence, since, contrary to the assertions of nationalist doctrine, mankind is not naturally divided into distinct 'nations,' each with its own exclusive territory, and the attempt to make the political map conform to some linguistic criterion is bound to be a brutal and sanguinary affair." [12]

Since the middle of the nineteenth century, Canada has been the stage for exactly this conflict over the meaning of the term "nation" that has been central to European thought. Those who believed that a nation is "self-determined" have had both spokesmen and practitioners. The same is true of the doctrine of the predetermined nation. Both views have been expressed in English, and both have been presented in French. Theories of nationalism, when they are something more than mere rationalizations, are apparently not controlled by national patents.

In the century following the British Conquest of New France, British policy toward Canada vacillated between acceptance of the French and Catholic culture of the new colony and the desire to transform these new subjects into English-speaking Protestants. These policies were motivated by a combination of ignorance, prejudice, and calculation. Almost predictably, the leadership of the French-speaking community responded by developing a protective nationalist ideology and strategy based on their distinctive language, customs, and, to some extent, religion. Louis-Joseph Papineau was the movement's leader; the historian, François-Xavier Garneau, its theoretician. In 1834 Papineau stated the essence of the nineteenth-century nationalist creed: "One nation ought never to govern another." [13]

Paradoxically Lord Durham, whose famous report of 1839 advocated the assimilation of the French Canadians, agreed with

Papineau. He found "two nations warring in the bosom of a single state" and concluded that until that number was halved, and Canada a uniformly Anglo-Saxon nation, there would be no peace. Papineau had wished to subordinate the English; Durham demanded the extinction of the French. Both exhibited that nationalist tendency described by a French political scientist when he wrote of "the tendency, whether it be on the ethnic, social, political, administrative, linguistic or sometimes religious level, to reduce differences, to suppress the seeds of internal conflict." [14]

The defeat of the rebellion in 1837-38 marked the failure of Papineau's plan, though the seed he had planted remained in the ground. The passage of the Rebellion Losses Bill in 1849, whereby Louis-H. LaFontaine gave proof that "French power" supported by sympathetic English Canadians could make a binational political system work, marked the defeat of Durham's plan.

But his ideas also retained life. The politicians who learned their trade under the Union of 1841 concluded that co-operation between what they called the "two races" offered the only practical approach to building a stable and prosperous colony. They had no well-devised conception of nationhood – except perhaps intellectuals like Etienne Parent and Bishop Laflèche – but they did have the practical politician's normal desire to achieve results and to stay in power. Although he was speaking only of Lower Canada at the time, John A. Macdonald perhaps came as close to defining his conception of Canada as he ever did when he wrote in 1856 that the English Canadian "must make friends with the French, without sacrificing the status of his race or language, he must respect their nationality. Treat them as a nation and they will act as a free people generally do – generously." [15]

It is nevertheless true that by 1867 two conceptions of "nation" and "nationalism" existed in Canada. Both were expressed with greater or lesser degrees of clarity in the debates that took place over the Confederation proposals, and each had its supporters in the two linguistic communities. As is usual in Canada, theoretical views were expressed most explicitly and carefully by French Canadians. No politician stated with greater clarity than George-Etienne Cartier the conception of nationhood as a self-determined political community. In the Confederation debates he went out of his way to emphasize that "the idea of unity of races was utopian – it was impossible," and offered as the only workable scheme for Canada one in which "we would form a political nationality with which neither the national origin, nor the religion of any individual would interfere."[16] With this sentiment Macdonald and most of his colleagues appear to have agreed, though it must have strained the tolerance of some of them, notably George Brown. Even the critics of the new scheme, such as the *rouges* Dorion brothers, were willing to accept the idea of a political community housing more than one cultural nation, though they feared that the Confederation plan was too centralized to guarantee French-Canadian rights. The most thoroughgoing statement of the predetermined concept of nation came not from any politician but rather from a brilliant ecclesiastic, the Vicar-General of Trois-Rivières, Louis Laflèche. In a series of newspaper articles, collected in book form in 1866, Laflèche elucidated in detail, and with erudition, the French-Canadian claim to recognition as a nation. He explored the religious, historical, geographical, and social claims to nationhood, and expounded at length upon his people's uniqueness and sense of mission. The argument was long and subtle, but the essence was simple enough. A nation, Laflèche wrote, "is a people who speak the same language, who have the same faith, and whose morals, customs and laws are uniform."[17] Despite the completeness of his definition Laflèche did not draw what might have seemed the logical conclusion: that French Canada as a nation had a right to sovereign statehood. Instead, the ecclesiastical leader gave his support to Confederation, which he apparently felt provided sufficient guarantees for the future security of the French-Canadian nation. It is probably also fair to say that Laflèche believed that French Canadians already had national institutions sufficient for their protection in the form of the Church.

A similar conception of nation and nationalism, though more oriented toward the future than to the past, also animated some English-Canadian intellectuals in the years immediately after Confederation. For the most part the members of the Canada First movement seemed to have had a vision of Canada that left only a rather restricted place for French Canadians. Charles Mair, a nationalist poet, was one of their number and his poetry was shot through with an ethnically inspired nationalism. So, too, was a revealing essay he published under the title of "The New Canada" in 1875. Since he was especially concerned about the future of western Canada, he took the view that, outside of Quebec, French would have to be treated as any other immigrant language, and suppressed. "In order to build up a great nation," he wrote in words reminiscent of much nationalist literature, "minor nationalities are no doubt called upon to make heavy sacrifices."[18] These sacrifices were made explicit in a speech D'Alton McCarthy delivered in the House of Commons in 1890 supporting the abolition of the French language in the Northwest Territories. His contention was that "we cannot have, and never will have in this country, two nationalities." He was learned and logical, larding his oration with numerous citations from European nationalist authors. He called on his fellow members of the House to support a resolution asserting that "it is expedient in the interests of the national unity of the Dominion that there should be a community of language among the people of Canada."[19] Convictions like those led to the radical reduction of French-language educational rights outside of Quebec between 1890 and 1927. Most English-Canadian provinces, in sharp contrast to Quebec, acted on the principle that Canada was, or ought to be, a culturally homogeneous nation.[20]

This view of nation and nationalism has found exponents in every generation of Canadians. For every Francophone Jules-Paul Tardivel, whose 1894 novel, *Pour la Patrie*, presented the case for "the establishment of a New France on the border of the St. Lawrence,"[21] there has been at least one Goldwin Smith or George Parkin advocating some form of Anglo-Saxon nationalism as Canada's proper destiny.[22] For every Lionel Groulx, a Donald Creighton. For every George Grant, a Marcel Rioux.[23] So, too, the ideal of a self-determined political-constitutional nation had many exponents, though none, perhaps, so consistent as the French-Canadian journalist and intellectual, Henri Bourassa. He summarized one Canadian tradition when he responded to his contemporary, Tardivel, who insisted that only those of the same language, culture, religion, and historical tradition could be considered members of a nation. Bourassa insisted:

> Our nationalism is Canadian nationalism, founded on the duality of cultures and on the particular traditions that this duality implies. The fatherland, for us, is the whole of Canada, that is a federation of distinct cultures and provinces. The nation which we wish to see develop is the Canadian nation, composed of French Canadians and English Canadians. That is of two elements separated by language and religion and by the legal arrangements necessary for the conservation of their respective traditions, but united in a sense of brotherhood, and in an attachment to a common fatherland.[24]

These, then, are the essentials of the two ideological traditions that have dominated thinking in Canada about the nature of nation and nationalism. I have used the rather clumsy Germanic terms "predetermined" and "self-determined" to distinguish these conflicting currents, and, as with all categorization, this has ridden roughshod over differences that have existed within particular traditions. At the very least I should perhaps have said something about "regional" resistance to the concept of a Canadian nation, for that would once again underline the manner in which even the most carefully conceived theories of Canadian nationalism are perceived as too uniform in a country as diverse in region and ethnicity as Canada. To the regions, "national" policies sometimes seem nothing more than the will of the central Canadian majority dressed up in the respectable rhetoric of "Canadianism."[25] But this would be the subject for another discussion that would examine nationalism as a mere rationalization of self-interest. What I have tried to do in examining "nationalism" as an ideology may seem to be mere historical interest at best, or an academic exercise at worst. No conclusion could be more unfortunate. The nature of nationalism, the ideological framework within which Canadian leaders, often unconsciously, operate, is fundamental to any discussion of the issues brought to a head by the Quebec election of November 15, 1976.

The two schools of thought I have delineated, in fact, lie behind the central conflict in Canada today. The only difference is that each of these concepts is armed with more political power than at any time in our past. To be specific, the concept of "nation" as a predetermined, culturally homogeneous community was basic to the philosophy of the Parti Québécois government of Quebec. It is expressed most explicitly in that government's White Paper on Language Policy and in the unamended version of the language act, which began by asserting that "the National Assembly states that French is, and always has been, the language of the people of Quebec, and that is what permits the Quebec people to express its identity."[26] The same philosophy can be found in other statements by members of that government, including the remark of Dr. Camille Laurin that "all nations are founded on the principle of ethnocentricity," and Premier Lévesque's references to his party's victory as a "sort of national mandate by the French majority in Quebec."[27] The opposing view, not surprisingly, finds equally vigorous expression in the recent policy paper on language issued by the government of Canada entitled *Un Choix national/A National Understanding*, where the argument rests on the distinction, now familiar, between political nationhood and cultural distinctiveness.[28]

There is something nearly as significant about these statements as the contents themselves: here are two government policy statements on fundamental cultural questions. In each case the state is taking a much more interventionist approach to the promotion of a conception of nation than has been traditional. Of course, as far back as 1867 the British North America Act set out certain rather limited provisions concerning the official use of the French and English languages in Canada. But before 1960 neither Ottawa nor Quebec made any very sustained effort to legislate or act in this area, apparently assuming that the matter was self-regulating.

The same, incidentally, was not true of the other provinces, which, through educational legislation, implemented language policies. For the most part these policies established English as the priority language – in some cases the only language – with occasional exceptions for French-language or, more probably, bilingual education. For historical reasons of a constitutional, political, economic, and religious nature, Quebec, until recently, was the only province that offered anything like equal status to the two language groups. Even the controversial new language legislation, Bill 101, provides more generous treatment for the English-speaking minority in Quebec than is provided for French-language minorities in many of the other provinces.

It is well known that the major change in Quebec since 1960, the very essence of the Quiet Revolution, has been the discovery and use of the state as an instrument for the achievement of social and national goals. Moreover, it is plain that the rise of the positive state in Quebec has been a major factor in the crisis the Canadian federal system has been experiencing during the past dozen or so years.[29] Increasingly, an identification has been made between "nation" (i.e., Francophone Quebec) and state. That in turn has led, among other things, to the conclusion that the state must take positive steps in the promotion of the French language, which, by definition, means the reduction of the status of the English language. At virtually the same time, and for somewhat similar reasons, the central government, which had played an interventionist role in culture at least since the establishment of the CBC and later the Canada Council, also decided that the traditional *laissez-faire* attitude to language policy was no longer acceptable. What this meant, in reality, was that under the title of bilingualism, the federal government would promote the French language, which had never achieved anything like the status of rough equality within federal institutions that the 1867 constitution had guaranteed. This also involved an effort, beginning in 1968, to convince the provinces that had adopted English as the dominant language to move in the direction of linguistic equality in education and some other public services. Thus in the field of language, as in many other fields, the emergence of the positive or welfare state in Canada greatly complicated both federal-provincial and French-English relations.

Once again it is useful to emphasize the contrasting philosophies that underlie the language policies of the two levels of government. The Quebec White Paper on Language Policy and the resulting legislation make the explicit claim that language policy is merely an instrument in promoting a national culture.[30] The federal government's statement on language derives from a different set of assumptions. It insists from the outset that "it is proper to make precise in the first place that the government thinks it necessary to establish a clear distinction between language and culture, though in practice the two are intimately connected."[31]

Thus language policy is presented as a logical consequence of a political-constitutional conception of Canadian nationhood rather than as a national cultural policy. Whether such fine distinctions are workable in practice could be the subject of another debate. But the very fact that the theoretical distinctions are made is one further recent evidence of the continuing existence of conflicting ideologies of nationalism in Canada.

Indeed, the experience of the Quebec government in attempting to translate a theory of nation based on cultural homogeneity into practice suggests the limitations of that theory. The province's Commission des Droits de la Personne, in a radical criticism of the original language act, offered a familiar counter-proposition about the relation of nation and state. "We believe that the confusion between belonging to a cultural group and to a civil society is indefensible and, even more, eminently dangerous. It contains the seeds of a discriminatory attitude toward those who have had the misfortune not to be part of the cultural group that has proclaimed itself the national group."[32]

A quite different, and even ironic, response was evoked from another group in Quebec. Nothing better illustrates the confusion that results from the attempt to apply the predetermined, culturally homogeneous concept of nation to the task of defining statehood and citizenship than a recent statement by the spokesmen for a group of Inuit villages on Hudson Bay (Povungnituk, Ivujivik, and Saglonc). This group rejected the leadership of the Northern Quebec Inuit Association at Fort Chimo, opposed the James Bay Agreement, and insisted that neither French nor English but rather the Inuit language is the only language essential to their people. In words that unconsciously demonstrate the impact of the white man's thought on the Inuit, the dissidents declare:

> We, the Esquimo, have a distinct culture and language and like all other people, we are convinced that it belongs to us and to us alone to defend our culture. We, the first concerned, we want the same chances as the Quebecers to take the necessary measures to protect our language. And like the Quebecers, we do not want the responsibility and the task of passing laws concerning our language and our culture to belong to anyone but ourselves. . . . What we want is rather the creation by the Esquimo of New Quebec, of a genuine regional government with all the powers needed to assure its development of our society, of our culture and of our language. [33]

These Inuit, small in number but ancient in culture, dramatically focus attention on the central Canadian issue: if the Inuit claim to a predetermined, culturally homogeneous nation-state is denied, on what principal can other culturally homogeneous nations assert their right to statehood?[34] If, on the other hand, the claim is conceded, on what principle can the demands of any group claiming cultural nationhood be denied?[35] Here is the fundamental dilemma of the geographical entity called Canada, and the geographical entity called Quebec. Since neither entity is culturally homogeneous, claims to nationhood, if they are to rest on anything more substantial than the tyranny of majorities, must find sanctions of some other sort. Otherwise the clumsy magic of that "sorcerer's apprentice," as a European writer has called nationalism, may lead along unpredictable and even dangerous courses. [36]

FIFTEEN

Nation, Identity, Rights: Reflections on W.L. Morton's *The Canadian Identity*

"The sovereignty of the community, the region, the state – any higher sovereignty in fact – makes sense only if it derives from the one genuine sovereignty of the human being, which finds its political expression in civil sovereignty."

Vaclav Havel, *Summer Meditations* (1992)

"But Europe is exactly what people don't seem to want today. They want identities. The great modern and murderous delirium in Europe is the folly of ethnic identity."

Bernard-Henri Lévy, *The New York Times*, December 13, 1992

"It has taken a lot for us to realize why we've been made into sacrificial animals. Because somebody somewhere decided that the bestial concept of a herd composed of only one color, all speaking the same language, all thinking along similar lines, all believing in the same god, must wipe out everything else."

Zlatko Dizdarevic, *Sarajevo: A War Journal* (1993)

BEFORE W.L. MORTON decided to devote his 1960 lectures at the University of Wisconsin to the topic of the Canadian identity, he had doubtless considered, and dismissed, at least two objections to that theme. The first was that the "Canadian identity" was a somewhat hackneyed subject, one over which much ink had been spilled by successive generations of Canadian nationalists, and especially by historians. Morton, whose own work was changing focus from "region" to "nation" at that point, probably dismissed that objection on the grounds that there was always something new to say even about an old topic. And he was right, for he had developed a perspective that was his own. The second objection related to his audience. For Americans, the question of national identity – or way of life, as they preferred to call it – had long since been settled, if not by the speculations of Emerson and Whitman, then surely on the bloody battlegrounds of the Civil War. Would they not think that the Canadian preoccupation with this topic was merely a sign of immaturity or self-indulgence? That objection Morton probably accepted as a challenge, one more reason for explaining why two nations, not one, existed in North America. To define the Canadian identity, an identity distinct from the American way of life, would be a demonstration of maturity and independence.

Thirty years after the first publication of those lectures two thoughts occur to me about these hypothetical objections. First, it is depressingly obvious that the question of the Canadian identity retains a pertinence in the 1990s that would have surprised W.L. Morton. What would surely have astonished him even more is the obvious state of disarray that exists on that very question – as evidenced by our continuing constitutional instability – and I will return to that.

Before I take it up, however, I want to point to an even greater irony. Those very Americans who firmly believed in the early 1960s that their own way of life was settled and secure – congealed, to use the late Louis Hartz's phrase – are today at least as confused about the issue of identity as Canadians. Hector St. John de Crèvecoeur's famous question – "What then is the American, this new man?" – first posed in 1782, is very far from finding an unambiguous answer today. Let me illustrate. Recently two of what might be called periodicals of the cultural avant-garde published special issues on what one, *October*, called "The Identity in Question" and the other, *Critical Inquiry*, simply dubbed "Identities." What the contributors to these two magazines are preoccupied with is the issue of what is sometimes called "multiculturalism," sometimes "diversity." (It is reported, in another discussion of this subject, that one midwestern university now has a Dean of Diversity!) The difference between multiculturalism and diversity is, I believe, that the latter includes sexual and/or gender differences, or what that great American political philosopher, Pat Buchanan, prefers to call "sexual proclivities." This debate raged through the universities and schools of the United States during most of the Reagan-Bush years. While it has all sorts of ramifications and, in typical American fashion, has been conducted with an intensity that often verges on hysteria, producing such words and phrases as "logocentric hierarchies," "hegemonic discourse," "Eurocentric," "Dead White Males," "political correctness," "tenured radicals," and "the closing of the American Mind," it is a critical debate. Underneath the rhetoric there is a serious attempt to redefine the nature of the American identity. And the reason is obvious. As Andrew Hacker wrote recently, "Each year this country becomes less white, less 'European,' and less tightly bound by a single language. The United States now has a greater variety of cultures than at any time in its history." [1]

The issues at stake are neatly though not objectively summarized in *The Disuniting of America: Reflections on a Multicultural Society* by that now somewhat venerable paragon of American liberal nationalism, Arthur M. Schlesinger, Jr. His goal is a defence of the American way of life with its traditions, as he sees them, of individualism, equality of opportunity, and the merging of ethnic identities into the melting pot. For him, multiculturalism represents an attempt to substitute group rights for individual rights, special treatment for equality of opportunity, and ethnic tension for the good old harmony of the American way. While parading his inherited liberal credentials, Schlesinger nevertheless insists that the new emphasis on the preservation of difference can only lead to a distortion of the American past and the fragmentation of the nation. As an historian he is especially concerned about the "use" of history to promote a contentious, rather than merely a tolerant, past. And when he insists that "history can give a sense of national identity," [2] he clearly means a single, not a diverse, identity. But that, of course, is exactly the position that is contested both by those who insist on multiple and distinct identities and by those who, like Joan Scott in the United States and Audrey Kobayashi in Canada, see all identities as historically constructed, multiple, and changing. [3]

Here I have only touched on what is a vast ocean of controversy. But I want to move on and to suggest that such controversy is certainly not confined to North America. In these days when every news report brings fresh evidence of the corrosive capacity of aroused ethnicity to undermine established political systems, whether in bloodshed in Yugoslavia or in bitterness and bickering in Czechoslovakia, it is hardly necessary to insist that the question of identity is ubiquitous. Once again a spectre is haunting Europe, the spectre of nationalism. Again, examples are numerous. Writing in

Le Monde in July, 1992, the French sociologist Edgar Morin worried about the possible contradictions between "le processus métana-tionale" and the continued need for the nation-state to protect local culture and prevent the emergence of "une civilisation anonyme." A month later his colleague, Dominique Schnapper, daughter of Raymond Aron, told *Le Devoir* that the nation-state could only pre-serve its culture and its stability if it rejected the claims of groups, insisted on the equality of individuals, and promoted social integra-tion.[4] (This latter view Quebec nationalists applaud if applied to Quebec, but reject if applied to Canada.) For Europeans the prob-lem is one that is quite familiar to Canadians: on the one hand the economic pressures toward continental integration, on the other the question of the place of those internal communities – whether guest workers, immigrants, or refugees – in the host culture. In a world where cultures know few boundaries, a world where, as V.S. Naipaul once said, "Everywhere . . . men are in movement, the world is in movement, and the past can only cause pain,"[5] it is no wonder, perhaps, that so identity-conscious a writer as the Pales-tinian literary critic Edward Said is moved to ask: "Who cares about the labels of national identity anyway?"[6]

What is at issue in this debate, of course, is the resolution of radi-cally different views about the relationship between "identity" and "nation" at a time when what Michael Walzer has called "the new tribalism"[7] has asserted itself emphatically. For some intellectuals like Isaiah Berlin and Walzer, "nationalism" is irrepressible, a natu-ral way of defining community, agreeing apparently with Herder that "to be human must be to feel at home somewhere, with your own kind." For others, like the Czechoslovakian writer Vaclav Havel and his Polish counterpart Adam Michnik, "home" means more than ethnicity – house, family, occupation, behaviour, lan-guage – for all are encapsulated in "the civic principle" that places equally distributed rights of citizenship above ethnicity or religion.[8] What has reopened these old questions in Europe – one almost expects the 1848 Frankfurt Assembly to be reconvened – is, of course, the collapse of the Soviet empire in the East and the thrust toward unification in the West. Throughout Europe the established state system is in crisis. And that crisis is one of "identity"; on the one hand is the fear of cultural homogenization – the hegemony of EuroDisney – and on the other the fear that a reversion to past iden-tities, based on ethnic "purity" or religious fundamentalism, will produce a new world order riven by hatreds and jealousies that are all too familiar.

This crisis of state is one that, usually in a less dramatic way, is something of a commonplace in Canada. We often think that our parochial concerns are at least our own. But the fact is that our "constitutional crisis" is only our version of the identity crisis that besets much of the developed world and beyond. And that is what led me to think that a re-reading of W.L. Morton's *The Canadian Identity* could be useful.

Re-reading Morton's lectures – including his presidential address to the Canadian Historical Association in 1960 entitled "The Relevance of Canadian History" – one is immediately struck by how simple the world once was. I don't mean that Morton simplified it – I literally mean that, comparatively, Canada and the manner in which our history was presented and understood was simple and straightforward. Though Morton used the word "identity" in his title, I don't think he ever repeated it in the lectures themselves. Indeed, he might more adequately have described the contents of his book if he had pre-empted Donald Smiley by using the title *The Canadian Political Nationality*. Morton's aim was to devise a political definition of Canada, rather than to speak about matters we now subsume in "identity." In stressing, as he did, Canada's British heritage, our northern geography, our dependent economic life, and our conservative, evolutionary political instincts – matters he thought were shared by English- and French-speaking Canadians – Morton's principal objective was to distinguish Canada from the people who formed his audience in Madison, Wisconsin.

Oddly, perhaps, he came closest to defining what he meant by identity when he used a word that often falls from American lips – "destiny." Here is what he said:

> Canadian destiny is an evolution in progress. It has not yet been defined. It cannot yet be defined. But certain elements may be perceived. It is part of Canada's destiny to be an independent nation in America. Canadian nationhood consists of a political nationality resting on two cultures. There are other diversities too, but none not subsumed in the political nationality.

He continued, stressing Canada's northern economy, its "monarchical and parliamentary democracy," the importance of membership in the Commonwealth "because it is an antidote to the isolationism and continentalism that Canada's American character and affinities breed." And finally, given the exigencies of the Cold War, Canada had a special role in its alliance system. Ultimately, Morton asserted a few pages later, the essential difference between the United States and Canada lay in the fact that "America is united at bottom by the covenant, Canada is united at the top by allegiance" – that allegiance to monarchy Morton called "the moral core of Canadian nationhood."[9]

These passages make it obvious that Morton, most often, conceived of "identity" or "political nationality" as a matter of "allegiance" to the Canadian state rather than being based on cultural or linguistic distinctions. Citizenship defined political identity, not vice versa. What he was expounding was, in effect, a subtle version of Canadian "nationality" very similar to that laid down by John A. Macdonald and especially George-Étienne Cartier in the Confederation debates of 1865. It was an elegant and convincing exposition of that position, part of which Morton had already developed in what I have always considered one of his most thoughtful essays, the one entitled "Clio in Canada," first published in 1946.[10] There he had set out, in firm opposition to the "imperialist" implication of the Creighton-Innis Laurentian thesis, a conception of a pluralistic Canada founded on Lord Acton's famous critique of the homogenizing liberal nationalism expounded by J.S. Mill in his *Political Economy*. (In passing, I cannot resist remarking that it has always amused me, and sometimes irritated me, that nationalists in Canada have often pointed to Acton as evidence of the supposed incompatibility of liberalism and nationalism – blind to the fact that it was Mill's position, not Acton's, that was much more characteristic of the nineteenth-century liberal view of nationalism.)

Though Morton's recapitulation of the 1865 recipe for Canadian nationality was intellectually impressive, it was out of step with the developing temper even of his times in its separation of political nationality from cultural and especially ethnic identity. On one significant matter, however, it was quite in tune with that temper: the concern to distinguish and defend Canada from the increasing impact of the United States. Here his voice joined a larger, sometimes dissonant, Greek chorus that included George Grant, Walter Gordon, Cy Gonick, Donald Creighton, and the two Mels – Hurtig and Watkins. For these nationalists, and I think for Morton, the outstanding challenge to Canada's survival in the 1960s and later came from the United States. That challenge was both cultural and economic.

I think that preoccupation, valid as it was, prevented Morton, and others who thought like him, from recognizing the seriousness – I believe more serious than the U.S. threat – of the new nationalism in Quebec. And the growing intensity of that nationalism contributed to, but did not create, regional and ethnocultural discontents elsewhere in Canada. Certainly each of these discontents – Quebec, regionalism, and ethnic revival – represented a challenge to Morton's conception of Canada, and together they made responding to the influence of the United States more difficult.

While I have lumped Morton together with a number of other public figures and intellectuals, I want to make one thing clear. Neither in his attitude to the United States nor toward Quebec nationalism, and certainly not to the voices of regional and ethnic dissatisfaction, was Morton ever shrill or intolerant. But he was firm even while recognizing that the ground under him was shifting. Quebec gave him the greatest difficulty, as it did most other Canadians. In Morton's case a gradual recognition of the potential of Quebec nationalism provoked a very striking public response from him.

The occasion was a conference sponsored by the Canadian Union of Students at Laval University in the summer of 1964. The topic, of course, was "A New Concept of Confederation?" The two faculty members advising the students were Professor Jacques-Yvan Morin, who subsequently served in René Lévesque's government, and myself. In his surprising speech Morton confessed that he was passing through a state of depression brought on by the realization that his world, "the English-Canadian world," had collapsed and that he was "a man without a world." He went on to say:

> I have become aware over the past few months that a prestige I once unconsciously possessed, I have now consciously not got. I have become a Canadian like any other, a member of an ethnic minority, and am obliged to make such way in the world as my personal merit permits. It is of no significance any more that the English conquered New France, or that most of the laws and constitution of Canada derive from English origin, that English happens to be my own mother tongue. I am now – I never knew this was not true of me before – I am now a Canadian like any other. [11]

It was a strange – and moving – confession, though I think the students, French and English, were utterly puzzled by it. It began with the arrival of his grandparents in Manitoba in the 1860s and 1870s and moved on to explain his conviction that Canada could only continue to exist on the basis of a "dualism of culture and a federalism of power" – a strong federal government in a bilingual country. Morton's dramatic confession produced an equally dramatic response. Professor Gérard Bergeron of Laval, commenting on Morton's speech, began his remarks by noting that Morton's ancestors had arrived in 1870. His, Bergeron stated, had arrived in 1663! The comment was a friendly one, meant only to emphasize that the idea of a single Canadian nation was a difficult one. But it was telling. In that exchange the two speakers offered an insight into the debate about "identity" that has not been much improved upon in the subsequent decades. Yet the exchange did not, I think, much alter Morton's view about the way that a new accommodation between French and English could be worked out.

Morton's thinking about Quebec was clear and direct. He recognized that nationalism in Quebec, based as it was on "language and culture . . . could only operate to divide English Canadians from French, and to destroy the Canadian political nationality." [12] He therefore resisted the temptation, often favoured by "moderate" French- and English-Canadian federalists, to accept a "two nations" concept advocating a transfer of federal powers to Quebec that would not be available to other provinces – "special status," "associate states," or, these days, "asymmetrical federalism." He was, however, quite open – unlike his friend D.G. Creighton – to a policy recognizing increased rights for the French language in Canada. He had always blamed the Manitoba school and language controversy of the 1890s on transplanted Ontario Grits, and he was entirely willing to undo that mistake.

Another aspect of his response to Quebec nationalism revealed, I think, a fundamental misunderstanding of the nature of nationalism, especially of Quebec nationalism. This response – one he shared with many Canadian nationalists – was to argue that a vigorous resistance to the United States influence in Canada would restore French-Canadian confidence in Canada and, though he didn't use the term, a new Canadian nationalism could be fostered. What he was saying was that, in essence, the source of the Canadian malaise was really English Canada's infatuation with the United States. "Both French and English Canada are being 'colonized,'" he wrote in a new chapter added to the 1971 edition of *The Cana-dian Identity*, "the former by Anglo-Canadian capital, the latter by American. French Canada resists; will English Canada?"[13]

The difficulty with this solution, as events have demonstrated, was at least twofold. The first was that French Canadians, apart from some members of their declining traditional leadership class, did not really share Morton's reservations about the United States or, for that matter, about United States capital investment. René Lévesque often made a point of emphasizing his preference for New York over Toronto, Old Orchard Beach, Maine, for the beaches of Nova Scotia – and in this he was fairly typical of French-speaking Quebecers. Those who found support for free trade with the United States among nationalists in Quebec surprising – Philip Resnick, for example – only revealed their ignorance. Morton's pre-scription for dealing with U.S. influence in Canada implied that the federal government should exercise direct authority in economic and cultural matters. Quebec nationalists, anxious to construct their own state cultural and economic institutions, scorned that solution. As a nationalist Morton simply could not see that nation-alism was no substitute for nationalism. In reality, for all of his com-mitment to "political nationality," Morton was also often a cultural nationalist – and remained one even after his English world had disappeared. That made coming to terms with a competing – Fran-cophone – cultural nationalism nearly impossible.

In the years after the Laval conference the discussion of "iden-tity" in Canada moved a considerable distance from the assump-tion articulated by W.L. Morton in those stimulating University of Wisconsin lectures. Morton's position, at least in general terms, did not disappear, but it was certainly sharply challenged. To repeat, for Morton "identity" was mainly a matter of allegiance, citizen-ship, the sharing of common political values. Within that capacious tent, diversity could be allowed to flourish. In 1971 in the new chap-ter he added to his earlier lectures he spelled this out in a fashion that had only been implicit earlier. There he wrote of "a concept of a nationality made up of a mosaic of peoples and a plurality of cul-tures . . . an unusual concept, which flew in the face of most human experience and had in fact cost Canada much." Nevertheless, he saw it as a positive, even distinguishing Canadian characteristic. "Basic to Canadian life was the duality of English and French and the indefinite perpetuation of the cultures of other groups. In this fact, not in a failure of assimilation, was the root of the mosaic principle. Because it was so integral a part of Canadian life, obviously Canada stood or fell with the success or failure of the mosaic."[14]

Morton believed, by 1971, that a mosaic, or multicultural society, where the rights of citizenship were enjoyed equally by all, could even survive the decline of monarchical sentiment. Nor did he see any contradiction between bilingualism and ethnic equality, suggesting that he viewed bilingualism as a legitimate public policy, multiculturalism as a voluntary association. But the important point is that for Morton citizenship, nationality, commitment to the values of the Canadian political community – "allegiance" was the word he preferred – took definite precedence over those other, and for citizenship purposes, lesser loyalties or identities.

Over against this conception of "identity" or "allegiance," a conception Morton rather uncomfortably shared with Pierre Trudeau (he always felt that Trudeau lacked sufficient respect for British parliamentary traditions, including the monarchy, and would doubtless have objected to the Charter and especially to Trudeau's plebiscitary tendencies), the other versions of identity in Canada, always present but usually muted, grew apace. That conception of identity, which I once called "limited identities" – the phrase is usually attributed to J.M.S. Careless and I have decided that he is welcome to it! – was based on smaller communities of affiliation: region, ethnicity, class, and, increasingly, gender (one originally neglected by me).

Why these allegiances gradually began to challenge the ideal of a civic nationality is a subject of very great complexity. Any full explanation would include at least the following factors: regional reaction to Quebec's claim to what was often perceived as "special" treatment and regional economic differences sometimes accentuated by the debate over U.S. investment; the uncomfortable suspicion among what the B&B Commission called "the other ethnic groups" that bilingualism placed them at a disadvantage; political opportunism; renewed immigration, sometimes from new sources; the new radicalism of the late sixties and seventies that revived academic and non-academic interest in class analysis; and, finally, that combination of social, physiological, and intellectual changes that created feminism. Increasingly these "limited" – if they are "limited" – identities came to be seen as competing with "the Canadian identity" rather than existing harmoniously under its broad umbrella.

Though the small-is-beautiful school of "limited identities" takes a variety of forms, its most systematic version is one advanced by the distinguished McGill political philosopher Charles Taylor. It underlies his much-praised book, *Sources of the Self* and his Massey lectures published as *The Modern Malaise*. Most recently in a volume entitled *Multiculturalism and "The Politics of Recognition,"* Taylor argues that the modern need for self-recognition, both as individuals and as collectivities, has produced what he calls two competing conceptions of "rights-liberalism." The first, "the politics of universalism" or "equal dignity," insists that all citizens be treated equally. The second, "the politics of difference," though growing out of the "politics of universality," insists that equality must include the acceptance of difference especially in matters of "collective rights." Taylor uses this framework to analyse the conflict between Quebec and the rest of Canada especially in the matter of language laws, taking the position that the collective rights of French Canadians can, without a breach of liberty, take precedence over individuals' right to express themselves freely on commercial signs.

Clear-eyed philosopher that he is, Taylor is not unaware of the potential danger to democracy that arises when collective rights are used to trump individual rights. His answer is an attempt to combine the two versions of liberalism. His formula recognizes that certain rights are fundamental and not subject to variation. The only example he offers is *habeas corpus* – and I find this troubling, for I would have expected him to include at least the "Fundamental Freedoms" that begin our Charter, all of which are now subject to the notwithstanding provisions of section 33. Taylor then continues by distinguishing

> these fundamental rights from the broad range of immunities and presumptions of uniform treatment that have sprung up in modern cultures of judicial review. They are willing to weigh the importance of certain forms of uniform treatment against the importance of cultural survival and to opt sometimes in favour of the latter. They are thus in the end not procedural models of liberalism, but are grounded very much on judgments of what makes a good life – judgments in which the integrity of cultures has an important place.[15]

As Taylor admits, this statement leaves many unanswered questions – including the meaning of the "integrity of cultures" – but it is clear that for him it would certainly mean, for Canada, some arrangement like that proposed by the Meech Lake or Charlotte-town Accords.

His view is explicitly applied to Canada in an essay he prepared for the Macdonald Commission in 1985 entitled "Alternative Futures: Legitimacy, Identity, and Alienation in Late Twentieth Century Canada." There Taylor contends that the essence of the Canadian problem is an identity crisis that is characteristic of con-temporary societies. Modern, rational, secular, and bureaucratic society has resulted in political alienation, loss of allegiance to established, often large state structures, and a search for identity in some new form. He argues that there are two possible cures for this modern malaise. One is what he calls the "rights model," where cit-izenship is defined in a clear set of rights, as in the Canadian Charter of Rights and Freedoms. The other is the "community model," where people of common background, and here he seems to mean ethnic background, though not exclusively, live in organic, partici-patory societies. In a general sense, these are the contrasting posi-tions of Herder and Havel. The first emphasizes, if not centraliza-tion, then at least a uniform set of rights within a large political com-munity. The second emphasizes decentralization and diversity of collectivities. For Taylor, and others of similar outlook – similar, but not identical – like the philosopher Will Kymlicka, whose *Liber-alism, Community and Culture* makes a similar argument from a lib-eral perspective, the concept of decentralization, diversity of com-munities, and what might be called "multiple special statuses" is best suited to today's Canada. Kymlicka, who avoids any detailed discussion of Quebec, is especially anxious to find a place for a part of the mosaic that went almost totally unnoticed in Morton's dis-cussion of the Canadian identity, namely the Native peoples.[16]

Neither Taylor nor Kymlicka draws an unbreachably stark con-trast between the two versions of liberalism, for each believes that they can be combined, though not without difficulty. Taylor, rather grudgingly, admits that although the "politics of equal respect" is "inhospitable" to collective diversities, it does not seek to "abolish" those differences. He is, however, seemingly less willing to admit that the "politics of difference" can also be "inhospitable" to the rights so crucial to the "politics of equal respect." The problem is that though in earlier essays Taylor critically dissected Quebec nationalism, in his latest work he makes no real effort to analyse the issues of "equal respect" and "difference" in relation to the essentially homogenizing goals of modern ethnic nationalism – and he believes that Quebec nationalism is grounded in ethnicity. For Taylor, Herder rather than Kant is the best guide to the good society. [17]

While Morton, whose own view was "liberal" and pluralistic, might not have seen any contradiction between "political nationality," which he might have called an "allegiance" model rather than a "rights" model, and "community identity," it is surely the case that there is a potential conflict. That is what we have, in some ways, been confronting – or avoiding – over the last thirty years. It can be seen most obviously in the conflict between the ideal of equal citizenship, advocated by most English Canadians, and the concept of "distinct societies" put forward first, in a variety of formulae, by some French Canadians and especially Quebec nationalists. Something of this sort also explains the insistence of some western provinces, notably Manitoba, or at least Sterling Lyon, and Saskatchewan, or at least Allan Blakeney, on the inclusion of a notwithstanding clause applicable to part of the Charter. A similar difference, in another form, explains the decision of the Native Women's Association of Canada to take the Assembly of First Nations to court to determine whether gender rights, as defined by the Charter, take precedence over the "inherent right to self-government." For women who have seen their human rights infringed by traditional forms of Native government, the argument advanced by the brilliant young lawyer Mary Ellen Turpel, [18] that the Charter embodies bourgeois liberal values that are foreign to Native societies, is not very convincing. This argument, of course, merely repeats similar claims since 1982 made by Quebec nationalists. It should, however, be noted that Quebec nationalists often favour the "rights model" within Quebec at the same time as they advocate a version of the "community model" for Quebec's relations with Canada. Similarly, proponents of Native self-government often claim that the new Native communities will enact their own charters of rights.

What this suggests to me is that over the past few decades a serious confusion has developed over the relationship between citizens' rights and collective identities, and the distinction between individual and collective rights has become muddled. Let me deal with the latter point – individual and collective rights – first. The Charter, especially because it is so often associated with Pierre Elliott Trudeau's brand of liberalism, which is said to be entirely concerned with the individual, is frequently characterized as the protector of individual rights to the exclusion of collective rights. This view is regularly argued by Quebec nationalists for whom collective rights are those of the Francophone majority in Quebec. To them, the Charter, especially the provisions protecting the English language in Quebec, represents a dilution of their collective rights. In fact, of course, the Charter contains both sections that guarantee individual rights and others that protect collective rights. Among the latter are minority language rights, which are *collective*, not *individual* rights. Thus the language dispute in Quebec is not between advocates of collective rights and the proponents of individual rights, but between the advocates of the majority and the supporters of the minority – two collectivities. The same observation could be made about the dispute over "gender equality" and the "inherent right to self-government": two kinds of collectivities, or identities, have come into conflict. Aboriginal rights, gender equality, language rights, multicultural guarantees, the rights of the disabled – these are all collective rights. The Charter thus enshrines *both* individual and collective rights, the latter most often being the collective rights of minority communities. Therefore, it seems to me, the Charter articulates both a "rights model" and a "community model," though not in the fashion preferred by those who agree with Charles Taylor.

The Charlottetown "Canada clause" in a confused fashion attempted to reassert, at least in part, the superiority of "collective rights" of majorities over the Charter provisions that protect minority "collective rights." Of course, nothing is quite that simple since this Canada clause was a bizarre assortment of the supposed distinguishing "characteristics" of virtually any group with sufficient clout to achieve mention. It also included an affirmation by "Canadians" (not their "governments") of "respect for individual and collective human rights and freedoms of all people." Whether this means just in Canada or was intended to be a foreign policy statement is unspecified! Nor can I imagine what it can possibly mean to declare that "Canadians affirm the equality of the provinces at the same time as recognizing their diverse characteristics." Only the disabled, a group that may not define Canada (unless it refers to intellectual disability) but that should stand near the top of any list of people in need of protection, were ignored.

Doubtless, this grab-bag was assembled in an attempt to respond to what I earlier called the crisis of the state. But rather than an adequate response, it strikes me as little more than a summary of the crisis. That crisis is, in simplified terms, an inability to distinguish between a clear statement of the values of a civic culture or political nationality and a list of the anxieties of a number of groups about their "identities." Instead of setting out what Canadians have in common as members of a political community, the Charlottetown Canada clause focused heavily on diversity and therefore set out both to constitutionalize conflict and to guarantee continuing competition for inclusion.

For a country like Canada, and for many others struggling for stability and peace, there must be a distinction between those identities based on tribal allegiances and a civic culture that all can share. We – and here I don't merely mean Canadians, for the tendency is widespread – have accepted uncritically the validity of certain claims about "identity," especially ethnic identity, as though it were something permanent and unambiguous, rather than something malleable, something that is historically constructed and therefore changing. In a brilliant analysis of the apparent inability of Western nations to respond effectively to such crises as Lebanon and Yugoslavia, the French historian Georges Corm has recently argued that part of the problem lies in the failure of democratic philosophy to distinguish clearly between the individual rights of man and the collective rights of national communities, and especially the failure to establish priorities in the conflict between them. That failure, he contends, arises from a willingness to "*essentialiser*" religious and ethnic difference and an inability to dissect the "mythico-political" nature of the entity we call the "nation."[19] A similar failure, I think, mars much of Canadian discussion of these matters. Indeed, as the document called the Charlottetown Accord demonstrated, we don't even want to face the possibility that choices have to be made. For my part, I agree entirely with James Rule, who, in a sharp disagreement with his colleague Michael Waltzer's optimistic assessment of "the new tribalism," writes, "We must do everything in our power to prevent the state from becoming the vehicle for implementing visions of ethnic, religious, or national domination."[20] That seems to me to be an equally valid goal for a "united Canada," an independent Quebec, or the various forms that Native self-government might take.

I guess that what I have been saying, in summary, is that while Canada has become a far more complex and troubled country than the one W.L. Morton analysed in his Wisconsin lectures, his basic formula, his essential political philosophy, remains a convincing one. He went to the heart of our past – and our potential future – when he argued that our success as a country was founded on ensuring that "nationality did not descend into nationalism."[21] For Morton in 1960, just as for Vaclav Havel in 1989, the "civic principle" held out the best hope not only for Canadians, but for many other peoples. I entirely agree. "A Canadian," Mavis Gallant once wrote, "is someone who has a logical reason to think he is one."[22] Now *there* is a Canada clause I could learn to live with, and even to love.

SIXTEEN

Civic Nations and Distinct Societies

"There are no liberals here. There are only nationalists. We are victims of a long lasting nationalistic idea, impossible to get rid of. It is the true state of mind of the people of Serbia."

Professor Vladimir Goati in *The New York Times*,
April 10, 1994

". . . and I therefore now no longer attach any value to any kind of ethnicity."

Nelson Mandela in *The New York Times*, May 1, 1994

As I THINK back on more than thirty years of the debate over the status of Quebec one event stands out vividly in my memory. In November, 1967, the students of Glendon College, York University, organized a conference called "Quebec: Year VIII." The conference took place against the background of René Lévesque's departure from the Quebec Liberal Party and the founding of the Mouvement souveraineté-association, the hearings of the États généraux, Jacques-Yvan Morin's attempt to sell his concept of associate states, and the beginnings of the campaign to convince Pierre Trudeau to run for the federal Liberal leadership. Many political luminaries, some now justly forgotten, were present: Robert Cliche, Gilles Grégoire, Jean-Luc Pepin, Claude Ryan, Eric Kierans, and René Lévesque, who spoke for twice as long and three times as entertainingly as any other speaker. (Since a good part of Lévesque's speech was taken from a paper by Professor Jacques Parizeau, even he was there in sharp mind if not in stout body.)

Lévesque's speech deserves to be recalled because he told his mainly English-speaking audience something important that many refused to hear. The speech was typically disorganized, often witty, occasionally angry, and always a performance. But it did set out the issues that have been debated ever since. First he turned his fire on the ever-smiling Jean-Luc Pepin, that master of the fuzzy ambiguity, who had spoken about the need to guarantee equality for French Canadians. "What is equality," Lévesque demanded, "equality applied to individuals as citizens, to cultural groups, to political society, or to political groups?" The federalists, he said, referring disdainfully to the absent Pierre Trudeau, attempted to confine equality to individuals and cultural groups, but that was a false solution. Quebec would only be satisfied if equality was applied to political societies, to political groups. Equality meant the right to self-determination. And if anyone believed that a halfway house between these types of equality would ever be sufficient – here Claude Ryan was being scourged – Lévesque provided an example of the kind that had made him the star of *Point de Mire*. "All of this leads to a dead end which is called special status," he argued.

> Quebec gets power on immigration. Quebec gets power on social policies. Quebec has got everything more or less. What does Quebec want? Quebec wants more all the time – because more and more she can do her job and nobody else is going to do it the way she wants it to be done. This is called special status. It raises up a monster, a monster because Quebec will be half in and half out of federal structure. Mr. Pepin would be elected to Ottawa in that kind of special status which is the only kind which Quebec would accept, and the rest of Canada would say: 'What the hell is Pepin doing in Ottawa in a structure three quarters of which is under special status, Quebec being out of it?' What would he be minister of when four departments out of five would be siphoned out of Ottawa in special status and be administered in Quebec? He would be minister more and more of nine provinces but not Quebec. Which means that special status is a constitutional-political monstrosity. The only courageous thing is to look things in the face and say: 'Inevitably this movement of Quebec is going to lead to independence, to political sovereignty.' Can we, when that comes in two to four years, be wise enough to see it coming and maintain some association that ensures continued progress in both Canada and Quebec?[1]

On that night in November, 1967, René Lévesque defined the problem, set aside irrelevant solutions, and defended his option. He proclaimed his wager that a genuine nationalist movement had been born in Quebec, that he would succeed in convincing Quebecers that real nations don't eat kitsch – halfway measures. On that topic, though on few others, he agreed with his old associate Pierre Trudeau, who had told audiences of constitutional lawyers and political scientists in 1964 that "when a tightly knit minority within a state begins to define itself forcefully and consistently as a nation it is triggering a mechanism which will tend to propel it towards full statehood."[2]

But where Lévesque viewed nationalism positively, Trudeau judged it an ideology of the elite – *la nouvelle trahison des clercs* – that was neither rooted in the popular consciousness nor suited to resolving the real socio-economic problems of French Canadians. He fully agreed with his friend Charles Taylor, who, in a brilliant article published in 1965, concluded that Quebec nationalism like "modern nationalism is primarily a middle class phenomenon" whose goals only superficially resembled those of social democrats.[3] As an alternative to the retrograde idea that every nation required a state, Trudeau argued that federalism, with its division of powers, provided both a guarantee of cultural survival and for individual liberty. Special status, as he inelegantly put it, was a con game, a mere disguise for incremental separation, a temporary stopping place for those without the courage or clarity to make up their minds. Since none of its proponents would ever define special status, state its goals, and set its limits, the Trudeau-Lévesque position rang true. Even Claude Ryan, once its most persuasive proponent, dropped it from his now forgotten Beige Paper in 1980.

Lévesque and Trudeau were agreed on another point: constitutions and public institutions shape societies, they don't merely reflect them, a viewpoint that is central to the superb constitutional writings of Alan C. Cairns.[4] Lévesque believed that full sovereignty was required to shape his province into a homogeneous French-speaking nation, though he always insisted that English-language minority rights would be respected. (The first version of the Lévesque language law – Bill 1, revised after criticism from civil rights groups to become 101 – revealed this goal most clearly.) That *projet de société* could only be achieved after full statehood had been established. Trudeau countered with the offer of a federal system guided by a constitutionally entrenched Charter of Rights that would preserve and promote a diverse society of the kind that Canada, including Quebec, was becoming. Lévesque was a nationalist in the traditional sense: his ideal society was founded on linguistic and cultural commonalities. Trudeau rejected nationalism, whether French-Canadian, English-Canadian, or Canadian, and sought to replace it with the ideal of a civic nation where the guarantee of individual freedom and cultural diversity was itself the bond binding a political community together. He would certainly second Alan Cairns's motion that "In Quebec, as in Canada, the community must be defined in civic terms, applicable to all, if it is not to be an instrument of exclusion."[5] Similarly, he would reject Charles Taylor's alternative "participatory model" on the grounds that Taylor, by 1985, had forgotten the lessons he once taught about the nature of modern nationalism.[6]

The conflict, or at least contrast, between "the rights model" and the "participatory model," sometimes defined as "individual rights" versus "collective rights" or, in Taylor's most recent version, as "the politics of equal respect" and "the politics of difference,"[7] has come to dominate much of the current discussion of politics and the constitution in Canada. And, as this has happened, a new effort has been made to revive that concept that Lévesque and Trudeau dismissed so long ago: special status. The revival began with the Meech Lake Accord and, though the term "special status" has been banished, the idea is so intoxicating that it has resurfaced as "distinct society" and "asymmetrical federalism." This revival has a strikingly curious aspect: it is almost exclusively among English Canadians. The two leading proponents of the "participatory politics of difference model," Charles Taylor and Jeremy Webber, live and teach in Quebec; the other, Will Kymlicka, whose *Liberalism, Community and Culture* provides a philosophical argument for a collectivist liberalism that would encourage special status for minority cultures – his example is Native people – teaches in Ottawa.

Many of those Francophones who might once have welcomed the Taylor-Webber-Kymlicka approach – Guy Laforest and Christian Dufour, for example – appear to have concluded that if Canadian duality is an impossible dream, then independence is preferable. Interestingly, they seem also tempted to adopt a rights model of civic nationalism for an independent Quebec. That is understandable since an independent Quebec based on "the politics of difference" and "collective rights" would imply a "right" to special status for minority collectivities – Native people, Anglos, and allos! As Lysianne Gagnon shrewdly observed:

Nowadays, the 'correct' way to be a sovereignist is to emphasize the territorial, rather than the ethnic dimension. For right-thinking sovereignists, the rationale for sovereignty is not rooted in the French Canadian nation, as it was in previous times, but in the fact that Quebec as a whole, including its minorities, is a distinct society with its own culture and institutions. This is highly debatable, but it has become a given, something that is not even discussed. [8]

Much of the argument about collective and individual rights turns on the nature of the Charter. Quebec nationalists and others, including Taylor and Webber, contend that the Charter, in establishing what Webber calls "a unitary conception of Canadian citizenship," is an instrument of homogenization. [9] Though his argument is more subtle, Alan Cairns concurs, as does Peter Russell. [10] To some extent the charge can be sustained: the Charter does give Canadian citizens, wherever they live, a defined set of rights free from the infringement of either federal or provincial governments "subject only to such reasonable limits prescribed by law as can demonstrably be justified in a free and democratic society." Subject also, alas, to a partial provincial override.

But does the Charter protect only individuals against collectivities? The answer, Pierre Trudeau to the contrary notwithstanding, is no. It protects both: the language rights of French and English Canadians, the equality rights of men and women, the Aboriginal rights of Native Canadians, and the rights of some other collectivities. These are guarantees of diversity, not homogeneity. Moreover, those who argue that the Charter's "individualism" is an homogenizing assault on collective cultural rights are themselves the defenders of "homogeneity" – the right of a majority culture to impose its norms on minority cultures. Or even on a minority gender, as Native women observed in the debate over the Charter and the "inherent right to self-government." Once again Alan Cairns is the best guide to Charter federalism: the Charter, he writes, "is a Janus-faced document, presenting both liberal individualism and a constitutionalization of the linguistic, ethnic, racial, cultural and sex identities of Canadians." [11] Too much of our constitutional debate has been conducted in unexamined simplifications as though words were things, forgetting as Vaclav Havel's warning "that to be wary of words and the horrors that might slumber inconspicuously within them – isn't this, after all, the true vocation of the intellectual?"[12] (Here Jeremy Webber seems especially guilty writing about Quebec's "traditional concerns," "traditional grievances," and "centralist visions" without definition, about "identity" as though it had an essential, unproblematic meaning, confusing "citizenship" with "nationalism" and Quebecers with Quebec.)[13]

There is no convincing reason why a constitution should not recognize both individual and collective rights. Nor, as Joseph Raz argues in a recent issue of *Dissent*, is it necessary for liberals to choose individual over cultural rights; in modern societies "liberal multiculturalism" is the ideal.[14] In Canada the issue has never really been one of whether collective rights should be recognized, but rather how. The 1982 constitution answers that question with the Charter. Its critics – the special status-Meech Lake-asymmetrical federalism proponents – agree with Ken McRoberts's contention that that answer merely avoids the question. McRoberts tries to make the case that since 1968 English Canadians, misled by Pierre Trudeau (who did have some support in Quebec!), have ignored the obvious: it is Quebec, not French Canadians, that should have been recognized as special or distinct. McRoberts articulates – and Webber repeats – a view held by many English-Canadian nationalists: the federal government should retain, perhaps even increase, its jurisdiction over the rest of Canada while allowing, even encouraging, Quebec to opt for its own course as the national homeland of French Canada, a distinct society. Implicit in this view – McRoberts's is explicit – is the contention that language belongs to territories, not to people. The supposed failure of bilingualism should be recognized. Thus what the Charter protects as a fundamental human right is summarily dismissed.[15]

Charles Taylor's case for asymmetrical federalism – he doesn't use the term, being satisfied to urge an apparently unlimited decentralization – is philosophical rather than constitutional. Alienation, the modern malaise of contemporary societies, is best relieved, he argues, by affirming community cultural values rather than guaranteeing rights. Small is unalienated. Apart from a commitment to a Meech-style arrangement, Taylor is distressingly vague about details. To some extent those details are sketched in by his McGill colleague, Jeremy Webber, a professor of law. His book, *Reimagining Canada: Language, Culture, Community, and the Canadian Constitution*, might have been entitled *Lament for Meech Lake*. It is an ingenious, but not entirely successful attempt to replace the concepts of nation and nationalism in our constitutional debate with language, culture, and community, concepts that are sometimes viewed as the essence of nation and, in combination with a particular historical understanding, nationalism. Second, he contends, somewhat unoriginally, that in a federal system loyalties are not singular but at least dual. In his view Trudeau's Charter and Lévesque's *indépendantisme* both failed to recognize this principle, a contention that in Trudeau's case is unfounded unless one insists, as Webber apparently does, that there should be no commonly held rights of Canadian citizenship. Webber then argues in favour of an asymmetrical federalism applied to Quebecers and Native people based on the proposition that language, culture, and community justify special status.

Most of these arguments are familiar, though Webber often has an original slant and a naive enthusiasm that unintentionally reveals the softness of his arguments. Here, for example, is what he has to say about culture, a concept that lies at the heart of his justification for special status. "I will speak of 'culture'," he writes, "because that is the term commonly used in the discussion of these issues. But note that in this context the range of things marked by culture may be very broad indeed, much broader than the narrow definition of specifically linguistic or folkloric characteristics. Furthermore, this idea of culture is not static, not frozen in the past. Culture, as it is used here, is essentially the same as the distinctive characteristics of a particular community's public debate through time." [16] Culture is everything, and nothing. Who said that at the mention of "culture" he reached for his dictionary? Webber's vagueness tails off into a smoky evanescence, often making the Meech Lake Accord seem an example of clarity. In a constitution with that definition of culture as an interpretive clause and a provincial government empowered to preserve and promote it, one can imagine a very, very special status!

Webber also contends, as do McRoberts and other proponents of special status, that the Trudeau-Lévesque argument against it, which claims that it would make federal MPs from Quebec irrelevant, is unconvincing. (In fact, proponents of special status rarely care much about the federal Parliament.) After all, Webber argues, federal MPs often vote on legislation that applies to only one part of the country, nor does the constitution require that all provinces be the same. But this is just obfuscation. Special status refers to a differential division of powers between the federal government and one province. When the federal Parliament legislates for the Atlantic fishery or prairie grain growers it does so not because of a differential division of powers, but because it is empowered to do so. It is not saying that this is a national policy, except for one province; it is saying that this is a national policy that applies where it is relevant, the latter being determined by geography.

The second argument often advanced for special status–asymmetrical federalism is the example of the Canada/Quebec pension plan. There is no doubt that that agreement has worked. But how far could it be extended? It is also worth noting that the funds acquired by Quebec through the pension plan – the funds in the Caisse de Dépôt – have been used to promote Quebec Inc., to build a national Quebec economy. And the success of that project, nationalists in English Canada might remember, is what encouraged so many Quebec business people to support free trade with the United States: sovereignty-association.

Another example of the workings of special status or, at least, special arrangements is in the field of immigration. Here, as Monique Nemni has shown, the increased power of Quebec has resulted in the virtual disappearance of Canada from the programs the Quebec government has designed to integrate new immigrants into the host society. Where immigrants are taught that they are to become *citoyens* of Quebec who will soon join other Quebec *citoyens* in the goal of *bâtir Québec*, it is perhaps desirable to have a Charter that sets out the rights of all Canadians in the country in which immigrants are, after all, seeking to become *citoyens*.[17]

What these two examples underline is that any discussion of special status–asymmetry that ignores the dynamic nature and the final goals of nationalism is, in the pejorative sense, academic. The evidence of nationalism's destructive nature can be seen across the world. The example of the former Yugoslavia, where Germany's vulgar haste in recognizing Croatia's claim to the right of national self-determination set off a brutal series of crimes against humanity unequalled since 1945, is only the most obvious. ("They will go on destroying," writes Zlatko Dizdarevic, "until all that remains is evil, hatred, nationalism, and fascism.")[18] Spain, so recently released from the chains of fascism, moves gradually toward a special status-style crisis. Recently Jordi Pujol, the Catalan nationalist leader, whose region already has special powers, demanded more. "Catalonia is a nation," he insisted in familiar terms, "with its language, culture, historical identity, and traditional institutions."

Since by the 1979 constitution the Basque country, Galicia, Andalusia, and Catalonia all enjoy special status, more power for one means more for all. And nationalist movements have appeared in the Canary Islands, Aragon, the Balearic Islands, and Valencia demanding equality with the special![19] In Czechoslovakia first there was the hyphen, then the "and," and finally dissolution without even an appeal to the people. The quest for special status is naturally contagious. Nothing reveals it more than the debate between Quebec nationalists and spokespeople for the "First Nations." "Unless the First Nations right to self-determination is fully recognized and respected by the National Assembly," Ovide Mercredi said to that body's members in February, 1992, "the right to self-determination for French Canadians cannot legitimately exist." And he went on to describe his people's national characteristics in terms interchangeable with those of Quebec or Catalan nationalists. The geese and the ganders are deep in the sauce.[20]

The curious innocence of many intellectuals in Canada about the expansive thrust of nationalism is a subject that begs investigation. Perhaps this naiveté is the result of our longtime colonial status, the French-English duality, the heterogeneous population, and the federal form of government. But an unrequited nationalist love for a nation that has yet to be imagined apparently blinds many to reality. As René Lévesque made plain in 1968, nationalism is a force that demands not special status or asymmetry, but equal status, sovereignty, and, all too often, "ethnic cleansing," though not necessarily of the brutal Serbian variety. Even those for whom special status of the Meech Lake variety is only symbolic miss the point: a symbol is symbolic of something: according to *Le Petit Robert,* "distinct" implies "*autre, différent, indépendant, séparé.*" That is what "*société distinct*" symbolized; that is what the government of Quebec was to be empowered to "preserve and promote."[21]

It has taken nearly a quarter-century for the clarity that Lévesque and Trudeau hoped to impose on the Canadian constitutional debate in the 1960s to come to fruition. The attempt to avoid the issue, to appease rather than restrain nationalism, has been costly – how costly only time will reveal. The dynamic of Quebec politics, a dynamic driven by each party's attempt to outbid its rival through appeals to nationalist sentiment – our party can win a more distinct status than yours – has finally run its course. The long Meech-Allaire-Campeau-Bélanger-Charlottetown episode made the obvious unavoidable. Quebecers now have a choice between provincial status in an evolving Canadian federal system, two official languages in a multicultural society, and a Charter that guarantees defined individual and collective rights . . . or independence.

It could be worse. My other main memory of Quebec: Year VIII at Glendon College is of a plea made by a newly minted External Affairs officer about to take up his first posting in Belgrade. His preparatory reading, he told us, convinced him that the future of Canada lay in the Yugoslavian solution! With or without Tito? someone asked.

Notes

(All translations from the French by the author.)

1 Who Belongs Where?

1. Grahame Clark and Stuart Piggott, *Prehistoric Societies* (New York, 1965), chs. 4, 5; W.H. McNeill, *The Great Frontier* (Princeton, N.J., 1983).
2. Elie Kedourie, *Nationalism* (London, 1960), p. 9.
3. Shlomo Avineri, *The Making of Modern Zionism* (New York, 1981).
4. Michel Foucault, *The Order of Things. The Archeology of the Human Sciences* (New York, 1973).
5. Ernest Gellner, *Nations and Nationalism* (Ithaca, N.Y., 1983), p. 44.
6. Kedourie, *Nationalism*, p. 101.
7. Francis Jennings, *The Invasion of America* (New York, 1975); Tzvetan Todorov, *The Conquest of America* (New York, 1984).
8. McNeill, *The Great Frontier*, p. 9.
9. François Vaillancourt, "Le statut du Français et des francophones au Québec, 1960-1980," unpublished ms.
10. Anthony D. Smith, *The Ethnic Revival in the Modern World* (Cambridge, 1981), p. 28.
11. *Kontinent. The Alternative Voice of Russia and Eastern Europe* (New York, 1974), p. 29.
12. Zlatko Dizdarevic, *Sarajevo: A War Journal* (New York, 1993), p. 112.
13. Walker Connor, *Ethnonationalism* (Princeton, N.J., 1994), p. 25.
14. William Johnson, *A Canadian Myth: Quebec, Between Canada and the Illusion of Utopia* (Montreal and Toronto, 1994). This is an excellent chronicle of Quebec politics since 1960, and especially since 1984, though his concentration on "Anglophobia" as the source of nationalism among Francophones is exaggerated. Read together with Stevie Cameron, *On the Take: Crime, Corruption and Greed in the Mulroney Years* (Toronto, 1994), the real nature of

Mulroney's *beau risque* – his alliance with Quebec nationalists – becomes appallingly clear.

15. Daniel Patrick Moynihan, *Pandaemonium. Ethnicity in International Politics* (New York, 1994), p. 173.

16. Canada, *House of Commons Debates*, 133,051, Monday, April 18, 1994, pp. 3137-41, 3166-92.

17. Tony Judt, "The New Old Nationalism," *New York Review of Books*, XLI, 10, May 26, 1994, p. 50.

18. Tzvetan Todorov, *On Human Diversity. Nationalism, Racism and Exoticism in French Thought* (New York, 1993), p. 241.

19. Alain Finkielkraut, *The Undoing of Thought* (London, 1988), p. 105.

20. E.J. Hobsbawm, *The Age of Empire* (London, 1987), p. 142.

2 The White Man Cometh

1. Bernard W. Sheehan, "Indian-White Relations in Early America: A Review Essay," *William and Mary Quarterly*, 26, 2 (April, 1969), p. 285.

2. Ronald H. Frame, ed., *The Complete Works of Montaigne* (Stanford, Calif., 1957), vol. 3, p. 693.

3. R. Cole Harris, "The Extension of France into Rural Canada," in James R. Gibson, ed., *European Settlement and Development in North America* (Toronto, 1978), pp. 27-45.

4. John Locke, *Two Treatises of Government* (Cambridge, 1960), p. 298.

5. Frederick Jackson Turner, *The Frontier in American History*, ed., R.A. Billington (New York, 1962), p. 3; John C. Juricek, "American Usage of the word 'Frontier' from Colonial Times to Frederick Jackson Turner," *Proceedings of the American Philosophical Association*, 110 (1966), pp. 10-34.

6. Harold Adams Innis, *The Fur Trade in Canada* (Toronto, 1961), pp. 384, 392; see also W.J. Eccles, "A Belated Review of Harold Adams Innis, *The Fur Trade in Canada*," *Canadian Historical Review*, 60, 4 (December, 1979), pp. 419-41.

7. Turner, *The Frontier*, pp. 11-14.

8. Frederick Jackson Turner, *The Character and Influence of the Indian Trade in Wisconsin* (Norman, Okla., 1977), pp. 77-79. Turner and Innis agreed on another fundamental matter, for Turner wrote, "The water system composed of the St. Lawrence and the Great Lakes is the key to the continent" (p. 21). Innis's "Laurentian thesis" was founded on that concept.

9. Innis, *Fur Trade in Canada*, p. 15.

10. Turner, *The Frontier*, p. 3.

11. Nancy Oestreich Lurie, "Indian Cultural Adjustment to European Civilization" in James Morton Smith, *Seventeenth-Century America* (Chapel Hill,

N.C., 1959), p. 39; see also Erna Gunther, *Indian Life on the Northwest Coast of North America* (Chicago, 1972), pp. 249-62; T.J. Brasser, "Early Indian-European Contacts," in Bruce G. Trigger, *Handbook of the North American Indians*, vol. 15 (Washington, D.C., 1978), pp. 78-88 (*The Northeast*).

12. Carl Otto Sauer, *Sixteenth-Century North America* (Berkeley, Calif., 1971), p. 303; see also Cornelius J. Jaenen, "Amerindian Views of French Culture in the Seventeenth Century," *Canadian Historical Review*, 55, 3 (September, 1974), pp. 361-91.

13. H.P. Biggar, ed., *The Voyages of Jacques Cartier* (Ottawa, 1924), pp. 53, 55-56, 61, 57, 66. Marcel Trudel, *Histoire de la Nouvelle-France*, vol. 1: *Les Vaines Tentatives. 1534-1603* (Montréal, 1963), pp. 81-82. Brian Slattery, "French Claims in North America, 1500-59," *Canadian Historical Review*, 59, 2 (June, 1978), p. 147, argues for a literal interpretation of Cartier's intent, but that only seems tenable in a strict legal sense. Wilcomb E. Washburn, "The Moral and Legal Justification for Dispossessing the Indians," in Smith, *Seventeenth-Century America*, pp. 15-32.

14. Jesse D. Jennings, *Prehistoric North America* (New York, 1968); J.V. Wright, *Six Chapters of Canada's Prehistory* (Ottawa, 1976).

15. Conrad Heidenreich, *Huronia* (Toronto, 1971), p. 283; Elizabeth Tooker, *An Ethnography of the Huron Indians, 1615-49* (Washington, D.C., 1964), pp. 58-66.

16. John S. Ewers, *The Horse in Blackfoot Indian Culture* (Washington, D.C., 1955), p. 300.

17. Philip Drucker, *Cultures of the North Pacific Coast* (San Francisco, Calif., 1965); Wilson Duff, *Images Stone B.C. Thirty Centuries of Northwest Coast Indian Sculpture* (Toronto, 1975).

18. Diamond Jenness, "The Indian's Interpretation of Man and Nature," *Transactions of the Royal Society of Canada*, 3rd ser., 26, 2 (1930), pp. 57-62.

19. Wilcomb E. Washburn, *The Indian in America* (New York, 1975), pp. 10-65. Of the many studies of Indian art, a particularly useful one is Ted J. Brasser, *"Bo'jou, Neejee"* (Ottawa, 1976), which is especially good on the question of contact. Norman Feder's *American Indian Art* (New York, 1971) is also excellent.

20. Alfred W. Crosby, Jr., *The Columbian Exchange* (Westport, Conn., 1972); R.M. Saunders, "The First Introduction of European Plants and Animals to Canada," *Canadian Historical Review*, 16, 4 (December, 1935), pp. 388-401.

21. Ralph Davis, *The Rise of the Atlantic Economies* (London, 1973). There is a substantial and controversial literature on the topic of the comparative economic organization and motivation of Europeans and Amerindians. It is conveniently summarized and discussed in Arthur J. Ray and Donald Freeman, *'Give Us Good Measure.' An Economic Analysis of Relations between the Indians*

and the Hudson's Bay Company before 1763 (Toronto, 1978), pp. 10-18. Another viewpoint is presented in Marshall Sahlins, *Stone Age Economics* (Chicago, 1972). On this topic and other aspects of contact, there is much useful information in Carol M. Judd and Arthur J. Ray, eds., *Old Trails and New Directions*, Papers of the Third North American Fur Trade Conference (Toronto, 1980).

22. This generalization is, of course, subject to many exceptions, for a few Amerindians have entered the capitalist system at almost every level, from high finance to high steel. One interesting study, which demonstrates some of the problems, is Rolf Knight, *Indians at Work: An Informal History of Native Labour in British Columbia* (Vancouver, 1978).

23. Alden T. Vaughan, *New England Frontier: Puritans and Indians 1620-1675* (Boston, 1965), pp. 211-34; Innis, *Fur Trade in Canada*.

24. W.J. Eccles, *The Canadian Frontier 1534-1760* (New York, 1969), p. 24: "The French were far more dependent upon the Indians than the Indians on them."

25. Innis, *Fur Trade in Canada*, p. 389; James Axtell, "The Scholastic Philosophy of the Wilderness," *William and Mary Quarterly*, 29, 3 (July, 1972), pp. 335-66; Eric Ross, *Beyond the River and the Bay* (Toronto, 1973), p. 6.

26. Innis, *Fur Trade in Canada*, cited on p. 49. Champlain's point is dramatically seconded by a modern birchbark-canoe maker. See John McPhee, *The Survival of the Bark Canoe* (New York, 1975), p. 21. For a thorough account of cultural contact in early New France, see Marcel Trudel, *Histoire de la Nouvelle France*, vol. 2: *Le Comptoir 1604-1627* (Montréal, 1966), pp. 353-403.

27. Gabriel Sagard, *The Long Journey to the Country of the Huron*, ed. G.M. Wrong (Toronto, 1939), p. 60. Corn was nearly as important in early New England, where the first settlers learned corn cultivation from the Indians. A.C. Parker, "Iroquois Use of Maize and Other Food Plants," in W.N. Fenton, ed., *Parker on the Iroquois* (Syracuse, N.Y., 1968), pp. 14-15; Bernard Sheehan, *Savagism and Civility: Indians and Englishmen in Colonial Virginia* (Cambridge, 1980), pp. 101-09.

28. Harold Adams Innis, *Peter Pond. Fur Trader and Adventurer* (Toronto, 1930), pp. 84-86; Grace Lee Nute, *Voyageurs* (New York, 1931), p. 54.

29. George T. Hunt, *The Wars of the Iroquois. A Study in Inter-Tribal Trade Relations* (Madison, Wis., 1940), pp. 53-65.

30. Bruce G. Trigger, *The Children of Aataentsic*, 2 vols. (Montreal, 1976), 1, p. 175. In *Huronia*, p. 219, Conrad Heidenreich argues that the Huron trading network was less developed than Trigger suggests, but he agrees that a pre-contact network did exist.

31. John Phillip Reid, *A Law of Blood: Primitive Law of the Cherokee Nation* (New York, 1965), p. 124.

32. John C. Ewers, "The Indian Trade of the Upper Missouri before Lewis and Clark," *Bulletin of the Missouri Historical Society*, 10, 4 (1954), pp. 429-46.

33. John C. Ewers, "The Influence of the Fur Trade upon the Indians of the Northern Plains," in Malvina Bolus, *People and Pelts* (Winnipeg, 1972), cited on p. 3.

34. Trigger, *Children of Aataentsic*, 1, p. 187.

35. Arthur J. Ray, *Indians in the Fur Trade* (Toronto, 1974), pp. 51-57.

36. Wilson Duff, *The Indian History of British Columbia*, vol. 1: *The Impact of the White Man*, Anthropology in British Columbia, Memoir no. 5 (Victoria, 1964), p. 58; Gunther, *Indian Life*, pp. 119-38.

37. Eccles, *Canadian Frontier, 1534-1760*, pp. 24-25.

38. John C. Ewers, "Inter-Tribal Warfare as the Precursor of Indian-White Warfare on the Great Plains," *Western Historical Quarterly*, 6, 4 (October, 1975), pp. 397-410. P. Richard Metcalf, "Who Should Rule at Home? Native American Politics and Indian-White Relationships," *Journal of American History*, 61, 3 (December, 1974), pp. 651-65.

39. Robin Fisher, *Contact and Conflict, Indian-European in British Columbia, 1774-1890* (Vancouver, 1977), pp. 42-43; Ray, *Indians*, pp. 14-16; but see also Bruce G. Trigger, "The Mohawk-Mohican War (1624-28): The Establishment of a Pattern," *Canadian Historical Review*, 52, 3 (September, 1971), pp. 276-86, for a careful examination of the way the trade rivalries of Dutch, French, and British led to the Iroquois wars.

40. Francis Jennings, *The Invasion of America: Indians, Colonialism and the Cant of Conquest* (New York, 1976), pt. 2, *passim*.

41. Bernard G. Hoffman, *Cabot to Cartier* (Toronto, 1961), p. 214.

42. Andrew Hill Clark, *Acadia: The Geography of Early Nova Scotia* (Madison, Wis., 1968), p. 361. For a full account, see L.F.S. Upton, *Micmacs and Colonists, Indian-White Relations in the Maritimes, 1713-1867* (Vancouver, 1979).

43. T.J.C. Brasser, "The Coastal Algonkians: People of the First Frontier," in Eleanor Burke Leacock and Nancy Oestreich Lurie, *North American Indians in Historical Perspective* (New York, 1971), p. 73.

44. A.G. Bailey, "Social Revolution in Early Canada," *Canadian Historical Review*, 19, 3 (September, 1938), pp. 264-76.

45. Lurie, "Indian Cultural Adjustment," p. 28; Fisher, *Contact and Conflict*, *passim*.

46. H.P. Biggar, *The Works of Samuel de Champlain* (Toronto, 1925), II, p. 171.

47. Ray, *Indians*, p. 69; Arthur J. Ray, "Fur Trade History as an Aspect of Native History," in Ian A.L. Getty and Donald B. Smith, *One Century Later* (Vancouver, 1978), p. 10; for an excellent example, see Samuel Hearne, *A Journey to the Northern Ocean, 1769-71-72*, ed. Richard Glover (Toronto, 1958), p. 187.

48. Eccles, *Canadian Frontier, 1534-1760*, p. 6.

49. Heidenreich, *Huronia*, p. 293.

50. Sagard, *Country of the Huron*, p. 125; Wallis Smith, "The Fur Trade and Frontier: A Study in Inter-Cultural Alliance," *Anthropologica*, n.s. 15 (1973), pp. 21-36.

51. R.M. Saunders, "The Emergence of the Coureur de Bois as a Social Type," *Canadian Historical Association Report* (1939), p. 26; Normand Lafleur, *La Vie traditionnelle du coureur de bois aux XIXe et XXe siècles* (Montréal, 1973), pp. 29-70; Louise Déchêne, *Habitants et marchands de Montréal au XVIIe siècle* (Montréal, 1974), pp. 217-26.

52. Bruce Trigger, "The Jesuits and the Fur Trade," *Ethnohistory*, 12, 1 (Winter, 1965), p. 38.

53. Heidenreich, *Huronia*, p. 282. For a parallel in New England, see Vaughan, *New England Frontier*, p. 234.

54. Trigger, *Children of Aataentsic*, I, pp. 361-65, 425-30.

55. Hunt, *Wars of the Iroquois*, pp. 66-104; Trigger, *Children of Aataentsic*, II, p. 664.

56. Trigger, *Children of Aataentsic*, II, p. 601.

57. L.J. Burpee, ed., *Journals and Letters of Pierre Gaultier de Varennes de la Vérendrye and His Sons* (Toronto, 1927), p. 146.

58. Ray, "Fur Trade History," cited on p. 11. E.E. Rich, *The Fur Trade and the Northwest to 1857* (Toronto, 1967), p. 103; Edward Umfreville, *The Present State of Hudson's Bay containing a Full Description of That Settlement and Adjacent Country: And Likewise of the Fur Trade and Hints for Its Improvement*, ed. W.S. Wallace (Toronto, 1954), pp. 31-32.

59. Ewers, "The Influence of the Fur Trade," cited on p. 9.

60. Ray and Freeman, '*Give Us Good Measure,*' p. 236.

61. John S. Galbraith, *The Little Emperor, Governor Simpson of the Hudson's Bay Company* (Toronto, 1976), pp. 188-208.

62. Duff, *Indian History*, p. 53.

63. Arthur J. Ray, "Diffusion of Diseases in the Western Interior of Canada, 1830-1850," *Geographical Review*, 66, 2 (April, 1976), pp. 139-57.

64. Henry F. Dobyns, "Estimating Aboriginal American Population: An Appraisal of Techniques with a New Hemispheric Estimate," *Current Anthropology*, 7 (1966), pp. 395-416. For a survey of the literature, see Dobyns, *Native American Historical Demography* (Chicago, 1976). My figures are taken from William N. Denevan, ed., *The Native Population of the Americas* (Madison, Wis., 1976), p. 291.

65. After an extended examination of the discussion of pre-contact population, Woodrow Borah concluded that only after a great deal of additional research

will it be possible to arrive at a hemispheric figure with a margin of error between 30 per cent and 50 per cent. Denevan, *Native Population*, p. 34.

66. These figures, taken from Denevan, are about 25 per cent higher than the now commonly accepted, and very judicious, estimate contained in Harold E. Driver, *Indians of North America*, 2nd ed. (Chicago, 1975), pp. 63-64.

67. Driver, *Indians of North America*, p. 257; F.W. Hodge, *Handbook of the Indians of Canada* (Ottawa, 1911), p. 390. By the mid-1960s, the Indian population of the United States had grown to 600,000. In Canada the figure was 200,000 (Driver, *Indians of North America*, pp. 527, 539).

68. See, for example, Lewis Henry Morgan, *The League of the Iroquois* [1851] (Secaucus, N.J., 1975), p. 145; and Diamond Jenness, *The Indians of Canada* [1932] (Toronto, 1977), p. 264.

69. Wilbur R. Jacobs, "The Indian and the Frontier in American History – A Need for Revision," *Western Historical Quarterly*, 4, 1 (January, 1973), p. 46. See also Alfred W. Crosby, "Virgin Soil Epidemics as a Factor in the Aboriginal Depopulation of America," *William and Mary Quarterly*, 33, 2 (April, 1976), pp. 289-99.

70. Denevan, *Native Population*, cited on p. 5.

71. Crosby, *Columbian Exchange*, pp. 122-64. The most convincing, perhaps even conclusive discussion of this issue is Francisco Guerra, "The Problem of Syphilis," in Fredi Chiappelli, ed., *First Images of America: The Impact of the New World on the Old* (Berkeley, Calif., 1976), II, pp. 845-51.

72. Virgil J. Vogel, *American Indian Medicine* (Norman, Okla., 1970), p. 211.

73. Shelburne F. Cook, "The Significance of Disease in the Extinction of the New England Indians," *Human Biology*, 14 (1973), pp. 487-91; Trigger, *Children of Aataentsic*, II, pp. 499-501; Reid, *A Law of Blood*, p. 6; Howard R. Lamar, ed., *The American West* (New York, 1977), pp. 702-03; John C. Ewers, *The Blackfeet: Raiders of the Plains* (Norman, Okla., 1958), pp. 65-66; L.S.F. Upton, "The Extermination of the Beothuks," *Canadian Historical Review*, 58, 2 (June, 1977), pp. 133-53; Wilson Duff, *The Indian History*, pp. 42-43.

74. J.B. Tyrrell, ed., *David Thompson's Narrative, 1784-1812* (Toronto, 1916), p. 323.

75. John F. Taylor, "Sociocultural Effects of Epidemics on the Northern Plains, 1734-1850," *Western Canadian Journal of Anthropology*, 7, 4 (1977), p. 78.

76. Ray, *Indians in the Fur Trade*, pp. 188-91.

77. Edwin T. Denig, *Five Tribes of the Upper Missouri* (Norman, Okla., 1961), p. 72.

78. Taylor, "Sociocultural Effects of Epidemics," p. 65; Ray, *Indians*, pp. 183-91.

79. Reuben Thwaites, ed., *The Jesuit Relations and Allied Documents*, 73 vols. (Cleveland, Ohio, 1898), XVI, p. 39.

80. Vogel, *American Indian Medicine*, p. 35; Trigger, *Children of Aataentsic*, II, pp. 592-30.

81. Tyrrell, *David Thompson's Narrative*, p. 324; Alfred Goldsworthy Bailey, *The Conflict of European and Eastern Algonkian Cultures 1504-1700*, 2nd ed. (Toronto, 1969), p. 81; Calvin Martin, *Keepers of the Game, Indian-Animal Relations and the Fur Trade* (Berkeley, Calif., 1978), p. 146.

82. Vogel, *American Indian Medicine*, p. 35. In August, 1979, a government hospital in Kenora, Ontario, agreed to allow an Ojibwa medicine man to practise in the mental health unit. Though not attempting to cure "white man's diseases," George Councillor said, "there are Indian sicknesses that doctors can't see, like when a bad medicine man puts a curse on somebody. White men call them emotional problems and hallucinations. In our culture you can get sick from many things. If you hurt a small animal or bird you might have problems many years later. It's forbidden by the Great Spirit to be cruel. You have to fit in with the way things work." The local clergymen, equally in keeping with their own traditions, opposed recognition of this contemporary Midewiwin. *Globe and Mail* (Toronto, August 29, 1979), p. 9.

83. Tyrrell, *David Thompson's Narrative*, p. 110. Victor G. Hopwood, in *David Thompson: Travels in Western North America, 1784-1812* (Toronto, 1971), p. 32, interprets this passage as evidence that the Indians had developed a myth of a "golden age" before the white man arrived. He neglects to observe that the white man also witnessed this "golden age." Calvin Martin, in *The Keepers of the Game*, pp. 113-56, argues that the relations between the decline in the number of animals and disease can be explained by the destruction of the Indians' belief system, which could not deal with the fact that the Europeans brought disease. The result was that war was declared on the animals, which seemed to have been held responsible. That may be so, but as a speculation it is certainly no more convincing than the argument for an ecological interpretation presented here and based on Aldo Leopold's essay, "Thinking like a Mountain," in *A Sand County Almanac* (New York, 1976), pp. 129-33.

84. Cornelius J. Jaenen, *Friend and Foe* (Toronto, 1976), cited on p. 104. See also J. H. Kennedy, *Jesuit and Savage in New France* (New Haven, Conn., 1950), p. 107.

85. Vogel, *American Indian Medicine*, cited on p. 190; Anthony F.C. Wallace, *The Death and Rebirth of the Seneca* (New York, 1972), p. 63.

86. Biggar, *Works of Samuel de Champlain*, pp. 212-13; Vogel, *American Indian Medicine*, pp. 111-23; John J. Heagarty, *Four Centuries of Medical History in Canada* (Toronto, 1928), I, p. 269. See also William N. Fenton, "Contacts between Iroquois Herbalism and Colonial Medicine," in *Smithsonian Institution Annual Report 1941* (Washington, D.C., 1942), pp. 503-26; Raymond D.

Fogelson, "Change, Persistence and Accommodation in Cherokee Medico-Magical Beliefs," in William N. Fenton and John Gulich, eds., *Symposium on Cherokee and Iroquois Cultures* (Washington, D.C., 1961), pp. 215-25.

87. Jaenen, *Friend and Foe*, cited on p. 110.

88. Trigger, *Children of Aataentsic*, I, p. 433; André Vachon, "L'Eau-de-Vie dans la société indienne," *Canadian Historical Association Report* (1960), pp. 28-29; Thomas D. Graves, "Acculturation, Access and Alcoholism in a Tri-Ethnic Community," *American Anthropologist*, 69, 3-4 (June-August, 1967), pp. 307-21; David G. Mandelbaum, "Alcohol and Culture," *Current Anthropology*, 6 (1965), pp. 281-92; Nancy Lurie, "The World's Oldest Ongoing Protest Demonstration: North American Indian Drinking Patterns," *Pacific Historical Review*, 40, 3 (August, 1971), pp. 311-32. All deviate from the alienation explanation presented in most work on the Indian and alcohol.

89. E.E. Rich, "Trade Habits and Economic Motivations among the Indians of North America," *Canadian Journal of Economics and Political Science*, 26, 1 (February, 1960), pp. 50-53.

90. Arthur J. Ray, "The Hudson's Bay Company Fur Trade in the Eighteenth Century," in Gibson, *European Settlement and Development in North America*, pp. 134-35.

91. A.S. Morton, ed., *The Journal of Duncan M'Gillivray of the Northwest Company at Fort George on the Saskatchewan 1794-5* (Toronto, 1929), p. 47.

92. Paul Sharp, *Whoop Up Country: The Canadian and American West* (Norman, Okla., 1973), pp. 43-50; Ewers, *Blackfeet*, p. 261.

93. Thwaites, *Jesuit Relations and Allied Documents*, VII, p. 57. On the Indian and conservation, see Martin, *Keepers of the Game*, pp. 157-88.

94. Robin F. Wells, "Castoreum and the Steel Trap," *American Anthropologist*, 74, 2 (June, 1972), pp. 479-83; Carl P. Russell, *Firearms, Traps and Tools of the Mountain Men* (New York, 1967), chs. 2 and 3.

95. Tyrrell, *David Thompson's Narrative*, pp. 204-06.

96. Ray, *Indians*, p. 105.

97. Frank G. Roe, *The North American Buffalo: A Critical Study of the Species in the Wild State* (Toronto, 1970), cited on p. 609.

98. Innis, *Fur Trade*, pp. 2, 235.

99. Ray, *Indians*, pp. 205-13.

100. Frank Gilbert Roe, *The Indian and the Horse* (Norman, Okla., 1974), pp. 332-75; Ewers, *The Horse*, p. 318.

101. William N. Fenton and Merle Deardorff, "The Last Passenger Pigeon Hunt of the Cornplanter Senecas," *Journal of the Washington Academy of Sciences*, 33, 10 (October 15, 1943), pp. 289-315. In *The Passenger Pigeon* (Norman, Okla., 1973), A.W. Schorger writes: "It has been said that the Indian was

the most dangerous of the wild enemies of the pigeon. While possibly true in a literal sense, there is no reason to believe that their raids had an appreciable effect until a large commerce was established by the whites" (p. 137).

102. Mandelbaum, *The Plains Cree*, pp. 51-52; Alexander Ross, *The Red River Settlement* (London, 1856), p. 267.

103. Thwaites, *Jesuit Relations and Allied Documents*, VI, p. 297.

104. Peter Kalm, *Travels into North America* (Barre, Mass., 1972), p. 489.

105. Tyrrell, *David Thompson's Narrative*, p. 113.

106. Ewers, *The Horse*, p. 13.

107. Mandelbaum, *The Plains Cree*, pp. 30-31. Ewers, *Blackfeet*, p. 297.

108. Ewers, *The Horse*, p. 114.

109. Ewers, *Blackfeet*, cited on p. 223.

110. Harold Hickerson, "The Chippewa of the Upper Great Lakes," in Leacock and Lurie, *North American Indians*, pp. 183-89.

111. John Phillip Reid, *A Better Kind of Hatchet: Law, Trade and Diplomacy in the Cherokee Nation during the Early Years of European Contact* (Philadelphia, 1976), p. 189.

112. Thomas Hatley, "The Dividing Path: The Direction of Cherokee Life in the Eighteenth Century" (M.A. thesis, University of North Carolina, 1977), chs. 1 and 11. There is sometimes a curious twist to the European impact on North American life. It was the writings of a Jesuit missionary in China in the early eighteenth century that brought ginseng to the attention of a fellow missionary and botanist, Father Joseph-François Lafiteau, in New France. Subsequently, the demands of the China trade, via Europe, became so great that the plant became virtually extinct in Canada. William N. Fenton, "Contacts between Iroquois Herbalism and Colonial Medicine," pp. 517-20; and William N. Fenton, "Joseph-François Lafiteau," in *Dictionary of Canadian Biography* (Toronto, 1974), pp. 334-38.

113. Reid, *A Better Kind of Hatchet*, p. 192.

114. Fred Gearing, *Priests and Warriors, Social Structures for Cherokee Politics*, American Anthropological Association Memoir no. 93, 1962, pp. 79-105.

115. William G. McLoughlin, "Thomas Jefferson and the Beginning of Cherokee Nationalism, 1806 to 1809," *William and Mary Quarterly*, 32, 4 (October, 1975), pp. 550-51.

116. Reid, *A Law of Blood*, p. 276.

117. Howard R. Lamar, *The Trader and the American Frontier: Myth's Victim* (College Station, Tex., 1977), p. 52.

118. Kahn, *Travels into North America*, p. 492. James Axtell, "The White Indians of Colonial America," *William and Mary Quarterly*, 3rd ser., 32, 1 (January, 1975), pp. 55-88. An ingenious and entirely improbable explanation for the liaisons between whites and Indians was offered by a British nobleman at the

end of the eighteenth century. He wrote that "[concerning] the infecundity of the North American savages, M. Buffon, a respectable author, and for that reason often quoted, remarks that the males are feeble in the organs of generation, that they have no ardor for the female sex, and that they have few children. . . . A woman never admits her husband till the child she is nursing be three years old, and this led Frenchmen to go often astray from their Canadian wives" (Lord Henry Home Kames, *Sketches of the History of Man* [London, 1807], p. 364). The classic study of intercultural sexual relations in New France and the Canadian West is Marcel Giraud, *Les Métis canadien. Son Rôle dans l'histoire de l'Ouest* (Paris, 1945). Strongly influenced by F.J. Turner, Giraud's work will long remain a seminal study of the social history of the fur trade.

119. Vaughan, *New England Frontier*, p. 209. But see also Axtell, "White Indians of Colonial America," pp. 58-88. The assumption that Amerindians were always eager for these marriage alliances is not correct. See Jaenen, "Amerindian Views of French Culture," pp. 283-84.

120. Merle H. Deardorff, "The Religion of Handsome Lake: Its Origin and Development," in William N. Fenton, ed., *Symposium on Local Diversity in Iroquois Culture* (Washington, D.C., 1951), p. 83; Grace S. Woodward, *The Cherokees* (Norman, Okla., 1963), p. 86; William F. Wheeler, "Sacajaweah: A Historical Sketch," *Contributions to the Historical Society of Montana*, 7 (1919), pp. 271-96; Anne W. Hafen, "Jean-Baptiste Charbonneau," in LeRoy R. Hafen, ed., *The Mountain Men and the Fur Trade in the Far West* (Glendale, Calif., 1965), pp. 205-24. William T. Hagen, "Squaw Men on the Kiowa, Comanche, Apache Reservation: Advance Agents of Civilization or Disturbers of the Peace?" in John G. Clark, *The Frontier Challenge* (Lawrence, Kan., 1971), p. 173; Ewers, *Blackfeet*, p. 71; Mandelbaum, *The Plains Cree*, p. 10.

121. W. Kaye Lamb, ed., *Sixteen Years in Indian Country: The Journals of Daniel William Harmon, 1800-1816* (Toronto, 1957), pp. 28-29, 62-63, 98, 195.

122. Harvey L. Carter and Marcia C. Spencer, "Stereotypes of the Mountain Men," *Western Historical Quarterly*, 6, 1 (January, 1975), p. 31, estimate that 36 per cent of the mountain men in their sample had Indian wives.

123. John S. Ewers, "Mothers of the Mixed Bloods," in his *Indian Life on the Upper Missouri* (Norman, Okla., 1968), pp. 62-64; Lewis O. Saum, *The Fur Trader and the Indian* (Seattle, 1965), pp. 85-86.

124. Galbraith, *The Little Emperor*, pp. 67-71.

125. Sylvia Van Kirk, "The Custom of the Country: An Examination of Fur Trade Marriages," in Lewis H. Thomas, *Essays in Western History* (Edmonton, 1976), pp. 49-68; Sylvia Van Kirk, "Women and the Fur Trade," *The Beaver* (Winter, 1972), pp. 4-21; Jennifer Brown, "A Demographic Transition in Fur

Trade Country: Family Size and Fertility of Company Officers and Country Wives," *Western Canadian Journal of Anthropology*, 6, 1 (1976), pp. 61-71; Jennifer S.H. Brown, *Strangers in Blood: Fur Trade Company Families in Indian Country* (Vancouver, 1980).

126. Jennifer Brown, "Ultimate Respectability: Fur Trade Children in the Civilized World," *The Beaver* (Winter, 1977), pp. 4-10, (Spring, 1978), pp. 48-55.

127. John E. Foster, "The Origins of Mixed Bloods in the Canadian West," in Thomas, *Essays in Western History*, pp. 71-80; John E. Foster, "The Country-Born in Red River, 1820-1850" (Ph.D. thesis, University of Alberta, 1973), pp. 66-70. In Red River alone the Métis population grew from 500 in 1821 to 12,000 in 1870, an astonishing rate of increase, especially when contrasted with the parallel decline of Indian populations (Ray, *Indians*, p. 205). See also Margaret McLeod and W.L. Morton, *Cuthbert Grant of Grantown* (Toronto, 1963); George Woodcock, *Gabriel Dumont* (Edmonton, 1975).

128. Fisher, *Contact and Conflict*, pp. 113, 209.

129. Washburn, *The Indian in America*, p. 94; Edmund Wilson, *Apologies to the Iroquois* (New York, 1960), p. 171; Howard Adams, *Prison of Grass* (Toronto, 1975); Maria Campbell, *Halfbreed* (Toronto, 1973).

130. Benjamin Drake, *The Life of Tecumseh and His Brother the Prophet* (Cincinnati, 1852), p. 124.

131. Driver, *Indians of North America*, pp. 269-83; Reid, *A Law of Blood*, pp. 131-41; George S. Snyderman, "Concepts of Land Ownership among the Iroquois and Their Neighbours," in Fenton, *Symposium on Local Diversity*, pp. 15-34.

132. Jenness, *Indians*, p. 124; Eleanor Leacock, *The Montagnais "Hunting Territory" and the Fur Trade*, American Anthropological Association Memoir no. 78, 1954, pp. 1-23; Rolf Knight, "A Re-Examination of Hunting, Trapping, and Territoriality among the Northern Algonkian Indians," in Anthony Leeds and Andrew P. Vayda, *Man, Culture and Animals* (Washington, D.C., 1965), pp. 27-42.

133. For a survey of this controversial topic, see A.G. Bailey, "Retrospective Thoughts of an Ethnohistorian," Canadian Historical Association, *Historical Papers* (1977), pp. 14-29; and the essays by Frank Speck, Eleanor Leacock, and Adrian Tanner, in Bruce Cox, ed., *Cultural Ecology* (Toronto, 1973), pp. 58-114.

134. William N. Fenton, "Locality as a Basic Factor in the Development of Iroquois Social Structure," in Fenton, *Symposium on Local Diversity*, p. 43.

135. Reid, *Law of Blood*, p. 68.

136. Martha Champion Rundle, "Iroquois Women, Then and Now," in Fenton, *Symposium on Local Diversity*, p. 174.

137. Ewers, *Blackfeet*, p. 214.

138. Duff, *Indian History*, p. 8.

139. Vaughan, *New England Frontier*, p. 105.

140. Jennings, *The Invasion of America*, pp. 128-45.

141. *Journals, Legislative Assembly, Canada*, 1844-45, "Report on the Affairs of the Indians of Canada," Appendix E.E.E.

142. Charles M. Johnston, ed., *The Valley of the Six Nations* (Toronto, 1964), pp. lv-lxix, 120-92; Sally Weaver, "Six Nations of Grand River, Ontario," in Trigger, *Handbook*, pp. 525-36.

143. Fisher, *Contact and Conflict*, pp. 175-201.

144. Frances Paul Prucha, "Andrew Jackson's Indian Policy: A Reassessment," *Journal of American History*, 56 (1969), pp. 527-39.

145. Washburn, *The Indian in America*, pp. 197-208; R.C. MacLeod, *The North-West Mounted Police and Law Enforcement, 1873-1905* (Toronto, 1976), pp. 27-31.

146. René Fumoleau, *As Long as the Land Shall Last* (Toronto, 1973), cited on p. 24. Fumoleau's study and Alexander Morris, *The Treaties of Canada with the Indians* (Toronto, 1880), provide an account of the dispossession process. In "Protection, Civilization, Assimilation: An Outline History of Canada's Indian Policy," *Western Canadian Journal of Anthropology*, 6, 2 (1976), pp. 13-30, John Tobias looks at post-treaty treatment.

147. John MacLean, *Canadian Savage Folk* (Toronto, 1896), p. 302.

148. Of course, even today the "frontier" is not entirely closed. The search for oil in northern and Arctic territories has raised again all of the old problems of contact. See *Northern Frontier, Northern Homeland. The Report of the Mackenzie Valley Pipeline Inquiry*, vol. 1 (Ottawa, 1977).

149. William N. Fenton, "This Island, The World on the Turtle's Back," *Journal of American Folklore*, 75, 298 (October-December, 1961), pp. 283-300.

150. Dee Brown, *Bury My Heart at Wounded Knee* (New York, 1970), p. 13; Hugh Dempsey, *Crowfoot* (Edmonton, 1972), pp. 154-94.

151. V.S. Naipaul, *A Bend in the River* (New York, 1979), p. 249.

3 Making a Garden out of a Wilderness

1. Fernand Braudel, *The Perspective of the World* (London, 1985), pp. 387, 388.

2. Cecil Jane, ed., *The Journal of Christopher Columbus* (New York, 1989), p. 191; Patricia Seed, "Taking Possession and Reading Texts: Establishing the Authority of Overseas Empires," *William and Mary Quarterly*, XLIX, 2 (April, 1992), p. 199.

3. Marc Lescarbot, *History of New France* (Toronto, 1914), III, p. 246. The theme of my lecture might have benefited had I been able to substantiate the claim, sometimes made, that "Acadie" is a corruption of "Arcadie" – an ideal,

rural paradise. Unfortunately the claim, sometimes made on the basis of Verrazzano's 1524 voyage when he described the coast of present-day Virginia as "Arcadie," is unfounded. "Acadie" likely is derived from the Micmac word "Quoddy" or "Cadie," meaning a piece of land. The French version became "la Cadie" or "l'Acadie," even though the French sometimes thought of the area as a potential "Arcadie." See Andrew Hill Clark, *Acadia: The Geography of Early Nova Scotia* (Madison, Wisconsin, 1968), p. 71.

4. J.G.A. Pocock, "Deconstructing Europe," *London Review of Books*, 19 December 1991, pp. 6-10.

5. J.H. Elliott, *The Old World and the New, 1492-1650* (Cambridge, 1989), p. 10.

6. Alfred W. Crosby, Jr., *The Columbian Exchange: Biological and Cultural Consequences of 1492* (Westport, Conn., 1972), p. 67.

7. Tzvetan Todorov, *The Conquest of America* (New York, 1984), ch. 1, n. 7: p. 146.

8. Kirkpatrick Sale, *The Conquest of Paradise: Christopher Columbus and the Columbian Legacy* (New York, 1991), p. 129.

9. William Cronon, *Changes in the Land Indians: Colonists and Ecology in New England* (New York, 1983), p. 12.

10. Leslie Upton, *Micmacs and Colonists: Indian-White Relations in the Maritimes, 1713-1867* (Vancouver, 1979), p. 25.

11. Peter Mason, *Deconstructing America: Representations of the Other* (London, 1990); Antonello Gerbi, *Nature in the New World* (Pittsburgh, 1985).

12. *The Works of Samuel D. Champlain* (Toronto, 1922), I, p. 243 (hereafter Champlain).

13. Lescarbot, III, pp. 484-85; Nicholas Denys, *Description and Natural History of the Coasts of North America (Acadia)* (Toronto, 1908), pp. 393, 390; Hugh Honour, *The New Golden Land: European Images of America from the Discovery to the Present Time* (New York, 1975), pp. 36-37.

14. Denys, pp. 362-69; Le Clercq, *New Relation of Gaspesia* (Toronto, 1910), p. 279.

15. Le Clercq, p. 275; Denys, pp. 257-340; Champlain, pp. 368, 247; Denys, p. 199.

16. Champlain, p. 327. For a discussion of the distribution of Native peoples, see Bruce J. Bourque, "Ethnicity in the Maritime Peninsula, 1600-1759," *Ethnohistory*, 36 (1989), pp. 257-84.

17. Sieur de Dièreville, *Relation of the Voyage to Port Royal in Acadia* (Toronto, 1933), pp. 130-41; Lescarbot, III, pp. 54, 205, 164; Karen Anderson, *Chain Her by One Foot* (London, 1990).

18. Lescarbot, III, pp. 200-02; Le Clercq, p. 243.

19. Le Clercq, pp. 135-39; Denys, p. 420; Marc Lescarbot, *The Conversion of the Savages*, in Reuben Gold Thwaites, ed., *The Jesuit Relations and Allied*

Documents (New York, 1959), I, p. 101; *Jesuit Relations*, III, p. 83; Le Clercq, pp. 265, 273.

20. Le Clercq, p. 243; Lescarbot, III, p. 333.

21. Lescarbot, III, pp. 365, 27, 113; *Jesuit Relations*, III, p. 21; Todorov, *Conquest*, pp. 27-33; Marshall Sahlins, *Islands of History* (Chicago, 1985), p. 10.

22. *Jesuit Relations*, III, pp. 33-35.

23. *Ibid.*, p. 33.

24. Champlain, p. 295.

25. Clarence J. Glacken, "Changing Ideas of the Habitable World," in William L. Thomas, ed., *Man's Role in Changing the Face of the Earth* (Chicago, 1956), pp. 70-92; Lescarbot, III, pp. 241, 351, 363-64; Alfred W. Crosby, Jr., *Ecological Imperialism: The Biological Expansion of Europe, 900-1900* (Cambridge, 1986); A. Bartlett Giamatti, *The Earthly Paradise of the Renaissance Epic* (Princeton, N.J., 1969); Hugh Johnson, *The Principles of Gardening* (London, 1979), p. 8.

26. *Jesuit Relations*, III, p. 63; Denys, p. 303; Lescarbot, I, p. xii.

27. Denys, pp. 149-50; Dièreville, pp. 94-95. See Clark, *Acadia*, pp. 24-31.

28. Lescarbot, II, p. 317; John Hemming, *The Conquest of the Incas* (London, 1983), pp. 77-88.

29. Champlain, p. 272; Jane, ed., *Columbus*, p. 24; Le Clercq, p. 115; *Jesuit Relations*, III, p. 111; Le Clercq, p. 205; Lescarbot, III, p. 487.

30. Denys, p. 156; Dièreville, pp. 75-77, 102, 122-23.

31. William M. Denevan, "The Pristine Myth: the Landscape of the Americas in 1492," *Annals of the Association of American Geographers*, 82, 3 (1992), pp. 369-85; Keith Thomas, *Man and the Natural World* (New York, 1983), p. 274; Le Clercq, p. 331; Marshall Sahlins, *Stone Age Economics* (Chicago, 1972); Denys, p. 403; Clarence J. Glacken, *Traces on the Rhodian Shore: Nature and Culture in Western Thought from Ancient Times until the End of the Eighteenth Century* (Berkeley, 1967), p. 494; Lescarbot, III, p. 137. See also Richard White, "Native Americans and the Environment," in W.E. Swagerty, ed., *Scholars and the Indian Experience* (Bloomington, Indiana, 1984), pp. 179-204; Lescarbot, III, p. 137.

32. Lescarbot, III, pp. 94, 127; J.G.A. Pocock, "Tangata Whenua and Enlightenment Anthropology," *New Zealand Journal of History*, 26, 1 (April, 1992), pp. 35, 36, 41. Pocock bases much of his intricate argument on late seventeenth-century and eighteenth-century sources, yet Marc Lescarbot's *History of New France*, first published in 1609, already articulates and assumes, though in a somewhat unsystematic way, a fairly full-blown version of the theory. See also John Locke's chapter "Of Property" in his *Essay Concerning the True Original Extent of Civil Government* (1640).

33. Lescarbot, III, p. 254; *Jesuit Relations*, I, p. 177.

34. Denys, p. 415; Lescarbot, III, p. 163; Le Clercq, p. 151; Lescarbot, III, p. 227.

Professor John Marshall has pointed to the importance of domestic animal imports as disease carriers by drawing my attention to Jared Diamond, "The Arrow of Disease," *Discover* (October, 1992), pp. 64-73.

35. Le Clercq, pp. 254-55; Dièreville, p. 77.

36. Dean R. Snow and Kim M. Lamphear, "European Contact and Indian Depopulation in the Northeast," *Ethnohistory*, 35 (1988), pp. 15-33; Virginia P. Miller, "Aboriginal Micmac Population: A Review of Evidence," *Ethnohistory*, 23 (1976), pp. 117-27, and "The Decline of Nova Scotia Micmac Population, A.D. 1600-1850," *Culture*, 3 (1982), pp. 107-20; John D. Daniels, "The Indian Population of North America in 1492," *William and Mary Quarterly*, XLIX, 2 (April, 1991), pp. 298-320.

37. Bruce G. Trigger, *Natives and Newcomers* (Montreal, 1985), pp. 183-94.

38. Le Clercq, p. 255; Denys, pp. 449-50.

39. Denys, p. 442.

40. Calvin Martin, "Four Lives of a Micmac Copper Pot," *Ethnohistory*, 22 (1975), pp. 111-33; Le Clercq, p. 277; Denys, p. 452. See also Wilson D. Wallis and Ruth S. Wallis, *The Micmac Indians of Eastern Canada* (Minneapolis, 1945); Bruce J. Bourque and Ruth Holmes Whitehead, "Tarrentines and the Introduction of European Trade Goods in the Gulf of Maine," *Ethnohistory*, 32 (1985), pp. 327-41.

41. *Jesuit Relations*, I, pp. 166-67; Le Clercq, pp. 193-94.

42. Denys, p. 437; *Jesuit Relations*, III, p. 135; Lescarbot, III, p. 189; Elliott, *The Old World*, p. 27.

43. Le Clercq, pp. 125, 104.

44. Lescarbot, III, pp. 256-57, 229.

45. Rev. Silas Tertius Rand, *Legends of the Micmacs* (London, 1894), 279.

4 *Sauvaiges*, Indians, Aboriginals, Amerindians, Native Peoples, First Nations

1. Georges E. Sioui Wendayete, "1992: The Discovery of Americity," in Gerald McMaster and Lee-Ann Martin, *Indigena: Contemporary Native Perspectives* (Hull, Quebec, 1992), pp. 59-70. There are two good general histories of Native peoples in Canada: James Miller, *Skyscrapers Hide the Heavens: A History of Indian-White Relations in Canada* (Toronto, 1989); Olive Patricia Dickason, *Canada's First Nations: A History of Founding Peoples from Earliest Times* (Toronto, 1992).

2. See ch. 2, above. According to the 1991 census, 1,002,675 people, an increase of 41 per cent over the 1986 count, acknowledged Native ancestry. *Globe and Mail*, March 31, 1993, p. 7. Some portion of this increase can be attributed to

the increasing respectability – even chic – of such ancestry. See Denis Vaugeois, "Québec pure laine . . . ou délicatement métisses," *Le Devoir*, 30 août 1993, p. 14.

3. Martine J. Reid, "Silent Speakers: Arts of the Northwest Coast," in Julia D. Harrison, ed., *The Spirit Sings: Artistic Traditions of Canada's First Peoples* (Toronto, 1987), p. 203.

4. Stewart Raby, "Indian Land Surrenders in Southern Saskatchewan," *Canadian Geographer*, XVII (1973), pp. 37-38.

5. Paul Tennant, *Aboriginal Peoples and Politics: The Indian Land Question in British Columbia, 1849-1989* (Vancouver, 1990), *passim*.

6. Ramsay Cook, ed., *The Voyages of Jacques Cartier* (Toronto, 1993), pp. 22, 70.

7. Miller, *Skyscrapers*, p. 207.

8. Tzvetan Todorov, *The Conquest of America* (New York, 1984), p. 42.

9. Tennant, *Aboriginal Peoples*, p. 84 *et seq.*

10. Cited in *Report of the Aboriginal Justice Inquiry of Manitoba*, Volume I: *The Justice System and the Aboriginal People* (Altona, Manitoba, 1991), p. 65.

11. Cited in Miller, *Skyscrapers*, p. 196.

12. Celia Haig-Brown, *Resistance and Renewal: Surviving the Indian Residential School* (Vancouver, 1988).

13. Douglas Cole, *Captured Heritage: The Scramble for Northwest Coast Artifacts* (Vancouver, 1985); Douglas Cole and Ira Chaikin, *An Iron Hand upon the People: The Law against the Potlach on the Northwest Coast* (Vancouver, 1990); Daisy (My-yah-nelth) Sewid-Smith, *Persecution or Prosecution* (Nu-Yum-Baleess Society, 1979). See also Ralph T. Coe, *Lost and Found Traditions: Native American Art, 1965-85* (Vancouver, 1986), for a study of the role of the arts in the revival of Native cultures.

14. Sarah Carter, *Lost Harvests: Prairie Indian Reserve Farmers and Government Policy* (Montreal, 1990), p. 210. See also Helen Buckley, *From Wooden Ploughs to Welfare* (Montreal, 1992).

15. Hana Samek, *The Blackfoot Confederacy, 1880-1920: A Comparative Study of Canadian and U.S. Indian Policy* (Albuquerque, 1987), pp. 56-86.

16. *Report of the Aboriginal Justice Inquiry*, I, pp. 9-10.

17. *Ibid.*, Volume II: *The Deaths of Helen Betty Osborne and John Joseph Harper*. See also Rupert Ross, *Dancing with a Ghost* (Toronto, 1992).

18. *To the Source, Commissioners' Report, Assembly of First Nations* (Ottawa, 1992), pp. 3-4. For an analysis of comparative provincial treatment of Native people, see Bradford Morse, "Indigenous Peoples in Quebec and Canada," *Literary Review of Canada* (October, 1992), pp. 9-12. The same author provides international comparisons in an excellent unpublished paper entitled "Comparative Assessments of Indigenous Peoples in Quebec, Canada and Abroad." "Canada," Morse writes, "looks very enlightened and positive in relation to

Scandinavia and Australia but far less so when examined in comparison to many aspects of American and New Zealand policy."

19. Brian Slattery, "Understanding Aboriginal Rights," *Canadian Bar Review*, 66 (1987), pp. 727, 736-48; Tennant, *Aboriginal Peoples*, pp. 213-26.

20. Paul Tennant, Sally M. Weaver, Roger Gibbins, and J. Rick Ponting, "The Report of the House of Commons Special Committee on Indian Self-Government: Three Comments," *Canadian Public Policy*, x, 2: pp. 211-15.

21. Dickason, *Canada's First Nations*, pp. 243-46; James Miller, "The Oka Controversy and the Federal Land Claims Process," in Ken Coates, ed., *Aboriginal Land Claims in Canada* (Toronto, forthcoming). For a taste of Quebec opinion, see Robin Philpot, *Oka: dernier alibi du Canada anglais* (Montréal, 1991).

22. Ovide Mercredi, "Pour une entente honorable," *Le Devoir*, 23 juillet 1992, p. 15.

23. *Le Devoir*, 13 février 1992, p. B10. See, for example, Lise Bissonnette, "Questions aux premiers peuples," *Le Devoir*, 16 mars 1992, p. 12, and a contrasting view, Paul Dionne, "Il faut lâcher du lest face aux Amérindiens," *Le Devoir*, 7 mai 1982, p. B-8.

24. *To the Source*, p. 23.

25. *To the Source*, p. 54.

26. Mary Ellen Turpel, "Aboriginal Peoples and the Canadian *Charter*: Interpretive Monopolies, Cultural Differences," *Canadian Human Rights Year Book*, 1989-90, pp. 3-45.

27. *Globe and Mail*, July 13, 1992, p. 6.

28. *To the Source*, p. 29.

5 The Evolution of Nationalism in Quebec

1. Hubert, Aquin, "L'existence politique," in *Blocs erratique* (Montréal, 1977), p. 57; Pierre Elliott Trudeau, *Le fédéralisme et la société canadienne-française* (Montréal, 1967), esp. p. 161.

2. E.J. Hobsbawn, *The Age of Empire 1875-1914* (London, 1987) p. 144.

3. Dale Miquelon, *New France 1701-1744: "A Supplement to Europe"* (Toronto, 1987), p. 5.

4. Jean-Pierre Wallot, *Un Québec qui bouge* (Montréal, 1975), pp. 264-74.

5. Thomas Chapais, "La Nationalité canadienne-française," *Discours et Conférences* (Montréal, 1880), p. 34.

6. Fernand Ouellet, *Lower Canada 1791-1840: Social Change and Nationalism* (Toronto, 1980), pp. 275-328.

7. François-Xavier Garneau, *Histoire du Canada* (5 ème édition, Paris, 1913), pp. xlv, xlviii.

8. Louis-Edmond Hamelin, "Evolution numérique séculaire du clergé catholique dans le Québec," *Recherches sociographiques*, II (1961), pp. 189-211.

9. L'Abbé L.-A. Laflèche, *Quelques Considérations sur les Rapports de la société civile avec la Religion et la famille* (Montréal, 1866), p. 47; Nadia Eid, *Le clergé et le pouvoir politique au Québec* (Montréal, 1978), cited p. 241.

10. Guy LaFlèche, *Les Saints martyrs Canadiens* (Laval, 1988), pp. 281-84.

11. Ramsay Cook, ed., *French-Canadian Nationalism: An Anthology* (Toronto, 1969), p. 126; Paul-Emile Borduas, *Refus global* (Montréal, 1959); Marcel Rioux, ed., *L'Eglise et le Québec* (Montréal, 1961); Pierre Maheu, "Le Pouvoir cléricale," in Parti Pris, *Les Québécois* (Montréal, 1971), pp. 171-90.

12. Jules-Paul Tardivel, *Pour La Patrie* (Montréal, 1895); Alonie de Lestres (Lionel Groulx), *L'Appel de la race* (Montréal, 1922).

13. Cook, *French-Canadian Nationalism*, pp. 118-52.

14. Yolande Lavoie, *L'émigration des québécois aux Etats Unis de 1840 à 1930* (Québec, 1979), p. 45; William Ryan, *The Clergy and Economic Growth in Quebec, 1846-1914* (Quebec, 1966).

15. Susan M. Trofimenkoff, ed., *Groulx: Variations on a Nationalism Theme* (Toronto, 1973), pp. 188-90.

16. Michael Oliver, "The Social and Political Ideas of French Canadian Nationalists" (Ph.D. thesis, McGill University, 1956).

17. *Royal Commission of Enquiry on Constitutional Problems* (Quebec, 1956), II, p. 33.

18. Michael D. Behiels, *Prelude to Quebec's Quiet Revolution* (Montreal and Kingston, 1985).

19. Michel Brunet, *La Présence anglaise et les Canadiens* (Montréal, 1958), pp. 113-66.

20. Michel Brunet, *Canadians et canadiens* (Montréal, 1954), p. 30.

21. Ramsay Cook, *Canada and the French Canadian Question* (Toronto, 1966), pp. 119-42.

22. Pierre E. Trudeau, ed., *La Grève de l'amiante* (Montréal, 1956), pp. 13-14.

23. Trudeau, *Le fédéralisme et la société canadienne-française*.

24. See Chapter Eight.

25. René Lévesque, "For an Independent Quebec," *Foreign Affairs*, LIV (1976), p. 739.

26. Dominique Clift, *Le déclin du nationalisme au Québec* (Montréal, 1981), p. 165.

27. Alain G. Gagnon and Khayyam Z. Paltiel, "Towards *Maître chez nous*: the ascendency of the Balzacian Bourgeoisie in Quebec," *Queen's Quarterly* (1986), pp. 731-49.

28. Graham Fraser, *René Lévesque and the Parti Québécois in Power* (Toronto, 1984).

29. *L'Evolution de la Population de Québec et ses Conséquences*, Secrétariat de Développement social (Québec, 1984); Marc G. Termote, "Why are Quebeckers dying out even faster than other Canadians?" *Transactions of the Royal Society of Canada*, F, 5th series, III (1985), pp. 81-94.

30. Jean-Louis Roy, "Le Nationalisme Québécois dans les Années 80," *Le Devoir*, 1 juin 1985; Jean-Claude Leclerc, 'L'Effondrement Démographique,' *Le Devoir*, 8 novembre 1985.

31. This undocumented assertion would seem to find some support in the survey research that underlies "Les valeurs des jeunes," *L'actualité* (juin 1989), pp. 28-48. Current attitudes in Quebec to nationalism and/or independence are revealed in *L'actualité* (mai 1990), pp. 7-22.

6 The Paradox of Quebec

1. Jean-Guy Pilon, "Quebec and the French Fact," in Philip Stratford and Michael Thomas, eds., *Voices From Quebec* (Toronto, 1977), pp. 2-3.

2. François-Marc Gagnon, "Borduas: Father of Quebec Separatism?" *Vanguard* (June-July, 1977).

3. Michel Morin et Claude Bertrand, *Le Territoire imaginaire de la culture* (Montréal, 1979).

4. Maurice Pinard and Richard Hamilton, "The Parti Québécois Comes to Power," *Canadian Journal of Political Science*, XI, 4 (December, 1978), pp. 739-75.

5. Pierre Vadeboncoeur, *La dernière heure et la première* (Montréal, 1970), p. 7.

6. Pierre Drouilly, "Le paradoxe québécois," *Le Devoir*, 14 février 1980, p. 5.

7. See, for example, Gilles Bourque et Anne Legaré, *Le Québec, la question nationale* (Paris, 1978); Henry Milner, *Politics in the New Quebec* (Toronto, 1978); and Denis Monière, *Le développement des ideologies au Quebec* (Montréal, 1977).

8. Jacques Monet, *The Last Cannon Shot* (Toronto, 1969), p. 25.

9. J. Huston, ed., *Le Répertoire national* (Montréal, 1893), I, pp. 172-75.

10. François-Marc Gagnon, "The Hidden Image of Early French Canadian Nationalism: A Parable," *Arts Canada* (December, 1979-January, 1980), pp. 11-14.

11. Camille Laurin, *Ma Traversée du Québec* (Montréal, 1970), p. 85.

12. *La politique québécoise du développement culturel* (Québec, 1978), I, pp. 50-51.

13. *Quebec-Canada: A New Deal* (Quebec, 1979), pp. 3-4.

14. Robert-Lionel Seguin, *La Victoire de Saint-Denis* (Montréal, 1964), p. 45; Marcel Rioux, *La Question du Québec* (Paris, 1969), pp. 70-71.

15. Michel Brunet, *Canadians et canadiens* (Montréal, 1954), p. 30. Maurice Seguin, *l'idée de l'indépendance au Québec* (Montréal, 1968). See also Michael D. Behiels, "Prelude to Quebec's 'Quiet Revolution'; the Re-emergence of Liberalism and the Rise of Neo-Nationalism, 1940-1960" (PH.D. thesis, York University, 1978), I, pp. 130-91.

16. Fernand Ouellet, *Le Bas Canada 1791-1840* (Ottawa, 1976), pp. 214ff.

17. F.-X. Garneau, *Histoire du Canada* (5th edition, Paris, 1920), II, p. 392; Philippe Reid, "François-Xavier Garneau et l'infériorité numérique des Canadiens Français," *Recherches Sociographiques*, XV, 1, pp. 31-39.

18. Jacques Henripin, "From Acceptance of Nature to Control: The Demography of the French Canadians Since the Seventeenth Century," *Canadian Journal of Economics and Political Science*, XXIII, 1 (February, 1957), pp. 10-19.

19. Yolande Lavoie, *L'émigration des Canadiens aux Etats-Unis avant 1930* (Montréal, 1972).

20. E. Hamon, *Les Canadiens-Français de la Nouvelle Angleterre* (Québec, 1891), pp. 155-56.

21. Christian Morissonneau, *La Terre Promise: Le Mythe du Nord québécois* (Montréal, 1978), p. 78.

22. Jacques Henripin, "Evolution de la composition ethnique et linguistique de la population canadienne," *Relations*, XXIe année, 248 (août 1961), pp. 207-09.

23. *La Situation de la Langue française au Québec*, I, *La Langue de Travail* (Québec, 1972), p. 301.

24. "La Politique québécoise de la Langue française," *Le Devoir*, 2 avril 1977, p. 7; *A New Deal*, pp. 29-30.

25. J.-P. Bernard, *Les Rouges* (Montréal, 1971), p. 265.

26. Fernand Ouellet, "Nationalism canadien-français et Laicisme au XIXe Siècle," *Recherches Sociographiques*, IV, 1 (janvier-avril 1963), pp. 44-70.

27. Jules-Paul Tardivel, *For My Country, Pour la Patrie* (1895) (Toronto, 1975), p. 39. Translation by Sheila Fishman.

28. *Notre Avenir Politique* (Montréal, 1923), p. 29.

29. André Laurendeau, *Notre Nationalisme* (Montréal, 1935), p. 50.

30. Pierre Vallières, *Un Québec Impossible* (Montréal, 1977), p. 71.

31. Robert Gurik, *Hamlet, Prince de Québec* (Montréal, 1968).

32. Fernand Ouellet, *Louis-Joseph Papineau, Un Etre Divisé* (CHA Booklet, Ottawa, 1961), p. 22.

33. Garneau, *Histoire*, p. 33.

34. Lionel Groulx, "Un Chef de trente-trois ans," in *Notre Maître, le Passé* (2ième Série, Montréal, 1936), p. 150.

35. The Constitutional Committee of the Quebec Liberal Party, *A New Canadian Federation*, 1980, p. 12.
36. Hubert Aquin, "The Cultural Fatigue of French Canada," in Larry Shouldice, *Contemporary Quebec Criticism* (Toronto, 1979), pp. 55-82.
37. Morin et Bertrand, *Le Territoire*, pp. 154-55.

7 The Coming of the Quiet Revolution

1. Georges-Emile Lapalme, *le bruit des choses reveillées: mémoires* (Montréal, 1969).
2. Vincent Lemieux, *Quatre Elections provinciale au Québec* (Québec, 1970), pp. 6-10.
3. Gérard Dion and Louis O'Neill, *Two Priests Censure Political Immorality in Quebec* (Montreal, 1956), p. 16.
4. *Les Insolence du Frère Untel* (Montréal, 1960), p. 16.
5. Cited in H.F. Quinn, *The Union Nationale* (Toronto, 1963), pp. 117-18.
6. Cited in Camille Laurin, "Autorité et personalité au Canada français," in *Ma Traversée du Québec* (Montréal, 1970), p. 21.
7. *Le Devoir*, 8 août 1956.
8. *Le Devoir*, 14 janvier 1954.
9. Pierre Elliott Trudeau, "Politique fonctionnelle," *Cité libre*, I, 1 (juin 1950), p. 21.
10. *Le Vrai*, 3 novembre 1956.
11. *Le Devoir*, 14 septembre 1956.
12. Gérard Bergeron, "Political Parties in Quebec," *University of Toronto Quarterly* (April, 1958), p. 366.
13. Pierre Elliott Trudeau, "Un Manifest démocratique," *Cité libre* (octobre 1958), p. 21.
14. Pierre Elliott Trudeau, *Les Cheminements de la Politique* (Montréal, 1970), p. 29.
15. *Le Devoir*, 1 décembre 1958.
16. *Le Devoir*, 11 avril 1959.
17. Bergeron, "Political Parties," p. 356.

8 "Au Diable avec le Goupillon et la Tuque"

1. These figures are found in Kenneth McRoberts and Dale Posgate, *Quebec: Social Change and Political Crisis* (Toronto, 1980), p. 51; and Pierre E. Trudeau, ed., *La Grève de l'amiante* (Montréal, 1956), pp. 4-5.

2. *Le Devoir*, 1 juillet, 1927.

3. Trudeau, *La Grève*, pp. 165-212; Renaude Lapointe, *l'Histoire bouleversante de Mgr. Charbonneau* (Montréal, 1962).

4. François-Marc Gagnon, *Paul-Emile Borduas* (Montréal, 1978), pp. 4-64; see also André-G. Bourassa, *Surrealism and Quebec Literature* (Toronto, 1984), pp. 80-155.

5. Paul-Emile Borduas, *Ecrits 1942-1958* (Halifax, 1978), pp. 45-54.

6. Christian Morissonneau, *La Terre promise: Le Myth du nord québécois* (Montréal, 1978); Maurice Tremblay, "Orientations de la Pensée sociale," in Jean-Charles Falardeau, ed., *Essais sur le Québec contemporain* (Québec, 1953), pp. 193-208.

7. *La Presse*, 1 juillet 1927, cited in Geoffrey Kelley, "Developing a Canadian National Feeling: The Diamond Jubilee Celebrations of 1927" (M.A. thesis, McGill University, 1984), p. 76. For examples of traditional nationalism, see Ramsay Cook, ed., *French-Canadian Nationalism: An Anthology* (Toronto, 1969).

8. For example, Henri Bourassa, *Que devons-nous à l'Angleterre?* (Montréal, 1915); Henri Bourassa, *Les Ecoles du Nord-Ouest* (Montréal, 1905).

9. Joseph Levitt, *Henri Bourassa and the Golden Calf* (Ottawa, 1969).

10. René Durocher et Michèle Jean, "Duplessis et la Commission royale d'enquête sur les problèmes constitutionels, 1953-1956," *Revue d'histoire de l'Amérique française*, 25, 3 (décembre 1971), pp. 237-64; *Royal Commission of Enquiry on Constitutional Problems, Quebec* (Quebec, 1956), II, pp. 33, 67, 44.

11. *Ibid.*, pp. 61, 85, 87.

12. *Ibid.*, pp. 65, 72.

13. Robert Parisé, *Georges-Henri Lévesque* (Montréal, 1976); Michael Beheils, "Le Père Georges-Henri Lévesque et l'établissement des sciences sociales à Laval, 1938-1955," *Revue de l'Université d'Ottawa*, 52, 3 (octobre-décembre 1982), pp. 355-76; Falardeau, ed., *Essais*; Maurice Tremblay, "Reflexions sur le Nationalisme," *Ecrits du Canada français*, V (Montréal, 1959), pp. 9-44.

14. Trudeau, *La Grève*, pp. 14, 403.

15. Maurice Lamontagne, *Le Fédéralisme canadien* (Québec, 1954).

16. *Le Devoir*, 6 mai 1959.

17. Michel Brunet, *Canadians et canadiens* (Montréal, 1954); *La présence Anglaise et les canadiens* (Montréal, 1958); Ramsay Cook, "L'Historien et le Nationalisme," *Cité libre*, XV, 73 (janvier 1965), pp. 5-14; Serge Gagnon, "Pour une conscience historique de la révolution québécoise," *Cité libre*, XVI, 83 (janvier 1966), pp. 4-19.

18. Michael Beheils, *Prelude to Quebec's Quiet Revolution: Liberalism versus Neo-Nationalism, 1940-1960* (Montreal, 1985)

19. Jean Hamelin, *Histoire du catholicisme québécois: Le XXe Siècle*, Tome 2 (Montréal, 1984), p. 139.

20. *Ibid.*, p. 134; *commission d'Etude sur les Laics et l'Eglise* (Montréal, 1972), p. 23.

21. Louis-Edmond Hamelin, "Evolution Numerique Seculaire du Clergé Catholique dans le Québec," *Recherches Sociographiques*, 2, 2 (1961), pp. 189-242; Hamelin, *Histoire*, p. 135; Anthony D. Smith, *The Ethnic Revival in the Modern World* (London, 1981), p. 104; Pierre E. Trudeau, "Some Obstacles to Democracy in Quebec," in Trudeau, *Federalism and the French Canadians* (Toronto, 1968), pp. 103-21; and Trudeau, *Les Cheminements de la Politique* (Montréal, 1970).

22. For a detailed account of the policies of the Lesage government, see Dale C. Thomson, *Jean Lesage and the Quiet Revolution* (Toronto, 1984); and McRoberts and Posgate, *Quebec*, pp. 94-123.

23. *Report of the Royal Commission of Enquiry on Education, Quebec* (Quebec, 1963), I, pp. 75, 81, 72, 64.

24. Léon Dion, *le bill 60 et la société québécoise* (Montréal, 1967), pp. 144-45; Thomson, *Jean Lesage*, p. 310.

25. Clarence Hogue, *Québec un siècle d'électricité* (Montréal, 1979), pp. 269, 386; Paul Sauriol, *La Nationalisation de l'électricité* (Montréal, 1962), p. 86.

26. Albert Breton, "The Economics of Nationalism," *Journal of Political Economy*, LXXII, 4 (August, 1964), pp. 376-86.

27. Boyce Richardson, *James Bay* (Toronto, 1972)

28. Antonin Dupont, *Les relations entre l'Eglise et l'Etat sous Louis-Alexandre Taschereau 1920-1936* (Montréal, 1972).

29. Thomson, *Jean Lesage*, pp. 184-89.

30. Henri Bourassa, *Réligion, Langue, Nationalité* (Montréal, 1910); Bourassa, *La Langue Gardienne de la Foi* (Montréal, 1918).

31. Raymond Barbeau, *Le Québec Bientôt Unilingue?* (Montréal, 1965).

32. *Rapport de la Commission d'Enquête sur la Situation de la Langue française et sur les Droits linguistiques au Québec* (Québec, 1972), 3 vols. See especially vol. 1, *La Langue de Travail.*

33. "La Politique québécoise de la langue française," *Le Devoir*, 2 avril 1977.

34. William D. Coleman, *The independence movement in Quebec* (Toronto, 1984), p. 182.

35. Ernest Gellner, *Nations and Nationalism* (Ithaca, N.Y., 1983), pp. 57, 125.

36. Charles Taylor, "Nationalism and the Political Intelligentsia," *Queen's Quarterly*, LXXII, I (Spring, 1965), p. 152.

37. In *Entre l'Eden et l'Utopie* (Montréal, 1984), Luc Bureau offers a satirical and humorous account of the failures of planning. See especially pp. 200-03.

38. Lionel Groulx, *Chemins de l'Avenir* (Montréal, 1964), p. 22. The following

year the conservative philosopher George Grant offered a similar reflection on Canada as a whole in his *Lament for a Nation* (Toronto, 1965).

39. Lionel Groulx, *Mes Mémoires* (Montréal, 1974), pp. 4, 298.
40. Smith, *Ethnic Revival*, p. 25.
41. André J. Bélanger, "Le Nationalisme au Québec: Histoire en Cinq Temps d'un Imaginaire," *critère*, 28 (printemps 1980), p. 58. See also Maurice Pinard and Richard Hamilton, "The Class Basis of Quebec's Independence Movement," *Ethnic and Racial Studies*, 7, 1 (January, 1984), pp. 19-54; Kenneth McRoberts, "The Sources of Neo-Nationalism in Quebec," *ibid.*, 57-85.

9 The Trudeau-Lévesque Debate

1. *Le Devoir*, 17 juillet 1980 [translation].
2. René Lévesque, "Quebec's Economic Future," in *The Montreal Star, Seminar on Quebec* (Montreal, 1963), p. 78.
3. Albert Breton, "The Economics of Nationalism," *Journal of Political Economy*, 72 (August, 1964), pp. 376-86.
4. Jacques Lazure, *La Jeunesse de Québec en révolution* (Montréal, 1970), pp. 23-62.
5. Quoted in Gérard Bergeron, *Notre miroir à deux faces* (Montréal, 1985), p. 42.
6. Quoted in Gérard Pelletier, *Les Années d'impatience 1950-1960* (Montréal, 1983), p. 49 [translation].
7. *Ibid.*, pp. 50-51 [translation].
8. Gérard Pelletier, *Le Temps de choix 1960-68* (Montréal, 1986), p. 214.
9. Pierre Elliott Trudeau, *Federalism and the French Canadians* (Toronto, 1968), p. 179. For detailed accounts of Trudeau's ideas, see Reg Whitaker, "Reason, Passion and Interest: Pierre Trudeau's Eternal Liberal Triangle," *Canadian Journal of Political and Social Theory*, 4 (Winter, 1980), pp. 5-32; Ramsay Cook, *The Maple Leaf Forever* (Toronto, 1977), pp. 22-44.
10. René Lévesque, *Option Québec* (Montréal, 1968), p. 14.
11. Jacques Guay, "Comment René Lévesque est devenu indépendantiste," *Le Magazine Maclean* (février 1969), p. 27 [translation].
12. Jean Provencher, *René Lévesque: portrait d'un Québécois* (Montréal, 1973), p. 33 [translation].
13. René Lévesque, *Memoirs* (Toronto, 1986), p. 74. Lévesque doesn't help much by writing that "the nation-state has had its day" and that "one cannot be anything but federalist . . . at least in world terms" (p. 117).
14. Quoted in Jean-Louis Rioux, "Radio-Canada, 1959," in *En Grève* (Montréal, 1963), p. 265. It is interesting that the editor of the nationalist daily, *Le Devoir*,

Gérard Filion, rejected Lévesque's claim, writing sarcastically, "when honour is lost, nothing is left but shame." *Ibid.* [translation].

15. *La Presse*, 2 novembre 1967 [translation].
16. René Lévesque, "For an Independent Quebec," *Foreign Affairs*, 54 (1976), pp. 737, 742.
17. Pierre Elliott Trudeau, "L'Ascéticisme en canot," *JEC*, 6 (juin 1944), p. 5 [translation]. The official English version (not this translation) appears in Borden Spears, ed., *Wilderness Canada* (Toronto, 1970), p. 5.
18. Spears, ed., *Wilderness Canada*, p. 5.
19. Pierre Elliott Trudeau, ed., *La Grève de l'amiante* (Montréal, 1956), p. 41 [translation].
20. *Ibid.*, p. 404 [translation].
21. "Manifeste pour une politique fonctionelle," *Cité libre* (mai 1964) [translation].
22. Quoted in Pelletier, *Le Temps*, p. 222; Dorval Brunelle, *Les Trois Colombes: essai* (Montréal, 1985), p. 18 [translation].
23. Trudeau, *Federalism*, p. 211.
24. *Ibid.*, pp. 31-32.
25. Bergeron, *Notre miroir*, p. 124 [translation].
26. Pierre Elliott Trudeau, "La Consolidation du Canada passe par le renforcement organique de la fédération," *Le Devoir*, 2 avril 1984, p. 8 [translation].
27. Hubert Aquin, "L'Existence politique," *Liberté*, 21 (mars 1962), p. 69 [translation]. See also Elie Kedourie, *Nationalism* (London, 1960), p. 101: "These movements are ostensibly directed against the foreigner, the outsider, but they are also the manifestation of a species of civil strife between the generations; nationalist movements are children's crusades. . . ." Brunelle, in *Les Trois Colombes*, also touches on this theme of generational conflict. No one has applied it, in detail, to Quebec and it could not be done mechanically, since Trudeau and Lévesque were of the same generation.
28. Bergeron, *Notre miroir* [translation].
29. *Le Devoir*, 16 novembre 1976; *Le Devoir*, 22 mai 1980 [translation].

10 Language Policy and the Glossophagic State

1. [1985] 1 SCR 721 at 744.
2. Camille Laurin, Minister of State for Cultural Development, *Québec's Policy on the French Language* (March, 1977).
3. Janet Ajzenstat, *The Political Thought of Lord Durham* (Kingston, 1988).
4. Sir C.P. Lucas, ed., *Lord Durham's Report on the Affairs of British North America* (Oxford, 1912), II, 292.

5. See, for example, A. Raynauld, G. Marion et R. Béland, "La Répartition des Revenus Selon Les Groupes Ethniques Au Canada," an unpublished research report prepared for the B&B Commission, reviewed in Kenneth McRoberts, *Quebec: Social Change and Political Crisis*, 3rd ed. (Toronto, 1988), pp. 176-77.

6. See Serge Carlos, *L'utilisation du français dans le monde du Travail du Québec* (Québec, 1973), and the discussion in McRoberts, *Quebec*, pp. 177-80.

7. Laurin, *Québec's Policy*, p. 52. Emphasis added.

8. Jean Laponce, *Languages and their Territories*, 2nd ed. (Toronto, 1987), p. 1.

9. Henri Bourassa, *Religion, Langue, Nationalité* (Montréal, 1910).

10. Robert Craig Brown and Ramsay Cook, *Canada 1896-1921: A Nation Transformed* (Toronto, 1974), pp. 252-62.

11. John Porter, *The Vertical Mosaic* (Toronto, 1965).

12. RSC 1985, c. 0-3, repealed and replaced by SC 1988, c. 38.

13. See Jean Larose, *La Petite Noirceur* (Montréal, 1987), pp. 65-71; Richard Handler, *Nationalism and the Politics of Culture in Quebec* (Madison, Wisconsin, 1988).

14. RSQ 1977, c. C-11.

15. *Attorney General of Québec* v. *La Chaussure Brown's Inc. et al.* (1988), 54 DLR (4th) 577.

16. *Ibid.*, 604.

17. Joshua Fishman, *Sociology of Language* (Rowley, Mass., 1972).

18. RSQ 1977, c. C-11, s. 11.

11 Alice in Meechland

1. Michel Brunet, *La Présence Anglaise et les Canadiens* (Montréal, 1958), pp. 113-66; Pierre E. Trudeau, ed., *La Grève de l'amiante* (Montréal, 1956), pp. 3-91.

2. Ramsay Cook, *The Maple Leaf Forever* (Toronto, 1971), pp. 96-122.

3. C. Morissonneau, "Mobilité et Identité québécoise," *Cahiers de Géographie du Québec*, 23 (1979), pp. 29-38.

4. Michael Behiels, *Prelude to the Quiet Revolution* (Montreal, 1985).

5. Ramsay Cook, *Canada, Quebec, and the Uses of Nationalism* (Toronto, 1986), pp. 68-86.

6. Le Devoir, *Le Québec et le Lac Meech* (Montréal, 1987), p. 137.

7. *Royal Commission of Enquiry on Constitutional Problems* (Quebec, 1956), Vol. II.

8. Anthony Smith, *The Ethnic Revival in the Modern World* (Cambridge, 1981), ch. 6, "Bureaucracy and the Intelligentsia."

9. Ramsay Cook, *Canada and the French Canadian Question* (Toronto, 1966), pp. 62-78.

10. Dominique Clift, *Le déclin du nationalism au Québec* (Montréal, 1981); Gérard Bouchard, "Une ambiguité québécoise: les bonnes élites et le méchant peuple," *Présentations*, Société royale du Canada (1985-86), pp. 29-43.

11. Le Devoir, *Le Québec et le Lac Meech*, p. 53.

12. *Ibid.*, pp. 54-60.

13. See *ibid.*, *passim*, for expression of these conflicting views.

14. See *Canadian Parliamentary Review*, 10, 3 (Autumn, 1987), for an unofficial translation of this speech. Emphasis added.

15. *The 1987 Constitutional Accord Report of the Special Joint Committee of the Senate and the House of Commons* (Ottawa, 1987), p. 41.

16. *Ibid.*, 33.

17. *Ibid.*, 40.

18. Le Devoir, *Le Québec et le Lac Meech*, p. 70. In reference to this matter Professor Robert Décary of the Université de Montréal writes: "Thus, duality will be the business of the federal and provincial parliaments, while the distinct character of Quebec will be the business of Quebec alone, expressing itself by its National Assembly and *by its government.* . . . Quebec will become the only master of the protection and promotion of its distinct character. Moreover, the *government* of Quebec sees itself recognized by a constitutional status relative to this protection and promotion, which will signify, notably, the right to participate as such as the government in numerous international activities."

19. Lowell Murray, "Le Canada doit respondre 'oui' au Québec," *Le Devoir*, 28 août 1987.

20. 8 SCR at 123.

21. Le Devoir, *Le Québec et le Lac Meech*, p. 95.

22. *Ibid.*, p. 60. The position taken by the Lévesque government in 1985, while more restrictive than the Anglophone community in Quebec would find easily acceptable, represents a realistic basis on which to begin serious discussions about allowing Quebec the same power in language matters as is enjoyed by the other provinces. See *Projet d'accord Constitutionnel. Propositions du Gouvernement du Québec* (Québec, 1985), p. 20.

23. Le Devoir, *Le Québec et le Lac Meech*, p. 123.

12 Cultural Nationalism in Canada

1. Frederick Philip Grove, "Nationhood," in his *It Needs to Be Said* (Toronto, 1929), p. 142.

2. Raymond Williams, *Keywords. A Vocabulary of Culture and Society* (London, 1976), p. 76.

3. Margaret Atwood, *Survival* (Toronto, 1972).

4. Ramsay Cook, *The Maple Leaf Forever* (Toronto, 1971).

5. Robin Matthews and James Steele, *The Struggle for Canadian Universities* (Toronto, 1969). Michael Butler and David Shugarman, "Americanization and Scholarly Values," *Journal of Canadian Studies* (August, 1970), pp. 12-27; Alan Kornberg and Alan Tharp, "The American Impact on Canadian Political Science and Sociology," in R.A. Preston, *The Influence of the United States on Canadian Development* (Durham, N.C., 1972), pp. 55-98.

6. Wallace Clement, *The Canadian Corporate Elite* (Toronto, 1975).

7. Barry Lord, *The History of Painting in Canada: Towards a People's Art* (Toronto, 1974).

8. Bruce Kidd and John Macfarlane, *The Death of Hockey* (Toronto, 1972).

9. S.M. Crean, *Who's Afraid of Canadian Culture?* (Toronto, 1976).

10. Margaret Prang, "The Origins of Public Broadcasting in Canada," *Canadian Historical Review*, XLVI, 1 (March, 1965), pp. 1-31.

11. National Archives of Canada, Dafoe Papers, J.W Dafoe to Dr. H.L. McBain, January 20, 1934.

12. C.C. Berger, *The Sense of Power* (Toronto, 1969).

13. For a concise statement, see C.P. Stacey, *The Undefended Border: The Myth and the Reality*, CHA Historical Booklets (Ottawa, 1954); Robert Craig Brown, "Canada in North America," in John Braeman *et al.*, *20th Century American Foreign Policy* (Columbus, 1971), pp. 343-77.

14. Armand Lavergne, "National Defence as viewed by French Canadians," *Canadian Military Institute*, Selected Papers from the Transcriptions of the Canadian Military Institute, 1910 (Welland, 1910), pp. 98, 102.

15. F.W. Field, *Capital Investments in Canada* (Montreal, 1914), pp. 9-35. A.J. deBray, *L'Essor Industriel et Commercial du Peuple Canadien* (Montréal, n.d.).

16. J.M. Bliss, "Canadianizing American Business: The Roots of Branch Plant," in Ian Lumsden, ed., *Close the 49th Parallel* (Toronto, 1970), pp. 27-42. See also United States Tariff Commission, *Reciprocity with Canada: A Study in the Arrangement of 1911* (Washington, 1911), p. 76.

17. For a thorough discussion, see Hugh G.J. Aitken, *American Capital and Canadian Resources* (Cambridge, 1961).

18. Robert Babcock, *Gompers in Canada: A Study in American Continentalism before the First World War* (Toronto, 1974).

19. Irving Abella, "American Unionism, Communism and the Canadian Labour Movement: Some Myths and Realities," in R.A. Preston, *The Influence of the United States on Canadian Development* (Durham, N.C., 1972), p. 223. See

also I.M. Abella, "Lament for a Union Movement," in Lumsden, ed., *Close the 49th Parallel*, pp. 75-92.

20. Alfred Charpentier, *Ma Conversion au Syndicalisme Catholique* (Montréal, 1946).

21. Paul Sharp, *Agrarian Revolt in Western Canada* (Minneapolis, 1948).

22. *World's Work*, September, 1905; *World's Work*, January, 1903; *Cosmopolitan*, April, 1903.

23. J. Castell Hopkins, *Continental Influence in Canadian Development* (Toronto, 1908), p. 3.

24. *Kempville Advance*, December 7, 1911, cited in Peter Oliver, "The Making of a Provincial Premier: Howard Ferguson and Ontario Politics, 1870-1923" (PH.D. thesis, University of Toronto, 1969), p. 134.

25. Sir Reginald Coupland, ed., *The Durham Report* (Oxford, 1945), p. 43.

26. *Ottawa Citizen*, June 26, 1916.

27. André Siegfried, *Deux Mois en l'Amérique du Nord à la Veille de la Guerre* (Paris, 1916), p. 12.

28. Canada, Documents on External Affairs, II, *The Paris Peace Conference of 1919* (Ottawa, 1969), p. 17.

29. W.P. [Sir William Peterson], "English-speaking Solidarity," *The University Magazine*, XVI (April, 1917), p. 154.

30. Archibald MacMechan, "Canada as a Vassal State," *Canadian Historical Review*, I, 4 (December, 1920), p. 350.

31. Peter Mellen, *The Group of Seven* (Toronto, 1970), p. 104; Ann Davis, "The Wembley Controversy in Canadian Art," *Canadian Historical Review*, XIV, I (March, 1973).

32. F.B. Housser, *A Canadian Art Movement: The Story of the Group of Seven* (Toronto, 1926), pp. 13, 16, 17, 215.

33. Lawren Harris, "The Group of Seven in Canadian History," *CHA Report* (1948), p. 30. It is fairly clear that Harris thought not so much in terms of Canada vs. Europe, but rather of North America vs. Europe. In 1928 he wrote: "Just as we enter new relationships in space which evoke a new attitude and are giving rise to what we call the modern world, so there is a new race forming on this continent, the race of the new dispensation which will develop and embody the new attitude. It grows now largely within the swaddling clothes of European culture and tradition, but its ideals are not the same. Its attitude is not the same. Its direction is not the same, as both Lincoln and Whitman knew." Lawren Harris, "Creative Art and Canada," in Bertram Brooker, *Yearbook of the Arts in Canada 1928-1929* (Toronto, 1929), p. 181.

34. Hugh G.J. Aitken, "The Changing Structure of the Canadian Economy," in Aitken *et al.*, *The American Economic Impact on Canada* (Durham, N.C., 1959), p. 7.

35. J. Margorie Van derHoek, "The Penetration of American Capital in Canada," *Canadian Forum*, VI, 71 (August, 1926), p. 335.

36. H. Gordon Skilling, *Canadian Representation Abroad* (Toronto, 1945), pp. 185-233.

37. James Eayrs, *In Defence of Canada: From the Great War to the Great Depression* (Toronto, 1965), pp. 70-77.

38. Sir Robert Falconer, *The United States as a Neighbour* (Cambridge, 1925), pp. I, 242-51. The subject of U.S. influence on Canada was a popular one in the 1920s. W.B. Munro, in the Marfleet Lectures at the University of Toronto in 1929 and later published as *American Influences on Canadian Government* (Toronto, 1929), summed up a widely accepted view this way: "It is inevitable, of course, that the influence of American political practise upon Canada should be far-reaching. The juxtaposition of a neighbour which so far outranges Canada in population, wealth and world importance means that every branch of Canadian life and thought must be subjected to an overwhelming psychological pressure from south of the line. American influence upon Canada is more powerful than all the foreign influences combined. American newspapers, periodicals and American motion pictures are daily carrying American political ideas into every hamlet in the Dominion. The radio will accentuate this pressure, for the broadcasting stations pay no heed to international boundaries. One might, perhaps, generalize by saying that in the government and politics of Canada most of what is superimposed is British, but most of what works its way in from the bottom is American" (pp. 90-91). Of course, some Canadians hoped to resist the "inevitable." See John C. Weaver, "Canadians Confront American Mass Culture, 1918-30," paper presented to the annual meeting of the Canadian Historical Association, June, 1972. See also Carl Berger, "Internationalism, Continentalism and the Writing of History: Comments on the Carnegie Series and the Relations of Canada and the United States," in Preston, *Influence of the United States*, pp. 32-54.

39. John MacCormac, *Canada: America's Problem* (New York, 1940), p. 13.

40. Ramsay Cook, "From Lord Grey to Lloyd George," *International Journal*, XXVI, 1 (Winter, 1970), pp. 186-93.

41. J.W. Pickersgill and G.S. Forster, *The Mackenzie King Record*, III (Toronto, 1970), p. 95; see also D.G. Creighton, "Canada in the English-speaking World," *Canadian Historical Review*, XXVI, 2 (June, 1945), pp. 119-27.

42. W.L.M. King to Lord Moran, June 9, 1950, in *Churchill: Taken from the Diaries of Lord Moran: The Struggle for Survival 1940-1945* (Boston, 1966), p. 117, n. 3.

43. Privy Council Office, *Foreign Ownership and the Structure for Canadian Industry* (Ottawa, 1968), pp. 9-11.

44. A.E. Safarian, "Some Myths About Foreign Business Investment in Canada," *Journal of Canadian Studies*, VI, 3 (August, 1971), pp. 3-20.

45. George Grant, *Lament for a Nation* (Toronto, 1965). Part of Grant's argument is anticipated by Frederick Philip Grove's essay "Nationhood," in Grove, *It Needs to Be Said*, pp. 133-63.

46. George W. Ball, *The Discipline of Power* (Boston, 1968), p. 228; see also J.L. Granatstein, "Co-operation and Conflict: The Course of Canadian-American Relations since 1945," in Charles F. Doran and John H. Sigler, eds., *Canada and the United States* (Englewood Cliffs, N.J., 1985), pp. 45-68.

47. *Report of the Royal Commission on Publications* (Ottawa, 1961), pp. 5-6.

48. For a catalogue of concerns, see the essays in Lumsden, ed., *Close the 49th Parallel*.

49. Harold Adams Innis, *Essays in Canadian Economic History* (Toronto, 1956), p. 405.

50. Mel Watkins, "The American System and Canada's National Policy," *Canadian Association of American Studies Bulletin* (Winter, 1967).

51. Mel Watkins, "A New National Policy," in Trevor Lloyd and Jack McLeod, *Agenda 1970* (Toronto, 1968), p. 163.

52. John Porter, *The Vertical Mosaic* (Toronto, 1965), p. 56.

53. John Porter, "Canadian Character in the 20th Century," *Annals of the American Academy of Political and Social Science*, 370 (March, 1967), pp. 49-56.

54. Matthews and Steele, *The Struggle for Canadian Universities*.

55. Eugene Benson, "The House that Davis Built," *C.A.U.T. Bulletin*, 19, 3 (Spring, 1971), pp. 6-7.

56. Robert L. Perry, "Why Henry Lee Sold Foreign . . .," *Financial Post*, September 25, 1971, pp. 30-32. See also *Foreign Direct Investment in Canada* (Ottawa, 1972); and Pierre L. Bourgault, *Innovation and the Structure of Canadian Industry* (Ottawa, 1972).

57. S.F. Wise and R.C. Brown, *Canada Views the United States* (Seattle, 1967).

58. Senate of Canada, *Report of the Special Senate Committee on the Mass Media* (Ottawa, 1970), p. 194.

59. *US News & World Report*, June 21, 1976, p. 67.

13 Imagining a North American Garden

1. Joyce Carol Oates, *Crossing the Border* (New York, 1974), pp. 11, 12, 16.

2. Joyce Carol Oates, "One Half of Robertson Davies," *The New Republic*, 178 (April 15, 1978), pp. 22-25.

3. Northrop Frye, *The Bush Garden* (Toronto, 1971), p. 199.

4. See Chapter Two.

5. F.J. Turner, *Frontier and Section* (Englewood Cliffs, N.J., 1961), p. 39; Walt Whitman, *Collected Poetry and Selected Prose* (Boston, 1959), p. 11.

6. Doug Owram, *Promise of Eden* (Toronto, 1980), p. 127.

7. Ramsay Cook, *The Maple Leaf Forever*, revised edition (Toronto, 1977), pp. 148-57.

8. Barbara Novak, *Nature and Culture* (New York, 1980), p. 38. Perry Miller, *Nature's Nation* (Cambridge, Mass., 1967), p. 205; Ralph Waldo Emerson, *Nature Addresses and Lectures* (Boston, 1903), p. 10.

9. John Richardson, *Wacousta* (Toronto, 1964), p. 159.

10. Susanna Moodie, *Roughing it in the Bush* (Toronto, 1962), p. 237.

11. Novak, *Nature and Culture*, p. 41.

12. Catharine Parr Traill, *The Backwoods of Canada* (London, 1836), p. 153. In this section I have benefited from Marcia B. Kline, *Beyond the Land Itself. Views of Nature in Canada and the United States* (Cambridge, Mass., 1970).

13. Ann Davis, *A Distant Harmony* (Winnipeg, 1982), p. 3.

14. Cook, *The Maple Leaf Forever*, p. 156.

15. Goldwin Smith, *Canada and the Canadian Question* (Toronto, 1891).

16. Carl Berger, *The Sense of Power* (Toronto, 1970).

17. Davis, *A Distant Harmony*, p. 181.

18. Traill, *Backwoods*, p. 155.

19. D.C. Scott, *Poems of Archibald Lampman* (Toronto, 1900), pp. 6, 17, 179.

20. George Altmeyer, "Three Ideas of Nature in Canada," *Journal of Canadian Studies*, XI, 3 (August, 1976), pp. 21-36; Douglas Cole, "Artists, Patrons and Public: An Enquiry into the Success of the Group of Seven," *Journal of Canadian Studies*, XIII, 2 (Summer, 1976), pp. 69-78; Roderick Nash, *Wilderness and the American Mind* (New Haven, 1967).

21. Art Gallery of Ontario, N.G. Jackson Papers, A.Y. Jackson to cousin, September 23, 1910.

22. Ann Davis, "The Apprehended Vision: The Philosophy of the Group of Seven" (PH.D. thesis, York University, 1973).

23. F.B. Housser, *A Canadian Art Movement: The Story of the Group of Seven* (Toronto, 1926), pp. 13, 17. Arthur Lismer, "Art and Life," in *SCM, Foundations: Building the City of God* (Toronto, 1927), p. 74.

24. Carl Berger, "The True North Strong and Free," in Peter Russell, *Nationalism in Canada* (Toronto, 1966), pp. 3-26.

25. Lawren Harris, "Revelation of Art in Canada," *The Canadian Theosophist*, VII, 5 (July 15, 1926), pp. 85-86.

26. Michèle Lacombe, "Theosophy and the Canadian Idealist Tradition: A Preliminary Exploration," *Journal of Canadian Studies*, XVII, 2 (Summer, 1982), pp. 100-18.

27. Thomas A. Johnson, *The Complete Poems of Emily Dickinson* (Boston, 1960),

pp. 667-68; *The Collected Poems of Wallace Stevens* (Boston, 1972), p. 76.

28. Arthur Lismer, "Tom Thomson: Canadian Painter, 1877-1917," *Educational Review of the Province of Quebec*, LXXX, 3 (1954), pp. 170, 172; Maria Tippett, *Emily Carr* (Toronto, 1979), pp. 175-76; *Artscanada* (August, 1973), p. 22.

29. Lawren Harris, "The Group of Seven in Canadian History," *Report of the Canadian Historical Association* (1948), p. 29.

30. Sandra Djwa, "'A New Soil and a Sharp Sun': The Landscape in Modern Canadian Poetry," *Modernist Studies. Literature and Culture, 1920-1940*, 2, 2 (1977), p. 10; see also Sandra Djwa, "F.R. Scott," *Canadian Poetry*, 4 (Spring, 1979), pp. 1-16. In an uncanny way Scott here seems to be replying to Mrs. Traill, who wrote that "instead of poring with mysterious awe among our curious limestone rocks, that are often singularly grouped together, we refer them to the geologist to exercise his skill in accounting for their appearance: instead of investing them with the solemn characters of ancient temples or heathen altars, we look upon them with the curious eye of natural philosophy alone." Traill, *Backwoods*, pp. 153-54.

31. *The Collected Poems of F.R. Scott* (Toronto, 1981), p. 255.

32. *Ibid.*, p. 175.

33. Davis, *A Distant Harmony*, pp. 175, 169.

34. François-Marc Gagnon, "Painting in Quebec in the Thirties," *Journal of Canadian Art History*, III, 1 & 2 (Fall, 1976), pp. 2-4.

35. Frye, *Bush Garden*, pp. ii-iii.

36. Ramsay Cook, *William Kurelek. A Prairie Boy's Visions* (Toronto, 1980), p. 37.

37. Doris Shadbolt, *The Art of Emily Carr* (Vancouver, 1979), p. 196.

38. Paul-Emile Borduas, *Ecrits/Writings, 1942-58* (Halifax, 1978), p. 153. In an unpublished paper entitled "Paul-Emile Borduas et le Paysage de Sainte-Hilaire," François-Marc Gagnon argues convincingly that the mountain at Sainte-Hilaire informs Borduas's most *automatiste* work. LeMoine Fitzgerald wrote that "subconsciously the prairies and skies get into most things I do no matter how abstract they may be." Ann Davis, "Lionel LeMoine Fitzgerald, A North American Artist," in *Lionel LeMoine Fitzgerald: The Development of an Artist* (Winnipeg, 1978), p. 63.

39. Davis, *A Distant Harmony*, pp. 145, 149.

40. Ann Davis, *Frontiers of Our Dreams. Quebec Painting in the 1940's and 1950's* (Winnipeg, 1979), p. 14.

41. Eli Mandel, "The Inward, Northward Journey of Lawren Harris," *Artscanada* (October-November, 1978), p. 20.

42. Al Purdy, *Selected Poems* (Toronto, 1972), p. 77.

43. Borduas, *Ecrits/Writings*, p. 46.

14 Nationalist Ideologies in Canada

1. Alfred Cobban, *The Nation State and National Self-Determination* (London, 1969), pp. 128-29.
2. See, for example, Rupert Emerson, *From Empire to Nation* (Boston, 1962); Louis Snyder, *The New Nationalism* (Ithaca, N.Y., 1968).
3. Isaiah Berlin, "The Bent Twig," *Foreign Affairs*, 51, 1 (October, 1972), p. 30.
4. See K.H. Silvert, ed., *Expectant Peoples* (New York, 1967); David Apter, *The Politics of Modernization* (Chicago, 1965).
5. These and other theories of nationalism are critically discussed in A.D. Smith, *Theories of Nationalism* (London, 1971).
6. George Grant, *Lament for a Nation* (Toronto, 1965).
7. Marcel Rioux, *La Question du Québec* (Paris, 1969).
8. Hannah Arendt, *On Violence* (New York, 1970), p. 85.
9. Elie Kedourie, *Nationalism* (London, 1960), p. 9.
10. Otto Pflanze, "Nationalism in Europe, 1848-1871," *Review of Politics*, 28, 2 (April, 1966), pp. 129-42; Jacques Droz, "Concept français et concept allemand de l'idée de nationalité," *Europa und der Nationalismus*, Bericht urber des III, Internationale Historicker Treffen in Speyer – 17 bis 20 October 1949 (Baden-Baden, 1950), pp. 111-33.
11. Cited in Robert Berdahl, "New Thoughts on German Nationalism," *American Historical Review* (February, 1972), p. 66.
12. Elie Kedourie, *Nationalism in Asia and Africa* (New York, 1970), p. 35.
13. Fernand Ouellet, "Papineau," *Cahiers de l'Institut d'histoire*, Université Laval (Québec, n.d.), p. 65.
14. Raoul Girardet, "Autour de l'Idéologie Nationaliste," *Revue Française de science politique*, xv, 3 (June, 1965), p. 431.
15. Donald Creighton, *John A. Macdonald, The Young Politician* (Toronto, 1952), p. 227.
16. *Confederation Debates* (Ottawa, 1865), p. 60.
17. L'abbé L. Laflèche, *Quelques Considérations sur les Rapports de la Société Civile avec La Religion et La Famille* (Montréal, 1866), p. 24.
18. Charles Mair, "The New Canada," *Canadian Monthly and National Review*, VIII (1875), p. 161.
19. Canada, *House of Commons Debates*, 1890, I, p. 840.
20. Ramsay Cook, *Provincial Autonomy, Minority Rights and the Compact Theory, 1867-1921* (Ottawa, 1969).
21. Jules-Paul Tardivel, *Pour la Patrie* (Montréal, 1895), p. 7.
22. Carl Berger, *The Sense of Power* (Toronto, 1970).
23. Grant's identification of "nation" with cultural homogeneity is not very consistent though he certainly thinks of a nation as something more than a

"sovereign" state. But the identification of "nation" and culture is explicit when he writes that "indigenous cultures are dying everywhere in the modern world. French-Canadian nationalism is a last ditch stand." Grant, *Lament*, p. 76. Professor Rioux is more explicit: "One recognizes a nation when there is a collective plan to exist which is specific to a widespread historical group among whom subsist stable characteristics (language, outlook, customs, and traditions). The most important element which ties the members of this group together is, according to Renan, 'the desire to do great things together.'" Rioux, *La Question*, p. 109. Professor Rioux is, of course, misleading in citing Renan in his support since Renan specifically denied that nations were defined by the cultural characteristics mentioned by Rioux. Renan, of course, was arguing in favour of France's national claim to Alsace! See Ernest Renan, "Qu'est-ce qu'une nation?" *Oeuvres Complètes*, I, p. 891.

24. Henri Bourassa in *Le Nationaliste*, 3 avril 1904.
25. Ramsay Cook, *The Maple Leaf Forever* (Toronto, 1971), pp. 197-214.
26. "Projet de Loi No. 1," *Le Devoir*, 28 avril 1977.
27. *La Presse*, 30 avril 1977; *Globe and Mail*, Report on Business, January 1, 1977.
28. *Un Choix National/A National Understanding* (Ottawa, 1977).
29. Kenneth McRoberts and Dale Posgate, *Quebec: Social Change and Political Crisis* (Toronto, 1980).
30. "La Politique Québécoise de la Langue française," *Le Devoir*, 2 avril 1977.
31. *Un Choix National*, p. 17.
32. "La Charte du français et les Droits fondamentaux," *Le Devoir*, 17 juin 1977. See also Claude Ryan, "Qui est Québécois?" *Le Devoir*, 18 juin 1977.
33. "Les villages de Povungnituk, Ivujivik et Saglonc face au 'bill' 101," *Le Devoir*, 18 août 1977.
34. Rémi Savard, "Par delà les revendications de la NOIA, Québec saura-t-il discerner l'aspiration légitime des Inuits à la souveraineté," *Le Devoir*, 6 septembre 1977. In this article Yves Bérubé, the Quebec minister responsible for the new Quebec, is cited as saying, "One does not recognize the right of self-determination where we own the land. . . ." The principle here seems to be "heads I win, tails you lose."
35. Conor Cruise O'Brien, "In Secession, a Case for the Individual," *Globe and Mail*, January 27, 1973.
36. Godfried van Benthem van den Bergh, "Contemporary Nationalism in the Western World," *Daedelus* (Summer, 1966), p. 854.

15 Nation, Identity, Rights

This chapter is based on the W.L. Morton Lecture delivered at the University of Manitoba, October 28, 1992.

1. Andrew Hacker, "Transnational America," *New York Review of Books*, November 22, 1990, p. 19; John Searle, "The Storm Over the University," *New York Review of Books*, December 6, 1990, pp. 34-42.

2. Arthur Schlesinger, Jr., *The Disuniting of America: Reflections on a Multicultural Society* (New York, 1992), p. 137.

3. Joan Scott, "Multiculturalism and the Politics of Identity," *October*, 61 (Summer, 1992), p. 19; Audrey Kobayashi, "The Japanese Canadians' Redress Settlement and its Implications for Race Relations," *Canadian Ethnic Studies*, XXI, 2 (1989), pp. 9-12.

4. Edgar Morin, "Espoirs et peurs d'Europe," *Le Monde*, 1 juillet 1992, p. 2; "La Spectatrice engagée," *Le Devoir*, 3 août 1992, p. 9. See also Perry Anderson, *A Zone of Engagement* (London, 1992), pp. 261-78; Jurgen Habermas, *The New Conservatism: Cultural Criticism and the Historians' Debate* (Cambridge, Mass., 1989), pp. 249-67.

5. V.S. Naipal, *A Bend in the River* (New York, 1979), p. 141.

6. Edward Said, "The Anglo-Arab Encounter," *TLS*, 19 (June, 1992), p. 19. See also Edward Said, "The Politics of Knowledge," *Raritan*, XI, 1 (Summer, 1991), pp. 17-31.

7. Michael Walzer, "The New Tribalism," *Dissent* (Spring, 1992), pp. 164-72.

8. *New York Review of Books*, November 21, 1991, p. 19; *ibid.*, December 5, 1991, p. 49.

9. W.L. Morton, *The Canadian Identity* (Toronto, 1972), pp. 83-85, 88-89.

10. Brian McKillop, *Contexts of Canada's Past: Selected Essays of W.L. Morton* (Toronto, 1980), pp. 103-12.

11. *Ibid.*, p. 259. For the original text and Bergeron's commentary, see CUS/UCE, *A New Concept of Confederation?/Vers une nouvelle Confédération?* [1964], pp. 121-38.

12. Morton, *Canadian Identity*, p. 119.

13. *Ibid.* p. 150.

14. *Ibid.*, pp. 147-48.

15. Charles Taylor, *Multiculturalism and "The Politics of Recognition"* (Princeton, N.J., 1992), p. 61. Earlier in the same essay Taylor speaks of "life, liberty, due process, free speech, free practice of religion, and so on" as "fundamental and crucial." The "so on" is typical of Taylor's impatience with specifics when it comes to constitutional matters.

16. Charles Taylor, "Alternative Futures: Legitimacy, Identity and Alienation in Late Twentieth Century Canada," in Alan Cairns and Cynthia Williams, eds., *Constitutionalism, Citizenship and Society in Canada* (Toronto, 1985), pp. 183-230. For a critique of the historical claims made by Taylor, see Robert C. Vipond, *Liberty and Community and the Failure of the Constitution* (Albany, N.Y., 1991), pp. 143-49; Will Kymlicka, *Liberalism, Community, and Culture* (Oxford, 1989).

17. Taylor's analysis of nationalism is found in Chapters I and III of his *Reconciling the Solitudes: Essays on Canadian Federalism and Nationalism* (Montreal and Kingston, 1993). His clearest statement of the ethno-linguistic character of Quebec nationalism is on page 141. On Herder, see page 136. Both Ernest Gellner's *Nations and Nationalism* (Ithaca, N.Y., 1983) and Anthony D. Smith's *The Ethnic Revival in the Modern World* (Cambridge, 1981) stress the homogenizing character of nationalism.

18. Mary Ellen Turpel, "Aboriginal Peoples and the Canadian Charter: Interpretive Monopolies, Cultural Differences," *Canadian Human Rights Yearbook*, 1989-90, pp. 3-45.

19. Georges Corm, "L'Occident saisi par la violence des replis identitaires," *Le Monde Diplomatique* (mai 1992), pp. 18-19. See Alain Finkielkraut, *The Undoing of Thought* (London, 1988), p. 105; also Etienne Tassin, "Europe as a Political Community," in Chantal Mouffe, ed., *Dimensions of Radical Democracy* (London, 1992), pp. 169-92.

20. James Rule, "Tribalism and the State," *Dissent* (Fall, 1992), p. 521.

21. Morton, *Canadian Identity*, p. 138. That Morton did not free himself completely of nationalist assumptions is demonstrated in Lyle Dick, "The Seven Oaks Incident and the Construction of a Historical Tradition," *Journal of the Canadian Historical Association*, New Series, 2 (1991), pp. 107-10.

22. Mavis Gallant, *Home Truths* (Toronto, 1981), p. xiii. For a critique of my view, see Guy Laforest, "Herder, Kedourie et les errements de l'antinationalisme au Canada," in Raymond Hudon et Réjean Pelletier, *L'engagement intellectuel: Mélanges en l'honneur de Léon Dion* (Québec, 1991), pp. 313-38; also Laforest, *Trudeau et la Fin d'Un Rêve Canadien* (Montréal, 1992), pp. 233-51.

16 Civic Nations and Distinct Societies

1. *Quebec: Year VIII* (Toronto, 1968), pp. 49, 52, 56.

2. Pierre Elliott Trudeau, *Federalism and the French Canadians* (Toronto, 1968), p. 188.

3. Charles Taylor, *Reconciling the Solitudes* (Montreal, 1993), p. 21.

4. This theme underlies Cairns's four books of essays: *Constitution, Government, and Society in Canada* (Toronto, 1988); *Disruptions: Constitutional Struggles, from the Charter to Meech Lake* (Toronto, 1991); *Charter versus Federalism* (Montreal, 1992); *Reconfigurations: Canadian Citizenship and Constitutional Change* (Toronto, 1995).

5. Cairns, *Charter versus Federalism*, p. 60.

6. Taylor, *Reconciling the Solitudes*, pp. 59-119. For a convincing critique from an historical perspective, see Robert Vipond, *Liberty and Community* (Albany, N.Y., 1991), pp. 143-52.

7. Charles Taylor, *Multiculturalism and "the Politics of Recognition"* (Princeton, N.J., 1992), pp. 25-73.

8. Will Kymlicka, *Liberalism, Community and Culture* (Oxford, 1989); Guy Laforest, *Trudeau et la Fin d'un Rêve canadien* (Sillery, Québec, 1992); Christian Dufour, *A Canadian Challenge/Le défi québécois* (Lantzville, B.C., 1990); *Globe and Mail*, April 30, 1994, p. D3.

9. Jeremy Webber, *Reimagining Canada: Language, Culture, Community and the Canadian Constitution* (Montreal, 1994), p. 143.

10. Cairns, *Charter versus Federalism, passim*; Peter Russell, *Constitutional Odyssey* (Toronto, 1992), p. 111.

11. Cairns, *Charter versus Federalism*, p. 79.

12. Vaclav Havel, *Open Letters* (London, 1991), p. 287.

13. On the myth of Quebec's "traditional demands," see Max Nemni, "Canada in Crisis: the Destructive Power of Myth," *Queen's Quarterly*, 99, 1 (Spring, 1992), pp. 232-35. For serious discussions of "identity," see Perry Anderson, *A Zone of Engagement* (London, 1992), pp. 251-78; Joan Scott, "Multiculturalism and the Politics of Identity," *October*, 61 (Summer, 1992), pp. 12-19.

14. Joseph Raz, "Multiculturalism: A Liberal Perspective," *Dissent* (Winter, 1994), pp. 67-79. To the exaggerated expectations and fears that are often expressed in discussions of multiculturalism, Tzvetan Todorov's reply is the best: "multiculturalism is neither a panacea nor a threat, but simply the reality of all existing states." Todorov, *On Human Diversity* (Cambridge, Mass., 1993), p. 252.

15. Kenneth McRoberts, *English Canada and Quebec: Avoiding the Issue* (Toronto, 1991). For the argument that language is a human rather than a territorial right, see Leslie Green, "Are Language Rights Fundamental?" *Osgoode Hall Law Journal*, 25, 4 (Winter, 1987), pp. 639-69.

16. Webber, *Reimagining Canada*, pp. 237-38.

17. Monique Nemni, "Bienvenue au Québec! Le Canada connais pas," *Cité libre*, XXII, 2 (mars-avril 1994), pp. 12-17.

18. Zlatko Dizdarevic, *Sarajevo: A War Journal* (New York, 1993), p. 174.

19. *New York Times*, March 10, 1994, p. 46.

20. *Le Devoir*, 13 février 1992, p. B-10. See also Lise Bissonnette's reply rejecting the idea of "racial" nations and favouring a "political" nation. *Ibid.*, 16 mars 1992, p. 12.

21. *Le Petit Robert* (1977), p. 557.

Index

Abenaki, 57, 67

Aboriginal peoples, 10, 57, 71, 73

Acadia, 29, 30, 51, 71; early history of, 53-59; as wilderness, 60-66; native population decline, 67; disadvantages of contact, 69-70

Action française, 91, 106

Action libérale nationale, 91

Acton, Lord John E., 21, 147, 152, 212, 226

African Americans, 11

Ajzenstat, Janet, 151

Alaska Boundary Dispute (1903), 179

Algonkian, 28, 29, 30

Alliance Québec, 165

Altdorfer, Albrecht, 208

Althusser, Louis, 99

American Declaration of Independence, 197, 198

American Federation of Labor, 179, 180

American Historical Association, 181

Americanization, 172, 174, 181, 197, 198, 199, 211

Amerindians, 13, 22, 24, 52, 55, 67, 70, 73, 88, 100; cosmology of, 26; and trade, 27-33; population decline of, 33; and pathogens, 34; migration of, 35; social breakdown of, 36; and medicine, 37; and alcohol, 38; and conservation, 39-40; and dependence, 41; and social organization, 42-48; and reserves, 49

Andalusia, 245

Anderson, Karen, 58

Aquin, Hubert, 85, 109, 148

Arapaho, 35

Arctic, 17

Arendt, Hannah, 212

Arikara, 35

Asbestos strike, 119, 120, 124, 145, 146

Assembly of First Nations, 79, 80, 233; constitutional statement of, 82-83

Assimilation, 13, 73, 229; and *canadiens*, 14, 92, 93, 99, 102, 151, 152, 153, 213; and Canadians, 15; and Amerindians, 43; and immigrants, 156

Assiniboine, 28, 29, 35

Atahualpa, 62

Atwood, Margaret, 173

Autonomy Bills, 154

Bailey, Alfred G., 54

Balfour Declaration, 186

Ball, George, 190

Bancroft, George, 201

Barretto, Antonio, 117

Beige Paper (1980), 239

Bélanger, André-J., 136

Bennett, R.B., 183

Beothuk, 34, 74

Berger, Carl, 176, 202

Bergeron, Gérard, 115, 117, 149, 228

Berlin, Sir Isaiah, 211, 224

Bertrand, Guy, 109

Bertrand, Jean-Jacques, 103; administration of, 156

Biard, Father Pierre, 56, 59, 60, 61, 63, 65, 67, 69, 70

Bilingualism, 12, 153, 154, 158, 166, 219, 230, 242

Bill 101 (Charter of the French Language), 95, 103, 133, 156, 157, 158, 161, 218, 239

Bill 60, 128

Blackfoot, 29, 30, 34, 35, 39, 41, 44

Blake, Edward, 178

Blakeney, Allan, 233

Bloc populaire, 115

Bloc Québécois, 20, 21

Blood, 45

Boer War, 178

Borden, Sir Robert Laird, 176, 183, 189